36x (1/15) 4/15   43x (8/16)

W9-CBS-296

TORMENT

ALSO BY LAUREN KATE

FALLEN

LAUREN KATE

TORMENT

A FALLEN NOVEL

DELACORTE PRESS

TINDERBOX

All rights reserved. Published in the United States by Delacorte Press,
an imprint of Random House Children's Books,
a division of Random House, Inc., New York.

Delacorte Press is a registered trademark and the colophon is a trademark of
Random House, Inc.

WWW.RANDOMHOUSE.COM/TEENS
WWW.FALLENBOOKS.COM

Library of Congress Cataloging-in-Publication Data is available upon request.
ISBN: 978-0-385-73914-6 (trade)
ISBN: 978-0-385-90773-6 (lib. bdg.)
ISBN: 978-0-375-89717-7 (ebook)

The text of this book is set in 12-point Classical Garamond BT.

Book design by Angela Carlino

Printed in the United States of America

10 9 8 7 6 5 4 3 2 1

First Edition

Random House Children's Books supports the First Amendment
and celebrates the right to read.

FOR ELIZABETH, IRDY, ANNE, AND VIC.
I HAVE BEEN SO LUCKY TO HAVE YOU.

ACKNOWLEDGMENTS

First, inexpressible thanks to my readers for all the effusive and generous support. Because of you, I may just have to keep writing forever.

To Wendy Loggia, whose belief in this series was a great gift, and who knows just how to make it more like what it always wanted to be. To Beverly Horowitz for the sharpest pep talk I've ever received, and the dessert you stuffed into my purse. To Krista Vitola, whose good-news emails have made so many of my days. To Angela Carlino and the design team, for the jacket that could launch a thousand ships. To my traveling partner Noreen Marchisi, Roshan Nozari, and the rest of the tremendous marketing team at Random House. You are magicians. To Michael Stearns and Ted Malawer, tireless geniuses. Your wit and encouragement make you almost too much fun to work with.

To my friends, who keep me sane and inspired. To my family in Texas, Arkansas, Baltimore, and Florida for so much exuberance and love. And to Jason, for every single day.

For, if I imp my wing on thine

Affliction shall advance the flight in me.

☀☀

—Geⲟrge Herbert, *Easter Wings*

PROLOGUE

NEUTRAL WATERS

Daniel stared out at the bay. His eyes were as gray as the thick fog enveloping the Sausalito shoreline, as the choppy water lapping the pebble beach beneath his feet. There was no violet to his eyes now at all; he could feel it. She was too far away.

He braced himself against the biting gale off the water. But even as he tugged his thick black pea coat closer, he knew it was no use. Hunting always left him cold.

Only one thing could warm him today, and she was

out of reach. He missed the way the crown of her head made the perfect resting spot for his lips. He imagined filling the circle of his arms with her body, leaning down to kiss her neck. But it was a good thing Luce couldn't be here now. What she'd see would horrify her.

Behind him, the bleat of sea lions flopping in heaps along the south shore of Angel Island sounded the way he felt: jaggedly lonely, with no one around to hear.

No one except Cam.

He was crouched in front of Daniel, tying a rusty anchor around the bulging, wet figure at their feet. Even engaged in something so sinister, Cam looked good. His green eyes had a sparkle and his black hair was cut short. It was the truce; it always brought a brighter glow to the angels' cheeks, a shinier sheen to their hair, an even sharper cut to their flawless muscled bodies. Truce days were to angels what beach vacations were to humans.

So even though Daniel ached inside each time he was forced to end a human life, to anyone else he looked like a guy coming back from a week in Hawaii: relaxed, rested, tan.

Tightening one of his intricate knots, Cam said, "Typical Daniel. Always stepping aside and leaving me to do the dirty work."

"What are you talking about? I'm the one who finished him." Daniel looked down at the dead man, at the wiry gray hair matted to his pasty forehead, at his gnarled hands and cheap rubber galoshes, at the dark red tear across his chest. It made Daniel feel cold all over again. If the killing weren't necessary to ensure Luce's safety, to save her, Daniel would never raise another weapon. Never fight another fight.

And something about killing this man did not feel quite right. In fact, Daniel had a vague, troubling sense that something was profoundly wrong.

"Finishing them is the fun part." Cam looped the rope around the man's chest and tightened it under his arms. "The dirty work is seeing them off to sea."

Daniel still gripped the bloodied tree branch in his hand. Cam had snickered at the choice, but it never mattered to Daniel what he used. He could kill with anything.

"Hurry up," he growled, sickened by the obvious pleasure Cam took in human bloodshed. "You're wasting time. The tide's going out."

"And unless we do this my way, high tide tomorrow will wash Slayer here right back ashore. You're too impulsive, Daniel, always were. Do you ever think more than one step ahead?"

Daniel crossed his arms and looked back out at the white crests of the waves. A tourist catamaran from the San Francisco pier was gliding toward them. Once, the vision of that boat might have brought back a flood of memories. A thousand happy trips he'd taken with

Luce across a thousand lifetimes' seas. But now—now that she could die and not come back, in this lifetime when everything was different and there would be no more reincarnations—Daniel was always too aware of how blank *her* memory was. This was the last shot. For both of them. For everyone, really. So it was Luce's memory, not Daniel's, that mattered, and so many shocking truths would have to be gently brought to the surface if she was going to survive. The thought of what she had to learn made his whole body tense up.

If Cam thought Daniel wasn't thinking of the next step, he was wrong.

"You know there's only one reason I'm still here," Daniel said. "We need to talk about her."

Cam laughed. "I *was*." With a grunt, he hoisted the sopping corpse up over his shoulder. The dead man's navy suit bunched up around the lines of rope Cam had tied. The heavy anchor rested on his bloody chest.

"This one's a little gristly, isn't he?" Cam asked. "I'm almost insulted that the Elders didn't send a more challenging hit man."

Then—as if he were an Olympic shot-putter—Cam bent his knees, spun around three times to wind up, and launched the dead man out across the water, a hundred feet clear into the air.

For a few long seconds, the corpse sailed over the bay. Then the weight of the anchor dragged it down . . .

down . . . down. It splashed grandly into the deep aqua-marine water. And instantly sank out of sight.

Cam wiped his hands. "I think I've just set a record."

They were alike in so many ways. But Cam was something worse, a demon, and that made him capable of despicable acts with no remorse. Daniel was crippled by remorse. And right now, he was further crippled by love.

"You take human death too lightly," Daniel said.

"This guy deserved it," Cam said. "You really don't see the sport in all of this?"

That was when Daniel got in his face and spat, "She is not a game to me."

"And that is exactly why you will lose."

Daniel grabbed Cam by the collar of his steel-gray trench coat. He considered tossing him into the water the same way he'd just tossed the predator.

A cloud drifted past the sun, its shadow darkening their faces.

"Easy," Cam said, prying Daniel's hands away. "You have plenty of enemies, Daniel, but right now I'm not one of them. Remember the truce."

"Some truce," Daniel said. "Eighteen days of others trying to kill her."

"Eighteen days of you and me picking them off," Cam corrected.

It was angelic tradition for a truce to last eighteen

days. In Heaven, eighteen was the luckiest, most divine number: a life-affirming tally of two sevens (the archangels and the cardinal virtues), balanced with the warning of the four horsemen of the Apocalypse. In some mortal languages, eighteen had come to mean life itself—though in this case, for Luce, it could just as easily mean death.

Cam was right. As the news of her mortality trickled down the celestial tiers, the ranks of her enemies would double and redouble each day. Miss Sophia and her cohorts, the Twenty-four Elders of Zhsmaelin, were still after Luce. Daniel had glimpsed the Elders in the shadows cast by the Announcers just that morning. He had glimpsed something else, too—another darkness, a deeper cunning, one he hadn't recognized at first.

A shaft of sunlight punctured the clouds, and something gleamed in the corner of Daniel's vision. He turned and knelt down to find a single arrow planted in the wet sand. It was slimmer than a normal arrow, a dull silver color, laced with swirling etched designs. It was warm to the touch.

Daniel's breath caught in his throat. It had been eons since he'd seen a starshot. His fingers quaked as he gently drew it from the sand, careful to avoid its deadly blunt end.

Now Daniel knew where that other darkness had come from in this morning's Announcers. The news was even grimmer than he'd feared. He turned to Cam, the feather-light arrow balanced in his hands. "He wasn't acting alone."

Cam stiffened at the sight of the arrow. He moved toward it almost reverently, reaching out to touch it the same way Daniel had. "Such a valuable weapon to leave behind. The Outcast must have been in a great hurry to get away."

The Outcasts: a sect of spineless, waffling angels, shunned by both Heaven and Hell. Their one great strength was the reclusive angel Azazel, the only remaining starsmith, who still knew the art of producing starshots. When loosed from its silver bow, a starshot could do little more than bruise a mortal. But to angels and demons, it was the deadliest weapon of all.

Everyone wanted them, but none were willing to associate with Outcasts, so bartering for starshots was always done clandestinely, via messenger. Which meant the guy Daniel had killed was no hit man sent by the Elders. He was merely a barterer. The Outcast, the real enemy, had spirited away—probably at the first sight of Daniel and Cam. Daniel shivered. This was not good news.

"We killed the wrong guy."

"What 'wrong'?" Cam brushed him off. "Isn't the world better off with one less predator? Isn't Luce?" He stared at Daniel, then at the sea. "The only problem is—"

"The Outcasts."

Cam nodded. "So now they want her too."

Daniel could feel the tips of his wings bristling under his cashmere sweater and heavy coat, a burning itch that made him flinch. He stood still, with his eyes closed and his arms at his sides, straining to subdue himself before his wings burst forth like the violently unfurling sails of a ship and carried him up and off this island and over the bay and away. Straight toward her.

He closed his eyes and tried to picture Luce. He'd had to tear himself away from that cabin, from her peaceful sleep on the tiny island east of Tybee. It would be evening there by now. Would she be awake? Would she be hungry?

The battle at Sword & Cross, the revelations, and the death of her friend—it had taken quite a toll on Luce. The angels expected her to sleep all day and through the night. But by tomorrow morning, they would need to have a plan in place.

This was the first time Daniel had ever proposed a truce. To set the boundaries, make the rules, and draw up a system of consequences if either side transgressed— it was a huge responsibility to shoulder with Cam. Of course he would do it, he would do anything for her . . . he just wanted to make sure he did it *right*.

"We have to hide her somewhere safe," he said. "There's a school up north, near Fort Bragg—"

"The Shoreline School." Cam nodded. "My side has

looked into it as well. She'll be happy there. And educated in a way that won't endanger her. And, most importantly, she'll be shielded."

Gabbe had already explained to Daniel the type of camouflage Shoreline could provide. Soon enough, word would spread that Luce was hidden away there, but for a time at least, within the school's perimeter, she would be nearly invisible. Inside, Francesca, the angel closest to Gabbe, would look after Luce. Outside, Daniel and Cam would hunt down and kill anyone who dared draw near the school's boundaries.

Who would have told Cam about Shoreline? Daniel didn't like the idea of their side knowing more than his. He was already cursing himself for not visiting the school before they made this choice, but it had been hard enough to leave Luce when he did.

"She can start as early as tomorrow. Assuming"—Cam's eyes ran over Daniel's face—"assuming you say yes."

Daniel pressed a hand to the breast pocket of his shirt, where he kept a recent photograph. Luce on the lake at Sword & Cross. Wet hair shining. A rare grin on her face. Usually, by the time he had a chance to get a picture of her in one lifetime, he had lost her again. This time, she was still here.

"Come on, Daniel," Cam was saying. "We both know what she needs. We enroll her—and then let her be. We can do nothing to hasten this part but leave her alone."

"I can't leave her alone that long." Daniel had tossed out the words too quickly. He looked down at the arrow in his hands, feeling ill. He wanted to fling it into the ocean, but he couldn't.

"So." Cam squinted. "You haven't told her."

Daniel froze. "I can't tell her anything. We could lose her."

"*You* could lose her," Cam sneered.

"You know what I mean." Daniel stiffened. "It's too risky to assume she could take it all in without . . ."

He closed his eyes to banish the image of the agonizing red-hot blaze. But it was always burning at the back of his mind, threatening to spread like wildfire. If he told her the truth and killed her, this time she would *really* be gone. And it would be his fault. Daniel couldn't do anything—he could not exist—without her. His wings burned at the thought. Better to shelter her just a little longer.

"How convenient for you," Cam muttered. "I just hope she isn't disappointed."

Daniel ignored him. "Do you really believe she'll be able to learn at this school?"

"I do," Cam answered slowly. "Assuming we agree she'll have no external distractions. That means no Daniel, and no Cam. That has to be the cardinal rule."

Not see her for eighteen days? Daniel couldn't fathom it. More than that, he couldn't fathom Luce's ever agreeing to it. They had only just found each other in this lifetime and finally had a chance to be together. But, as usual, explaining the details could kill her. She couldn't hear about her past lives from the mouths of angels. Luce didn't know it yet, but very soon, she would be on her own to figure out . . . everything.

The buried truth—specifically what Luce would think of it—terrified Daniel. But Luce's uncovering it by herself was the only way to break free from this horrible cycle. This was why her experience at Shoreline would be crucial. For eighteen days, Daniel could kill as many Outcasts as came his way. But when the truce was over, everything would be in Luce's hands again. Luce's hands alone.

The sun was setting over Mount Tamalpais and the evening fog was rolling in.

"Let me take her to Shoreline," Daniel said. It would be his last chance to see her.

Cam looked at him strangely, wondering whether to concede. A second time, Daniel had to physically force his aching wings back into his skin.

"Fine," Cam said at last. "In exchange for the starshot."

Daniel handed over the weapon, and Cam slipped it inside his coat.

"Take her as far as the school and then find me. Don't screw up; I'll be watching."

"And then?"

"You and I have hunting to do."

Daniel nodded and unfurled his wings, feeling the deep pleasure of their release all through his body. He stood for a moment, gathering energy, sensing the wind's rough resistance. Time to flee this cursed, ugly scene, to let his wings carry him back to a place where he could be his true self.

Back to Luce.

And back to the lie he would have to live a little while longer.

"The truce begins at midnight tomorrow," Daniel called, kicking back a great spray of sand on the beach as he lifted off and soared across the sky.

ONE

EIGHTEEN DAYS

Luce planned on keeping her eyes closed all six hours of the cross-country flight from Georgia out to California, right up until the moment when the wheels of the plane touched down in San Francisco. Half asleep, she found it so much easier to pretend she was already reunited with Daniel.

It felt like a lifetime since she'd seen him, though it had really only been a few days. Ever since they'd said goodbye at Sword & Cross on Friday morning, Luce's whole body had felt groggy. The absence of his voice, his warmth, the touch of his wings: it had sunk into her bones, like a strange illness.

An arm brushed against hers, and Luce opened her eyes. She was face to face with a wide-eyed, brown-haired guy a few years older than her.

"Sorry," they both said at the same time, each retreating a few inches on either side of the plane's armrest.

Out the window, the view was startling. The plane was making its descent into San Francisco, and Luce had never seen anything like it before. As they traced the south side of the bay, a winding blue tributary seemed to cut through the earth on its way to the sea. The stream divided a vibrant green field on one side from a swirl of something bright red and white on the other. She pressed her forehead to the double plastic pane and tried to get a better view.

"What is that?" she wondered aloud.

"Salt," the guy answered, pointing. He leaned in closer. "They mine it out of the Pacific."

The answer was so simple, so . . . human. Almost a surprise after the time she'd spent with Daniel and the other—she was still unpracticed at using the terms literally—angels and demons. She looked out across the midnight-blue water, which seemed to stretch forever west. Sun-over-water had always meant *morning* to Atlantic coast–raised Luce. But out here, it was almost night.

"You're not from around here, are you?" her seat-mate asked.

Luce shook her head but held her tongue. She kept staring out the window. Before she'd left Georgia this morning, Mr. Cole had coached her about keeping a low profile. The other teachers had been told that Luce's parents had requested a transfer. It was a lie. As far as Luce's parents, Callie, and anyone else knew, she was still enrolled at Sword & Cross.

A few weeks before, this would have infuriated her. But the things that had happened in those final days at Sword & Cross had left Luce a person who took the world more seriously. She had glimpsed a snapshot of another life—one of so many she'd shared with Daniel before. She'd discovered a love more important to her than anything she'd ever thought possible. And then she'd seen all of that threatened by a crazy, dagger-wielding old woman whom she'd thought she could trust.

There were more out there like Miss Sophia, that Luce knew. But no one had told her how to recognize them. Miss Sophia had seemed normal, up until the end. Could the others look as innocent as . . . this brown-haired guy sitting next to her? Luce swallowed, folded her hands on her lap, and tried to think about Daniel.

Daniel was taking her someplace safe.

Luce pictured him waiting for her in one of those gray plastic airport chairs, elbows on knees, his blond head tucked between his shoulders. Rocking back and forth in his black Converse sneakers. Standing up every few minutes to pace around the baggage carousel.

There was a jolt as the plane touched down. Suddenly she was nervous. Would he be as happy to see her as she was to see him?

She focused on the brown and beige pattern on the cloth seat in front of her. Her neck felt stiff from the long flight and her clothes had a stale, stuffy airline smell. The navy-blue-suited ground crew outside the window seemed to be taking an abnormally long time to direct the plane to its Jetway. Her knees bobbed with impatience.

"I take it you're staying in California for a while?" The guy next to her offered a lazy smile that only made Luce more anxious to get up.

"Why would you say that?" she asked quickly. "What would make you think that?"

He blinked. "With that huge red duffel bag and all."

Luce inched away from him. She hadn't even noticed this guy until two minutes ago when he'd jarred her awake. How did he know about her luggage?

"Hey, nothing creepy." He shot her a strange look. "I was just standing behind you in line when you checked in."

Luce smiled awkwardly. "I have a boyfriend" streamed from her mouth. Instantly, her cheeks reddened.

The guy coughed. "Got it."

Luce grimaced. She didn't know why she'd said that. She didn't want to be rude, but the seat belt light went off and all she wanted to do was barrel past this guy and right off the plane. He must have had the same idea, because he edged backward in the aisle and swept his hand forward. As politely as she could, Luce pushed past and bounded toward the exit.

Only to get caught in a bottleneck of agonizing slowness on the Jetway. Silently cursing all the casual Californians shuffling in front of her, Luce stood on her toes and shifted from foot to foot. By the time she stepped into the terminal, she'd driven herself half insane with impatience.

Finally, she could move. She wove expertly through the crowd and forgot all about the guy she'd just met on the plane. She forgot to feel nervous that she'd never been to California in her life—never been further west than Branson, Missouri, that time when her parents dragged her to see Yakov Smirnoff doing standup. And for the first time in days, she even briefly forgot the horrible things she'd seen at Sword & Cross. She was headed toward the only thing in the world that had the power to make her feel better. The only thing that could make her feel that all the anguish she'd been through— all the shadows, that unreal battle in the cemetery, and worst of all, the heartbreak of Penn's death—might be worth surviving.

There he was.

Sitting exactly as she'd imagined he would, on the last in a block of sad gray chairs, next to an automatic sliding door that kept opening and closing behind him. For a second, Luce stood still and just enjoyed the view.

Daniel was wearing flip-flops and dark jeans she'd never seen before, and a stretched-out red T-shirt that was ripped near the front pocket. He looked the same, yet somehow different. More rested than he had when they'd said goodbye the other day. And was it just that she'd missed him so much, or was his skin even more radiant than she remembered? He looked up and finally saw her. His smile practically gleamed.

She took off running toward him. Within a second, his arms were around her, her face buried in his chest, and Luce let out the longest, deepest breath. Her mouth found his and they sank into a kiss. She went slack and happy in his arms.

She hadn't realized it until now, but a part of her had wondered whether she'd ever see him again, whether the whole thing might have been a dream. The love she felt, the love that Daniel reciprocated, all still felt so surreal.

Still caught up in his kiss, Luce lightly pinched his bicep. Not a dream. For the first time in she didn't even know how long, she felt like she was home.

"You're here," he whispered into her ear.

"*You're* here."

"We're both here."

They laughed, still kissing, eating up every bit of the sweet awkwardness at seeing each other again. But when Luce was least expecting it, her laugh turned into a sniffle. She was looking for a way to say how hard the last few days had been for her—without him, without anyone, half asleep and groggily aware that everything had changed—but in Daniel's arms now, she failed to find the words.

"I know," he said. "Let's get your bag and get out of here."

Luce turned toward the baggage carousel and found her neighbor from the plane standing in front of her, the straps of her huge duffel gripped in his hands. "I saw this go by," he said, a forced smile on his face, like he was hell-bent on proving his good intentions. "It's yours, isn't it?"

Before Luce had time to answer, Daniel relieved the guy of the unwieldy bag, using only one hand. "Thanks, man. I'll take it from here," he said, decisively enough to end the conversation.

The guy watched as Daniel slid his other hand around Luce's waist and steered her away. This was the first time since Sword & Cross that Luce had been able to see Daniel as the world did, her first chance to wonder whether other people could tell, just by looking, that there was something extraordinary about him.

Then they were through the sliding glass doors and

she took her first real breath of the West Coast. The early-November air felt fresh and brisk and somehow healthy, not soggy and chilled like the Savannah air this afternoon when her plane had taken off. The sky was a brilliant bright blue, no clouds on the horizon. Everything looked new-minted and clean—even the parking lot held row after row of recently washed cars. A line of mountains framed it all, tawny brown with scraggly dots of green trees, one hill rolling into the next.

She was not in Georgia anymore.

"I can't decide whether to be surprised," Daniel teased. "I let you out from under my wing for two days and another guy swoops in."

Luce rolled her eyes. "Come on. We barely spoke. Really, I slept the whole flight." She nudged him. "Dreaming of you."

Daniel's pursed lips turned into a smile and he gave the top of her head a kiss. She stood still, wanting more, not even realizing that Daniel had stopped in front of a car. And not just any car.

A black Alfa Romeo.

Luce's jaw dropped when Daniel unlocked the passenger door.

"Th-this . . . ," she stammered. "This is . . . did you *know* this is my absolute dream car?"

"More than that," Daniel laughed. "This used to *be* your car."

He laughed when she practically jumped at his

words. She was still getting used to the reincarnation part of their story. It was so unfair. A whole car she had no memory of. Whole *lives* she couldn't recall. She was desperate to know about them, almost like her former selves were siblings she'd been separated from at birth. She rested her hand on the windshield, searching for a wisp of something, for déjà vu.

Nothing.

"It was a sweet sixteen present from your folks a couple of lifetimes ago." Daniel looked sideways, like he was trying to decide how much to say. Like he knew she was hungry for the details but might not be able to swallow too many at once. "I just bought it off this guy in Reno. He bought it after you, uh . . . Well, after you . . ."

Spontaneously combusted, Luce thought, filling in the bitter truth that Daniel wouldn't speak. That was the one thing about her past lives: The ending rarely changed.

Except, it seemed, this time it could. This time they could hold hands, kiss, and . . . she didn't know what else they could do. But she was dying to find out. She caught herself. They had to be careful. Seventeen years was not enough, and in this lifetime, Luce was adamant about sticking around to see what it was like to really be with Daniel.

He cleared his throat and patted the gleaming black hood. "Still drives like a champ. The only problem is . . ." He looked at the convertible's tiny trunk, then at Luce's duffel bag, then back at the trunk.

Yes, Luce had a terrible habit of overpacking, she'd be the first to admit. But for once, this wasn't her fault. Arriane and Gabbe had packed her things from her dorm room at Sword & Cross, every black and nonblack piece of clothing she'd never had a chance to wear. She'd been too busy saying goodbye to Daniel, and to Penn, to pack. She winced, feeling guilty for being out here in California with Daniel, so far from where she'd left her friend buried. It didn't seem fair. Mr. Cole had kept assuring her that Miss Sophia would be dealt with for what she'd done to Penn, but when Luce had pressed him about what exactly that meant, he'd tugged at his mustache and clammed up.

Daniel glanced suspiciously around the parking lot. He popped the trunk, Luce's massive duffel bag in hand. It was an impossible fit, but then a soft sucking sound came from the back of the car and Luce's bag began to shrink. A moment later, Daniel snapped the trunk shut.

Luce blinked. "Do that again!"

Daniel didn't laugh. He seemed nervous. He slid into the driver's seat and started the car without a word. It was a strange, new thing for Luce: seeing his face look so serene on the surface, but knowing him well enough to sense something deeper underneath.

"What's wrong?"

"Mr. Cole told you about keeping a low profile, didn't he?"

She nodded.

Daniel backed out of the spot, then wheeled around to the parking lot's exit, slipping a credit card into the machine on their way out. "That was stupid. I should have thought—"

"What's the big deal?" Luce tucked her dark hair behind her ears as the car began to pick up speed. "You think you're going to attract Cam's attention by stuffing a bag into a trunk?"

Daniel got a faraway look in his eyes and shook his head. "Not Cam. No." A moment later, he squeezed her knee. "Forget I said anything. I just— We *both* just have to be cautious."

Luce heard him but was too overwhelmed to listen too closely. She loved watching Daniel expertly work the gearshift as they took the ramp onto the freeway and zipped through traffic; loved feeling the wind whipping through the car as they sped toward the towering San Francisco skyline; loved—most of all—just being with Daniel.

In San Francisco proper, the road turned much hillier. Every time they crested one peak and started careening down another, Luce caught a different glimpse of the city. It looked old and new at the same time: Mirror-windowed skyscrapers backed right up against restaurants and bars that looked a century old. Tiny cars lined the streets, parked at gravity-defying angles. Dogs and strollers everywhere. The sparkle of blue water all around the city's edge. And the first candy-apple-red glimpse of the Golden Gate Bridge in the distance.

Her eyes darted around to keep up with all the sights. And even though she had spent most of the past few days sleeping, she suddenly felt a wave of exhaustion.

Daniel stretched his arm around her and guided her head toward his shoulder. "Little-known fact about angels: We make excellent pillows."

Luce laughed, lifting her head to kiss his cheek. "I couldn't possibly sleep," she said, nuzzling his neck.

On the Golden Gate Bridge, throngs of pedestrians, spandexed bicyclers, and joggers flanked the cars. Far below was the brilliant bay, dotted with white sailboats and the beginning notes of a violet sunset. "It's been days since we've seen each other. I want to catch up," she said. "Tell me what you've been doing. Tell me everything."

For an instant, she thought she saw Daniel's hands tighten around the steering wheel. "If your goal is *not* to go to sleep," he said, cracking a smile, "then I really shouldn't delve into the minutiae of the eight-hour-long Council of the Angels meeting I was stuck in all day yesterday. See, the board met to discuss an amendment to proposition 362B, which details the sanctioned format for cherubic participation in the third circuit of—"

"Okay, I get it." She swatted him. Daniel was joking,

but it was a strange new kind of joke. He was actually being open about being an angel, which she loved—or at least she *would* love it, once she'd had a little more time to process it. Luce still felt like her heart and brain were both struggling to catch up to the changes in her life.

But they were back together for good now, so everything was infinitely easier. There was nothing to hold back from one another anymore. She pulled on his arm. "At least tell me where we're going."

Daniel flinched, and Luce felt a knot of cold unfold inside her chest. She moved to put her hand on his, but he pulled away to downshift.

"A school in Fort Bragg called Shoreline. Classes start tomorrow."

"We're enrolling at another school?" she asked. "Why?" It sounded so permanent. This was supposed to be a provisional trip. Her parents didn't even know she'd left the state of Georgia.

"You'll like Shoreline. It's very progressive, and a lot better than Sword and Cross. I think you'll be able to . . . develop there. And no harm will come to you. The school has a special, protective quality. A camouflage-like shield."

"I don't get it. Why do I need a protective shield? I thought coming out here, away from Miss Sophia, was enough."

"It's not just Miss Sophia," Daniel said quietly. "There are others."

"Who? You can protect me from Cam, or Molly, or whoever." Luce laughed, but the cold feeling in her chest was spreading to her gut.

"It's not Cam or Molly, either. Luce, I can't talk about it."

"Will we know anyone else there? Any other angels?"

"There are some angels there. No one you know, but I'm sure you'll get along. There's one more thing." His voice was flat as he stared straight ahead. "I won't be enrolling." His eyes didn't once veer off the road. "Just you. It's only for a little while."

"How little?"

"A few . . . weeks."

Had Luce been the one behind the wheel, this was when she would have slammed on the brakes.

"A few *weeks*?"

"If I could be with you, I would." Daniel's voice was so flat, so steady, that it made Luce even more upset. "You saw what just happened with your duffel bag and the trunk. That was like my shooting up a flare into the sky to let everyone know where we are. To alert anyone who is looking for me—and by me, I mean you. I am too easy to find, too easy for others to track down. And that bit with your bag? That is nothing compared to the things I do every day that would draw the attention of . . ." He shook his head sharply. "I won't put you in danger, Luce, I won't."

"Then *don't.*"

Daniel's face looked pained. "It's complicated."

"And let me guess: You can't explain."

"I wish I could."

Luce drew her knees to her chest, leaned away from him and against the passenger-side door, feeling somehow claustrophobic under the big blue California sky.

※

For half an hour, the two of them rode in silence. In and out of patches of fog, up and down the rocky, arid terrain. They passed signs for Sonoma, and as the car cruised through lush green vineyards, Daniel spoke. "It's three more hours to Fort Bragg. You going to stay mad at me the whole time?"

Luce ignored him. She thought of and refused to give voice to hundreds of questions, frustrations, accusations, and—ultimately—apologies for acting like such a spoiled brat. At the turnoff for the Anderson Valley, Daniel forked west and tried again to hold her hand. "Maybe you'll forgive me in time to enjoy our last few minutes together?"

She wanted to. She really wanted to *not* be fighting with Daniel right now. But the fresh mention of there being such a thing as a "last few minutes together," of his leaving her alone for reasons she couldn't understand and that he *always* refused to explain—it made Luce nervous, then terrified, then frustrated all over again. In the roiling sea of new state, new school, new dangers everywhere, Daniel was the only rock she had to hold on to. And he was about to leave her? Hadn't she been through enough? Hadn't they both been through enough?

It was only after they'd passed through the redwoods and come out into a starry, royal-blue evening that Daniel said something that broke through to her. They'd just passed a sign that read WELCOME TO MENDOCINO, and Luce was looking west. A full moon shone down on a cluster of buildings: a lighthouse, several copper water towers, and rows of well-preserved old wooden houses. Somewhere out beyond all that was the ocean she could hear but couldn't see.

Daniel pointed east, into a dark, dense forest of redwood and maple trees. "See that trailer park up ahead?"

She never would have if he hadn't pointed it out, but now Luce squinted to see a narrow driveway, where a lime-caked wooden placard read in whitewashed letters MENDOCINO MOBILE HOMES.

"You used to live right there."

"What?" Luce sucked in her breath so quickly, she started to cough. The park looked sad and lonesome, a dull line of low-ceilinged cookie-cutter boxes set along a cheap gravel road. "That's awful."

"You lived there before it was a trailer park," Daniel said, easing the car to a stop by the side of the road.

"Before there were mobile homes. Your father in that lifetime brought your family out from Illinois during the gold rush." He seemed to look inward somewhere, and sadly shook his head. "Used to be a really nice place."

Luce watched a bald man with a potbelly tug a mangy orange dog on a leash. The man was wearing a white undershirt and flannel boxers. Luce couldn't picture herself there at all.

Yet it was so clear to Daniel. "You had a two-room cabin and your mother was a terrible cook, so the whole place always smelled like cabbage. You had these blue gingham curtains that I used to part so I could climb through your window at night after your parents were asleep."

The car idled. Luce closed her eyes and tried to fight back her stupid tears. Hearing their history from Daniel made it feel both possible *and* impossible. Hearing it also made her feel extremely guilty. He'd stuck with her for so long, over so many lifetimes. She'd forgotten how well he knew her. Better even than she knew herself. Would Daniel know what she was thinking now? Luce wondered whether, in some ways, it was easier to be her and to never have remembered Daniel than it was for him to go through this time and time again.

If he said he had to leave for a few weeks and couldn't explain why . . . she would have to trust him.

"What was it like when you first met me?" she asked.

Daniel smiled. "I chopped wood in exchange for meals back then. One night around dinnertime I was walking past your house. Your mother had the cabbage going, and it stank so badly I almost skipped your house. But then I saw you through the window. You were sewing. I couldn't take my eyes off your hands."

Luce looked at her hands, her pale, tapered fingers and small, square palms. She wondered if they'd always looked the same. Daniel reached for them across the console. "They're just as soft now as they were then."

Luce shook her head. She loved the story, wanted to hear a thousand more just like it, but that wasn't what she'd meant. "I want to know about the first time you met me," she said. "The *very* first time. What was that like?"

After a long pause, he finally said, "It's getting late. They're expecting you at Shoreline before midnight." He stepped on the gas, taking a quick left into downtown Mendocino. In the side mirror, Luce watched the mobile home park grow smaller, darker, until it disappeared completely. But then, a few seconds later, Daniel parked the car in front of an empty all-night diner with yellow walls and floor-to-ceiling front windows.

The block was full of quirky, quaint buildings that reminded Luce of a less stuffy version of the New England coastline near her old New Hampshire prep school, Dover. The street was paved with uneven cobblestones that glowed yellow in the light from the streetlamps overhead. At its end, the road seemed to drop straight into the ocean. A coldness sneaked up on her. She had to ignore her reflexive fear of the dark. Daniel had explained about the shadows—that they were nothing to be afraid of, merely messengers. Which should have been reassuring, except for the hard-to-ignore fact that it meant there were bigger things to be afraid of.

"Why won't you tell me?" She couldn't help herself. She didn't know why it felt so important to ask. If she was going to trust Daniel when he said he had to abandon her after longing all her life for this reunion—well, maybe she just wanted to understand the origins of that trust. To know when and how it had all begun.

"Do you know what my last name means?" he said, surprising her.

Luce bit her lip, trying to think back to the research she and Penn had done. "I remember Miss Sophia saying something about *Watchers*. But I don't know what it means, or if I'm even supposed to believe her." Her fingers went to her neck, to the place where Miss Sophia's knife had lain.

"She was right. The Grigoris are a clan. They're a clan named after me, actually. Because they watch and learn from what happened when . . . back when I was still welcome in Heaven. And back when you were . . .

well, this all happened a very long time ago, Luce. It's hard for me to remember most of it."

"Where? Where was I?" she pressed. "I remember Miss Sophia saying something about the Grigoris consorting with mortal women. Is that what happened? Did you . . . ?"

He looked over at her. Something changed on his face, and in the dim moonlight, Luce couldn't tell what it meant. It was almost like he was relieved that she had guessed it, so he didn't have to be the one to spell it out.

"The very first time I saw you," Daniel continued, "it wasn't any different than any other time I've seen you since. The world was newer, but you were just the same. It was—"

"Love at first sight." That part she knew.

He nodded. "Just like always. The only difference was, in the beginning, you were off-limits to me. I was being punished, and I'd fallen for you at the worst possible time. Things were very violent in Heaven. Because of who . . . I am . . . I was expected to stay away from you. You were a distraction. The focus was supposed to be on winning the war. It's the same war that's still going on." He sighed. "And if you haven't noticed, I'm still very distracted."

"So you were a very high angel," Luce murmured.

"Sure." Daniel looked miserable, pausing and then seeming, when he spoke again, to bite out the words: "It was a fall from one of the highest perches."

Of course. Daniel would have to be important in Heaven in order to have caused such a big rift. In order for his love of a mortal girl to be so off-limits.

"You gave it all up? For me?"

He touched his forehead to hers. "I wouldn't change a thing."

"But I was nothing," Luce said. She felt heavy, like she was dragging. Dragging him down. "You had to give up so much!" She felt sick to her stomach. "And now you're damned forever."

Turning off the car, Daniel gave her a sad smile. "It might not be forever."

"What do you mean?"

"Come on," he said, hopping out of the car and coming around to open her door. "Let's take a walk."

They ambled to the end of the street, which didn't dead-end after all, but led to a steep, rocky staircase going down to the water. The air was cool and moist with sea spray. Just to the left of the steps, a trail led away. Daniel took her hand and moved to the cliff's edge.

"Where are we going?" Luce asked.

Daniel smiled at her, straightening his shoulders, and unfurled his wings.

Slowly, they extended up and out from his shoulders, unfolding with an almost inaudible series of soft snaps and creaks. Fully flexed, they made a gentle, feathery *fwump* like a duvet being flung over a bed.

For the first time, Luce noticed the back of Daniel's t-shirt. There were two tiny, otherwise invisible slits, which parted now to let his wings slip through. Did all of Daniel's clothes have these angelic alterations? Or did he have certain, special things he wore when he knew he planned on flying?

Either way, his wings never failed to leave Luce speechless.

They were enormous, rising three times taller than Daniel, and curved up into the sky and to either side like broad white sails. Their broad expanse caught the light of the stars and reflected it more intensely, so that they glowed with an iridescent shimmer. Near his body they darkened, shading into a rich earthy cream color where they met his shoulder muscles. But along their tapered edges, they grew thin and glowed, becoming almost translucent at the tips.

Luce stared at them, rapt, trying to remember the line of every glorious feather, to hold all of it inside her for when he went away. He shone so bright, the sun could have borrowed light from him. The smile in his violet eyes told her how good it felt for him to let his wings out. As good as Luce felt when she was wrapped up in them.

"Fly with me," he whispered.

"What?"

"I'm not going to see you for a little while. I have to give you something to remember me by."

Luce kissed him before he could say anything else, lacing her fingers around his neck, holding him as tightly as she could, hoping to give him something to remember her by, too.

With her back pressed to his chest, and his head over her shoulder, Daniel traced a line of kisses down her neck. She held her breath, waiting. Then he bent his legs and gracefully pushed off the edge of the cliff.

They were flying.

Away from the rocky ledge of the coastline, over the crashing silver waves below, arcing across the sky as if they were soaring for the moon. Daniel's embrace shielded her from every rough gust of wind, every brush of ocean chill. The night was absolutely quiet. As if they were the only two people left in the world.

"This is Heaven, isn't it?" she asked.

Daniel laughed. "I wish it were. Maybe one day soon."

When they had flown out far enough that they couldn't see land on either side of them, Daniel banked gently north, and they swooped in a wide arc past the city of Mendocino, which glowed warmly on the horizon. They were far above the tallest building in town and moving incredibly fast. But Luce had never felt safer or more in love in her life.

And then, all too soon, they were descending, gradually nearing a different cliff's edge. The sounds of the ocean grew louder again. A dark single-lane road wound off the main highway. When their feet touched down lightly on a cool patch of thick grass, Luce sighed.

"Where are we?" she asked, though of course she already knew.

The Shoreline School. She could see a large building in the distance, but from here it looked completely dark, merely a shape on the horizon. Daniel held her pressed to him, as if they were still in the air. She craned her head around to look at his expression. His eyes were damp.

"The ones who damned me are still watching, Luce. They have been for millennia. And they don't want us to be together. They will do anything they can to stop us. That's why it isn't safe for me to stay here."

She nodded, her eyes stinging. "But why am *I* here?"

"Because I will do everything in my power to keep you safe, and this is the best place for you now. I love you, Luce. More than anything. I'll be back to you as soon as I can."

She wanted to protest, but stopped herself. He'd given up everything for her. When he let her out of his embrace, he opened his palm and a small red shape inside it began to grow. Her duffel bag. He'd taken it from the back of the car without her even knowing, carried it all the way here inside his hand. In just a few seconds, it had filled out entirely, back to its full size. If she hadn't been so heartbroken about what it meant for him to hand it over to her, Luce would have loved the trick.

A single light went on inside the building. A silhouette appeared in the doorway.

"It's not for long. As soon as things are safer, I'll come for you."

His hot hand clasped her wrist and before she knew it, Luce was caught up in his embrace, drawn to his lips. She let everything else fall away, let her heart brim over. Maybe she couldn't remember her former lives, but when Daniel kissed her, she felt close to the past. And the future.

The figure in the doorway was walking toward her, a woman in a short white dress.

The kiss Luce had shared with Daniel, too sweet to be so brief, left her just as out of breath as their kisses always did.

"Don't go," she whispered, her eyes closed. It was all happening too fast. She couldn't give Daniel up. Not yet. She didn't think she ever could.

She felt the rush of air that meant he'd already taken off. Her heart went after him as she opened her eyes and saw the last trace of his wings disappear inside a cloud, into the dark night.

TWO

❧ ‡ ☙

SEVENTEEN DAYS

Thwap.

Luce winced and rubbed her face. Her nose stung.

Thwap. Thwap.

Now it was her cheekbones. Her eyelids drifted open and, almost immediately, she scrunched up her face in surprise. A stocky dishwater-blond girl with a grimly set mouth and major eyebrows was leaning over her. Her hair was piled messily on top of her head. She wore yoga pants and a ribbed camouflage tank top that matched her green-flecked hazel eyes. She held a Ping-Pong ball between her fingers, poised to pelt.

Luce scrambled backward in her bedsheets and shielded her face. Her heart already hurt from missing Daniel. She didn't need any more pain. She looked down, still trying to get her bearings, and remembered the bed she had indiscriminately collapsed into the night before.

The woman in white who had appeared in Daniel's wake had introduced herself as Francesca, one of the teachers at Shoreline. Even in her stunned stupor, Luce could tell that the woman was beautiful. She was in her mid-thirties, with blond hair brushing her shoulders, round cheekbones, and large, soft features.

Angel, Luce decided almost instantly.

Francesca asked no questions on the way to Luce's room. She must have been expecting the late night drop-off, and she must have sensed Luce's utter exhaustion.

Now this stranger who'd pelted Luce back into con-sciousness looked ready to chuck another ball. "Good," she said in a gravelly voice. "You're awake."

"Who are you?" Luce asked sleepily.

"Who are *you,* is more like it. Other than the stranger I wake to find squatting in my room. Other than the kid disrupting my morning mantra with her weirdly personal sleep-babbling. I'm Shelby. *Enchantée.*"

Not an angel, Luce surmised. Just a Californian girl with a strong sense of entitlement.

Luce sat up in bed and looked around. The room was a little cramped, but it was nicely appointed, with light-colored hardwood floors; a working fireplace; a microwave; two deep, wide desks; and built-in bookshelves that doubled as a ladder to what Luce now realized was the top bunk.

She could see a private bathroom through a sliding wooden door. And—she had to blink a few times to be certain—an ocean view out the window. Not bad for a girl who had spent the past month gazing out at a rank old cemetery in a room more appropriate for a hospital than a school. But then, at least that rank cemetery and that room had meant she was with Daniel. She had barely begun getting comfortable at Sword & Cross. And now she was back to starting from scratch.

"Francesca didn't mention anything about me having a roommate." Luce knew instantly from the expression on Shelby's face that this was the Wrong Thing to Say.

So she took a quick glance at Shelby's décor instead. Luce had never trusted her own interior design instincts, or maybe she'd never had the chance to indulge them. She hadn't stuck around Sword & Cross long enough to do much decorating, but even before that, her room at Dover had been white-walled and bare. Sterile chic, as Callie had once said.

This room, on the other hand—there was something about it that was strangely . . . groovy. Varieties of potted plants she'd never seen before lined the window-sill; prayer flags were strung across the ceiling. A patch-work quilt in muted colors was sliding off the top bunk, half obstructing Luce's view of an astrology calendar taped over the mirror.

"What'd you think? They were going to clear out the dean's quarters just because you're Lucinda Price?"

"Um, no?" Luce shook her head. "That's not what I meant at all. Wait, how did you know my name?"

"So you *are* Lucinda Price?" The girl's green-flecked eyes seemed to fix on Luce's ratty gray pajamas. "Lucky me."

Luce was speechless.

"Sorry." Shelby exhaled and adjusted her tone, parking herself on the edge of Luce's bed. "I'm an only child. Leon—that's my therapist—he's trying to get me to be less harsh when I first meet people."

"Is it working?" Luce was an only child too, but she wasn't nasty to every stranger she came into contact with.

"What I mean is . . ." Shelby shifted uncomfortably. "I'm not used to sharing. Can we"—she tossed her head—"rewind?"

"That'd be nice."

"Okay." Shelby took a deep breath. "Frankie didn't mention your having a roommate last night because then she would have had to either notice—or, if she had already noticed, disclose—that I wasn't in bed when you arrived. I came in through that window"—she pointed—"around three."

Out the window, Luce could see a wide ledge connecting to an angled portion of the roof. She pictured Shelby darting across a whole network of ledges on the roof to get back here in the middle of the night.

Shelby made a show of yawning. "See, when it comes to the Nephilim kids at Shoreline, the only thing the teachers are strict about is the *pretense* of discipline. Discipline itself doesn't so much exist. Though, of course, Frankie's not going to advertise that to the new girl. Especially not Lucinda Price."

There it was again. That edge in Shelby's voice when she said Luce's name. Luce wanted to know what it meant. And where Shelby had been until three. And how she'd come in through the window in the dark without knocking over any of those plants. And who were the Nephilim kids?

Luce had sudden vivid flashbacks to the mental jungle gym Arriane had taken her through when they'd first met. Her Shoreline roommate's tough exterior was a lot like Arriane's, and Luce remembered a similar how-will-I-ever-be-friends-with-you feeling her first day at Sword & Cross.

But though Arriane had seemed intimidating and even a little dangerous, there had been something charmingly off-kilter about her from the start. Luce's new roommate, on the other hand, just seemed annoying.

Shelby popped off the bed and lumbered into the bathroom to brush her teeth. After digging through her duffel bag to find her toothbrush, Luce followed her in and gestured sheepishly at the toothpaste.

"I forgot to pack mine."

"No doubt the dazzle of your celebrity blinded you to the small necessities of life," Shelby replied, but she picked up the tube and extended it toward Luce.

They brushed in silence for about ten seconds until Luce couldn't take it anymore. She spat out a mouthful of froth. "Shelby?"

With her head in the belly of the porcelain sink, Shelby spat and said, "What?"

Instead of asking any of the questions that had been running through her head a minute before, Luce surprised herself and asked, "What was I saying in my sleep?"

This morning was the first in at least a month of vivid, complicated, Daniel-ridden dreams on which Luce had woken up unable to remember a single thing from her sleep.

Nothing. Not one brush of an angel wing. Not one kiss of his lips.

She stared at Shelby's gruff face in the mirror. Luce needed the girl to help jog her memory. She *must* have been dreaming about Daniel. If she hadn't been . . . what could it mean?

"Beats me," Shelby said finally. "You were all muffled and incoherent. Next time, try enunciating." She left the bathroom and slipped on a pair of orange flip-flops. "It's breakfast time. You coming or what?"

Luce scurried out of the bathroom. "What do I wear?" She was still in her pajamas. Francesca hadn't said anything last night about a dress code. But then, she'd also failed to mention the roommate situation.

Shelby shrugged. "What am I, the fashion police? Whatever takes the least amount of time. I'm hungry."

Luce hustled into a pair of skinny jeans and a black wraparound sweater. She would have liked to spend a few more minutes on her first-day-of-school look, but she just grabbed her backpack and followed Shelby out the door.

The dormitory hallway was different in the daylight. Everywhere she looked were bright, oversized windows with ocean views, or built-in bookshelves crammed full of thick, colorful hardcover books. The floors, the walls, the recessed ceilings and steep, curving staircases were all made from the same maple wood used to build the furniture inside Luce's room. It should have given the whole place a warm log cabin feel, except that the school's layout was as intricate and bizarre as Sword & Cross's dorm had been boring and straightforward. Every few steps, the hallway seemed to split off into small tributary hallways, with spiral staircases leading further into the dimly lit maze.

Two flights of stairs and what looked like one secret door later, Luce and Shelby stepped through a set of double-paned French windows and into the daylight. The sun was incredibly bright, but the air was cool enough that Luce was glad she'd worn a sweater. It smelled like the ocean, but not really like home. Less briny, more chalky than the East Coast shore.

"Breakfast is served on the terrace." Shelby gestured at a broad green expanse of land. This lawn was bordered on three sides by thick blue hydrangea bushes, and on the fourth by the steep, straight drop into the sea. It was hard for Luce to believe how very beautiful the school's setting was. She couldn't imagine being able to stay inside long enough to make it through a class.

As they approached the terrace, Luce saw another building, a long, rectangular structure with wooden shingles and cheery yellow-trimmed windowpanes. A large hand-carved sign hung over the entrance: "MESS HALL," it read in quotes, like it was trying to be ironic. It was certainly the nicest mess Luce had ever seen.

The terrace was filled with whitewashed iron lawn furniture and about a hundred of the most laid-back-looking students Luce had ever seen. Most of them had their shoes kicked off, their feet propped up on the tables as they dined on elaborate breakfast dishes. Eggs Benedict, fruit-topped Belgian waffles, wedges of rich-looking, flaky spinach-flecked quiche. Kids were reading the paper, gabbing on cell phones, playing croquet on the lawn. Luce knew from rich kids at Dover, but East Coast rich kids were pinched and snotty, not sun-kissed and carefree. The whole scene looked more like the first day of summer than a Tuesday in early November. It was all so pleasant, it was almost hard to begrudge the self-satisfied looks on these kids' faces. Almost.

Luce tried to imagine Arriane here, what she would think of Shelby or this oceanside dining, how she probably wouldn't know what to make fun of first. Luce wished she could turn to Arriane now. It would be good to be able to laugh.

Looking around, she accidentally caught the eyes of a couple of students. A pretty girl with olive skin, a polka-dot dress, and a green scarf tied in her glossy black hair. A sandy-haired guy with broad shoulders tackling an enormous stack of pancakes.

Luce's instinct was to turn her head away as soon as she made eye contact—always the safest bet at Sword & Cross. But . . . neither one of these kids glared at her. The biggest surprise about Shoreline was not the crystal sunshine or the cushy breakfast terrace or the buckets-of-money aura hovering over everyone. It was that the students here were smiling.

Well, most of them were smiling. When Shelby and Luce reached an unoccupied table, Shelby picked up a small placard and flung it to the ground. Luce leaned sideways to see the word RESERVED written on it just as a kid their age in a full-on black-tie waiter suit approached them with a silver tray.

"Um, this table is re—" he began to say, his voice cracking inopportunely.

"Coffee, black," Shelby said, then abruptly asked Luce, "What do you want?"

"Uh, same," Luce said, uncomfortable at being waited on. "Maybe a little milk."

"Scholarship kids. Gotta slave to get by." Shelby rolled her eyes at Luce as the waiter darted away to get their coffees. She picked up the *San Francisco Chronicle* from the middle of the table and unfolded the front page with a yawn.

It was right around then that Luce had had enough.

"Hey." She shoved Shelby's arm down so she could see her face behind the paper. Shelby's heavy eyebrows rose in surprise. "I used to *be* a scholarship kid," Luce told her. "Not at my last school, but the school before that—"

Shelby shrugged off Luce's hand. "Should I be impressed by that part of your résumé, too?"

Luce was just about to ask what it was Shelby had heard about her when she felt a warm hand on her shoulder.

Francesca, the teacher who'd met Luce at the door last night, was smiling down at her. She was tall, with an imperious bearing, and was put together with a style that came across as effortless. Francesca's soft blond hair was cleanly flipped to one side. Her lips were glossy pink.

She wore a cool fitted black sheath dress with a blue belt and matching peep-toe stilettos. It was the kind of outfit that would make anyone feel dowdy by comparison. Luce wished she'd at least put on mascara. And maybe not worn her mud-crusted Converses.

"Oh, good, you two connected." Francesca smiled. "I knew you'd become fast friends!"

Shelby was silent but rustled her paper. Luce just cleared her throat.

"I think you'll find Shoreline a very simple adjustment, Luce. It's designed that way. Most of our gifted students just ease right in." *Gifted?* "Of course, you can come to me with any questions. Or just lean on Shelby."

For the first time all morning, Shelby laughed. Her laugh was a gruff, gravelly thing, the kind of chortle Luce would have expected from an old man, a lifetime smoker, not a teenage yoga enthusiast.

Luce could feel her face pinching up into a scowl. The last thing she wanted was to "ease right in" to Shoreline. She didn't belong with a lot of spoiled gifted kids on a cliff overlooking the ocean. She belonged with real people, people with soul instead of squash rackets, who knew what life was like. She belonged with Daniel. She still had no idea what she was doing here, other than hiding out *very* temporarily while Daniel took care of his . . . war. After that, he was going to take her back home. Or something.

"Well, I'll see you both in class. Enjoy breakfast!" Francesca called over her shoulder as she glided away. "Try the quiche!" She waved her hand, signaling to the waiter to bring each girl a plate.

When she was gone, Shelby took a big slurp of her coffee and wiped her mouth with the back of her hand.

"Um, Shelby—"

"Ever heard of eating in peace?"

Luce banged her coffee cup back into its saucer and waited impatiently for the nervous waiter to put down their quiches and disappear again. Part of her wanted to find another table. There were happy buzzes of conversation going on all around her. And if she couldn't join one of them, even sitting alone would be better than this. But she was confused by what Francesca had said. Why pitch Shelby as some great roommate when it was clear the girl was a total hater? Luce milled a bite of quiche around in her mouth, knowing she wouldn't be able to eat until she spoke up.

"Okay, I know I'm new here, and for some reason that annoys you. I guess you had a single room before me, I don't know."

Shelby lowered the paper just below her eyes. She raised one giant eyebrow.

"But I'm not *that* bad. So what if I have a few questions? Forgive me for not coming into school knowing what the hell the Nephermans are—"

"*Nephilim.*"

"Whatever. I don't care. I have no interest in making you my enemy—which means some of this," Luce said, gesturing at the space between the two of them, "is coming from you. So what's your problem, anyway?"

The side of Shelby's mouth twitched. She folded and set down the paper and leaned back in her chair.

"You *should* care about the Nephilim. We're going to be your classmates." She flung out her hand, waving it at the terrace. "Look out at the pretty, privileged student body of the Shoreline School. Half of these dopes you'll never see again, except as the object of our practical jokes."

"Our?"

"Yes, you're in the 'honors program' with the Nephilim. But don't worry; in case you're not too bright"—Luce snorted—"the gifted track here is mostly a coverup, a place to stow away the Nephs without anyone getting too suspicious. In fact, the only person who's ever gotten suspicious is Beaker Brady."

"Who's Beaker Brady?" Luce asked, leaning in so she didn't have to shout over the rough static of the waves crashing on the shore below.

"That grade-A nerdo two tables over." Shelby nodded at a chubby kid dressed in plaid who'd just spilled yogurt all over a massive textbook. "His parents loathe the fact that he's never been accepted into the honors classes. Every semester, they wage a campaign. He brings in Mensa scores, results from science fairs, famous Nobelists he's impressed, the whole shebang. And every semester, Francesca has to make up some bunk unpassable test to keep him out." She snorted. "Like, 'Hey, Beaker, solve this Rubik's cube in under thirty seconds.'" Shelby clicked her tongue against her teeth. "Except the nimrod passed that one."

"But if it's a cover-up," Luce asked, feeling sort of bad for Beaker, "what's it a cover-up for?"

"People like me. I'm a Nephilim. *N-E-P-H-I-L-I-M.* That means anything with angel in its DNA. Mortals, immortals, transeternals. We try not to discriminate."

"Shouldn't the singular be, you know, *nephil,* like *cherub* from *cherubim* and *seraph* from *seraphim*?"

Shelby scowled. "Seriously? Would you want to be called a *nephil*? It sounds like a bag you carry your shame in. No, thanks. Nephilim it is, no matter how many of us you're talking about."

So Shelby *was* a sort of angel. Strange. She didn't look or act the part. She wasn't gorgeous like Daniel, Cam, or Francesca. Didn't possess the magnetism of someone like Roland or Arriane. She just seemed kind of coarse and cranky.

"So it's like angel prep school," Luce said. "But for what? Do you go on to angel college after this?"

"It depends on what the world needs. A lot of kids take a year off and do Nephilim Corps. You get to travel, have a fling with a foreigner, et cetera. But that's in times of, you know, relative peace. Right now, well . . ."

"Right now what?"

"Whatever." Shelby looked like she was biting the word. "It just depends on who you are. Everyone here has, you know, varying degrees of power," she went on, seeming to read Luce's mind. "A sliding scale depending on your family tree. But in your case—"

This Luce knew. "I'm just here because of Daniel."

Shelby tossed her napkin on her empty plate and stood up. "That's a real impressive way to pitch yourself, Luce. The girl whose big-shot boyfriend pulled some strings."

Was that what everyone thought about her here? Was that . . . the truth?

Shelby reached over and stole the last bite of quiche off Luce's plate. "If you want a Lucinda Price fan club, I'm sure you can find that here. Just leave me out of it, okay?"

"What are you talking about?" Luce stood up. Maybe she and Shelby needed to rewind again. "I don't want a fan club—"

"See, I *told* you," she heard a high but pretty voice say.

Suddenly, the girl with the green scarf was standing before her, grinning and nudging another girl forward. Luce glanced past them, but Shelby was already far away—and probably not worth catching up to. Up close, the green-scarf girl looked kind of like a young Salma Hayek, with full lips and an even fuller chest. The other girl, with her pale coloring, hazel eyes, and short black hair, looked kind of like Luce.

"Wait, so you're really Lucinda Price?" the pale girl asked. She had very small white teeth and was using them to hold a couple of sequin-tipped bobby pins while she twisted a few dark tendrils into little knots. "As in Luce-and-Daniel? As in the girl who just came from that awful school in Alabama—"

"Georgia." Luce sort of nodded.

"Same thing. Ohmigod, *what* was Cam like? I saw him once at this death metal concert . . . of course, I was too nervous to introduce myself. Not that you'd be interested in Cam, because obviously—*Daniel!*" She trilled a laugh. "I'm Dawn, b-t-dubs. This is Jasmine."

"Hi," Luce said slowly. This was new. "Um . . ."

"Don't mind her, she just drank, like, eleven coffees." Jasmine spoke about three times more slowly than Dawn did. "What she means is we're excited to meet you. We always say how you and Daniel are, like, the greatest love story. Ever."

"Seriously?" Luce cracked her knuckles.

"Are you kidding?" Dawn asked, though Luce kept expecting *them* to be the ones working up to some kind of joke. "All that dying again and again? Okay, does it make you want him even more? I bet it *does*! And ohhh, when that fire that burns you up"—she closed her eyes, put a hand over her stomach, then brushed it up her body, clasping a fist over her heart. "My mom used to tell me the story when I was a little girl."

Luce was shocked. She glanced around the busy terrace, wondering whether anyone could overhear them. Speaking of burning up, her cheeks must be beet red right now.

An iron bell rang from the roof of the mess hall to signal the end of breakfast, and Luce was glad to see that everyone else had other things to focus on. Like getting to class.

"Your mom used to tell you what story?" Luce asked slowly. "About me and Daniel?"

"Just some of the highlights," Dawn said, opening her eyes. "Does it feel like a hot flash? Like a menopause kind of thing, not that you would know—"

Jasmine smacked Dawn on the arm. "Did you just compare Luce's unbridled passion to a hot flash?"

"Sorry." Dawn giggled. "I'm just fascinated. It sounds so totally romantic and awesome. I'm envious— in a good way!"

"Envious that I die every time I try to get with the guy of my dreams?" Luce hunched up her shoulders. "It's actually kind of a buzz kill."

"Tell that to the girl whose only kiss to date was with Ira Frank of the Irritable Bowel Syndrome." Jasmine gestured teasingly at Dawn.

When Luce didn't laugh, Dawn and Jasmine filled in with a placating giggle, as if they thought she was just being modest. Luce had never been on the receiving end of one of those giggles before.

"What exactly did your mom say?" Luce asked.

"Oh, just the usual stuff: The war broke out, shit hit the fan, and when they drew a line in the clouds, Daniel was all 'Nothing can tear us apart,' and that pissed *everyone* off. 'Course it's *my* favorite part of the story. So now your love has to suffer this *eternal* punishment where you still *desperately* want each other but you can't, like, you know—"

"But in some lives they can." Jasmine corrected Dawn, then winked impishly at Luce, who almost couldn't move from the shock of hearing all of this.

"No way!" Dawn flung out a hand dismissively. "The whole point is that she bursts into flames when she—" Seeing Luce's horrified expression, Dawn winced. "*Sorry.* Not what you want to hear."

Jasmine cleared her throat and leaned in. "My older sister was telling me this one story from your past that I swear would—"

"Oooh!" Dawn linked her arm through Luce's, as if this knowledge—knowledge that Luce had *no* access to— made her a more desirable friend. This was maddening. Luce was fiercely embarrassed. And, okay, a little excited. And absolutely unsure whether any of it was true. One thing *was* sure: Luce was suddenly kind of . . . famous. But it felt strange. Like she was one of those unnamed bimbos next to the It-boy movie star in a paparazzi photo.

"You guys!" Jasmine was pointing exaggeratedly down at the clock on her phone. "We're so super-late! We've got to book it to class."

Luce grimaced, quickly grabbing her backpack. She had no idea what class she had first, or where to find it, or how to take Jasmine and Dawn's enthusiasm. She hadn't seen such extended, eager smiles since—well, maybe ever.

"Do either of you know how I figure out where my first class is? I don't think I got a schedule."

"Duh," Dawn said. "Follow us. We're all together. All the time! It's so fun."

The two girls walked with Luce, one on either side, and took her on a winding tour between the tables of other kids finishing their breakfasts. Despite being "so super-late," both Jasmine and Dawn practically sauntered across the freshly cut grass.

Luce thought about asking these girls what was up with Shelby, but she didn't want to start off looking like a gossip. Besides, the girls seemed nice and everything, but it wasn't like Luce needed to make any new best friends. She had to keep reminding herself: This was only temporary.

Temporary, but still stunningly beautiful. The three of them walked along the hydrangea path, which curved around the mess hall. Dawn was chattering about something, but Luce couldn't take her eyes off the bluffs' dramatic edge, how abruptly the terrain dropped hundreds of feet to the glittering ocean. The waves rolled toward the small stretch of tawny beach at the foot of the cliff almost as casually as the Shoreline student body rolled toward class.

"Here we are," Jasmine said.

An impressive two-story A-frame cabin stood alone at the end of the path. It had been built in the middle of a shady pocket of redwoods, so its steep, triangular roof and the vast open lawn in front of it were covered with a blanket of fallen needles. There was a nice grassy patch with some picnic tables, but the main attraction was the cabin itself: More than half of it looked like it was made of glass, all wide, tinted windows and open sliding doors. Like something Frank Lloyd Wright could have designed. Several students lounged on a huge second-story deck that faced the ocean, and several more kids were mounting the twin staircases that wound up from the path.

"Welcome to the Nephi-lodge," Jasmine said.

"*This* is where you guys have class?" Luce's mouth was agape. It looked more like a vacation home than a school building.

Next to her, Dawn squealed and squeezed Luce's wrist.

"Good morning, Steven!" Dawn called across the

lawn, waving to an older man who was standing at the foot of the stairs. He had a thin face, stylish rectangular glasses, and a thick head of wavy salt-and-pepper hair. "I just absolutely *love* it when he wears the three-piece suit," she whispered.

"Morning, girls." The man smiled at them and waved. He looked at Luce long enough to make her veer toward nervousness, but the smile stayed on his face. "See you in a few," he called, and started up the stairs.

"Steven Filmore," Jasmine whispered, filling Luce in as they trailed behind him up the stairs. "Aka S.F., aka the Silver Fox. He's one of our teachers, and yes, Dawn is truly, madly, deeply in love with him. Even though he's spoken for. She is shameless."

"But I love Francesca, too." Dawn swatted Jasmine, then turned to Luce, her dark eyes smiling. "I defy you not to develop a couples crush on them."

"Wait." Luce paused. "The Silver Fox and Francesca are our teachers? And you call them by their first names? And they're *together*? Who teaches what?"

"We call the whole morning block humanities," Jasmine said, "though *angelics* would be more appropriate. Frankie and Steven teach it jointly. Part of the deal here, sort of yin and yang. You know, so none of the students get . . . swayed."

Luce bit her lip. They'd reached the top of the stairs and were standing in a crowd of students on the deck.

Everyone else was starting to amble through the sliding glass doors. "What do you mean, 'swayed'?"

"They're both fallen, of course, but have picked different sides. She's an angel, and he's more of a demon." Dawn spoke nonchalantly, as if she were talking about the difference between frozen yogurt flavors. Seeing Luce's eyes bulge, she added, "It's not like they can get married or anything—though that would be the hottest wedding ever. They just sort of . . . live in sin."

"A demon is teaching our humanities class?" Luce asked. "And that's okay?"

Dawn and Jasmine looked at each other and chuckled. "*Very* okay," Dawn said. "You'll come around to Steven. Come on, we gotta go."

Following the flow of other kids, Luce entered the classroom. It was broad and had three shallow risers, with desks on them, that led down to a couple of long tables. Most of the light came in through skylights. The natural lighting and high ceilings made the room seem even bigger than it was. An ocean breeze blew in through the open doors and kept the air comfortable and fresh. It could not have been more different from Sword & Cross. Luce thought she could almost have liked Shoreline, if it hadn't been for the fact that her whole reason for being here—the most important person in her life—was missing. She wondered if Daniel was thinking about her. Did he miss her the way she missed him?

Luce chose a desk close to the windows, between Jasmine and a cute boy-next-door kind of guy who was wearing cutoffs, a Dodgers cap, and a navy sweatshirt. A few girls stood clustered near the door to the bathroom. One of them had curly hair and boxy purple glasses. When Luce saw the girl's profile, she nearly bolted from her seat.

Penn.

But when the girl turned toward Luce, her face was a little squarer and her clothes were a little tighter and her laugh was a little louder and Luce almost felt like her heart was wilting. Of course it wasn't Penn. It never would be, ever again.

Luce could feel the other kids glancing at her—some of them outright stared. The only one who didn't was Shelby, who gave Luce an acknowledging nod.

It wasn't a huge class, just twenty desks arranged on the risers, facing the two long mahogany tables at the front. There were two dry-erase white boards behind the tables. Two bookshelves on either side. Two trash cans. Two desk lamps. Two laptops, one on each table. And the two teachers, Steven and Francesca, huddled near the front of the room, whispering.

In a move Luce wasn't expecting, they turned and stared at her too, then glided to the tables. Francesca sat on top of one, with one leg tucked beneath her and one of her high heels skimming the wood floor. Steven leaned against the other table, opened a heavy maroon leather portfolio, and rested his pen between his lips. For an older man, he was good-looking, sure, but Luce almost wished he weren't. He reminded her of Cam, and of how deceptive a demon's charm could be.

She waited for the rest of the class to take out textbooks she didn't have, to plunge into some reading assignment she'd be behind on, so she could surrender to feeling overwhelmed and just daydream about Daniel.

But none of that happened. And most of the kids were still sneaking glances at her.

"By now you must all have noticed that we're welcoming a new student." Francesca's voice was low and honey-thick, like a jazz singer's.

Steven smiled, showing a flash of brilliant white teeth. "Tell us, Luce, how are you liking Shoreline so far?"

The color drained from Luce's face as the other students' desks made scraping sounds on the floor. They were actually turning in their seats to focus on her.

She could feel her heart race and her palms grow damp. She shrank in her seat, wishing she were just a normal kid at a normal school back home in normal Thunderbolt, Georgia. At times over the past few days, she'd wished she'd never seen a shadow, never gotten into the kind of trouble that left her dear friends dead, or got her involved with Cam, or made it impossible for

Daniel to be near her. But there was where her anxious, tumbling mind always came to a full stop: How to be normal and still have Daniel? Who was so very far from normal. It was impossible. So here she was, sucking it up.

"I guess I'm still getting used to Shoreline." Her voice wobbled, betraying her, echoing off the sloped ceiling. "But it seems all right so far."

Steven laughed. "Well, Francesca and I thought to help you get used to it, we'd change gears from our usual Tuesday-morning student presentations—"

From across the room, Shelby hooted, "Yes!" and Luce noticed that she had a stack of notecards on her desk and a big poster at her feet that read APPARITIONS AIN'T SO BAD. So Luce had just gotten her out of a presentation. That had to be worth something in roommate points.

"What Steven means," Francesca chimed in, "is that we're going to play a game, as an icebreaker." She slid down from her table and walked around the room, heels clicking as she distributed a sheet of paper to each student.

Luce expected the chorus of groans that those words usually evoked from a classroom of teens. But these kids all seemed so agreeable and well-adjusted. They were actually just going to go with the flow.

When she laid the sheet on Luce's desk, Francesca

said, "This should give you an idea of who some of your classmates are, and what goals we work toward in this class."

Luce looked down at the paper. Lines had been drawn on the page, dividing it into twenty boxes. Each box contained a phrase. It was a game she'd played before, once at summer camp in western Georgia as a little kid, and again a couple of times in her classes at Dover. The object was to go around the room and match a different student with each phrase. Mostly, she was relieved; there were definitely more embarrassing icebreakers out there. But when she looked more closely at the phrases—expecting normal things like "Has a pet turtle" or "Wants to go skydiving someday"—she was a little unnerved to see things like "Speaks more than eighteen languages" and "Has visited the outerworld."

It was about to be painfully obvious that Luce was the only non-Nephilim in the class. She thought back to the nervous waiter who had brought her and Shelby their breakfast. Maybe Luce would be more comfortable among the scholarship kids. Beaker Brady didn't even know he'd dodged a bullet.

"If no one has questions," Steven said from the front of the room, "you're welcome to begin."

"Go outside, enjoy yourselves," Francesca added. "Take all the time you need."

Luce followed the rest of the students onto the deck.

As they walked toward the railing, Jasmine leaned over Luce's shoulder, pointing a green-lacquered fingernail at one of the boxes. "I have a relative who's a full-blooded cherub," she said. "Crazy old Uncle Carlos."

Luce nodded, like she knew what that meant, and jotted in Jasmine's name.

"Ooh, and I can levitate," Dawn chirped, pointing to the top left corner of Luce's page. "Not, like, a hundred percent of the time, but usually after I've had my coffee."

"Wow." Luce tried not to stare—it didn't seem like Dawn was making a joke. She could *levitate*?

Trying not to show that she was feeling more and more inadequate, Luce searched the page for something, anything she knew anything about.

Has experience summoning the Announcers.

The shadows. Daniel had told her the proper name for them that last night at Sword & Cross. Though she'd never actually "summoned" them—they'd always just shown up—Luce did have some experience.

"You can write me in there." She pointed to the bottom left corner of the paper. Both Jasmine and Dawn looked up at her, a little awed but not disbelieving, before moving on to fill in the rest of their sheets. Luce's heart slowed down a little. Maybe this wasn't going to be so bad.

In the next few minutes she met Lilith, a prim redhead

who was one of three Nephilim triplets ("You can tell us apart by our vestigial tails," she explained. "Mine's curly"); Oliver, a deep-voiced, squat boy who had visited the outerworld on summer vacation last year ("So totally overrated I can't even begin to tell you"); and Jack, who felt like he was on the cusp of being able to read minds and thought it would be all right if Luce wrote him down for that. ("I sense that you're okay with that, am I right?" He made a gun out of his fingers and clicked his tongue.) She had three boxes left when Shelby tugged the paper out of her hands.

"I can do both of these," she said, pointing at two of the boxes. "Which one do you want me for?"

Speaks more than eighteen languages or *Has glimpsed a past life.*

"Wait a minute," Luce whispered. "You've . . . you can glimpse past lives?"

Shelby waggled her eyebrows at Luce and dashed her signature into the box, adding her name in the "eighteen languages" box for good measure. Luce stared at the paper, thinking about all her own past lives and how frustratingly off-limits they were to her. She had underestimated Shelby.

But her roommate was already gone. Standing in Shelby's place was the boy she'd sat next to inside the classroom. He was a good half foot taller than Luce, with a bright, friendly smile, a splash of freckles on his nose, and clear blue eyes. Something about him, even the way he was chewing on his pen, looked . . . sturdy. Luce realized this was a strange word to describe someone she'd never spoken to, but she couldn't help it.

"Oh, thank God." He laughed, smacking his forehead. "The one thing I can do is the one thing you have left."

"'Can reflect a mirror image of self or others'?" Luce read slowly.

He tossed his head from side to side and wrote his name in the box. Miles Fisher. "Real impressive to someone like you, I'm sure."

"Um. Yeah." Luce turned away. Someone like her, who didn't even know what that meant.

"Wait, hey, where are you going?" He tugged her sleeve. "Uh-oh. You didn't catch the self-effacing joke?" When she shook her head, Miles's face fell. "I just meant, compared to everyone else in the class, I'm barely hanging on. The only person I've ever been able to reflect other than myself was my mom. Freaked my dad out for about ten seconds, but then it faded."

"Wait." Luce blinked at Miles. "You made a mirror image of your mother?"

"By accident. They say it's easy to do with the people you, like, love." He blushed, the faintest rosy pink across his cheekbones. "Now you're going to think I'm some kind of mama's boy. I just mean 'easy' is about where my powers end. Whereas you—you're the famous

Lucinda Price." He waved his hands in a very masculine version of spirit fingers.

"I wish everyone would stop saying that," she snapped. Then, feeling rude, she sighed and leaned against the deck's railing to look out at the water. It was just so hard to process all these hints that other people here knew more about her than she knew about herself. She didn't mean to take it out on this guy. "I'm sorry, it's just, I thought I was the only one barely hanging on. What's your story?"

"Oh, I'm what they call 'diluted,'" he said, making exaggerated air quotes. "Mom has angel in her blood a few generations back, but all my other relatives are mortal. My powers are embarrassingly low-grade. But I'm here because my parents endowed the school with, um, this deck you're standing on."

"Whoa."

"It's really not impressive. My family's obsessed with me being at Shoreline. You should hear the pressure I get at home to date a 'nice Nephilim girl for once.'" Luce laughed—one of the first real laughs she'd had in days. Miles rolled his eyes good-naturedly. "So, I saw you having breakfast with Shelby this morning. She your roommate?"

Luce nodded. "Speaking of nice Nephilim girls," she joked.

"Well, I know she's kind of, um . . ." Miles hissed and made a clawing motion with one hand, causing Luce to crack up again. "Anyway, I'm not the star student here or anything, but I've been around a while, and half the time I still think this place is pretty crazy. So if you ever want to have a very normal breakfast or something—"

Luce found herself bobbing her head. *Normal.* Music to her mortal ears.

"Like . . . tomorrow?" Miles asked.

"That sounds great."

Miles grinned and waved goodbye, and Luce realized that all the other students had already gone back inside. Alone for the first time all morning, she looked down at the sheet of paper in her hand, unsure how to feel about the other kids at Shoreline. She missed Daniel, who could have decoded a lot of this for her if only he hadn't been—where *was* he, anyway? She didn't even know.

Too far away.

She pressed a finger to her lips, remembering his last kiss. The incredible embrace of his wings. She felt so cold without him, even in the California sunshine. But she was here because of him, accepted into this class of angels or whatever they were—complete with her bizarre new reputation—all thanks to him. In a weird way, it felt good to be connected to Daniel so inextricably.

Until he came for her, it was all she had to hold on to.

THREE

SIXTEEN DAYS

"Okay, hit me, what's the weirdest thing about Shore-line so far?"

It was Wednesday morning before class, and Luce was seated at a sunny breakfast table on the terrace, sharing a pot of tea with Miles. He was wearing a vin-tage yellow T-shirt with a Sunkist logo on it, a baseball cap pulled down just above his blue eyes, flip-flops, and frayed jeans. Feeling inspired by the very relaxed dress code at Shoreline, Luce had swapped out her standard black getup. She was wearing a red sundress with a short white cardigan, which felt kind of like the first day of sunshine after a long stretch of rain.

She dropped a spoonful of sugar into her cup and laughed. "I don't even know where to start. Maybe my roommate, who I think snuck in just before sunrise this morning and was gone again before I woke up. No, wait, it's taking a class taught by a demon-and-angel couple. Or"—she swallowed—"the way kids here look at me like I'm some legendary freak. Anonymous freak, I got used to. But notorious freak—"

"You are *not* notorious." Miles took a giant bite of his croissant. "I'm gonna tackle those one at a time," he said, chewing.

As he dabbed the side of his mouth with his napkin, Luce half-marveled, half-chuckled at his occasionally impeccable table manners. She couldn't help picturing him taking some fancy etiquette course at the golf club as a boy.

"Shelby's rough around the edges," Miles said, "but she can be cool, too. When she feels like it. Not like I've ever witnessed that side of her." He laughed. "But that's the rumor. And the Frankie/Steven thing weirded me out at first, too, but somehow they make it work. It's like a celestial balancing act. For some reason having both sides present gives students here the most freedom to develop."

There was that word again. *Develop*. She remembered that Daniel had used it when he first told her he wouldn't be joining her at Shoreline. But develop into what? It could only apply to the kids who were Nephilim. Not Luce, who was the lone full human in her class of almost-angels, waiting until *her* angel felt like swooping back in to save her.

"Luce," Miles said, interrupting her thoughts. "The reason people stare at you is because everyone's heard about you and Daniel, but no one knows the real story."

"So instead of just asking me—"

"What? Whether you two really do it on the clouds? Or whether his rampant, ya know, 'glory' ever overwhelms your mortal"—he stopped, catching the horrified look on Luce's face, then gulped. "Sorry. I mean, you're right, they let it blow up into some big myth. Everyone else, that is. I try not to, um, speculate." Miles put down his tea and stared at his napkin. "Maybe it feels too personal to ask about."

Miles shifted his gaze and was now staring at her, but it didn't make Luce feel nervous. Instead, his clear blue eyes and slightly lopsided smile felt like an open door, an invitation to talk about some of the things she hadn't been able to tell anyone yet. As much as it sucked, Luce understood why Daniel and Mr. Cole had forbidden her to reach out to Callie or her parents. But Daniel and Mr. Cole were the ones who had enrolled her at Shoreline.

They were the ones who'd said she'd be okay here. So she couldn't see any reason to keep her story a secret from someone like Miles. Especially since he already knew *some* version of the truth.

"It's a long story," she said. "Literally. And I still don't know all of it. But basically, Daniel is an important angel. I guess he was kind of a big deal before the Fall." She swallowed, not wanting to meet Miles's eyes. She felt nervous. "At least, he was until he fell in love with me."

It all began to pour out of her. Everything from her first day at Sword & Cross, to how Arriane and Gabbe took care of her, to how Molly and Cam taunted her, to the gut-wrenching feeling of seeing a photograph of herself in a former life. Penn's death and how it devastated her. The surreal battle in the cemetery. Luce left out some of the Daniel details, private moments they'd shared together . . . but by the time she finished, she thought she'd given Miles a pretty complete picture of what had happened—and hopefully dispelled the myth of her intrigue for at least one person.

At the end, she felt lighter. "Wow. I've never actually told this stuff to anyone. Feels really good to say it aloud. Like it's more real now that I've admitted it to someone else."

"You can keep going if you want to," he said.

"I know I'm only here for a short time," she said.

"And in a way, I think Shoreline will help me to get used to people—I mean angels like Daniel. And Nephilim like you. But I still can't help feeling out of place. Like I'm posing as something I'm not."

Miles had been nodding and agreeing with Luce the whole time she told her story, but now he shook his head. "No way—the fact that you're mortal makes the whole thing even more impressive."

Luce glanced around the terrace. For the first time, she noticed a clear line dividing the tables of the Nephilim kids from the rest of the student body. The Nephilim claimed all the tables on the west side, closest to the water. There were fewer of them, no more than twenty, but they took up a lot more tables, sometimes with just one kid at a table that could have seated six, while the rest of the kids had to cram into the remaining east-side tables. Take Shelby, for example, who sat alone, battling the fierce wind over the paper she was trying to read. There was a lot of musical chairs, but not one of the non-Nephilim seemed to consider crossing over to sit with the "gifted" kids.

Luce had met some of the other non-gifted kids yesterday. After lunch, classes were held in the main building, a much less architecturally impressive structure where more traditional subjects were taught. Biology, geometry, European history. Some of those students seemed nice, but Luce felt an unspoken distance—all because she was on the gifted track—that thwarted the possibility of a conversation.

"Don't get me wrong, I've gotten to be friends with some of those guys." Miles pointed to a crowded table. "I'd pick Connor or Eddie G. for a game of touch football any day over any of the Nephilim. But seriously, do you think anyone over there could have handled what you did, and lived to tell about it?"

Luce rubbed her neck and felt tears prick at the corners of her eyes. Miss Sophia's dagger was still fresh in her mind, and she could never think about that night without her heart aching over Penn. Her death had been so senseless. None of it was fair. "I barely lived," she said softly.

"Yeah," Miles said, wincing. "That part I heard about. It's weird: Francesca and Steven are big on teaching us about the present and the future, but not really the past. Something to do with empowering us."

"What do you mean?"

"Ask me anything about the great battle that's coming, and the role a strapping young Nephilim like myself might play in it. But the early stuff you were talking about? None of the lessons here ever really go into that. Speaking of which"—Miles pointed at the terrace, which was emptying out—"we should go. You want to do this again sometime?"

"Definitely." And Luce meant it; she liked Miles. He

was much easier to talk to than anyone else she'd met so far. He was friendly and had the kind of sense of humor that put Luce instantly at ease. But she was distracted by something he'd said. The battle that was coming. Daniel and Cam's battle. Or a battle with Miss Sophia's group of Elders? If even the Nephilim were preparing for it, where did that leave Luce?

⁂

Steven and Francesca had a way of dressing in complementary colors that made them look better outfitted for a photo shoot than a lecture. On Luce's second day at Shoreline, Francesca was wearing three-inch golden gladiator heels and a mod pumpkin-colored A-line dress. It had a loose bow around her neck and matched, almost exactly, the orange tie that Steven wore with his ivory oxford shirt and navy blazer.

They were stunning to look at, and Luce was drawn to them, but not exactly in the couples-crush way Dawn had predicted the day before. Watching her teachers from her desk between Miles and Jasmine, Luce felt drawn to Francesca and Steven for reasons closer to her heart: They reminded her of her relationship with Daniel.

Though she'd never seen them actually touch, when they stood close together—which was almost always— the magnetism between them practically warped the walls. Of course that had something to do with their powers as fallen angels, but it must also have had to do with the unique way they connected. Luce couldn't help resenting them. They were constant reminders of what she couldn't have right now.

Most of the students had taken their seats. Dawn and Jasmine were going on to Luce about joining the steering committee so she could help them plan all these amazing social events. Luce had never been a big extracurricular girl. But these girls had been so nice to her, and Jasmine's face looked so bright when she talked about a yacht trip they were planning later that week that Luce decided to give the committee a chance. She was adding her name to the roster when Steven stepped forward, tossed his blazer on the table behind him, and wordlessly spread his arms out at his sides.

As if summoned, a shard of deep black shadow seemed to part from the shadows of one of the redwoods right outside the window. It peeled itself off the grass, then took substance and whipped into the room through the open window. It was quick, and where it went the day blackened and the room fell into darkness.

Luce gasped out of habit, but she wasn't the only one. In fact, most of the students inched back nervously in their desks as Steven begin to twirl the shadow. He just reached his hands in and began wrenching faster and faster, seeming to wrestle with something. Soon the shadow was spinning around in front of him so quickly it went blurry, like the spokes of a turning wheel. A thick gust of mildewy wind was emitted from its core, blowing Luce's hair back from her face.

Steven manipulated the shadow, arms straining, from a messy, amorphous shape into a tight, black sphere, no bigger than a grapefruit.

"Class," he said, coolly bouncing the levitating ball of blackness a few inches above his fingers, "meet the subject of today's lesson."

Francesca stepped forward and transferred the shadow to her hands. In her heels, she was nearly as tall as Steven. And, Luce imagined, she was just as skilled at dealing with the shadows.

"You've all seen the Announcers at some point," she said, walking slowly along the half-moon of student desks so they could each get a better look. "And some of you," she said, eyeing Luce, "even have some experience working with them. But do you really know what they are? Do you know what they can do?"

Gossips, Luce thought, remembering what Daniel had told her the night of the battle. She was still too new to Shoreline to feel comfortable calling out the answer, but none of the other students seemed to know. Slowly she raised her hand.

Francesca cocked her head. "Luce."

"They carry messages," she said, growing surer as

she spoke, thinking back to Daniel's assurance. "But they're harmless."

"Messengers, yes. But harmless?" Francesca glanced at Steven. Her tone betrayed nothing about whether Luce was right or wrong, which made Luce feel embarrassed.

The entire class was surprised when Francesca stepped back alongside Steven, took hold of one side of the shadow's border while he gripped the other, and gave it a firm tug. "We call this glimpsing," she said.

The shadow bulged and stretched out like a balloon being blown up. It made a thick glugging sound as its blackness distorted, showing colors more vivid than anything Luce had seen before. Deep chartreuse, glittering gold, marbleized swaths of pink and purple. A whole swirling world of color glowing brighter and more distinct behind a disappearing mesh of shadow. Steven and Francesca were still tugging, stepping backward slowly until the shadow was about the size and shape of a large projector screen. Then they stopped.

They gave no warning, no "What you are about to see," and after a horrified moment, Luce knew why. There could be no preparation for this.

The tangle of colors separated, settled finally into a canvas of distinct shapes. They were looking at a city. An ancient stone-walled city . . . on fire. Overcrowded and polluted, consumed by angry flames. People cornered by the flames, their mouths dark emptinesses, raising their arms to the skies. And everywhere a shower of bright sparks and burning bits of fire, a rain of deadly light landing everywhere and igniting everything it touched.

Luce could practically smell the rot and doom coming through the shadow screen. It was horrific to look at, but the strangest part, by far, was that there wasn't any sound. Other students around her were ducking their heads, as if they were trying to block out some wail, some screaming that to Luce was indistinguishable. There was nothing but clean silence as they watched more and more people die.

When she wasn't sure her stomach could take much more, the focus of the image shifted, sort of zoomed out, and Luce could see it from a distance. Not one but two cities were burning. A strange idea came to her, softly, like a memory she'd always had but hadn't thought of in a while. She knew what they were looking at: Sodom and Gomorrah, two cities in the Bible, two cities destroyed by God.

Then, like turning off a light switch, Steven and Francesca snapped their fingers and the image disappeared. The remnants of the shadow shattered into a small black cloud of ash that settled eventually on the floor of the classroom. Around Luce, the other students all seemed to be catching their breath.

Luce couldn't take her eyes off the place where the

shadow had been. How had it done that? It was starting to congeal again, the pieces of dark pooling together, slowly returning to a more familiar shadow shape. Its services complete, the Announcer inched sluggishly along the floorboards, then slid right out of the classroom, like the shadow cast by a closing door.

"You may be wondering why we just put you through that," Steven said, addressing the class. He and Francesca shared a worried look as they glanced around the room. Dawn was whimpering at her desk.

"As you know," Francesca said, "most of the time in this class, we like to focus on what you as Nephilim have the power to do. How you can change things for the better, however each of you decide to define that. We like to look forward, instead of backward."

"But what you saw today," Steven said, "was more than just a history lesson with incredible special effects. And it wasn't just imagery we conjured up. No, what you were seeing was the actual Sodom and Gomorrah, as they were destroyed by the Great Tyrant when he—"

"Unh-unh-unh!" Francesca said, wagging a finger. "We don't go for easy name-calling in here."

"Of course. She's right, as usual. Even I sometimes lapse into propaganda." Steven beamed at the class. "But as I was saying, the Announcers are more than mere shadows. They can hold very valuable information. In a way, they *are* shadows—but shadows of the past, of long-ago and not-so-long-ago events."

"What you saw today," Francesca finished, "was just a demonstration of an invaluable skill some of you may be able to harness. Someday."

"You won't want to try it right now." Steven wiped his hands with a handkerchief he'd pulled from a pocket. "In fact, we forbid you to attempt this, lest you lose control and lose yourselves in the shadows. But someday, maybe, it will be a possibility."

Luce shared a glance with Miles. He gave her a wide-eyed smile, as if he were relieved to hear this. He didn't seem to feel at all shut out, not the way Luce did.

"Besides," Francesca said, "most of you will probably find that you feel fatigued." Luce looked around the room at the students' faces as Francesca talked. Her voice had the effect of aloe on a sunburn. Half of the kids had their eyes closed, as if they'd been soothed. "That's very normal. Shadow-glimpsing is not done without great cost. It takes energy to look back even a few days, but to look back millennia? Well, you can feel the effects yourselves. In light of that"—she looked at Steven—"we're going to let you out early today to rest."

"We'll pick up again tomorrow, so make sure you've done your reading on disapparition," Steven said. "Class dismissed."

Around Luce, students rose slowly from their desks.

They looked dazed, exhausted. When she stood up, her own knees were a little wobbly, but somehow she felt less shaken than the others seemed to be. She tightened her cardigan around her shoulders and followed Miles out of the classroom.

"Pretty heavy stuff," he said, taking the stairs down from the deck two at a time. "Are you okay?"

"I'm fine," Luce said. She was. "Are you?"

Miles rubbed his forehead. "It just feels like we were really there. I'm glad they let us out early. Feel like I need a nap."

"Seriously!" Dawn added, coming up behind them on the winding path back to the dorm. "That was the last thing I was expecting from my Wednesday morning. I am so conking out right now."

It was true: The destruction of Sodom and Gomorrah had been horrifying. So real, Luce's skin still felt hot from the blaze.

They took the shortcut back to the dorm, around the north side of the mess hall and into the shade of the redwoods. It was strange seeing the campus so empty, with all the other kids at Shoreline still in class in the main building. One by one, the Nephilim peeled off the path and headed straight to bed.

Except for Luce. She wasn't tired, not at all. Instead, she felt strangely energized. She wished, again, that Daniel were there. She badly wanted to talk to him about Francesca and Steven's demonstration—and to know why he hadn't told her sooner that there was more to the shadows than she could see.

In front of Luce were the stairs leading up to her dorm room. Behind her, the redwood forest. She paced outside the entrance to the dorm, unwilling to go inside, unwilling to sleep this off and pretend she hadn't seen it. Francesca and Steven wouldn't have been trying to scare the class; they must have intended to teach them something. Something they couldn't come right out and say. But if the Announcers carried messages and echoes of the past, then what was the point of the one they'd just been shown?

She went into the woods.

Her watch said 11 a.m., but it could have been midnight under the dark canopy of trees. Goose bumps rose on her bare legs as she pressed deeper into the shady forest. She didn't want to think about it too hard; thinking would only increase the odds of her chickening out. She was about to enter uncharted territory. Forbidden territory.

She was going to summon an Announcer.

She'd done things to them before. The very first time was when she pinched one during class to keep it from sneaking into her pocket. There was the time in the library when she'd swatted one away from Penn. Poor Penn. Luce couldn't help wondering what message that

Announcer had been carrying. If she had known how to manipulate it then, the way Francesca and Steven had manipulated the one today—could she have stopped what happened?

She closed her eyes. Saw Penn, slumped against the wall, her chest aproned with blood. Her fallen friend. *No.* Looking back on that night was too painful, and it never got Luce anywhere. All she could do now was look ahead.

She had to fight the cold fear clawing at her insides. A slinking, black, familiar shape lurking alongside the true shadow of a low redwood branch a mere ten yards in front of her.

She took a step toward it, and the Announcer shrank back. Trying not to make any sudden moves, Luce pressed on, closer, closer, willing the shadow not to slip away.

There.

The shadow twitched under its tree branch but stayed put.

Heart racing, Luce tried to calm herself down. Yes, it was dark in this forest; and yes, not a soul knew where she was; and okay, sure, there was a chance no one would miss her for a good while if anything happened— but there was no reason to panic. Right? So why did she feel gripped by a gnawing fear? Why was she getting the same tremor in her hands she used to get when she saw the shadows as a girl, back before she'd learned they were basically harmless?

It was time to make a move. She could either stand here frozen forever, or she could chicken out and go sulking back to the dorm, or—

Her arm shot out, no longer shaking, and took hold of the thing. She dragged it up and clutched it tightly to her chest, surprised by its heft, by how cold and damp it was. Like a wet towel. Her arms were shaking. What did she do with it now?

The image of those burning cities flashed into her mind. Luce wondered whether she could stand to see this message on her own. If she could even figure out how to unlock its secrets. How did these things work? All Francesca and Steven had done was pull.

Holding her breath, Luce worked her fingers along the shadow's feathery edges, gripped it, and gave it a gentle tug. To her surprise, the Announcer was pliant, almost like putty, and took whatever shape her hands suggested. Grimacing, she tried to manipulate it into a square. Into something like the screen she'd seen her teachers form.

At first it was easy, but the shadow seemed to grow stiffer the more she tried to stretch it out. And every time she repositioned her hands to pull on another part, the rest would recoil into a cold, lumpy black mass. Soon she was out of breath and using her arm to wipe the sweat off her brow. She did not want to give up. But when the shadow started to vibrate, Luce screamed and dropped it to the ground.

Instantly, it darted off into the trees. Only after it was gone did Luce realize: It hadn't been the shadow that was vibrating. It was the cell phone in her backpack.

She'd gotten used to not having one. Until that moment, she'd even forgotten that Mr. Cole had given her his old phone before he put her on the plane to California. It was almost completely useless, solely so that he would have a way to reach her, to keep her up to date on what stories he was feeding to her parents, who still believed she was at Sword & Cross. So that when Luce talked to them, she could lie consistently.

No one besides Mr. Cole even had her number. And for really annoying safety reasons, Daniel hadn't given her a way to reach him. And now the phone had cost Luce her first real progress with a shadow.

She pulled it out and opened the text Mr. Cole had just sent:

Call your parents. They think you got an A– on a history test I just gave. And that you're trying out for the swim team next week. Don't forget to act like everything's okay.

And a second one, a minute later:

Is everything okay?

Grouchily, Luce stuffed the phone in her backpack and started tramping through the thick mulch of redwood needles toward the edge of the forest, toward her dorm. The text made her wonder about the rest of the kids at Sword & Cross. Was Arriane still there, and if so, who was she sailing paper airplanes to during class? Had Molly found someone else to make her enemy now that Luce was gone? Or had both of them moved on since Luce and Daniel had left? Did Randy buy the story that Luce's parents had made her transfer? Luce sighed. She *hated* not telling her parents the truth, hated not being able to tell them how far away she felt, and how alone.

But a phone call? Every false word she said—A– on a made-up history test, tryouts for some bogus swim team—would only make her feel that much more homesick.

Mr. Cole must be out of his mind, telling her to call them and lie. But if she told her parents the truth—the real truth—they would think *she* was out of her mind. And if she didn't get in touch with them, they would know something was up. They'd drive out to Sword & Cross, find her missing, and then what?

She could email them. Lying wouldn't be so hard by email. It would buy her a few days before she had to call. She would email them tonight.

She stepped out of the forest, onto the path, and gasped. It *was* night. She looked back at the lush, shaded woods. How long had she been in there with the shadow? She glanced at her watch. It was half past eight. She'd missed lunch. And her afternoon classes. And dinner. It had been so dark in the woods, she hadn't noticed time passing at all, but now it all slammed into her. She was tired, cold, and hungry.

⚜

After three wrong turns in the mazelike dorm, Luce finally found her door. Silently hoping that Shelby would be wherever it was she disappeared to at night, Luce slipped her huge, old-fashioned key into the lock and turned the knob.

The lights were off, but a fire was burning in the hearth. Shelby was seated cross-legged on the floor, eyes closed, meditating. When Luce came in, one eye popped open, looking highly annoyed at the sight before it.

"Sorry," Luce whispered, sinking into the desk chair closest to the door. "Don't mind me. Pretend I'm not here."

For a little while, Shelby did just that. She closed her evil eye and went back to meditating, and the room was tranquil. Luce turned on the computer that came with her desk and stared at the screen, trying to compose in her head the most innocuous message possible to her parents—and, while she was at it, one to Callie, who'd been sending a steady stream of unread emails to Luce's in-box this past week.

Typing as slowly as she possibly could so her keyboard taps wouldn't give Shelby yet another reason to hate her, Luce wrote:

Dear Mom and Dad, I miss you guys so much. Just wanted to drop you a line. Life at Sword & Cross is good.

Her chest constricted as she strained to keep her fingers from typing: *As far as I know, no one else has died this week.*

Still doing fine in all my classes, she made herself write instead. Might even try out for the swim team!

Luce looked out the window at the clear, starry sky. She had to sign off fast. Otherwise, she'd lose it.

Wonder when this rainy weather will let up. . . . Guess that's November in Georgia! Love, Luce

She copied the message into a new email to Callie, changed a few choice words, moved her mouse over the Send button, closed her eyes, double-clicked, and hung her head. She was a horrible fake of a daughter, a liar of a friend. And what had she been thinking? These were the blandest, most red-flag-worthy emails ever written. They were only going to freak people out.

Her stomach growled. A second time, more loudly. Shelby cleared her throat.

Luce spun around in her chair to face the girl, only to find her in downward dog. Luce could feel the tears welling up in the corners of her eyes. "I'm hungry, okay? Why don't you file a complaint, get me transferred to another room?"

Shelby calmly hopped forward on her yoga mat, swooped her arms into a prayer position and said, "I was just going to tell you about the box of organic mac and cheese in my sock drawer. No need for the waterworks. Jeez."

Eleven minutes later, Luce was sitting under a blanket on her bed with a steaming bowl of cheesy pasta, dry eyes, and a roommate who'd suddenly stopped hating her.

"I wasn't crying because I was hungry," Luce wanted to clarify, though the mac and cheese was so good, the gift so unexpectedly kind of Shelby, it almost brought fresh tears to her eyes. Luce wanted to open up to someone, and Shelby was, well, there. She hadn't thawed out all the way, but sharing her stash of food was a huge step for someone who'd barely spoken to Luce so far. "I, um, I'm having some family issues. It's just hard being away."

"Boo-hoo," Shelby said, chomping on her own bowl of macaroni. "Let me guess, your parents are still happily married."

"That's not fair," Luce said, sitting up. "You have no idea what I've been through."

"And you have some idea what *I've* been through?" Shelby stared Luce down. "Didn't think so. Look, here's me: Only child raised by a single mom. Daddy issues? Maybe. A pain in the ass to live with because I hate to share? Almost certainly. But what I can't stand is some sweet-faced, spoon-fed sweetheart with a happy home life and some fancy boyfriend showing up on my turf to moan about her poor long-distance love affair."

Luce sucked in her breath. "That's not it at all."

"Oh no? Enlighten me."

"I'm a fake," Luce said. "I'm . . . lying to the people I love."

"Lying to your fancy boyfriend?" Shelby's eyes narrowed, in a way that made Luce think her roommate might actually be interested.

"No," Luce muttered. "I'm not even speaking to him."

Shelby leaned back on Luce's bed and propped her feet up so they rested on the underside of the top bunk. "Why not?"

"It's long, stupid, and complicated."

"Well, every girl with half a brain knows there's only one thing to do when you break up with your man—"

"No, we didn't break up—" Luce said, at the exact same time as Shelby said:

"Change your hair."

"*Change my hair?*"

"Fresh start," Shelby said. "I've dyed mine orange, chopped it off. Hell, once I even shaved it after this jerk really broke my heart."

There was a small oval mirror with an ornate wooden frame attached to the dresser across the room. From her position on the bed, Luce could see her reflection. She put down the bowl of pasta and stood up to move closer.

She had chopped her hair off after Trevor, but that was different. Most of it had been singed, anyway. And when she'd arrived at Sword & Cross, it had been Arriane's hair she cut. Yet Luce thought she understood what Shelby meant when she said "fresh start." You could turn into someone else, pretend you weren't the person who'd just been through so much heartache. Even though—thank God—Luce wasn't mourning the permanent loss of her relationship with Daniel, she was mourning all sorts of other losses. Penn, her family, the life she used to have before things got so complicated.

"You're really thinking about it, aren't you? Don't make me bust out the peroxide from under the sink."

Luce ran her fingers through her short black hair. What would Daniel think? But if he wanted her to be happy here until they could be together again, she had to let go of who she'd been at Sword & Cross.

She turned around to face Shelby. "Get the bottle."

FOUR

⁓ ✦ ⁓

FIFTEEN DAYS

She wasn't *that* blond.

Luce wet her hands in the sink and tugged her short bleached waves. She'd made it through a full load of classes on Thursday, which included an unexpectedly stiff two-hour safety lecture from Francesca to reiterate why the Announcers were not to be messed with casually (it almost seemed like she'd been addressing Luce directly); back-to-back pop quizzes in her "regular" biology and math classes in the main school building; and what felt like eight straight hours of aghast stares from her classmates, Nephilim and non-Neph kids alike.

Even though Shelby had acted cool about Luce's new look in the privacy of their dorm room the night before, she wasn't effusive with compliments the way Arriane was or reliably supportive the way Penn had been. Stepping out into the world this morning, Luce had been overcome by nerves. Miles had been the first to see her, and he'd given her a thumbs-up. But he was so nice, he'd never let on if he really thought she looked terrible.

Of course, Dawn and Jasmine had flocked to her side right after humanities, eager to touch her hair, asking Luce who her inspiration had been.

"Very Gwen Stefani," Jasmine had said, nodding.

"No, it's Madge, right?" Dawn said. "Like, 'Vogue' era." Before Luce could answer, Dawn gestured between Luce and herself. "But I guess we aren't Twinkies anymore."

"Twinkies?" Luce shook her head.

Jasmine squinted at Luce. "Come on, don't say you never noticed? You two look . . . well, *looked* so much alike. You practically could have been sisters."

Now, standing alone before the main school building's bathroom mirror, Luce gazed at her reflection and thought about wide-eyed Dawn. They had similar coloring: pale skin, flushed lips, dark hair. But Dawn was smaller than she was. She wore bright colors six days a week. And she was way more chipper than Luce could ever be. A few superficial aspects aside, Luce and Dawn couldn't have been more different.

The bathroom door swung open and a wholesome-looking brunette in jeans and a yellow sweater entered. Luce recognized her from European history class. Amy Something. She leaned against the sink next to Luce and began to fidget with her eyebrows.

"Why'd you do that to your hair?" she asked, eyeing Luce.

Luce blinked. It was one thing to talk about it with her sort-of friends at Shoreline, but she'd never even spoken to this girl before.

Shelby's answer, *fresh start,* popped into her mind, but who was she kidding? All that bottle of peroxide had done last night was make Luce look as phony on the outside as she already felt on the inside. Callie and her parents would hardly recognize her right now, which wasn't the point at all.

And Daniel. What would Daniel think? Luce suddenly felt so transparently fake; even a stranger could see through her.

"I don't know." She pushed past the girl and out the bathroom door. "I don't know why I did it."

Bleaching her hair wouldn't wash away the dark memories of the past few weeks. If she really wanted a fresh start, she'd have to make one. But how? There was so little she actually had control over at the moment. Her whole world was in the hands of Mr. Cole and Daniel. And they were both far away.

It was scary how quickly and how much she'd come to rely on Daniel, scarier still that she didn't know when she'd see him next. Compared to the bliss-filled days with him she'd been expecting in California, this was the loneliest she'd ever been.

She trudged across the campus, slowly realizing that the only time she'd felt any independence since she'd arrived at Shoreline had been . . .

Alone in the woods with the shadow.

After yesterday's in-class demonstration, Luce had been expecting more of the same from Francesca and Steven. She had hoped that maybe the students would have a chance to experiment with the shadows on their own today. She'd even had the briefest fantasy of being able to do what she'd done in the forest in front of all the Nephilim.

None of that had happened. In fact, class today had felt like a big step back. A boring lecture about Announcer etiquette and safety, and why the students should never, under any circumstances, try on their own what they'd seen the day before.

It was frustrating and regressive. So now, instead of heading back to the dorm, Luce found herself jogging behind the mess hall, down the trail to the edge of the bluff, and up the wooden stairs of the Nephilim lodge. Francesca's office was in the annex on the second floor, and she'd told the class to feel free to come by anytime.

The building was remarkably different without the other students to warm it up. Dim and drafty and almost abandoned-feeling. Every noise Luce made seemed to carry, echoing off the sloping wooden beams. She could see a lamp on the landing one floor up and smell the rich aroma of brewing coffee. She didn't know yet whether she was going to tell Francesca what she'd been able to do in the forest. It might seem insignificant to someone as skilled as Francesca. Or it might seem like a violation of her instructions to the class today.

Part of Luce just wanted to feel her teacher out, to see whether she might be someone Luce could turn to when, on days like today, she started to feel as if she might fall apart.

She reached the top of the stairs and found herself at the head of a long, open hallway. On her left, beyond the wooden banister, she looked down at the dark, empty classroom on the second story. On her right was a row of heavy wooden doors with stained-glass transoms over them. Walking quietly along the floorboards, Luce realized she didn't know which office was Francesca's. Only one of the doors was ajar, the third one from the right, with light emanating from the pretty stained-glass scene in the transom. She thought she heard a male voice inside. She was poised to knock when a woman's sharp tone made her freeze.

"It was a mistake to even try," Francesca practically hissed.

"We took a chance. We got unlucky."

Steven.

"Unlucky?" Francesca scoffed. "You mean reckless. From a purely statistical standpoint, the odds of an Announcer bearing bad news were far too great. You saw what it did to those kids. They weren't ready."

A pause. Luce inched a little closer along the Persian rug in the hall.

"But she was."

"I won't sacrifice all the progress an entire class has made just because some, some—"

"Don't be shortsighted, Francesca. We came up with a beautiful curriculum. I know that as well as you. Our students outperform every other Nephilim program in the world. You did all that. You have a right to feel a sense of pride. But things are different now."

"Steven's right, Francesca." A third voice. Male. Luce thought it sounded familiar. But who was it? "Might as well throw your academic calendar out the window. The truce between our sides is the only timeline that matters anymore."

Francesca sighed. "You really think—"

The unknown voice said, "If I know Daniel, he'll be

right on time. He's probably counting down the minutes already."

"There's something else," Steven said.

A pause, then what sounded like a drawer sliding open, then a gasp. Luce would have killed to be on the other side of the wall, to see what they could see.

"Where did you get that?" the other male voice asked. "Are you trading?"

"Of course he's not!" Francesca sounded stung. "Steven found it in the forest during one of his rounds the other night."

"It's authentic, isn't it?" Steven asked.

A sigh. "Been too long for me to say," the stranger hedged. "I haven't seen a starshot in ages. Daniel will know. I'll take it to him."

"That's all? What do you suggest we do in the meantime?" Francesca asked.

"Look, this isn't my thing." The familiarity of that male voice was like an itch at the back of Luce's brain. "And it's really not my style—"

"Please," Francesca pleaded.

The office was silent. Luce's heart was pounding.

"Okay. If I were you? Step things up around here. Tighten their supervision and do everything you can to get *all* of them ready. End Times aren't supposed to be very pretty."

End Times. That was what Arriane had said would

happen if Cam and his army won that night at Sword &
Cross. But they hadn't won. Unless there'd already been
another battle. But then, what would the Nephilim need
to get ready for?

The sound of heavy chair legs scraping along the
floor made Luce jump back. She knew she should not be
caught eavesdropping on this conversation. Whatever it
was about.

For once, she was glad of the endless supply of mysterious alcoves in the Shoreline architecture. She ducked
under a decorative wood-shingled cornice between two
bookshelves and pressed herself into the recess of the
wall.

A single set of footsteps exited the office, and the
door closed firmly. Luce held her breath and waited for
the figure to descend the stairs.

At first, she could see only his feet. Brown European
leather boots. Then a pair of dark-wash jeans came into
view as he curved around the banister toward the second
story of the lodge. A blue-and-white-striped button-
down shirt. And finally, the distinctly recognizable mane
of black-and-gold dreadlocks.

Roland Sparks had turned up at Shoreline.

Luce jumped out from her hidden perch. She might
still be on nervous best behavior in front of Francesca
and Steven, who were dauntingly gorgeous and powerful and mature . . . and her teachers. But Roland didn't

intimidate her—not much, anyway—not anymore. Besides, he was the closest to Daniel she had been in days.

She slunk down the interior steps as silently as she could, then burst through the lodge door to the deck. Roland was moseying toward the ocean like he didn't have a care in the world.

"Roland!" she shouted, thundering down the last flight of stairs to the ground and breaking into a jog. He stood where the path ended and the bluff dropped down to steep and craggy rocks.

He was standing so still, looking out at the water. Luce was surprised to feel butterflies in her stomach when, very slowly, he began to turn around.

"Well, well." He smiled. "Lucinda Price discovers peroxide."

"Oh." She clutched at her hair. How stupid she must look to him.

"No, no," he said, stepping toward her, fluffing her hair with his fingers. "It suits you. A hard edge for hard times."

"What are you doing here?"

"Enrolling." He shrugged. "I just picked up my class schedule, met the teachers. Seems like a pretty sweet place."

A woven knapsack was slung over one of his shoulders with something long and narrow and silver sticking out of it. Following her eyes, Roland switched the bag to his other shoulder and tightened the top flap with a knot.

"Roland." Her voice quaked. "You left Sword and Cross? Why? What are you doing here?"

"Just needed a change of pace," he offered cryptically.

Luce was going to ask about the others—Arriane and Gabbe. Even Molly. Whether anyone had noticed or cared that she'd left. But when she opened her mouth, what came out was very different from what she had expected. "What were you talking about in there with Francesca and Steven?"

Roland's face changed suddenly, hardened into something older, less carefree. "That depends. How much did you hear?"

"Daniel. I heard you say that he . . . You don't have to lie to me, Roland. How much longer until he comes back? Because I don't think I can—"

"Come take a walk with me, Luce."

As awkward as it would have felt for Roland Sparks to put his arm around her shoulders back at Sword & Cross, that was how comforting it was when he did it that day at Shoreline. They were never really friends, but he was a reminder of her past—a bond she couldn't help turning to now.

They walked along the bluff's edge, around the breakfast terrace, and along the west side of the dorms, past a rose garden Luce had never seen before. It was dusk and the water to their right was alive with colors, reflecting the rose and orange and violet clouds gliding in front of the sun.

Roland led her to a bench facing the water, far away from all the campus buildings. Looking down, she could see a rugged set of stairs carved into the rock, starting just below where they were sitting, and leading all the way down to the beach.

"What do you know that you aren't saying?" Luce asked when the silence began to get to her.

"That water is fifty-one degrees," Roland said.

"Not what I meant," she said, looking him right in the eyes. "Did he send you here to watch over me?"

Roland scratched his head. "Look. Daniel's off doing his thing." He made a flitting motion at the sky. "In the meantime"—and she thought he cocked his head toward the forest behind the dorm—"you got your own thing to take care of."

"What? No, I don't have a thing. I'm just here because—"

"Bullshit." He laughed. "We all have our secrets, Luce. Mine brought me to Shoreline. Yours has been leading you out to those woods."

She started to protest, but Roland waved her off, that ever-cryptic look in his eyes.

"I'm not going to get you in trouble. In fact, I'm

rooting for you." His eyes moved past her, out to sea. "Now, back to that water. It's frigid. Have you been in it? I know you like to swim."

It struck Luce that she'd been at Shoreline for three days, with the ocean always visible, the waves always audible, the salt air always coating everything, but she still hadn't set foot on the beach. And it wasn't like at Sword & Cross, where a laundry list of things were off-limits. She didn't know why it hadn't even occurred to her.

She shook her head.

"About all you can do with a beach that cold is build a bonfire." Roland glanced at her. "You made any friends here yet?"

Luce shrugged. "A few."

"Bring them by tonight, after dark." He pointed to a narrow peninsula of sand at the foot of the rocky stairs. "Right down there."

She peered at Roland sideways. "What exactly do you have in mind?"

Roland grinned devilishly. "Don't worry, we'll keep it innocent. But you know how it is. I'm new in town; I'd like to make my presence known."

※

"*Dude.* Stomp down on my heel one more time, and I'm seriously going to have to break your ankle."

"Maybe if you weren't hogging the *entire* beam of

the flashlight up there, Shel, the rest of us could see where we were going."

Luce tried to stifle her laugh as she followed a bickering Miles and Shelby across campus in the dark. It was almost eleven, and Shoreline was pitch-black and silent, except for the hoot of an owl. An orange gibbous moon was low in the sky, cloaked by a veil of fog. Between the three of them, they'd only been able to come up with one flashlight (Shelby's), so only one of them (Shelby) had a clear view of the path down to the water. For the other two, the grounds—which had seemed so lush and well tended in the daylight—were now booby-trapped with fallen bristlecones, thick-rooted ferns, and the backs of Shelby's feet.

When Roland had asked her to bring some friends tonight, Luce had gotten a sinking feeling in her stomach. There were no hall monitors at Shoreline, no terrifying security cameras recording the students' every move, so it wasn't the threat of getting caught that made her nervous. In fact, sneaking out of the dorm had been relatively easy. It was drawing a crowd that was a bigger challenge.

Dawn and Jasmine seemed like the most likely candidates for a party on the beach, but when Luce went by their fifth-floor room, the hallway was dark and no one answered her knock. Back in her own room, Shelby had been tangled up in some sort of tantric yoga pose that hurt Luce just to look at. Luce hadn't wanted to break her roommate's fierce concentration by inviting her to some unknown party—but then a loud knock at their door had made Shelby fall crossly from her pose anyway.

Miles, asking Luce if she wanted to get some ice cream.

Luce looked back and forth between Miles and Shelby and smiled. "I've got a better idea."

Ten minutes later, bundled up in hooded sweatshirts, a backward Dodgers cap (Miles), and wool socks with individual toe shapes sewn in so she could still wear her flip-flops (Shelby), and with a nervous feeling in the gut about mingling Roland with the Shoreline crew (Luce), the three of them tramped toward the bluff's edge.

"So who is this guy again?" Miles asked, pointing out a dip in the rocky path just before Luce would have gone flying.

"He's just . . . a guy from my last school." Luce searched for a better description as the three of them started down the rocky stairs. Roland wasn't exactly her friend. And even though kids at Shoreline seemed pretty open-minded, she wasn't sure she should tell them which side of the fallen angel divide Roland fell on. "He was friends with Daniel," she said finally. "It'll probably be a pretty small party. I don't think he knows anyone here but me."

They could smell it before they could see it: the tell-tale hickory smoke of a good-sized bonfire. Then, when they were almost at the foot of the steep stairs, they wound around a bend in the rocks and froze as the sparks from a wild orange blaze finally came into view.

There must have been a hundred people gathered on the beach.

The wind was wild, like an untamed animal, but it was no match for the rowdiness of the partygoers. At one end of the gathering, closest to where Luce stood, a crowd of hippie guys with long, thick beards and ratty woven shirts had formed a makeshift drum circle. Their steady beat provided a nearby group of kids with a constantly changing groove to dance to. At the other end of the party was the bonfire itself, and when Luce stood on her toes, she recognized a lot of Shoreline kids crowded around the fire, hoping to beat out the cold. Everyone was holding a stick in the flames, jockeying for the best spot to roast their hot dogs and marshmallows, their cast-iron kettles full of beans. It was impossible to guess how they'd all found out about it, but it was clear that everyone was having a good time.

And in the middle of it all, Roland. He'd changed out of his pressed button-down shirt and expensive leather boots and was dressed, like everyone else there, in a hooded sweatshirt and shredded jeans. He was standing on a boulder, making riotous, exaggerated gestures, telling a story Luce couldn't quite hear. Dawn and Jasmine were among the captivated listeners; their fire-lit faces looked pretty and alive.

"This is your idea of a small party?" Miles asked.

Luce was watching Roland, wondering what story he was telling. Something about the way he was taking charge made Luce think back to Cam's room, to the first and only real party she'd ever gone to at Sword & Cross, and it made her miss Arriane. And, of course, Penn, who'd been nervous when she first arrived at the party but ended up having a better time than anyone. And Daniel, who would barely speak to Luce back then. Things were so different now.

"Well, I don't know about you guys," Shelby said, kicking off her flip-flops and padding onto the sand in her socks, "but I'm going to get myself a drink, then a hot dog, then maybe a lesson from one of those drum circle guys."

"Me too," Miles said. "Except for the drum circle part, in case that wasn't obvious."

"Luce." Roland waved from his position on the boulder. "You made it."

Miles and Shelby were already way ahead of her, heading toward the hot dog station, so Luce trekked over a dune of cool, damp sand toward Roland and the others.

"You weren't kidding when you said you wanted to make your presence known. This is really something, Roland."

Roland nodded graciously. "Something, huh? Something good, or something bad?"

It seemed like a loaded question, and what Luce wanted to say was that she couldn't tell anymore. She thought about the heated conversation she'd overheard in the teacher's office. How sharp Francesca's voice had sounded. The line between what was good and what was bad felt incredibly blurry. Roland and Steven were fallen angels who'd gone over. Demons, right? Did she even know what that meant? But then there was Cam, and . . . what did Roland mean by that question? She squinted at him. Maybe he was really only asking whether Luce was having fun?

A myriad of colorful partygoers swirled around her, but Luce could feel the endless black waves nearby. The air near the water was whipping and cold, but the bonfire was hot on her skin. So many things seemed to be at odds right now, all shoving up against her at once.

"Who are all these people, Roland?"

"Let's see." Roland pointed at the hippie kids in the drum circle. "Townies." To their right, he gestured at a big group of guys trying to impress a much smaller group of girls with a few very bad thrusting dance moves. "Those guys are marines stationed in Fort Bragg. From the way they're partying, I hope they're on leave for the weekend." When Jasmine and Dawn sidled up next to him, Roland put one arm around each of their shoulders. "These two, I believe you know."

"You didn't tell us you were such big friends with the celestial social director, Luce," Jasmine said.

"Seriously." Dawn leaned in to whisper loudly to Luce, "Only my diary knows how many times I've wished to go to a Roland Sparks party. And my diary will never tell."

"Oh, but I might," Roland joked.

"Is there no relish at this party?" Shelby popped up behind Luce with Miles at her side. She was holding two hot dogs in one hand and stuck out her free one to Roland. "Shelby Sterris. Who are you?"

"Shelby Sterris," Roland repeated. "I'm Roland Sparks. You ever live in East L.A.? Have we met before?"

"No."

"She has a photographic memory," Miles supplied, slipping Luce a veggie hot dog, which was not her favorite, but a nice gesture nonetheless. "I'm Miles. Cool party, by the way."

"Very cool," Dawn agreed, swaying with Roland to the drumbeat.

"What about Steven and Francesca?" Luce had to practically shout to Shelby. "Won't they hear us down here?" It was one thing to sneak out under the radar. It was another to plant a sonic boom directly on that radar.

Jasmine glanced back toward the campus. "They'll hear us, sure, but our leash is pretty long at Shoreline. At least for the Nephilim kids. As long as we stay on campus, under their umbrella of surveillance, we can pretty much do as we please."

"Does that include a limbo contest?" Roland grinned impishly, producing a long, thick branch from behind him. "Miles, you going to hold the other end for me?"

Seconds later, the branch was raised, the drumbeat changed, and it seemed like the whole party had dropped what they were doing to form one long, animated limbo line.

"Luce," Miles called to her. "You're not just going to stand there, are you?"

She studied the crowd, feeling stiff and rooted to her spot in the sand. But Dawn and Jasmine were making an opening for her to squeeze into line between the two of them. Already in competition mode—probably born in competition mode—Shelby was stretching out her back. Even the buttoned-up marine guys were going to play.

"Fine." Luce laughed and got in line.

Once the game began, the line moved quickly; for three rounds, Luce shimmied easily under the branch. The fourth time, she made it under with only a little trouble, having to tilt her chin back far enough to see the stars, and got a round of cheers for doing so. Soon she was cheering on the other kids too, only a little surprised to find herself jumping up and down when Shelby made it through. There was something amazing about arching out of the limbo stance after a successful turn—the whole party seemed to feed off it. Each time, it gave Luce a surprising rush of adrenaline.

Having fun wasn't usually such a simple thing. For so long, laughter had usually been closely followed by guilt, some nagging feeling that she wasn't supposed to be enjoying herself for one reason or another. But somehow tonight she felt lighter. Without even realizing it, she'd been able to shrug off the darkness.

By the time Luce looped around for her fifth turn, the line was significantly shorter. Half the kids at the party had already gotten out, and everyone was crowded around either Miles or Roland, watching the last kids standing. At the back of the line, Luce was giddy and a little light-headed, so the hard grip she felt on her arm almost made her lose her balance.

She started to scream, then felt fingers clamp over her mouth.

"Shhh."

Daniel was tugging her out of line and away from the party. His strong, warm hand sliding down her neck, his lips brushing the side of her cheek. For just a moment, the touch of his skin on hers, coupled with the bright violet glow of his eyes, and her days-old rising need to grab hold of him and never let go—it all made Luce divinely dizzy.

"What are you doing here?" she whispered. She meant to say *Thank God you're here* or *It's been so hard to be apart* or what she really meant, *I love you*. But there were also *You abandoned me* and *I thought it wasn't safe* and *What's this about a truce?* all knocking around in her brain.

"I had to see you," he said. As he led her behind a large volcanic rock on the beach, there was a conspiratorial smile on his face. The kind of smile that was contagious, finding its way onto Luce's lips too. The kind of smile that acknowledged not just that they were breaking Daniel's rule—but that they were enjoying doing it.

"When I got close enough to see this party, I noticed everyone dancing," he said. "And I got a little jealous."

"Jealous?" Luce asked. They were alone now. She threw her arms around his broad shoulders and looked deep into his violet eyes. "Why would you be jealous?"

"Because," he said, rubbing his hands across her back. "Your dance card is full. For all eternity."

Daniel held her right hand in his, wrapped her left around his shoulder, and started a slow two-step in the sand. They could still hear the music from the party, but from this side of the rock it felt like a private concert. Luce closed her eyes and melted against his chest, finding the place where her head fit into his shoulder like a puzzle piece.

"No, this isn't quite right," Daniel said after a moment. He pointed down at her feet. She noticed he was barefoot. "Take off your shoes," he said, "and I'll show you how angels dance."

Luce slipped off her black flats and tossed them aside

on the beach. The sand between her toes was soft and cool. When Daniel pulled her close, her toes overlapped with his and she almost lost her balance, but his arms held her steady. When she looked down, her feet were on top of his. And when she looked up: the sight she yearned for night and day. Daniel unfurling his silver-white wings.

They filled her plane of vision, stretching twenty feet into the sky. Broad and beautiful, glowing in the night, they must have been the most glorious wings in all of Heaven. Underneath her own feet, Luce felt Daniel's lift just barely off the ground. His wings beat lightly, almost like a heartbeat, holding both of them inches above the beach.

"Ready?" he asked.

Ready for what, she didn't know. It didn't matter.

Now they were moving backward in the air, as smoothly as figure skaters moved on ice. Daniel glided out over the water, holding her in his arms. Luce gasped as the first frothy wave skimmed their toes. Daniel laughed and lifted them a little higher in the sky. He dipped her backward. He spun them both around in circles. They were dancing. *On the ocean.*

The moon was like a spotlight, shining down on only them. Luce was laughing from sheer joy, laughing so much that Daniel started laughing too. She'd never felt lighter.

"Thank you," she whispered.

His answer was a kiss. He kissed her softly at first. On her forehead, then on her nose, then finally found his way to her lips.

She kissed him back deeply and hungrily and a bit desperately, throwing her whole body into it. This was how she came home to Daniel, how she touched that easy love they'd shared for so long. For a moment, the whole world went quiet; then Luce came up gasping for air. She hadn't even noticed they were back on the beach.

His hand cupped the back of her head, the ski cap she had tugged down over her ears. The cap concealing her bleached-blond hair. He pulled it off and a blast of ocean breeze hit her head. "What did you do to your hair?"

His voice was soft, but somehow it sounded like an accusation. Maybe it was because the song had ended, and the dance and the kiss had too, and now they were just two people standing on a beach. Daniel's wings were arched back behind his shoulders, still visible but out of reach.

"Who cares about my hair?" All she cared about was holding him. Wasn't that all he should care about too?

Luce reached to take back the ski cap. Her bare blond head felt too exposed, like a glowing red flag warning Daniel that she might be falling apart. As soon as she started to turn away, Daniel put his arms around her.

"Hey," he said, pulling her close again. "I'm sorry."

She exhaled, drew into him, and let his touch wash over her. She tipped her head up to meet his eyes.

"Is it safe now?" she asked, wanting Daniel to be the one to bring up the truce. Could they finally be together? But the worn look in his eyes gave her the answer before he opened his mouth.

"I shouldn't be here, but I worry about you." He held her at arm's length. "And from the looks of things, I'm right to worry." He fingered a lock of her hair. "I don't understand why you did this, Luce. It isn't you."

She pushed him away. It had always bothered her when people said that. "Well, I'm the one who dyed it, Daniel. So, technically, it *is* me. Maybe not the 'me' you want me to be—"

"That's not fair. I don't want you to be anyone other than who you are."

"Which is who, Daniel? Because if you know the answer to that, feel free to clue me in." Her voice grew louder as frustration overtook the passion slipping through her fingers. "I'm on my own here, trying to figure out why. Trying to figure out what I'm doing here with all these . . . when I'm not even . . ."

"When you're not what?"

How had they gone so quickly from dancing on air to this?

"I don't know. I'm just trying to take it day by day. Make friends, you know? Yesterday I joined a club, and we're planning a yacht trip somewhere. Things like that." What she really wanted to tell him about were the shadows. And especially what she'd done in the woods. But Daniel had narrowed his eyes like she'd already done something wrong.

"You're not going on a yacht trip anywhere."

"What?"

"You'll stay right here on this campus until I say so." He exhaled, sensing her rising anger. "I hate giving you these rules, Luce, but . . . I'm doing so much to keep you safe. I won't let anything happen to you."

"Literally." Luce gritted her teeth. "Good or bad or otherwise. Seems like when you're not around you don't want me doing anything at all."

"That's not true." He shook a finger at her. She'd never seen him lose his temper so quickly. Then he looked up at the sky, and Luce followed his gaze. A shadow zipped over their heads—like an all-black firework leaving a deadly, smoky tail. Daniel seemed to be able to read it instantly.

"I have to go," he said.

"How shocking." She turned away. "Turn up out of nowhere, pick a fight, then duck out. This must be real, true love."

He grabbed her shoulders and shook them until she met his eyes. "It *is* true love," he said, with such desperation that Luce couldn't tell whether it chipped away at or added to the pain in her heart. "You know it is." His eyes burned violet—not with anger but with intense desire. The kind of look that made you love a person so much, you missed him even when he was standing right in front of you.

Daniel ducked his head to kiss her cheek, but she was too close to tears. Embarrassed, she turned away. She heard his sigh, and then: the beat of wings.

No.

When she whipped her head around, Daniel was soaring across the sky, halfway between the ocean and the moon. His wings were lit bright white under a moonbeam. A moment later, it was hard to tell him apart from any of the stars in the sky.

FIVE

FOURTEEN DAYS

During the night, a windless layer of fog moved in like an army, settling over the town of Fort Bragg. It didn't lift with the sunrise, and its gloom seeped into everything and everyone. So all day Friday in school, Luce felt like she was being dragged along by a slow-moving tide. The teachers were out of focus, noncommittal, and slow with their lectures. The students sat in a heap of lethargy, struggling to stay awake though the long, damp drone of the day.

By the time classes let out, the dreariness had penetrated Luce to her very core. She didn't know what she was doing at this school that wasn't really hers, in this temporary life that only highlighted her lack of a real, permanent one. All she wanted to do was crawl into her bottom bunk and sleep it all away—not just the weather or her long first week at Shoreline, but also the argument with Daniel and the jumble of questions and anxieties that had shaken loose in her mind.

Sleep the night before had been impossible. In the darkest hours of the morning she'd stumbled alone back to her dorm room. She'd tossed and turned without ever really dozing off. Daniel's shutting her out no longer surprised her, but that didn't mean it had gotten any easier. And that insulting, chauvinistic *order* he'd given her to stay on the school grounds? What was this, the nineteenth century? It crossed her mind that maybe Daniel *had* spoken to her like that centuries ago, but—like Jane Eyre or Elizabeth Bennet—Luce was certain no former self of hers would ever have been cool with that. And she certainly wasn't now.

She was still angry and annoyed after class, moving through the fog toward the dorm. Her eyes were bleary and she was practically sleepwalking by the time her hand clasped her doorknob. Tumbling into the dim, empty room, she almost didn't see the envelope someone had slipped under the door.

It was cream-colored, flimsy and square, and when she flipped it over, she saw her name typed on the front in small, blocky letters. She tore into it, wanting an apology from him. Knowing she owed him one too.

The letter inside was typewritten on cream-colored paper and folded into thirds.

```
Dear Luce,
    There's something I've been waiting
too long to tell you. Meet me in town,
near Noyo Point, around six o'clock
tonight? The #5 bus along Hwy 1 stops a
quarter of a mile south of Shoreline.
Use this bus pass. I'll be waiting by
the North Cliff. Can't wait to see you.
                        Love, Daniel
```

Shaking the envelope, Luce felt a small slip of paper inside. She pulled out a thin blue-and-white bus ticket with the number five printed on its front and a crude little map of Fort Bragg drawn on its back. That was it. There was nothing else.

Luce couldn't figure it out. No mention of their argument on the beach. No indication that Daniel even understood how erratic it was to practically vanish into thin air one night, then expect her to travel at his whim the next.

No apology at all.

Strange. Daniel could turn up anywhere, anytime. He was usually oblivious to the logistical realities that normal human beings had to deal with.

The letter felt cold and stiff in her hands. Her more reckless side was tempted to pretend she'd never received it. She was tired of arguing, tired of Daniel's not trusting her with details. But that pesky in-love side of Luce wondered whether she was being too harsh on him. Because their relationship was worth the effort. She tried to remember the way his eyes had looked and his voice had sounded when he told her the story about the lifetime she'd spent in the California gold rush. The way he'd seen her through the window and fallen in love with her for something like the thousandth time.

That was the image she took with her when she left her dorm room minutes later to creep along the path toward Shoreline's front gates, toward the bus stop where Daniel had instructed her to wait. An image of his pleading violet eyes tugged at her heart while she stood under a damp gray sky. She watched colorless cars materialize in the fog, peel around the hairpin turns on guardrailless Highway 1, and vanish again.

When she looked back at Shoreline's formidable campus in the distance, she remembered Jasmine's words at the party: *As long as we stay under their umbrella of surveillance, we can pretty much do as we please.* Luce was stepping out from under the umbrella, but where was the harm? She wasn't really a student there; and anyway, seeing Daniel again was worth the risk of getting caught.

A few minutes past the half hour, the number five bus pulled up to the stop.

The bus was old and gray and rickety, as was the driver who heaved the levered door open to let Luce board. She took an empty seat near the front. The bus smelled like cobwebs, or a rarely used attic. She had to clutch the cheap leatherette seat cushion as the bus barreled around the curves at fifty miles an hour, as if just inches beyond the road, the cliff didn't drop a mile straight down into the jagged gray ocean.

It was raining by the time they got to town, a steady sideways drizzle just shy of a real downpour. Most of the businesses on the main street were already closed up for the night, and the town looked wet and a little desolate. Not exactly the scene she'd had in mind for a happy makeup conversation.

Climbing down from the bus, Luce pulled the ski cap out of her backpack and tugged it over her head. She could feel the chill of the rain on her nose and her fingertips. She spotted a bent green metal sign and followed its arrow toward Noyo Point.

The point was a wide peninsula of land, not lush green like the terrain on Shoreline's campus, but a mix of patchy grass and scabs of wet gray sand. The trees thinned out here, their leaves stripped away by the fitful ocean wind. There was one lone bench on a patch of mud all the way at the edge, about a hundred yards from the road. That must have been where Daniel meant for them to meet. But Luce could see from where she stood that he wasn't there yet. She looked down at her watch. She was five minutes late.

Daniel was never late.

The rain seemed to settle on the tips of her hair instead of soaking into it the way rain usually did. Not even Mother Nature knew what to do with a dyed-blond Luce. She didn't feel like waiting for Daniel out in the open. There was a row of shops on the main street. Luce hung back there, standing on a long wooden porch under a rusty metal awning. FRED'S FISH, the closed shop's sign read in faded blue letters.

Fort Bragg wasn't quaint like Mendocino, the town where she and Daniel had stopped before he'd flown her up the shoreline. It was more industrial, a real old-fashioned fishing village with rotting docks fitted into a curved inlet where the land tapered down toward the water. While Luce waited, a boatful of fishermen were stepping ashore. She watched the line of rail-thin, hardened men in their soaking-wet slickers come up the rocky stairs from the docks below.

When they reached the street level, they walked

alone or in silent clusters, past the empty bench and the sad slanted trees, past the shut-up storefronts to a gravel parking lot at the south edge of Noyo Point. They climbed into beat-up old trucks, turned over the engines, and drove away, the sea of grim-set faces thinning until one stood out—and he wasn't coming off any schooner. In fact, he seemed to have appeared suddenly out of the fog. Luce jumped back against the metal shutter of the fish store and tried to catch her breath.

Cam.

He was walking west along the gravel road right in front of her, flanked by two dark-clad fishermen who didn't seem to notice his presence. He was dressed in slim black jeans and a black leather jacket. His dark hair was shorter than when she'd last seen him, shining in the rain. A hint of the black sunburst tattoo was visible on the side of his neck. Against the colorless backdrop of the sky, his eyes were as intensely green as they had ever been.

The last time she'd seen him, Cam had been standing at the front of a sickening black army of demons, so callous and cruel and just plain . . . evil. It had made her blood run cold. She had a string of curses and accusations ready to fling at him, but it would be better still if she could just avoid him altogether.

Too late. Cam's green gaze fell on her—and she froze. Not because he turned on any of the fake charm

that she'd come too close to falling for at Sword &
Cross. But because he looked genuinely alarmed to see
her. He swerved, moving against the flow of the few
final straggling fishermen, and was at her side in an
instant.

"What are you doing here?"

Cam looked more than alarmed, Luce decided—he
looked almost afraid. His shoulders were bunched up
around his neck and his eyes wouldn't settle on anything
for longer than a second. He hadn't said a thing about
her hair; it almost seemed as if he hadn't noticed it. Luce
was certain Cam was not supposed to know that she was
out here in California. Keeping her away from guys like
him was the whole point of her relocation. Now she'd
blown that.

"I'm just—" She eyed the white gravel path behind
Cam, cutting through the grass bordering the cliff's
edge. "I'm just going for a walk."

"You are not."

"Leave me alone." She tried to push past him. "I
have nothing to say to you."

"Which would be fine, since we're not supposed to
be talking to one another. But you're not supposed to
leave that school."

Suddenly she felt nervous, like he knew something she didn't. "How did you know I'm even going to
school here?"

Cam sighed. "I know everything, okay?"

"Then you're here to fight Daniel?"

Cam's green eyes narrowed. "Why would I— Wait, are you saying *you're* here to see him?"

"Don't sound so shocked. We *are* together." It was like Cam still hadn't gotten over that she'd picked Daniel instead of him.

Cam scratched his forehead, looking concerned. When he finally spoke, his words were rushed. "Did he send for you? Luce?"

She winced, buckling under the pressure of his gaze. "I got a letter."

"Let me see it."

Now Luce stiffened, examining Cam's peculiar expression to try to understand what he knew. He looked about as uneasy as she felt. She didn't budge.

"You were tricked. Grigori wouldn't send for you right now."

"You don't know what he would do for me." Luce turned away, wishing Cam had never seen her, wishing herself far away. She felt a childish need to brag to Cam that Daniel had visited her last night. But the bragging would end there. There wasn't much glory in relaying the details of their argument.

"I know he would die if you died, Luce. If you want to live another day, you'd better show me the letter."

"You would kill me over a piece of paper?"

"I wouldn't, but whoever sent you that note probably intends to."

"What?" Feeling it almost burning in her pocket, Luce resisted the urge to thrust the letter into his hands. Cam didn't know what he was talking about. He couldn't. But the longer he stared at her, the more she began to wonder about the strange letter she was holding. That bus ticket, the directions. It *had* been weirdly technical and formulaic. Not like Daniel at all. She fished it out of her pocket, fingers trembling.

Cam snatched it from her, grimacing as he read. He muttered something under his breath as his eyes darted around the forest on the other side of the road. Luce looked around too, but she could see nothing suspicious about the few remaining fishermen loading their gear into rusty truck beds.

"Come on," he said finally, grabbing her by the elbow. "It's past time to get you back to school."

She jerked away. "I'm not going anywhere with you. I hate you. What are you even doing here?"

He stepped around her in a circle. "I'm hunting."

She sized him up, trying not to let on that he still made her nervous. Slim, punk-rock-dressed, *gunless* Cam. "Really?" She cocked her head. "Hunting what?"

Cam stared past her, toward the dusk-swept forest. He nodded once. "Her."

Luce craned her neck to see who or what Cam was

talking about, but before she could see anything, he pushed her sharply. There was a weird huff of air, and something silver zipped past her face.

"Get down!" Cam yelled, pressing hard on Luce's shoulders. She sank to the porch floor, feeling his weight on top of her, smelling the dust on the wood planks.

"Get off me!" she shouted. As she writhed in disgust, cold fear pressed into her. Whoever was out there must be really bad. Otherwise she'd never be in a situation where *Cam* was the one protecting her.

A moment later, Cam was sprinting across the empty parking lot. He was racing toward a girl. A very pretty girl about Luce's age, dressed in a long brown cloak. She had delicate features and white-blond hair pulled high into a ponytail, but something was strange about her eyes. They held a vacant expression that, even from this distance, struck Luce rigid with fear.

There was more: The girl was armed. She held a silver bow and was hurriedly nocking an arrow.

Cam barreled forward, his feet crunching on the gravel lot as he moved straight toward the girl, whose bizarre silver bow gleamed even in the fog. Like it was not of this earth.

Wresting her eyes away from the lunatic girl with the arrow, Luce rolled to her knees and scanned the parking lot to see whether anyone else looked as panicked as she felt. But the place was empty, eerily quiet.

Her lungs felt tight—she could hardly breathe. The girl moved almost like a machine, with no hesitation. And Cam was unarmed. The girl was pulling back on the bowstring and Cam was in point-blank range.

But it took her a split second too long. Cam plowed into her, knocking her onto her back. He brutally wrestled the bow out of her hands, snapping his elbow against her face until she let go. The girl yelped—a high, innocent sound—and recoiled on the ground as Cam turned the bow on her. She raised her open hand in supplication.

Then Cam loosed the arrow straight into her heart.

Across the parking lot, Luce cried out and bit down on her fist. Though she wanted to be far, far away, she found herself lumbering to her feet and jogging closer. Something was wrong. Luce expected to find the girl lying there bleeding, but this girl did not struggle, did not cry.

Because she was no longer there at all.

She, and the arrow that Cam had shot into her, had vanished.

Cam scoured the parking lot, snatching up the arrows the archer had spilled as if it was the most urgent task he'd ever performed. Luce crouched down where the girl had fallen. She traced the rough gravel with her finger, baffled and more terrified than she'd been a moment before. There was no sign that anyone had ever been there.

Cam returned to Luce's side with three arrows in one hand and the silver bow in the other. Instinctively, Luce reached out to touch one. She'd never seen anything like it. For some reason, it sent a strange ripple of fascination through her. Goose bumps rose on her skin. Her head swam.

Cam jerked the arrows away. "Don't. They're deadly."

They didn't look deadly. In fact, the arrows didn't even have heads. They were just silver sticks that dead-ended in a flat tip. And yet one had made that girl disappear.

Luce blinked a few times. "What just happened, Cam?" Her voice felt heavy. "Who was she?"

"She was an Outcast." Cam wasn't looking at her. He was fixated on the silver bow in his hands.

"A what?"

"The worst kind of angel. They sided with Satan during the revolt but wouldn't actually set foot in the underworld."

"Why not?"

"You know the type. Like those girls who want to be invited to the party but don't actually plan to show up." He grimaced. "As soon as the battle ended, they tried to backpedal up to Heaven pretty fast, but it was already too late. You only get one shot at those clouds." He glanced at Luce. "Most of us do, anyway."

"So, if they're not with Heaven . . ." She was still

getting used to talking concretely about these things. "Are they . . . with Hell?"

"Hardly. Though I remember when they came crawling back." Cam gave a sinister laugh. "Usually, we'll take just about anyone we can get, but even Satan has his limits. He cast them out permanently, struck them blind to add injury to insult."

"But that girl wasn't blind," Luce whispered, recalling the way her bow had followed Cam's every move. The only reason she hadn't hit him was because he'd moved so fast. And yet Luce had known there was *something* off about that girl.

"She was. She just uses other senses to feel her way through the world. She can *see* after a fashion. It has its limitations and its benefits."

His eyes never stopped combing the tree line. Luce clammed up at the thought of more Outcasts nested in the forest. More of those silver bows and arrows.

"Well, what happened to her? Where is she now?"

Cam stared at her. "She's dead, Luce. *Poof.* Gone."

Dead? Luce looked at the place on the ground where it had happened, now just as empty as the rest of the lot. She dropped her head, feeling dizzy. "I . . . I thought you couldn't kill angels."

"Only for lack of a good weapon." He flashed the arrows at Luce one last time before wrapping them up in a cloth he pulled from his pocket and tucking them inside his leather jacket. "These things are hard to come by. Oh, stop trembling, I'm not going to kill *you*." He turned away and started testing the doors of the cars in the lot, smirking when he spotted the rolled-down driver's-side window of a gray-and-yellow truck. He reached inside and flipped the lock. "Be thankful you don't have to walk back to school. Come on, get in."

When Cam popped open the passenger-side door, Luce's jaw dropped. She peered in through the open window and watched him jimmying the ignition. "You think I'm just going to get in some hot-wired car with you right after I watched you murder someone?"

"If I hadn't killed her"—he fumbled around beneath the steering wheel—"she would have killed you, okay? Who do you think sent you that note? You were lured out of school to be murdered. Does that make it go down any easier?"

Luce leaned against the hood of the truck, not knowing what to do. She thought back to the conversation she'd had with Daniel, Arriane, and Gabbe right before she'd left Sword & Cross. They'd said Miss Sophia and the others in her sect might come after her. "But she didn't look like—are the Outcasts part of the Elders?"

By then Cam had the engine running. He quickly hopped out, walked around, and hustled Luce into the passenger seat. "Move along, chop-chop. This is like herding a cat." Finally he had her sitting and pulled her seat belt around her. "Unfortunately, Luce, you've got more than one kind of enemy. Which is why I'm taking you back to school where it's safe. Right. Now."

She didn't think it would be smart to be alone in a car with Cam, but she wasn't sure staying here on her own was any smarter. "Wait a minute," she said as he turned back toward Shoreline. "If these Outcasts aren't part of Heaven or Hell, whose side are they on?"

"The Outcasts are a sickening shade of gray. In case you hadn't noticed, there are worse things out there than me."

Luce folded her hands on her lap, anxious to get back to her dorm room, where she could feel—or at least pretend to feel—safe. Why should she believe Cam? She'd fallen for his lies too many times before.

"There's nothing worse than you. What you want . . . what you tried to do at Sword and Cross was horrible and wrong." She shook her head. "You're just trying to trick me again."

"I'm not." His voice had less argument in it than she would have expected. He seemed thoughtful, even glum. By then, he had pulled into Shoreline's long, arched driveway. "I never wanted to hurt you, Luce, never."

"Is that why you called all those shadows to battle when I was in the cemetery?"

"Good and evil aren't as clear-cut as you think." He

looked out the window toward the Shoreline buildings, which appeared dark and uninhabited. "You're from the South, right? This time around, anyway. So you should understand the freedom that the victors have to rewrite history. Semantics, Luce. What you think of as evil— well, to my kind, it's a simple problem of connotation."

"Daniel doesn't think so." Luce wished she could have said *she* didn't think so, but she didn't know enough yet. She still felt like she was taking so much of Daniel's explanations on faith.

Cam parked the truck on a patch of grass behind her dorm, got out, and walked around to open the passenger door. "Daniel and I are two sides of the same coin." He offered his hand to help her down; she ignored him. "It must pain you to hear that."

She wanted to say it couldn't possibly be true, that there were no similarities between Cam and Daniel no matter how Cam tried to whitewash things. But in the week she'd been at Shoreline, Luce had seen and heard things that conflicted with what she'd once believed. She thought of Francesca and Steven. They were born of the same place: Once upon a time, before the war and the Fall, there had only been one side. Cam wasn't the only one who claimed that the divide between angels and demons wasn't entirely black and white.

The light was on in her window. Luce imagined Shelby on the orange area rug, her legs crossed in the lotus position, meditating. How could Luce go in and pretend she hadn't just seen an angel die? Or that everything that had happened this week hadn't left her riddled with doubts?

"Let's keep this evening's happenings between us, shall we?" Cam said. "And going forward, do us all a favor and stay on campus, where you won't get into trouble."

She pushed past him, out of the beam of the stolen truck's headlights and into the shadows cloaking the walls of her dorm.

Cam got back into the truck, revving the engine obnoxiously. But before he pulled away, he rolled down the window and called out to Luce, "You're welcome."

She turned around. "For what?"

He grinned and hit the gas. "For saving your life."

SIX

⁂

THIRTEEN DAYS

"It's *here*," a loud voice sang outside Luce's door early the next morning. Someone was knocking. "It's finally here!"

The knocking grew more insistent. Luce didn't know what time it was, other than way too early for all the giggling she could hear on the other side of the door.

"*Your* friends," Shelby called from the top bunk.

Luce groaned and slid out of bed. She glanced up at

Shelby, who was propped up on her stomach on the top bunk, already fully dressed in jeans and a puffy red vest, doing the Saturday crossword.

"Do you ever sleep?" Luce muttered, reaching into her closet to yank on the purple tartan robe her mother had sewn for her thirteenth birthday. It still fit her—sort of.

She pressed her face against the peephole and saw the convex smiling faces of Dawn and Jasmine. They were geared up with bright scarves and fuzzy earmuffs. Jasmine raised a cup holder with four coffees as Dawn, who had a large brown paper bag in her hand, knocked again.

"Are you going to shoo them away or should I call campus security?" Shelby asked.

Ignoring her, Luce swung open the door and the two girls flooded past her into the room, talking a mile a minute.

"Finally." Jasmine laughed, handing Luce a cup of coffee before plopping down on the unmade bottom bunk. "We have so much to discuss."

Neither Dawn nor Jasmine had ever come over before, but Luce was enjoying the way they acted right at home. It reminded her of Penn, who'd "borrowed" the spare key to Luce's room so she could barrel in whenever the need arose.

Luce looked down at her coffee and swallowed hard.

No way could she get emotional here, now, in front of these three.

Dawn was in the bathroom, rooting through the cupboards next to the sink. "As an integral member of the planning committee, we think you should be a part of the welcome address today," she said, looking up at Luce in disbelief. "How are you not even dressed yet? The yacht leaves in, like, under an hour."

Luce scratched her forehead. "Remind me?"

"Ugh." Dawn groaned dramatically. "Amy Branshaw? My lab partner? The one whose father owns the monster yacht? Is any of this ringing a bell?"

It was all coming back to her. Saturday. The yacht trip up the coast. Jasmine and Dawn had pitched the distantly educational idea to Shoreline's events committee—aka Francesca—and had somehow gotten it approved. Luce had agreed to help, but she hadn't done a thing. All she could think about now was Daniel's face when she'd told him about it, instantly dismissing the idea of Luce's having fun without him.

Now Dawn was rifling through Luce's closet. She pulled out a long-sleeved eggplant-colored jersey dress, tossed it at Luce, and shooed her into the bathroom. "Don't forget leggings underneath. It's cold out on the water."

On her way, Luce grabbed her cell phone from its charger. Last night, after Cam had dropped her off, she'd felt so terrified and alone, she'd broken Mr. Cole's number one rule and texted Callie. If Mr. Cole knew how badly she needed to hear from a friend . . . he'd probably still be furious with her. Too late now.

She opened her text message folder and recalled how her fingers had been shaking when she wrote the lie-filled text:

Finally scored a cell phone! Reception's spotty, but I'll call when I can. Everything's great here, but I miss you! Write soon!

No response from Callie.

Was she sick? Busy? Out of town?

Ignoring Luce for ignoring her?

Luce glanced in the mirror. She looked and felt like crap. But she'd agreed to help Dawn and Jasmine, so she tugged on the jersey dress and twisted her blond hair back with a few bobby pins.

By the time Luce came out of the bathroom, Shelby was helping herself to the breakfast the girls had brought with them in the paper bag. It did look really good—cherry Danishes and apple fritters and muffins and cinnamon rolls and three different kinds of juice. Jasmine handed her an oversized bran muffin and a tub of cream cheese.

"Brain food."

"What's all this?" Miles stuck his head in through the slightly ajar door. Luce couldn't see his eyes under his tugged-down baseball cap, but his brown hair was flipping up on the sides and his giant dimples showed when he smiled. Dawn went into an instant fit of giggles, for no other reason than that Miles was cute and Dawn was Dawn.

But Miles didn't seem to notice. He was almost more relaxed and casual around a group of very girly girls than Luce was herself. Maybe he had a whole bunch of sisters or something. He wasn't like some of the other kids at Shoreline, whose coolness seemed to be a front. Miles was genuine, the real thing.

"Don't you have any friends your own gender?" Shelby asked, pretending to be more annoyed than she really was. Now that she knew her roommate a little better, Luce was starting to find Shelby's abrasive humor almost charming.

"'Course." Miles stepped into the room totally unfazed. "It's just, my guy friends don't usually show up with breakfast." He slid a huge cinnamon roll out of the bag and took a giant bite. "You look pretty, Luce," he said with his mouth full.

Luce blushed and Dawn stopped giggling and Shelby coughed into her sleeve: "Awkward!"

At the first sound of the loudspeaker in the hallway, Luce jumped. The other kids looked at her like she was nuts, but Luce was still used to Sword & Cross's punishing PA pronouncements. Instead, Francesca's amber voice poured into the room:

"Good morning, Shoreline. If you're joining us on today's yachting trip, the bus to the marina leaves in ten minutes. Let's convene at the south entrance for a head count. And don't forget to dress warmly!"

Miles grabbed another pastry for the road. Shelby pulled on a pair of polka-dot galoshes. Jasmine tightened the band of her pink earmuffs and shrugged at Luce. "So much for planning! We'll have to wing the welcome address."

"Sit by us on the bus," Dawn instructed. "We'll totally map it out on the way to Noyo Point."

Noyo Point. Luce had to force herself to swallow a mouthful of bran muffin. The Outcast girl's dead expression even when she was alive; the awful ride home with Cam—the memory brought goose bumps to Luce's skin. It didn't help that Cam had rubbed it in about saving her life. Right after he told her not to leave campus again.

Such a weird thing to say. Almost like he and Daniel were in cahoots.

Stalling, Luce sat on the edge of her bed. "So we're all going?"

She'd never broken a promise to Daniel before. Even though she'd never really promised *not* to go on the yacht. The restriction felt so harsh and out of line, her instinct was to blow it off. But if she agreed to play by Daniel's rules, maybe she wouldn't have to face someone else's getting killed. Though that was probably just her paranoia rearing up again. That note had deliberately lured her off campus. A school yacht trip was something else entirely. It wasn't as though the Outcasts were piloting the boat.

"Of course we're all going." Miles grabbed Luce's hand, pulling her to her feet and toward the door. "Why wouldn't we?"

This was the moment of choice: Luce could stay safely on campus the way Daniel (and Cam) had told her. Like a prisoner. Or she could walk out this door and prove to herself that her life was her own.

❊

Half an hour later, Luce was staring, along with half of Shoreline's student body, at a shining white 130-foot Austal luxury yacht.

The air up at Shoreline had been clearer, but down on the water at the marina adjacent to the docks, there was still a thin felt of fog left over from the day before. When Francesca descended from the bus, she muttered, "Enough is enough," and raised her palms in the air.

Very casually, as if she were pushing aside curtains from a window, she literally parted the fog with her fingers, opening up a rich plane of clear sky directly over the gleaming boat.

It was done so subtly, none of the non-Nephilim students or teachers could tell that anything other than nature was at work. But Luce gaped, not sure she had just seen what she thought she had seen until Dawn started clapping very quietly.

"Stunning, as usual."

Francesca smiled slightly. "Yes, that's better, isn't it?"

Luce was beginning to notice all the small touches that could have been the work of an angel. The chartered coach ride had been so much smoother than the public bus she'd taken in the rain the day before. The storefronts seemed refreshed, as if the whole town had gotten a new coat of paint.

The students lined up to board the yacht, which was dazzling in the way very expensive things were. Its sleek profile curved like a seashell, and each of its three levels had its own broad white deck. From where they entered on the foredeck, Luce could see through the enormous windows into three plushly furnished cabins. In the warm, still sunshine down at the marina, Luce's worries about Cam and the Outcasts seemed ridiculous. She was surprised to feel them melt away.

She followed Miles into the cabin on the second level of the yacht. The walls were a sedate taupe, with long black-and-white banquettes hugging the curved walls. A half dozen students had already thrown themselves down on the upholstered benches and were picking at the huge array of food that covered the coffee tables.

At the bar, Miles popped open a can of Coke, split it between two plastic glasses, and handed one to Luce. "So the demon says to the angel: '*Sue me? Where do you think you're going to have to go to find a lawyer?*'" He nudged her. "Get it? 'Cause lawyers are supposed to all . . ."

A punch line. Her mind had been elsewhere and she'd missed the fact that Miles had even been telling a joke. She forced herself to crack up, laughing loudly, even slapping the top of the bar. Miles looked relieved, if not a little suspicious of her overblown reaction.

"Wow," Luce said, feeling crummy as she scaled back her fake laughter. "That was a good one."

To their left, Lilith, the tall redheaded triplet Luce had met on the first day of school, stopped the bite of tuna tartare on its way into her mouth. "What kind of lame half-breed joke is that?" She was scowling mostly at Luce, her glossy lips set in a snarl. "You actually think that's funny? Have you ever even *been* to the under-world? It's no laughing matter. We expect that from Miles, but I would have thought you had better taste."

Luce was taken aback. "I didn't realize it was a question of taste," she said. "In that case, I'm definitely sticking with Miles."

"Shhhh." Francesca's manicured hands were suddenly on both Luce's and Lilith's shoulders. "Whatever this is about, remember: You're on a ship with seventy-three non-Nephilim students. The word of the day is *discretion*."

That was still one of the weirdest parts about Shoreline as far as Luce was concerned. All the time they spent with the regular kids at the school, pretending they weren't doing whatever it was they were actually doing inside the Nephilim lodge. Luce still wanted to talk to Francesca about the Announcers, to bring up what she had done earlier that week in the woods.

Francesca glided away and Shelby shoved up next to Luce and Miles. "Exactly how discreet do you think I need to be while giving seventy-three non-Nephilim swirlies in the cabin toilets?"

"You're bad." Luce laughed, then did a double take when Shelby held out her plate of antipasti. "Look who's sharing," Luce said. "And you call yourself an only child."

Shelby jerked the plate back after Luce had helped herself to one olive. "Yeah, well, don't get used to it or anything."

When the engine revved beneath their feet, the whole boatful of students cheered. Luce preferred moments like this at Shoreline, when she really couldn't tell who was Nephilim and who wasn't. A line of girls braved the cold outside, laughing as their hair tumbled in the wind. Some of the guys from her history class were getting a game of poker together in one corner of the main cabin. That table was where Luce would have expected to find Roland, but he was conspicuously absent.

Near the bar, Jasmine was taking pictures of the whole scene while Dawn motioned to Luce, miming with a pen and paper in the air that they still had to write out their speech. Luce was heading over to join them when, out of the corner of her eye, she spotted Steven through the windows.

He was by himself, leaning against the railing in a long black trench coat, a fedora capping his salt-and-pepper hair. It still made her nervous to think of him as a demon, especially because she genuinely liked him—or at least, what she knew of him. His relationship with Francesca confused her even more. They were such a unit: It reminded her of what Cam had said the night before about him and Daniel not being all that different. The comparison was still nagging at her as she slid open the tinted-glass door and stepped out on the deck.

All she could see on the westward side of the yacht was the endless blue on blue of ocean and clear sky. The water was calm, but a brisk wind tore around the sides of the boat. Luce had to hold on to the railing, squinting in the bright sunlight, shielding her eyes with her hand as she approached Steven. She didn't see Francesca anywhere.

"Hello, Luce." He smiled at her and took off his hat when she reached the railing. His face was tan for November. "How is everything?"

"That's a big question," she said.

"Have you felt overwhelmed this week? Our demonstration with the Announcer didn't upset you too much? You know"—he lowered his voice—"we've never taught that before."

"Upset me? No. I loved it," Luce said quickly. "I mean—it was difficult to watch. But also fascinating. I've been wanting to talk about it with someone. . . ." With Steven's eyes on her, she remembered the conversation she'd overheard her two teachers having with Roland. How it had been Steven, not Francesca, who'd been more open to including Announcers in the curriculum. "I want to learn all about them."

"All about them?" Steven tilted his head, catching the full sun on his already golden skin. "That could take a while. There are trillions of Announcers, one for almost every moment in history. The field is endless. Most of us don't even know where to begin."

"Is that why you haven't taught them before?"

"It's controversial," Steven said. "There are angels who don't believe the Announcers have any value. Or that the bad things they often herald outweigh the good.

They call advocates like me historical pack rats, too obsessed with the past to pay attention to the sins of the present."

"But that's like saying . . . the past doesn't have any value."

If that were true, it would mean that all of Luce's former lives didn't add up to anything, that her history with Daniel was also worthless. So all she'd have to go on was what she knew of Daniel in this lifetime. And was that really enough?

No. It wasn't.

She had to believe there was more to what she felt for Daniel: a valuable, locked-away history that added up to something bigger than a few nights of blissful kissing and a few more nights of arguing. Because if the past had no value, that was really all they had.

"Judging from the look on your face," Steven said, "it seems like I've got another one on my side."

"I hope you're not filling Luce's head with any of your devilish filth." Francesca appeared behind them. Her hands were on her hips and a scowl was on her face. Until she started laughing, Luce had no idea she was teasing.

"We were talking about the shadows—I mean, the Announcers," Luce said. "Steven just told me he thinks there are trillions of them."

"Steven also thinks he doesn't need to call a plumber

when the toilet overflows." Francesca smiled warmly, but there was an undercurrent in her voice that made Luce feel embarrassed, like she'd spoken too boldly. "You want to bear witness to more gruesome scenes like the one we examined in class the other day?"

"No, that's not what I meant—"

"There's a reason why certain things are best left in the hands of experts." Francesca looked at Steven. "I'm afraid that, like a broken toilet, the Announcers as a window on the past are just one of those things."

"Of course we understand why you in particular might be interested in them," Steven said, drawing Luce's full attention.

So Steven got it. Her past lives.

"But *you* must understand," Francesca added, "that glimpsing shadows is highly risky without the proper training. If you are interested, there are universities, rigorous academic programs, even, that I would be happy to talk to you about *down the road*. But for now, Luce, you must forgive our mistake for showing it prematurely to a high school class, and then you must leave it at that."

Luce felt strange and exposed. Both of them were watching her.

Leaning over the railing a little, she could see some of her friends on the ship's main deck below. Miles had a pair of binoculars pressed to his eyes and was trying to point something out to Shelby, who ignored him behind her giant Ray-Bans. At the stern, Dawn and Jasmine were seated on a ledge with Amy Branshaw. They were bent over a manila folder, making hurried notes.

"I should go help out with the welcome address," Luce said, backing away from Francesca and Steven. She could feel their eyes on her all the way down the winding staircase. Luce reached the main deck, ducked under a row of furled sails, and squeezed past a group of non-Nephilim students standing in a bored circle around Mr. Kramer, the beanpole-thin biology teacher, who was lecturing on something like the fragile ecosystem right below their feet.

"There you are!" Jasmine pulled Luce into their powwow. "A plan is finally taking shape."

"Cool. How can I help?"

"At twelve o'clock, we're going to ring that bell." Dawn pointed at a huge brass bell hung from a white beam by a pulley near the ship's bow. "Then I'm going to welcome everyone, Amy's going to speak about how this trip came to be, and Jas is going to talk about this semester's upcoming social events. All we need is someone to say something environmentally friendly." All three girls looked at Luce.

"Is this a hybrid yacht or something?" Luce asked.

Amy shrugged and shook her head.

Dawn's face lit up with an idea. "You could say something about how being out here is making us all greener because he who lives closer to nature acts closer to nature?"

"Are you any good at writing poems?" Jasmine asked. "You could try to make it, you know, fun?"

Guilty of totally bailing on any real responsibilities, Luce felt the need to be amenable. "Environmental poetry," she said, thinking the only thing she was worse at than poetry and marine biology was public speaking. "Sure. I can do that."

"Okay, phew!" Dawn wiped her forehead. "Then here's my vision." She hopped up on the ledge where she'd been sitting and started making a list of things on her fingers.

Luce knew she should be paying attention to Dawn's requests ("Wouldn't it be l'awesome if we lined up shortest to tallest?"), especially since, in a very short time, she was slated to say something intelligent—and rhyming—about the environment in front of a hundred of her classmates. But her mind was still clouded by that bizarre conversation with Francesca and Steven.

Leave the Announcers to the experts. If Steven was right, and there really was an Announcer out there for every moment in history—well, that was like telling her to leave the entire past to the experts. Luce wasn't trying to claim expertise on Sodom and Gomorrah; it was just her own past—hers and Daniel's—she was interested in. And if anyone was going to be an expert on that, Luce figured it should be her.

But Steven had said it himself: There were a trillion shadows out there. It would be close to impossible to even locate the ones that had anything to do with her and Daniel, let alone know what to do with them if she ever found the right ones.

She glanced up at the second-story deck. She could see only the tops of Francesca's and Steven's heads. If Luce let her imagination run freely, she could make up a sharp conversation between them. About Luce. And about the Announcers. Probably agreeing not to bring them up with her ever again.

She was pretty sure that when it came to her past lives, she was going to be on her own.

Wait a minute.

The first day of class. During the icebreaker. Shelby had said—

Luce rose to her feet, forgetting completely that she was in the middle of a meeting, and was already crossing the deck when a piercing scream rang out behind her.

As she whipped around toward the sound, Luce saw a flash of something black dip off the bow of the boat.

A second later, it was gone.

Then a splash.

"Oh my God! *Dawn!*" Both Jasmine and Amy were leaning halfway over the prow, looking down into the water. They were screaming.

"I'll get the lifeboat!" Amy yelled, running into the cabin.

Luce hopped up on the ledge beside Jasmine and gulped at what she saw. Dawn had tumbled overboard and was thrashing in the water. At first, her dark head of hair and flailing arms were all that was visible, but then she glanced up and Luce saw the terror on her white face.

A horrible second later, a big wave overtook Dawn's tiny body. The boat was still moving, pulling further away from her. The girls trembled, waiting for her to resurface.

"What happened?" Steven demanded, suddenly at their side. Francesca was loosening a foam-ringed life preserver from its ties under the bow.

Jasmine's lips quivered. "She was trying to ring the bell to get everyone's attention for the speech. She b-b-barely leaned out—I don't know how she lost her balance."

Luce took another painful glance over the ship's bow. The drop into the icy water was probably thirty feet. There was still no sign of Dawn. "Where is she?" Luce cried. "Can she swim?"

Without waiting for an answer, she grabbed the life preserver out of Francesca's hands, looped one arm through it, and climbed to the top of the bow.

"Luce—stop!"

She heard the cry behind her, but it was already too late. She dove into the water, holding her breath, thinking on her way down of Daniel, and their last dive at the lake.

She felt the cold in her rib cage first, a harsh tightening around her lungs from the shock of the temperature. She waited until her descent slowed, then kicked for the surface. The waves poured over her head, spewing salt into her mouth and up her nose, but she clutched the life preserver tight. It was cumbersome to swim with, but if she found Dawn—*when* she found Dawn—they would both need it to stay afloat while they waited for the lifeboat.

She could vaguely sense a clamoring up on the yacht, people shouting and scurrying around the deck, calling down to her. But if Luce was going to be any help to Dawn, she had to tune all of them out.

Luce thought she saw the dark dot of Dawn's head in the freezing water. She tore forward, against the waves, toward it. Her foot connected with something—a hand?—but then it was gone and she wasn't sure whether it had been Dawn at all.

Luce couldn't go underwater while holding on to the life preserver, and she had a bad feeling that Dawn was deeper down. She knew she shouldn't let go of the life preserver. But she couldn't save Dawn unless she did.

Tossing it aside, Luce filled her lungs with air, then plunged down deep, swimming hard until the surface warmth disappeared and the water became so cold it hurt. She couldn't see a thing, just grasped everywhere she could, hoping to reach Dawn before it was too late.

It was Dawn's hair that Luce felt first, the thin shock of short, dark waves. Probing lower with her hand, she felt her friend's cheek, then her neck, then her shoulder. Dawn had sunk pretty far in such a short time. Luce slipped her arms under Dawn's armpits, then used all her strength to pull her up, kicking powerfully toward the surface.

They were far underwater, the daylight a distant shimmer.

And Dawn felt heavier than she could possibly be, like a great weight was attached to her, dragging both of them down.

At last Luce broke the surface. Dawn sputtered, spewing water out of her mouth and coughing. Her eyes were red and her hair was matted on her forehead. With one arm looped across Dawn's chest, Luce gently paddled them both toward the life preserver.

"Luce," Dawn whispered. In the tumbling waves, Luce couldn't hear her, but she could read her lips. "What's happening?"

"I don't know." Luce shook her head, straining to keep them both afloat.

"Swim to the lifeboat!" The call came from behind. But swimming anywhere was impossible. They could barely keep their heads above water.

The crew was lowering an inflatable life raft. Steven was inside it. As soon as the boat met the ocean, he began paddling briskly toward them. Luce closed her eyes and let the palpable relief wash over her with the next wave. If she could just hold on a little longer, they were going to be okay.

"Grab my hand," Steven shouted to the girls. Luce's legs felt like she'd been swimming for an hour. She pushed Dawn toward him so that Dawn could be the first one out.

Steven had stripped down to his slacks and white oxford shirt, which was wet now and clinging to his chest. His muscled arms were huge as he reached for Dawn. His face red with exertion, he grunted and heaved her up. When Dawn was draped over the gunwale, far enough that she wouldn't fall back in, Steven turned and quickly took hold of Luce's arms.

She felt weightless, practically soaring out of the water with his help. It was only when she felt her body slipping the rest of the way into the boat that she realized how sopping wet and freezing she was.

Except for where Steven's fingers had been.

There the drops of water on her skin were steaming.

She sat up, moving to help Steven pull the shivering Dawn the rest of the way into the raft. Exhausted, Dawn could barely drag herself upright. Luce and Steven each had to take her by an arm and heave. She was almost all the way inside the boat when Luce felt a shocking jerk pull Dawn back into the water.

Dawn's dark eyes bulged and she cried out as she slipped backward. Luce was not prepared: Dawn slipped out of her wet grip, and Luce fell back against the side of the raft.

"Hold on!" Steven caught hold of Dawn's waist just in time. He stood up, almost capsizing the raft. As he strained to lift Dawn out of the water, Luce saw the briefest flash of gold extend from his back.

His wings.

The way they jutted out instantly, at the moment when Steven needed the most strength—it seemed to happen almost against his will. They were gleaming, the color of the kind of expensive jewelry Luce had only seen behind glass cases at department stores. They were nothing like Daniel's wings. Daniel's were warm and welcoming, magnificent and sexy; Steven's were raw and intimidating, jagged and terrifying.

Steven grunted, the muscles in his arms strained, and his wings beat just once, giving him enough upward momentum to fly Dawn out of the water.

The wings stirred up enough wind to flatten Luce against the other side of the raft. As soon as Dawn was safe, Steven's feet touched down again on the floor of the raft. His wings immediately slid back into his skin. They left two small tears in the back of his dress shirt, the only proof that what Luce had seen had been real. His face was washed out and his hands were shaking.

The three of them collapsed inside the raft. Dawn had noticed nothing, and Luce wondered whether anyone watching from the boat had either. Steven looked at Luce as if she'd just seen him naked. She wanted to tell him it had been startling to see his wings; she hadn't known until then that even the dark side of the fallen angels could be so breathtaking.

She reached for Dawn, partly expecting to see blood somewhere on her skin. It really felt like *something* had taken her in its jaws. But there was no sign of any wound.

"Are you okay?" Luce finally whispered.

Dawn shook her head, sending droplets of water flying off her hair. "I can swim, Luce. I'm a good swimmer. Something had me—something—"

"Is still down there," Steven finished, picking up the paddle and hauling them back toward the yacht.

"What did it feel like?" Luce asked. "A shark or—"

Dawn shuddered. "Hands."

"Hands?"

"Luce!" Steven barked.

She turned to him: He seemed like a different being than the one she'd been talking to minutes earlier on the deck. There was a hardness in his eyes she'd never seen before.

"What you did today was—" He broke off. His dripping face looked savage. Luce held her breath, waiting for it. *Reckless. Stupid. Dangerous.* "Very brave," he finally said, his cheeks and forehead relaxing into their usual expression.

Luce exhaled, having a hard time even finding the voice to say thank you. She couldn't take her eyes off Dawn's trembling legs. And the rising thin red marks that looped around her ankles. Marks that looked like they'd been left by fingers.

"I'm sure you girls are scared," Steven said quietly. "But there's no reason to bring a general hysteria upon the whole school. Let me have a talk with Francesca. Until you hear from me: Not a word about this to anyone else. Dawn?"

The girl nodded, looking terrified.

"Luce?"

Her face twitched. She wasn't sure about keeping this secret. Dawn had almost died.

"Luce." Steven gripped her shoulder, removed his square-framed glasses, and stared into Luce's hazel eyes with his own dark brown ones. As the life raft was winched up to the main deck, where the rest of the school waited, his breath was hot in her ear. "Not a word. To anyone. It's for your own protection."

SEVEN

TWELVE DAYS

"I don't get why you're being so weird," Shelby said to Luce the next morning. "You've been here, what, six days? And you're Shoreline's biggest hero. Maybe you're going to live up to your reputation after all."

The Sunday-morning sky was dotted with cumulus clouds. Luce and Shelby were walking along Shoreline's tiny beach, sharing an orange and a thermos of chai. A strong wind carried the earthy scent of old redwoods down from the woods. The tide was rough and high, kicking up long swaths of knotted black seaweed, jellyfish, and rotting driftwood into the girls' path.

"It was nothing," Luce muttered, which wasn't exactly true. Jumping into that icy water after Dawn had certainly been *something*. But Steven—the severity of his tone, the force of his grip on her arm—had put a fear into Luce about *ever* speaking of Dawn's rescue.

She eyed the salty foam left in the wake of a receding wave. She was trying not to look out at the deep, dark water beyond—so she wouldn't have to think about *hands* down in its icy depths. *For your own protection.* Steven must have meant *your* in its plural form. As in, it's for all the students' protection. Otherwise, if he only meant Luce . . .

"Dawn's okay," she said. "That's all that matters."

"Um, *yeah*, because of you, Baywatch."

"Do not start calling me Baywatch."

"You prefer to think of yourself as a jack-of-all-trades kind of savior?" Shelby had the most deadpan way of teasing. "Frankie says some mystery creep's been lurking around the school grounds the past two nights. You should give him what for—"

"What?" Luce almost spat out her chai. "Who is it?"

"I repeat: *Mystery* creep. They dunno." Shelby took a seat on a weathered flat of limestone, skipping a few stones expertly into the ocean. "Just some dude. I overheard Frankie talking to Kramer about it on the boat yesterday after all the hoopla."

Luce sat down next to Shelby and began to root around in the sand for stones.

Someone was sneaking around Shoreline. What if it was Daniel?

It would be just like him. So stubborn about keeping his own promise not to see her, but unable to stay away. The thought of him made her yearn for him that much more. She could feel herself almost on the brink of tears, which was crazy. Odds were the mystery creep wasn't even Daniel. It could be Cam. It could be anyone. It could be an Outcast.

"Did Francesca seem worried?" she asked Shelby.

"Wouldn't you be?"

"Wait a minute. Is that why you didn't sneak out last night?" It was the first night Luce hadn't been woken up by Shelby coming in through the window.

"No." Shelby's skipping arm was toned from all her yoga. Her next stone skipped six times in a wide arc, coming almost all the way back to them, like a boomerang.

"Where do you go every night, anyway?"

Shelby stuffed her hands in the pockets of her puffy red ski vest. She was staring at the gray waves so intensely that it was clear she'd either seen something out there—or she was avoiding the question. Luce followed her gaze, almost relieved to see nothing in the water but gray-and-white waves all the way to the horizon.

"Shelby."

"What? I don't go anywhere."

Luce started to stand up, annoyed that Shelby felt she couldn't tell her anything. Luce was brushing damp sand from the backs of her legs when Shelby's hand tugged her back down onto the rock.

"Okay, I *used* to go see my sorry-ass boyfriend." Shelby sighed heavily, pitching a rock artlessly into the water, nearly pelting a fat seagull swooping down for a fish. "Before he became my sorry-ass *ex*-boyfriend."

"Oh. Shel, I'm sorry." Luce chewed on her lip. "I didn't even know you had a boyfriend."

"I had to start keeping him at arm's length. He got way too into the fact that I had a new roommate. Kept bugging me to let him come over late at night. Wanted to meet you. I don't know *what* kind of girl he thinks I am. No offense, but three's a crowd in my book."

"Who is he?" Luce asked. "Does he go here?"

"Phillip Aves. He's a senior in the main school."

Luce didn't think she knew him.

"That pale kid with the bleached-blond hair?" Shelby said. "Kind of looks like an albino David Bowie? You can't really miss him." Her mouth twitched. "Unfortunately."

"Why didn't you tell me you broke up?"

"I prefer downloading Vampire Weekend songs that I lip-sync to when you're not around. Better for my chakras. Besides"—she pointed a stubby finger at Luce—"you're the one being all moody and weird today. Daniel treating you wrong or something?"

Luce leaned back on her elbows. "That would require us actually seeing each other, which apparently we aren't allowed to do."

If Luce closed her eyes, she could let the sound of the waves take her back to the very first night she'd kissed Daniel. In this lifetime. The humid tangle of their bodies on that languishing Savannah boardwalk. The hungry pressure of his hands pulling her in. Everything seemed possible then. She opened her eyes. She was so far away from all of that now.

"So your sorry-ass ex-boyfriend—"

"No." Shelby made a zip-it motion with her fingers. "I don't want to talk about SAEB any more than I guess you want to talk about Daniel. Next."

That was fair. But it wasn't exactly that Luce didn't want to talk about Daniel. It was more like, if she *started* talking about Daniel, she might not be able to shut up. She already sounded like a broken record in her own mind—cycling on repeat through the total of oh, four physical experiences she'd had with him in this life. (She chose only to start counting once he stopped pretending she didn't exist.) Imagine how quickly she would bore

Shelby, who'd probably had tons of boyfriends, tons of experience. Compared to Luce's next to none.

One kiss she could barely remember with a boy who'd burst into flames. A handful of very hot moments with Daniel. That just about summed it up. Luce was certainly no expert when it came to love.

Again she felt the unfairness of her situation: Daniel had all these great memories of them together to fall back on when things got rough. She had nothing.

Until she looked up at her roommate.

"Shelby?"

Shelby had her puffy red hood pulled over her head and was poking a stick into the wet sand. "I told you I don't want to talk about him."

"I know. I was wondering, remember when you mentioned that you knew how to glimpse your past lives?"

This was what she'd been about to ask Shelby when Dawn fell overboard.

"I never said that." The stick plunged deeper into the sand. Shelby's face was flushed and her thick blond hair was frizzing out of her ponytail.

"Yes . . . you did." Luce tilted her head. "You wrote it on my paper. That day when we were doing the ice-breaker? You grabbed it out of my hands and said you could speak more than eighteen languages and glimpse past lives and which one did I need you to fill out—"

"I remember what I said. But you misunderstood what I meant."

"Okay," Luce said slowly, "well—"

"Just because I *have* glimpsed *a* past life before doesn't mean I know how to do it, and it doesn't mean it was my own."

"So, it wasn't yours?"

"Hell no, reincarnation is for freaks."

Luce frowned and dug her hands into the wet sand, wanting to bury herself in it.

"*Hello,* that was a joke." Shelby nudged Luce playfully. "Tailored especially for the girl who's had to go through puberty a thousand times." She grimaced. "Once was enough for me, thank you very much."

So Luce was That Girl. The girl who'd had to go through puberty a thousand times. She'd never thought about it that way before. It was almost funny: From the outside, going through endless puberties seemed like the worst part of her lot. But it was so much more complicated than that. Luce started to say she'd go through a thousand more pimples and hormone fluctuations if she could look into her past lives and understand more about herself, but then she looked up at Shelby. "If it wasn't yours, then whose past life did you glimpse?"

"Why are you being so nosy? Damn."

Luce could feel her blood pressure rising. "Shelby, ohmigod, throw me a bone!"

"Okay," Shelby said finally, making a chill-out motion with her hands. "I was at this party one night in Corona. Things got pretty crazy, half-naked séances and shit, and—well, that's not really the story. So I remember taking a walk to get some air. It was raining, hard to see where I was going. I turned the corner in an alleyway and there was this guy, kind of beat-up-looking. He was bent over a sphere of darkness. I'd never seen anything like it, shaped like a globe, but glowing, kind of floating above his hands. He was crying."

"What was it?"

"I didn't know then, but now I know it was an Announcer."

Luce was mesmerized. "And you saw some of the past life he was glimpsing? What was it like?"

Shelby met Luce's eyes and swallowed. "It was pretty gruesome, Luce."

"I'm sorry," Luce said. "I was only asking because . . ."

It felt like a big deal to admit what she was about to admit. Francesca would definitely be opposed to this. But Luce needed answers, and she needed help. Shelby's help.

"I need to glimpse some of my past lives," Luce said. "Or I need to at least try. Things have been happening recently that I'm supposed to just accept because I don't know any better—only I *could* know better, a lot better, if I could just see where I come from. Where I've been. Does that make any sense?"

Shelby nodded.

"I need to know what I had in the past with Daniel so I can feel surer of what I have with him now." Luce took a breath. "That guy, the one in the alley . . . did you see what he did to the Announcer?"

Shelby scrunched her shoulders. "He just sort of guided it into shape. I didn't even know what it was at the time, and I don't know how he tracked it down. That's why Francesca and Steven's demonstration freaked me out so much. I saw what happened that one night, and I've been trying to forget about it ever since. I had no idea that what I was seeing was an Announcer."

"If I could track down an Announcer, do you think you could guide it?"

"No promises," Shelby said, "but I'll give it a shot. You know how to track them down?"

"Not really, but how hard can it be? They've been haunting me all my life."

Shelby cupped her hand over Luce's on the rock. "I want to help you, Luce, but it's weird. I'm scared. What if you see something you, you know, shouldn't?"

"When you broke up with SAEB—"

"I thought I told you not to—"

"Just listen: Aren't you glad you figured out whatever it was that made you break up with him, sooner rather than later? I mean, what if you got engaged or something and only then—"

"Blech!" Shelby put up a hand to stop Luce. "Point taken. Now, come on, find us a shadow."

⚹

Luce led Shelby back across the beach and up the steep stone stairs, where dashes of battered red and yellow verbenas had pushed up through the wet, sandy soil. They crossed the neat green terrace, trying not to interrupt a group of non-Nephilim students in a game of ultimate Frisbee. They passed their third-story dorm room window and wound around the back of the building. At the edge of the forest of redwoods, Luce pointed to a space between the trees. "That's where I found one the last time."

Shelby marched into the forest ahead of Luce, shoving through the long, clawlike leaves of the vine maple trees among the redwoods and stopping under a giant fern.

It was dark under the redwoods, and Luce was glad of Shelby's company. She thought back to the other day, how quickly time had passed while she was harassing that shadow, getting nowhere. Suddenly she felt overwhelmed.

"*If* we can find and catch an Announcer, and *if* we can even get a glimpsing to work," she said, "what do you think the chances are that the Announcer will have anything to show about me and Daniel? What if we just get another awful Bible scene like we saw in class?"

Shelby shook her head. "Daniel I don't know about. But *if* we can summon and then glimpse an Announcer, then it *will* have to do with you. They're supposed to be summoner-specific—though you won't always be interested in what they have to say. Like how you get junk mail mixed with your important mail, but it's still addressed to you."

"How can they be . . . summoner-specific? That would mean Francesca and Steven were at the destruction of Sodom and Gomorrah."

"Well, yeah. They *have* been around forever. Rumor has it their résumés are pretty impressive." Shelby stared oddly at Luce. "Put your bug eyes back in your head. How else do you think they scored jobs at Shoreline? This is a really good school."

Something dark and slippery moved over them: a heavy cloak of an Announcer stretching sleepily in the lengthening shadows from the limb of a redwood tree.

"There." Luce pointed, not wasting any time. She swung herself up onto a low branch that stretched behind Shelby. Luce had to balance on one foot and lean out all the way to the left just to graze the Announcer with her fingertips. "I can't reach it."

Shelby picked up a pinecone and pitched it at the center of the shadow where it draped down from the branch.

"Don't!" Luce whispered. "You'll piss it off."

"It's pissing *me* off, being so coy. Just hold out your hand."

Grimacing, Luce did as she was told.

She watched the pinecone ricochet off the shadow's exposed side, then heard the soft swishing sound that used to fill her ears with dread. One side of the shadow was sliding, very slowly, away from the branch. It slipped off and landed across Luce's shaking extended arm. She pinched its edges with her fingers.

Luce hopped off the branch where she'd been standing and approached Shelby, her cold, musty offering in her hands.

"Here," Shelby said. "I'll take half and you take half, just like we saw in class. Ew, it's squishy. Okay . . . loosen your grip, he's not going anywhere. Let him just kind of chill and take shape."

It seemed like a long time passed before the shadow did anything at all. Luce felt almost like she was playing with the old Ouija board she'd had as a kid. An inexplicable energy on the tips of her fingers. The feeling of slight, continual movement before she could see any difference in the Announcer's shape.

Then there was a *whoosh:* It was contracting, folding slowly in on its dark self. Soon the whole thing had taken on the size and shape of a large box. It hovered just above their fingertips.

"Do you see that?" Shelby gasped. Her voice was almost inaudible over the whooshing sound of the shadow. "Look, there in the middle."

As had happened during class, a dark veil seemed to lift off the Announcer, revealing a shocking burst of color. Luce shielded her eyes, watching as the bright light seemed to settle back inside the shadow screen, into a foggy out-of-focus image. Then, finally, into distinct shapes in muted colors.

They were looking at a living room. The back of a blue plaid recliner with the footrest kicked up and a badly fraying bottom corner. An old wood-paneled television airing a rerun of *Mork & Mindy* with the volume off. A fat Jack Russell terrier curled on a round patchwork rug.

Luce watched a swinging door push open from what looked like a kitchen. A woman, older than Luce's grandmother had been when she died, walked through. She was wearing a pink-and-white patterned dress, heavy white tennis shoes, and thick glasses on a string around her neck. She was carrying a tray of cut fruit.

"Who are these people?" Luce wondered aloud.

When the old woman put down the tray on the coffee table, a liver-spotted hand extended from around the chair and selected a chunk of banana.

Luce leaned in to see more clearly, and the focus of the image shifted with her. Like a 3-D panorama. She hadn't even noticed the old man sitting in the recliner. He was frail, with a few thin patches of white hair and age spots all over his forehead. His mouth was moving, but Luce couldn't hear a thing. A row of framed pictures lined the mantel of the fireplace.

The whooshing in Luce's ears got louder, so loud it made her wince. Without her doing anything other than wonder about those pictures, the Announcer's image zoomed in. It left Luce with a feeling of whiplash—and an extreme close-up of one framed photograph.

A thin gold-plated frame around a smudged glass plate. Inside, the small photograph had a fine scalloped border around a yellowing black-and-white image. Two faces in the photograph: Hers and Daniel's.

Holding her breath, she studied her own face, which looked just a little younger than it did now. Dark shoulder-length hair set in pincurls. A white blouse with a Peter Pan collar. A wide A-line skirt brushing the middles of her calves. White-gloved hands, holding Daniel's. He was looking directly at her, smiling.

The Announcer started vibrating, then quaking; then the image inside started to flicker and fade away.

"No," Luce called, ready to lunge inside. Her shoulders connected with the edge of the Announcer, but that was as far as she got. A brush of bitter cold pushed her back and left her skin feeling damp. A hand clamped around her wrist.

"Don't get any wild ideas," Shelby warned.

Too late.

The screen went black and the Announcer dropped from their hands onto the forest floor, shattering into pieces like broken black glass. Luce suppressed a whimper. Her chest heaved. She felt like a part of her had died.

Lowering herself to all fours, she pressed her forehead to the ground and rolled onto her side. It was colder, murkier than it had been when they'd started. The watch on her wrist said it was after two o'clock, but it had been morning when they came into the forest. Looking west, toward the edge of the woods, Luce could see the difference in the light hitting the dorm. The Announcers swallowed time.

Shelby lay down next to her. "You okay?"

"I'm so confused. Those people—" Luce cupped her forehead. "I have no idea who they are."

Shelby cleared her throat and looked uncomfortable. "Don't you think, um, maybe you used to know them? Like, a long time ago. Like, maybe they were your . . ."

Luce waited for her to finish. "My what?"

"It really hasn't occurred to you that those were your parents from another life? That this is what they look like now?"

Luce's jaw dropped open. "No. Wait—you mean, I've had totally different parents in each of my past lives? I thought Harry and Doreen . . . I just assumed they would have been with me the whole time."

Suddenly she remembered something Daniel had said, about her mother making bad boiled cabbage in that past life. At the time, she hadn't dwelled on it, but now it made a little bit more sense. Doreen was an amazing cook. Everyone in east Georgia knew that.

Which meant Shelby must be right. Luce probably had a whole nation of past families she couldn't even remember.

"I'm so stupid," she said. Why hadn't she paid more attention to the way the man and woman looked? Why hadn't she felt the slightest connection to them? She felt like she'd lived her whole life and only now found out she was adopted. How many times had she been handed off to different parents? "This is— This is—"

"Totally messed up," Shelby said. "I know. On the bright side, you could probably save yourself a lot of money for therapy if you could look back at all your other families, see all the problems you had with hundreds of mothers before this one."

Luce buried her face in her hands.

"That is, if you need family therapy." Shelby sighed. "Sorry, who's talking about themselves again?" She raised her right hand, then slowly put it down. "You know, Shasta's not that far from here."

"What's Shasta?"

"Mount Shasta, California. It's just a few hours that-away." Shelby jerked her thumb toward the north.

"But the announcers only show the past. What

would be the point of going there now? They're probably—"

Shelby shook her head. "'The past' is a broad term. Announcers show the distant past right up to the events happening seconds ago, and everything in between. I saw a laptop on the desk in the corner, so there's a good chance . . . you know . . ."

"But we don't know where they live."

"Maybe you don't. Me, I zoomed in on a piece of their mail and got the address. Committed it to memory. 1291 Shasta Shire Circle, apartment 34." Shelby shrugged. "So, if you wanted to go visit them, we could totally drive there and back in a day."

"Right." Luce snorted. She desperately wanted to go visit them, but it just didn't seem possible. "In whose car?"

Shelby laughed a faux-sinister little laugh. "There was only one thing that wasn't sorry-ass about my sorry-ass ex-boyfriend." She dug into the pocket of her sweatshirt, pulling out a long key chain. "And that was his very sweet Mercedes, parked right here in the student lot. Lucky for you, I forgot to give him back the extra key."

❊

They tore down the road before anyone could stop them.

Luce found a map in the glove compartment and traced the line up to Shasta with her finger. She called out some directions to Shelby, who drove like a bat out of Hell, but the maroon Mercedes almost seemed to like the abuse.

Luce wondered how Shelby was staying so calm. If Luce had just broken up with Daniel and "borrowed" his car for the afternoon, she wouldn't be able to stop herself from remembering road trips they'd taken, or arguments they'd gotten into while driving to a movie, or what they'd done in the backseat that one time with all the windows rolled down. Surely Shelby was thinking about her ex. Luce wanted to ask, but Shelby had been clear that the topic was off-limits.

"Are you going to change your hair?" Luce asked finally, remembering what Shelby had said about getting over breakups. "I could help you, if you are."

Shelby's face pinched into a scowl. "That freak's not even worth it." After a long pause, she added, "But thank you."

The drive took most of the rest of the afternoon, and Shelby spent it working herself up, bickering with the radio, scanning the channels for the craziest nutjobs she could find. The air got colder, the trees thinned out, and the elevation of the landscape rose steadily the whole time. Luce focused on staying calm, imagining a hundred scenarios about meeting these parents. She tried to avoid thinking about what Daniel would say if he knew where she was going.

"There it is." Shelby pointed when a massive snow-capped mountain came into view directly in front of the road. "The town sits right in those foothills. We should be there just after sunset."

Luce didn't know how to thank Shelby for hauling her all the way up here on a whim. Whatever was behind Shelby's shift in attitude, Luce was grateful—she wouldn't have been able to do this on her own.

The town of Shasta was wacky and artistic, with a good number of elderly people walking leisurely down the wide avenues. Shelby rolled down the windows and let in the brisk early-evening air. It helped settle Luce's stomach, which was knotting up at the prospect of actually having to talk to the people she'd seen in the Announcer.

"What am I supposed to say to them? Surprise, I'm your daughter back from the dead," Luce practiced aloud as they were sitting at a stoplight.

"Unless you want to totally freak out a sweet old couple, we're going to have to work on that," Shelby said. "Why don't you pretend you're a solicitor, just to get in the door and feel them out?"

Luce looked down at her jeans, beat-up tennis shoes, and purple backpack. She didn't look like a very impressive salesperson. "What would I sell?"

Shelby started to drive again. "Hawk car washes or something cheesy like that. You can say you've got vouchers in your bag. I did that one summer, door to door. Almost got shot." She shuddered, then looked at Luce's white face. "Come on, your own mom and dad are not going to shoot you. Oh, hey, look, here we are!"

"Shelby, can we just sit in silence for a little while? I think I need to breathe."

"Sorry." Shelby pulled into a large parking lot facing a compound of small, single-story connected bungalow-style buildings. "Breathing I can do."

Through her nerves, Luce had to admit it was a pretty nice place. A series of the bungalows stood in a semicircle around a pond. There was a main lobby building with a row of wheelchairs lined up outside the doors. A big banner read WELCOME TO SHASTA SHIRE RETIREMENT COMMUNITY.

Her throat felt so dry it hurt to swallow. She didn't know if she even had it in her to say two words to these people. Maybe it was one of those things you just couldn't think about too much. Maybe she needed to get up there and force her hand down on that knocker and then figure out how to act.

"Apartment thirty-four." Shelby squinted at a square stucco building with a red Spanish-tile roof. "That looks like it over there. If you want me to—"

"Wait in the car till I get back? That would be great, thanks so much. I won't be long!"

Before Luce could lose her nerve, she was out the car door and jogging up the winding sidewalk toward the building. The air was warm and filled with a heady scent of roses. Cute old people were everywhere. Split into teams on the shuffleboard court near the entrance, taking an evening stroll through a neatly pruned flower garden next to the pool. In the early-evening light, Luce's eyes strained as she tried to locate the couple somewhere in this crowd, but no one looked familiar. She would have to go straight to their house.

From the footpath leading up to their bungalow, Luce could see a light on through the window. She stepped closer until she had a clearer view.

It was uncanny: the same room she'd seen earlier in the Announcer. Even down to the fat white dog asleep on the rug. She could hear dishes being washed in the kitchen. She could see the thin, brown-socked ankles of the man who had been her father however many years ago.

He didn't feel like her father. He didn't look like her father, and the woman hadn't looked at all like her mother. It wasn't that there was anything wrong with them. They seemed perfectly nice. Like perfectly nice . . . strangers. If she knocked on the door and made up some lie about car washes, would they become any less strange?

No, she decided. But that wasn't all. Even though *she* didn't recognize her parents, if they really were her parents, of course they would recognize *her*.

She felt stupid for not thinking about that before.

They'd take one look at her and know she was their daughter. Her parents were much older than most of the other people she'd seen outside. The shock of it might be too much for them. It was too much for Luce, and this couple had about seventy years on her.

By then she was pressed against their living room window, crouching behind a spiny sagebrush cactus bush. Her fingers were dirty from gripping the window-sill. If their daughter had died when she was seventeen, they must have been mourning her for close to fifty years. They'd be at peace with it by now. Wouldn't they? Luce popping up uninvited from behind a cactus plant would be the very last thing they needed.

Shelby would be disappointed. Luce herself was disappointed. It hurt to realize that this was as close as she was ever going to get to them. Hanging on the window-sill outside her former parents' house, she felt the tears roll down her cheeks. She didn't even know their names.

EIGHT

ELEVEN DAYS

To: thegaprices@aol.com
From: lucindap44@gmail.com
Sent: Monday, 11/15 at 9:49am
Subject: Hanging in there

Dear Mom and Dad,

I'm sorry I've been out of touch. Things at school have been busy, but I'm having a lot of good experiences. My favorite class these days is humanities. Right now I'm working on an extra-credit assignment that takes up a lot of my time. I miss you guys and hope to see you soon. Thanks for being such great parents. I don't think I tell you that enough.

Love,
Luce

Luce clicked Send on her laptop and quickly switched her browser back to the online presentation Francesca was giving at the front of the room. Luce was still getting used to being at a school where they handed out computers, complete with wireless Internet, right in the middle of class. Sword & Cross had a total of seven student computers, all of which were in the library. Even if you managed to get your hands on the encrypted password to access the Web, every site was blocked except for a few dry academic research ones.

The email to her parents had been prompted by guilt. The night before, she'd had the strangest feeling that merely by driving out to the retirement community in Mount Shasta, she was cheating on her *real* parents, the ones who had raised her in this lifetime. Sure, at some point, these other parents had been real, too. But that was still too strange a thought for Luce to really absorb.

Shelby hadn't been one-tenth as pissed off as she could have been about driving Luce all the way up there for no reason. Instead, she just fired up the Mercedes and drove to the nearest In-N-Out Burger so they could get a couple of off-the-menu grilled cheese sandwiches with special sauce.

"Do not give it a second thought," Shelby said, wiping her mouth with a napkin. "Do you know how many panic attacks my screwed-up family's given me? Believe me, I'm the last person who's going to judge you about this."

Now Luce looked across the classroom at Shelby and felt an intense gratitude for the girl who, a week before, had terrified her. Shelby's thick blond hair was pulled back by a terry-cloth headband, and she was taking diligent notes on Francesca's lecture.

Every screen Luce could see in her peripheral vision was fixed on the blue and gold PowerPoint presentation that Francesca was clicking through at a snail's pace. Even Dawn's. She looked especially spunky today in a hot-pink T-shirt dress and a high side ponytail. Was it possible she'd already recovered from what had happened on the boat? Or was she covering up the terror she must have felt—and maybe still felt?

Glancing over at Roland's monitor, Luce scrunched up her face. It didn't surprise her that he'd been mostly invisible since he arrived at Shoreline, but when he did turn up in class, she was actually upset to see her former reform school cohort following the rules.

At least Roland didn't look especially interested in the lecture on "Career Opportunities for Nephilim: How Your Special Skills Can Give You a Wing Up." In fact, the look on Roland's face was more disappointed than anything else. His mouth was set in a frown and he kept lightly shaking his head. Also strange was the fact that every time Francesca made eye contact with the students, she distinctly passed over Roland.

Luce pulled up the class chat room board to see whether Roland was logged on. It was supposed to be a tool for the class to bounce questions off each other, but the questions Luce had for Roland were not for class discussion. He knew something, something more than he'd let on the other day—surely it had to do with Daniel. She also wanted to ask him where he'd been on Saturday, whether he'd heard about Dawn's trip overboard.

Except Roland wasn't online. The only other person in the class who was logged on to the chat room was Miles. A text box with his name on it popped up on her screen:

Helloooo over there!

He was sitting right next to her. Luce could even hear him chuckling. It was cute that he got a kick out of his own dumb jokes. This was exactly the kind of goofy, teasing rapport she would love to have with Daniel. If he weren't so brooding all the time. If he were actually around.

But he wasn't.

She wrote back: *How's the weather in your neck of the woods?*

Getting sunnier now, he typed, still smiling. *Hey, what'd you do last night? I swung by your room to see if you wanted to grab dinner.*

She looked up from her computer, straight at Miles. His deep blue eyes were so sincere, she had an urge to turn to spill everything about what had happened. He'd been so amazing the other day, listening to her talk about her time at Sword & Cross. But there was no way to answer his question via chat. As much as she wanted to tell him, she didn't know whether she should talk about it. Even letting Shelby in on her secret project was practically wooing trouble from Steven and Francesca.

Miles's expression changed from his normal casual smile into an awkward frown. It made Luce feel terrible, and also slightly surprised, that she could elicit this kind of reaction in him.

Francesca clicked off the projector. When she crossed her arms over her chest, the pink silk sleeves of her peasant blouse bloomed out of her cropped leather jacket. For the first time, Luce noticed how far away Steven was. He was seated on the windowsill at the western corner of the room. He had barely said a word in class all day.

"Let's see how well you paid attention," Francesca

said, smiling widely at the students. "Why don't you break up into pairs and take turns conducting mock interviews."

At the sound of all the other students rising from their chairs, Luce groaned internally. She'd heard next to nothing of Francesca's lecture and had no idea what the assignment was.

Also, she knew she was just squatting in the Nephilim program temporarily, but was it too much to ask for her teachers to remember every once in a while that she wasn't like the rest of the kids in the class?

Miles tapped her computer screen where he had messaged her: *You wanna partner up?* Just then, Shelby appeared.

"I say we do CIA or Doctors Without Borders," Shelby said. She motioned for Miles to surrender the desk next to Luce. Miles stayed put. "There's no way I'm fictitiously applying for some lame dental hygienist position."

Luce looked back and forth between Shelby and Miles. Both of them seemed to feel proprietary about her, something she hadn't realized until now. Truthfully, she wanted to be partners with Miles—she hadn't seen him since Saturday. She'd kind of been missing him. In a friendly way. Like in a let's-catch-up-over-a-cup-of-coffee way, more than a let's-wander-along-the-beach-at-sunset-and-you-can-smile-at-me-with-those-incredible-blue-eyes way. Because she was with Daniel, she didn't think about other guys. She definitely didn't start blushing intensely in the middle of class while reminding herself that she didn't think about other guys.

"Is everything okay over here?" Steven laid his tan palm on Luce's desk and gave her a big-brown-eyed you-can-tell-me nod.

But Luce was still nervous around him after what he'd said to her and Dawn on the life raft the other day. Nervous enough that she'd even avoided bringing it up again with Dawn.

"Everything's great," Shelby responded. She took Luce by the elbow and jerked her toward the deck, where some of the other students were paired up, already conducting their mock interviews. "Luce and I were just about to talk résumés."

Francesca appeared behind Steven. "Miles," she said softly, "Jasmine still needs a partner if you'd like to pull up a desk next to her."

A few desks down, Jasmine said, "Dawn and I couldn't agree on who should play indie starlet and who should play"—her voice dropped an octave—"casting director. So she abandoned me for Roland."

Miles looked disappointed. "Casting director," he mumbled. "Finally, I've found my calling." He headed off to join his partner, and Luce watched him go.

With the situation diffused, Francesca steered Steven back to the front of the room. But even as he walked beside Francesca, Luce could feel him watching her.

She subtly checked her phone. Callie still hadn't texted her back. This wasn't like her, and Luce blamed herself. Maybe it would be better for both of them if Luce just kept her distance. It was only for a little while.

She followed Shelby outside to a seat on the wooden bench built into the curve of the deck. The sun was bright in the clear sky, but the only part of the deck that wasn't already packed with students was under the cool shade of a towering redwood. Luce brushed a layer of dull green needles off the bench and zipped her chunky sweater a little higher on her neck.

"You were really cool about everything last night," she said in a low voice. "I was . . . freaking out."

"I know," Shelby laughed. "You were all—" She made a trembling zombie face.

"Give me a break. That was rough. My one chance to learn something about my past, and I totally choked."

"You Southerners and your guilt." Shelby gave a one-shouldered shrug. "You gotta cut yourself some slack. I'm sure there are plenty more relatives where those two old geezers came from. Maybe even some who aren't so close to death's door." Before Luce's face could collapse, Shelby added, "All I'm saying is, if you ever feel up for tracking down another family member, just say the word. You're growing on me Luce, it's kinda weird."

"Shelby," Luce whispered suddenly, through clenched teeth. "Don't move." Beyond the deck, the biggest, most ominous Announcer Luce had ever seen was rippling in the long shadow cast by an enormous redwood tree.

Slowly, following Luce's eyes, Shelby looked out at the ground. The Announcer was using the real shadow of the tree as camouflage. Parts of it kept twitching.

"It looks sick, or skittish, or, I don't know . . ." Shelby trailed off, curling her lip. "There's something wrong with it, right?"

Luce was looking past Shelby at the staircase winding down to the ground level of the lodge. Below them were a bunch of unpainted wooden supports that propped up the deck. If Luce could get hold of the shadow, Shelby could join her under the deck before anyone saw anything. She could help Luce glimpse its message and they could make it back upstairs in time to rejoin the class.

"You're not seriously considering what I think you're seriously considering," Shelby said. "Are you?"

"Keep watch up here for a minute," Luce said. "Be ready when I call you."

Luce descended a few steps, so that her head was just level with the deck where the rest of the students were busy carrying out their interviews. Shelby had her back to Luce. She'd give a sign if anyone noticed Luce was gone.

Luce could hear Dawn in the corner, ad-libbing with Roland: "You know, I *was* stunned when I was nominated for a Golden Globe. . . ."

Luce looked back at the darkness stretched out along the grass. It occurred to her to wonder whether the other students had seen it. But she couldn't worry about that. She was wasting time.

The Announcer was a good ten feet away, but where she stood close to the deck, Luce was shielded from the other students' eyes. It would be too obvious if she walked right over to it. She was going to have to try to coax it off the ground and over to her without using her hands. And she had no idea how to do that.

That was when she noticed the figure leaning up against the other side of the redwood tree. Also hidden from the view of the students on the deck.

Cam was smoking a cigarette, humming to himself like he didn't have a care in the world. Except that he was covered entirely in blood and gore. His hair was matted to his forehead, his arms were scratched and bruised. His T-shirt was wet and stained with sweat, and his jeans were splattered too. He looked filthy and disgusting, as though he'd just emerged from battle. Only, there was no one else around—no bodies, no anything. Just Cam.

He winked at her.

"What are you doing here?" she whispered. "What did you *do*?" Her head swam from the sick reek coming off his bloodied clothes.

"Oh, just saved your life. Again. How many times

does this make?" He tapped ash off his cigarette. "Today it was Miss Sophia's crew, and I can't say I didn't enjoy it. Bloody monsters. They're after you, too, you know. Word has gotten out that you're here. And that you like to wander into that dark forest unchaperoned." He pointed.

"You just killed them?" She was horrified, glancing up at the deck to see whether Shelby, or anyone, could see them. *No.*

"A couple of them, yes, just now, with my own two hands." Cam showed off his palms, caked with something red and slimy that Luce really did not want to see. "I agree the woods are lovely, Luce, but they're also full of things that want you dead. So do me a favor—"

"No. You don't get to ask me for favors. Everything about you disgusts me."

"Fine." He rolled his eyes. "Then do it for Grigori. *Stay on campus.*" He flicked his cigarette onto the grass, rolled back his shoulders, and unfurled his wings. "I can't always be here to watch over you. And God knows Grigori can't."

Cam's wings were tall and narrow and pulled tight behind his shoulders, sleek and gold and flecked with brindled stripes of black. She wished they repulsed her, but they didn't. Like Steven's wings, Cam's were jagged, rough—they too looked as though they'd survived a lifetime of fights. The black stripes gave Cam's wings a dark, sensual quality. There was something magnetic about them.

But no. She *loathed* everything about Cam. She would forever.

Cam beat his wings once, lifting his feet off the ground. The wings' flapping was tremendously loud and kicked back a swirl of wind that raised leaves from the ground.

"Thank you," Luce said, crisply, before he coasted under the deck. Then he was gone in the shadows of the woods.

Cam was protecting her now? Where was Daniel? Wasn't Shoreline supposed to be safe?

In Cam's wake, the Announcer—the reason Luce had come down here in the first place—spiraled up from its shadow like a small black cyclone.

Closer. Then a little closer still.

Finally, the shadow wandered into the air just over her head.

"Shelby," Luce whispered loudly. "Get down here."

Shelby looked down at Luce. At the cyclone-shaped Announcer teetering over her. "What took you so long?" she asked, sprinting down the stairs just in time to watch the whole massive Announcer tumble down.

Straight into Luce's arms.

Luce screamed—but luckily, Shelby clapped a hand over her mouth.

"Thank you," Luce said, her words muffled against Shelby's fingers.

The girls were still huddled three steps down from the deck, in plain view of anyone who might cross over to the shady side. Luce couldn't straighten her knees under the weight of the shadow. It was the heaviest one she'd ever touched, and the coldest on her skin. It wasn't black like most of the others, but a sickly greenish gray. Parts of it were still twitching, lighting up like bolts of distant lightning.

"I don't have a good feeling about this," Shelby said.

"Come on," Luce whispered. "I summoned it. Now it's your turn to do the glimpsing."

"My turn? Who said anything about me having a turn? You're the one who dragged me down here." Shelby waved her hands like the last thing on earth she wanted to do was touch the beast in Luce's arms. "I know I said I'd help you track down your relatives, but whatever kind of relative you've got in here . . . I don't think either of us wants to meet."

"Shelby, please," Luce begged, groaning from the weight, the chill, and the general nastiness of the shadow. "I'm not a Nephilim. If you don't help me, I can't do this."

"What exactly are you trying to do?" A voice behind them from the top of the stairs. Steven had his hands clamped down on the banister and was glaring at the girls. He seemed larger than he did in class, towering over them, as if he had doubled in size. His deep brown eyes looked stormy, but Luce could feel the heat coming off them, and she was scared. Even the Announcer in her arms trembled and edged away.

Both girls were so startled they screamed.

Jarred by the sound, the shadow bolted from Luce's arms. It moved so fast she had no chance to stop it, and it left nothing behind but a freezing, foul-smelling wake.

In the distance, a bell rang. Luce could sense all the other kids trooping off toward the mess hall for lunch. On his way out, Miles stuck his head over the railing and peered down at Luce, but he took one look at Steven's red-hot expression, widened his eyes, and moved along.

"Luce," Steven said, more politely than she expected. "Would you mind seeing me after school?"

When he lifted his hands off the railing, the wood underneath them was scorched black.

⚡

Steven opened the door before Luce even knocked. His gray shirt was a bit wrinkled and his black knit tie was loosened at the neck. But he had regained the appearance of serenity, which Luce was beginning to realize took effort for a demon. He wiped his glasses on a monogrammed handkerchief and stepped aside.

"Please come in."

The office wasn't big, just wide enough for a large black desk, just long enough for three tall black bookshelves, each one crammed with hundreds of well-worn books. But it was comfortable and even welcoming—not like what Luce had imagined a demon's office would be like. There was a Persian carpet in the center of the room, a wide window looking east at the redwoods. Now, at dusk, the forest had an ethereal, almost lavender hue.

Steven sat down in one of two maroon desk chairs and motioned for Luce to take the other. She surveyed the framed pieces of art, jigsawed onto every spare inch of the wall. Most of them were portraits in varying degrees of detail. Luce recognized a few sketches of Steven himself and several flattering depictions of Francesca.

Luce took a deep breath, wondering how to begin. "I'm sorry I summoned that Announcer today; I—"

"Have you told anyone about what happened with Dawn in the water?"

"No. You told me not to."

"You haven't told Shelby? Miles?"

"I haven't told anyone."

He considered this for a moment. "Why did you call the Announcers the shadows the other day when we were talking on the boat?"

"It just slipped out. When I was growing up, they always were part of the shadows. They'd detach and come to me. So that's what I called them, before I knew what they were." Luce shrugged. "Stupid, really."

"It's not stupid." Steven stood up and went to the farthest bookshelf. He pulled down a thick book with a dusty red cover and brought it back to the desk. Plato: *The Republic*. Steven opened it to the exact page he'd been looking for, turning the book right side up in front of Luce.

It was an illustration of a group of men inside a cave, shackled beside one another, facing a wall. A fire blazed behind them. They were pointing at the shadows cast on the wall by a second group of men who walked behind them. Below the image, a caption read: *The Allegory of the Cave*.

"What is this?" Luce asked. Her knowledge of Plato started and ended with the fact that he palled around with Socrates.

"Proof of why your name for the Announcers is actually quite smart." Steven pointed at the illustration. "Imagine that these men spend their lives seeing *only* the shadows on this wall. They come to understand the world and what happens in it from these shadows, without ever seeing what casts the shadows. They don't even understand that what they are seeing *are* shadows."

She looked just beyond Steven's finger to the second group of men. "So they can never turn around, never see the people and things creating the shadows?"

"Exactly. And because they can't see what is actually casting the shadows, they assume that what they *can* see—these shadows on the wall—are reality. They have no idea that the shadows are mere representations and distortions of something much truer and more real." He paused. "Do you understand why I'm telling you this?"

Luce shook her head. "You want me to stop messing with the Announcers?"

Steven closed the book with a snap, then crossed to the other side of the room. She felt as if she'd disappointed him somehow.

"Because I don't believe you will stop . . . messing with the Announcers, even if I do ask you to. But I do want you to understand what you're dealing with the next time you summon one. The Announcers are *shadows* of past events. They can be helpful, but they also contain some very distracting, sometimes dangerous distortions. There's a lot to learn. A clean, safe summoning technique; then, of course, once you have honed your talents, the Announcer's noise can be screened out and its message be heard clearly through—"

"You mean that whooshing noise? There's a way to hear *through* that?"

"Never mind. Not yet." Steven turned and sank his hands into his pockets. "What were you and Shelby after today?"

Luce felt flushed and uncomfortable. This meeting

was not going at all as she'd expected. She'd thought maybe detention, some trash pickup.

"We were trying to learn more about my family," she finally managed to get out. Thankfully, Steven seemed to have no idea she had seen Cam earlier. "Or my families, I guess I should say."

"That's all?"

"Am I in trouble?"

"You weren't doing anything else?"

"What else would I be doing?"

It shot through her mind that Steven might think she was reaching out to Daniel, trying to send him a message or something. As if she'd even know how to do that.

"Summon one now," Steven said, opening the window. It was past dusk and Luce's stomach told her that most of the other students would be sitting down to dinner.

"I—I don't know if I can."

Steven's eyes looked warmer than they had earlier, excited almost. "When we summon Announcers, we're making a sort of wish. Not a wish for anything material, but a wish to better understand the world, our role in it, and what's to become of us."

Immediately, Luce thought of Daniel, what she wanted most for their relationship. She *didn't* feel she had much of a role in what was to become of them—and she wanted one. Was that why she'd been able to summon the Announcers before she'd even known how?

Nervously, she centered herself in her chair. She closed her eyes. She imagined a shadow detaching itself from the long darkness that stretched from the tree trunks outside, imagined it rolling away and rising, filling the space of the open window. Then floating closer to her.

She smelled the soft mildewy scent first, almost like black olives, then opened her eyes at the brush of coolness on her cheek. The temperature in the room had dropped a few degrees. Steven rubbed his hands together in the suddenly damp, drafty office.

"Yes, there you go," he murmured.

The Announcer was drifting in the air of his office, thin and transparent, no bigger than a silk scarf. It glided straight toward Luce, then wrapped a fuzzy tendril of nothingness around a blown-glass paperweight on the desk. Luce gasped. Steven was smiling when he stepped toward her, guiding it upright until it became a blank black screen.

Then it was in her hands, and she began to pull. The careful motion felt like trying to stretch out a piecrust without breaking it, something Luce had watched her mother do at least a hundred times. The darkness swirled into muted grays; then the faintest black-and-white image came into view.

A dark bedroom with a single bed. Luce—a former Luce, clearly—lying on her side, staring out the open window. She must have been sixteen years old. The door behind the bed opened, and a face, lit up by the hallway light, appeared in it. The mother.

The mother Luce had gone to see with Shelby! But younger, much younger—maybe by as many as fifty years, glasses perched at the end of her nose. She smiled, as if pleased to find her daughter sleeping, then pulled the door shut.

A moment later, a pair of fingertips gripped the bottom of the windowpane. Luce's eyes widened as the former Luce sat up in bed. Outside the window, the fingertips strained; then a pair of hands became visible, then two strong arms, lit up blue in the moonlight. Then Daniel's glowing face as he came in through the window.

Luce's heart was racing. She wanted to dive into the Announcer, as she'd wanted to yesterday with Shelby. But then Steven clicked his fingers and the whole thing snapped up like a venetian blind rolling to the top of a window frame. Then it broke apart and showered down.

The shadow lay in soft fragments on the desk. Luce reached for one, but it disintegrated in her hands.

Steven sat down behind his desk, probing Luce with his eyes as if to see what the glimpse had done to her. It suddenly felt very private, what she'd just witnessed in the Announcer; she didn't know whether she wanted Steven to know how powerfully it had rocked her. After all, he was technically on the other side. In the past few days she'd seen more and more of the demon in him. Not just the fiery temper, welling up until he literally steamed—but the dark-glorious golden wings, too. Steven was magnetic and charming, just like Cam—and, she reminded herself, just like Cam, a demon.

"Why are you helping me with this?"

"Because I don't want you to get hurt," Steven barely whispered.

"Did that really happen?"

Steven looked away. "It's a representation of something. And who knows how distorted it is. It's a shadow of a past event, not reality. There is always some truth to the Announcer, but it's never the *simple* truth. That's what makes Announcers so problematic, and so dangerous to those without proper training." He glanced at his watch. From below them came the sound of the door opening and closing on the landing. Steven stiffened when he heard a quick set of high heels clicking up the stairs.

Francesca.

Luce tried to read Steven's face. He handed her *The Republic,* which she slipped into her backpack. Just before Francesca's beautiful face appeared in the doorway, Steven said to Luce, "The next time you and Shelby choose not to complete one of your assignments, I will ask you to write a five-page research paper with citations. This time, I let you off with a warning."

"I understand." Luce caught Francesca's eye in the doorway.

She smiled at Luce—though whether it was an

off-you-go dismissal smile or a don't-think-you're-fooling-me-kid smile, it was impossible to tell. Trembling a little as she stood and flung her bag over her shoulder, Luce made for the door, calling back to Steven, "Thank you."

⁂

Shelby had the fire going in the hearth when Luce got back to her dorm room. The hot pot was plugged in next to the Buddha night-light and the whole room smelled like tomatoes.

"We were out of mac and cheese, but I made you some soup." Shelby ladled out a piping-hot bowlful, cracked some fresh black pepper on top, and brought it over to Luce, who'd collapsed on top of her bed. "Was it terrible?"

Luce watched the steam rise from her bowl and tried to figure out what to say. Bizarre, yes. Confusing. A little scary. Potentially . . . empowering.

But it hadn't been terrible, no.

"It was okay." Steven seemed to trust her, at least to the extent that he was going to allow her to continue summoning the Announcers. And the other students seemed to trust him, even admire him. No one else acted concerned about his motives or his allegiances. But with Luce he was so cryptic, so difficult to read.

Luce had trusted the wrong people before. *A careless*

pursuit at best. At worst, it's a good way to get yourself killed. That was what Miss Sophia had said about trust the night she'd tried to murder Luce.

It was Daniel who'd advised Luce to trust her instincts. But her own feelings seemed the most unreliable. She wondered whether Daniel had already known about Shoreline when he'd told her that, whether his advice was a way to prepare her for this long separation, when she would become less and less certain about everything in her life. Her family. Her past. Her future.

She looked up from the bowl at Shelby. "Thanks for the soup."

"Don't let Steven thwart your plans," Shelby huffed. "We should totally keep working on the Announcers. I am just so sick of these angels and demons and their power trips. 'Oooh, we know better than you because we're full-on angels and you're just the bastard child of some angel who got his rocks off.'"

Luce laughed, but she was thinking that Steven's mini-lecture on Plato and giving her *The Republic* tonight was the opposite of a power trip. Of course, there was no telling Shelby that now, not when she'd dropped into her usual I'm-on-a-tirade-against-Shoreline routine on Luce's bottom bunk.

"I mean, I know you have *whatever* going on with Daniel," Shelby continued, "but seriously, what good has an angel ever done for me?"

Luce shrugged apologetically.

"I'll tell you: nothing. Nothing besides knock up my mom and then totally ditch both of us before I was born. Real celestial behavior." Shelby snorted. "The kicker is, my whole life, my mom's telling me I should be grateful. For what? These watered-down powers and this enormous forehead I inherited from my dad? No thanks." She kicked the top bunk glumly. "I'd give anything to just be normal."

"Really?" Luce had spent the whole week feeling inferior to her Nephilim classmates. She knew the grass was always greener, but this she couldn't believe. What advantage could Shelby possibly see in *not* having her Nephilim powers?

"Wait," Luce said, "the sorry-ass ex-boyfriend. Did he . . ."

Shelby looked away. "We were meditating together, and, I don't know, somehow during the mantra, I accidentally levitated. It wasn't even a big deal, I was, like, two inches off the floor. But Phil wouldn't let it go. He started bugging me about what else I could do, and asking all these weird questions."

"Like what?"

"I don't know," Shelby said. "Some stuff about you, actually. He wanted to know if you'd taught me to levitate. Whether you could levitate too."

"Why me?"

"Probably more of his pervy roommate fantasies. Anyway, you should have seen the look on his face that day. Like I was some sort of circus freak. I had no choice but to break things off."

"That's awful." Luce squeezed Shelby's hand. "But it sounds like his problem, not yours. I know the rest of the kids at Shoreline look at the Nephilim funny, but I've been to a lot of high schools, and I'm starting to think that's just the way most kids' faces naturally bend. Besides, no one's 'normal.' Phil must have had something freakish about him."

"Actually, there was something about his eyes. They were blue, but faded, almost washed out. He had to wear these special contacts so people wouldn't stare at him." Shelby tossed her head to the side. "Plus, you know, that third nipple." She burst out laughing, was red in the face by the time Luce joined in and practically in tears when a light tapping on the windowpane shut both of them up.

"That *better* not be him." Shelby's voice instantly sobered as she hopped up from the bed and flung open the window, knocking over a potted yucca in her haste.

"It's for you," she said, almost numbly.

Luce was at the window in a heartbeat, because by then, she could *feel* him. Bracing her palms on the sill, she leaned forward into the brisk night air.

She was face to face, lip to lip, with Daniel.

For the briefest moment, she thought he was looking past her, into the room, at Shelby, but then he was kissing her, cupping the back of her head with his soft hands and pulling her to him, taking her breath away. A week's worth of warmth flowed through her, along with an unspoken apology for the harsh words they'd said the other night on the beach.

"Hello," he whispered.

"Hello."

Daniel was wearing jeans and a white T-shirt. She could see the cowlick in his hair. His tremendous pearl-white wings beat gently behind him, probing the black night, luring her in. They seemed to beat in the sky almost in time with her heart. She wanted to touch them, to bury herself in them the way she had the other night on the beach. It was a stunning thing to see him floating outside her third-story window.

He took her hand and pulled her over the windowsill and out into the air and his arms. But then he set her down on a wide, flat ledge under the window that she'd never noticed before.

She always felt the urge to cry when she was happiest. "You're not supposed to be here. But I'm so glad you are."

"Prove it," he said, smiling as he pulled her back against his chest so that his head was just over her shoulder. He looped one arm around her waist. Warmth radiated from his wings. When she looked over her shoulder, all she could see was white; the world was white, all softly textured and aglow with moonlight. And then Daniel's great wings began to beat—

Her stomach dropped a little and she knew she was being lifted—no, *rocketed,* straight into the sky. The ledge below them grew smaller and the stars above shone brighter and the wind ripped across her body, tousling her hair across her face.

Up they soared, higher into the night, until the school was just a black smudge on the ground below. Until the ocean was just a silver blanket on the earth. Until they pierced a feathery layer of cloud.

She wasn't cold or afraid. She felt free of everything that weighed her down on earth. Free of danger, free of any pain she'd ever felt. Free of gravity. And so in love. Daniel's mouth traced a line of kisses up the side of her neck. He wrapped his arms tight around her waist and turned her to face him. Her feet were on top of his, just as when they'd danced over the ocean at the bonfire. There was no wind anymore; the air around them was silent and calm. The only sounds were the beating of Daniel's wings as they hovered in the sky and the beating of her own heart.

"Moments like this," he said, "make everything we've had to go through worthwhile."

Then he kissed her as he'd never kissed her before. A

long, extended kiss that seemed to claim her lips forever. His hands traced the line of her body, lightly at first and then more forcefully, delighting in her curves. She melted into him, and he ran his fingers along the backs of her thighs, her hips, her shoulders. He took control of every part of her.

She felt the muscles beneath his cotton shirt, his taut arms and neck, the hollow at the small of his back. She kissed his jaw, his lips. Here in the clouds, with Daniel's eyes sparkling brighter than any star she had ever seen, this was where Luce belonged.

"Can't we just stay here forever?" she asked. "I'll never get enough of this. Of you."

"I hope not." Daniel smiled, but soon, too soon, his wings shifted, flattening out. Luce knew what was coming next. A slow descent.

She kissed Daniel one last time and loosened her arms from around his neck, preparing herself for flight—but then she lost her grip.

And fell.

It seemed to happen in slow motion. Luce tipping backward, her arms flailing wildly, and then the rush of cold and wind as she plummeted and her breath left her. Her last glimpse was of Daniel's eyes, the shock in his face.

But then everything sped up, and she was falling so furiously she couldn't breathe. The world was a spinning black void, and she felt nauseated and scared, her eyes burning from the wind, her vision dimming and tunneling. She was going to pass out.

And that would be it.

She would never know who she really was, never know whether it had all been worth it. Would never know whether she was worthy of Daniel's love, and he of hers. It was all over; this was it.

The wind was a fury in her ears. She closed her eyes and waited for the end.

And then he caught her.

There were arms around her, strong, familiar arms, and she was gently slowing, no longer falling—she was being cradled. By Daniel. Her eyes were closed, but Luce knew him.

She began to sob, so relieved that Daniel had caught her, had saved her. In that moment, she had never loved him more—no matter how many lifetimes she had lived.

"Are you okay?" Daniel whispered, his voice soft, his lips so close to hers.

"Yes." She could feel the beating of his wings. "You caught me."

"I will always catch you when you fall."

Slowly they dropped back to the world they'd left behind. To Shoreline and the ocean lapping up against the cliffs. When they neared the dormitory, he clasped her tightly, and gently coasted to the ledge, alighting with a feather-light touch.

Luce planted her feet on the ledge and looked up at

Daniel. She loved him. It was the only thing she was certain of.

"There," he said, looking serious. His smile hardened, and the sparkle in his eyes seemed to fade. "That should satisfy your wanderlust, at least for a little while."

"What do you mean, wanderlust?"

"The way you keep leaving campus?" His voice held a lot less warmth than it had a moment ago. "You have to stop doing that when I'm not around to look after you."

"Oh, come on, it was just a stupid field trip. Everyone was there. Francesca, Steven—" She broke off, thinking about the way Steven had reacted to what had happened to Dawn. She didn't dare bring up her road trip with Shelby. Or running into Cam under the deck.

"You've been making things very difficult for me," Daniel said.

"I haven't been having the easiest time either."

"I told you there were rules. I told you not to leave this campus. But you haven't listened. How many times have you disobeyed me?"

"*Disobeyed* you?" She laughed, but inside she felt dizzy and sick. "What are you, my boyfriend or my master?"

"Do you know what happens when you stray from here? The danger you put yourself in just because you're bored?"

"Look, the cat's out of the bag," she said. "Cam already knew I was here."

"Of course Cam knows you're here," Daniel said, exasperated. "How many times do I have to tell you Cam is not the threat right now? He won't try to sway you."

"Why not?"

"Because he knows better. And you should know better too than to sneak off like that. There are dangers you can't possibly fathom."

She opened her mouth but didn't know what to say. If she told Daniel she'd spoken with Cam that day, that he had killed several of Miss Sophia's entourage, it would only prove his point. Anger flared up in Luce, at Daniel, at his mysterious rules, at his treating her like a child. She would have given anything to stay with him, but his eyes had hardened into flat gray sheets and their time in the sky felt like a distant dream.

"Do you understand what kind of Hell I go through to keep you safe?"

"How am I supposed to understand when you don't tell me anything?"

Daniel's beautiful features distorted into a scary expression. "Is this her fault?" He jerked his thumb toward her dorm room. "What kind of sinister ideas has she been putting in your head?"

"I can think for myself, thank you." Luce narrowed her eyes. "But how do you know Shelby?"

Daniel ignored the question. Luce couldn't believe the way he was talking to her, like she was some kind of badly behaved pet. All the warmth that had filled her a moment ago when Daniel had kissed her, held her, looked at her—it wasn't enough when she felt this cold every time he spoke to her.

"Maybe Shelby is right," she said. She hadn't seen Daniel in so long—but the Daniel she wanted to see, the one who loved her more than anything, the one who'd followed her for millennia because he couldn't live without her—was still up there in the clouds, not down here, bossing her around. Perhaps, even after all these lifetimes, she didn't really know him. "Maybe angels and humans shouldn't . . ."

But she couldn't say it.

"Luce." His fingers wrapped around her wrist, but she shook him off. His eyes were open and dark, and his cheeks were white from the cold. Her heart was urging her to grab him and keep him close, to feel his body pressed against hers, but she knew deep down that this wasn't the kind of fight that could be cured with a kiss.

She pushed past him to a narrower part of the ledge and slid open her window, surprised to find that the room was already dark. She climbed inside, and when she turned back to Daniel, she noticed that his wings were trembling. Almost like he was about to cry. She wanted to go back to him, to hold and soothe and love him.

But she couldn't.

She closed the shutters and stood in her dark room alone.

NINE

~ ‡ ~

TEN DAYS

When Luce woke up on Tuesday morning, Shelby was already gone. Her bed was made, the handmade patchwork quilt folded at its foot, and her puffy red vest and tote bag had been plucked from their peg by the door.

Still in her pajamas, Luce stuck a mug of water in the microwave to make tea, then sat down to check her email.

To: lucindap44@gmail.com
From: callieallieoxenfree@gmail.com

Sent: Monday, 11/16 at 1:34am
Subject: Trying Not to Take It Personally

Dear L,

Got your text, and first things first, I miss you too. But I've got a really out-of-left-field suggestion: it's called you-and-I-catch-up. Crazy Callie and her wild ideas. I know you're busy. I know you're under heavy surveillance and it's hard to sneak away. What I don't know is a single detail about your life. Who do you eat lunch with? Which class do you like the most? What ever happened with that guy? See, I don't even know his name. I hate that.

I'm glad you got a phone, but don't text me to say you're going to call. Just call. I haven't heard your voice in ages. I ain't mad at ya. Yet.

xoC

Luce closed the email. It was next to impossible to piss Callie off. She'd never actually done it before. The fact that Callie didn't suspect that Luce was lying was only further proof of how distant they'd become. The shame Luce felt was heavy, settling right between her shoulders.

On to the next email:

To: lucindap44@gmail.com
From: thegaprices@aol.com

Sent: Monday, 11/16 at 8:30pm
Subject: Well, honey, we love you too

Luce Baby,

Your emails always brighten our days. How's the swim team going? Are you drying your hair now that it's cold outside? I know, I'm nagging, but I miss you.

Do you think Sword & Cross will grant you permission to leave campus for Thanksgiving next week? Dad could call the dean? We won't count our chickens yet, but your father did go out and buy a Tofurky just in case. I've been filling up the extra freezer with pies. Do you still like the one with the sweet potatoes? We love you and we think about you all the time.

Mom

Luce's hand hung frozen on her mouse. It was Tuesday morning. Thanksgiving was a week and a half away. It was the first time that her favorite holiday had even crossed her mind. But as quickly as it had come in, Luce tried to banish it. There was no way Mr. Cole would let her go home for Thanksgiving.

She was about to click Respond when a blinking orange box at the bottom of the screen caught her attention. Miles was online. He'd been trying to chat with her.

Miles (8:08): Mornin', Miss Luce.
Miles (8:09): I am STARVING. Do you wake up as hungry as I wake up?
Miles (8:15): Wanna get breakfast? I'll swing by your room on my way. 5 min?

Luce looked at her clock. 8:21. There was a booming knock on her door. She was still in her pajamas. Still had bed head. She opened the door a little.

The morning sun poured onto the hallway's hard-wood floors. It reminded Luce of coming down the always-sunlit wooden staircase at her parents' house for breakfast, the way the whole world looked brighter through the lens of one hallway filled with light.

Miles wasn't wearing his Dodgers cap today, so it was one of the few times she could clearly see his eyes. They were really deep blue, a nine-o'clock-in-summer sky blue. His hair was wet, dripping on the shoulders of his white T-shirt. Luce swallowed, unable to stop her mind from picturing him in the shower. He grinned at her, showing off a dimple and his super-white smile. He seemed so California today; Luce was surprised to real-ize how good he made it look.

"Hey." Luce wedged as much of her pajamaed body

as she could behind the door. "I just saw your messages. I'm in for breakfast, but I'm not dressed yet."

"I can wait." Miles leaned against the hallway wall. His stomach growled loudly. He tried to cross his arms over his waist to cover the sound.

"I'll hurry." Luce laughed, closing the door. She stood before her closet, trying not to think about Thanksgiving or her parents or Callie or why so many important people were slipping away from her at once.

She yanked a long gray sweater from her dresser and threw it on over a pair of black jeans. She brushed her teeth, put on big silver hoop earrings and a squirt of hand lotion, grabbed her bag, and studied herself in the mirror.

She didn't look like a girl who was stuck in some bickering power struggle of a relationship, or a girl who couldn't go home to her family for Thanksgiving. At the moment, she just looked like a girl who was excited to open a door and find a guy there who made her feel normal and happy and really sort of all-around wonderful.

A guy who was not her boyfriend.

She sighed, opening the door to Miles. His face lit up.

When they got outside, Luce realized the weather had changed. The sunlit morning air was just as brisk as it had been on the roof's ledge last night with Daniel. And it had felt icy then.

Miles held out his enormous khaki jacket to her,

but she waved it away. "I just need some coffee to warm me up."

They sat at the same table where they had sat the week before. Immediately, a couple of student waiters rushed over. Both guys seemed to be friends with Miles and had an easy joking manner. Luce certainly never got this level of service when she sat with Shelby. While the guys fired away with questions—how had Miles's fantasy football team done the night before, had he watched that YouTube clip of the guy pranking his girlfriend, did he have plans after class today—Luce looked around the terrace for her roommate but couldn't find her.

Miles answered all the guys' questions but seemed uninterested in extending the conversation any further. He pointed at Luce. "This is Luce. She wants a big cup of your hottest coffee and . . ."

"The scrambled eggs," Luce said, folding up the small menu that the Shoreline mess hall printed up each day.

"Same for me, guys, thanks." Miles handed back the two menus and turned full-focus on Luce. "Seems like I haven't seen you around much recently outside class. How are things?"

Miles's question surprised her. Maybe because she was already feeling like a guilt magnet this morning. She liked that there was no "Where have you been hiding?"

or "Are you avoiding me?" tacked on at the end. Just a question: "How are things?"

She beamed at him, then somehow lost track of her smile and was almost wincing by the time she said, "Things are okay."

"Uh-oh."

Horrible fight with Daniel. Lying to my parents. Losing my best friend. Part of her wanted to unleash all of that on Miles, but she knew she shouldn't. Couldn't. That would be taking their friendship to a level she wasn't sure was a good idea. She'd never had a really close guy friend before, the kind of friend you shared everything with and relied on like a girlfriend. Wouldn't things get . . . complicated?

"Miles," she finally said, "what do people do around here for Thanksgiving?"

"I don't know. I guess I've never stuck around to find out. I wish I could sometimes. Thanksgiving at my house is obnoxiously enormous. At least a hundred people. Like ten courses. And it's black-tie."

"You're joking."

He shook his head. "I wish I were. Seriously. We have to hire parking attendants." After a pause: "Why do you ask—wait, do you need a place to go?"

"Uhh . . ."

"You're coming." He laughed at her shocked expression. "Please. My brother's not coming home from college this year and he was my only lifeline. I can show you around Santa Barbara. We can ditch the turkey and get the world's best tacos at Super Rica." He raised an eyebrow. "It'll be so much less torturous to have you there with me. It might even be fun."

While Luce was mulling over his offer, she felt a hand on her back. She knew the touch by now—soothing to the point of having healing powers—Francesca's.

"I spoke to Daniel last night," Francesca said.

Luce tried not to react as Francesca leaned down. Had Daniel gone to see her after Luce had shut him out? The idea made her jealous, though she didn't really know why.

"He's worried about you." Francesca paused, seeming to search Luce's face. "I told him you're doing very well, considering your new surroundings. I told him I would make myself available to you for anything you need. Please understand that you should come to me with your questions." A sharpness entered her gaze, a hard, fierce quality. *Come to me instead of Steven* seemed to lie there, unspoken.

And then Francesca left, as quickly as she'd appeared, the silk lining of her white wool coat swishing against her black pantyhose.

"So . . . Thanksgiving," Miles finally said, rubbing his hands together.

"Okay, okay." Luce swallowed the rest of her coffee. "I'll think about it."

Shelby didn't show at the Nephilim lodge for that morning's class—a lecture on summoning angelic forebears, kind of like sending a celestial voice mail. By lunchtime, Luce was starting to get nervous. But heading into her math class, she finally spotted the familiar puffy red vest and practically sprinted toward it.

"Hey!" She tugged her roommate's thick blond ponytail. "Where've you been?"

Shelby turned around slowly. The look on her face took Luce back to her very first day at Shoreline. Shelby's nostrils were flared and her eyebrows were hunched forward.

"Are you okay?" Luce asked.

"Fine." Shelby turned away and started fiddling with the nearest locker, twirling a combination, then popping it open. Inside were a football helmet and about a case worth of empty Gatorade bottles. A poster of the Laker Girls was slapped on the inside of the door.

"Is that even your locker?" Luce asked. She didn't know a single Nephilim kid who used a locker, but Shelby was rooting through this one, tossing dirty sweat socks recklessly over her shoulder.

Shelby slammed the locker shut, then moved on to twirl the combination of the next one. "Now you're judging me?"

"No." Luce shook her head. "Shel, what is going on? You disappeared this morning, you missed class—"

"I'm here now, aren't I?" Shelby sighed. "Frankie

and Steven are a lot more lax about letting a girl take a personal day than the humanoids over here."

"Why do you need a personal day? You were fine last night, until—"

Until Daniel showed up.

Right around the time Daniel appeared at the window, Shelby had gone all pale and quiet and straight to bed and—

While Shelby stared at Luce as if her IQ had suddenly dropped by half, Luce became aware of the rest of the hall. Where the rust-colored lockers ended, the gray-carpeted walls were lined with girls: Dawn and Jasmine and Lilith. Preppy, cardiganed girls like Amy Branshaw from Luce's afternoon classes. Punky pierced girls who looked kind of like Arriane but were way less fun to talk to. A few girls Luce had never seen before. Girls with books clutched against their chests, gum popping in their mouths, and eyes darting at the carpet, at the wood-beamed ceiling, at each other. Anywhere but directly at Luce and Shelby. Though it was clear that all of them were eavesdropping.

A sick feeling in her stomach was starting to tell her why. It was the biggest collision of Nephilim and non-Nephilim Luce had seen so far at Shoreline. And every girl in this hallway had figured out before her:

Shelby and Luce were about to duke it out over a guy.

"Oh." Luce swallowed. "You and Daniel."

"Yeah. We. A long time ago." Shelby wouldn't look at her.

"Okay." Luce focused on breathing. She could handle this. But the whispers flying around the wall of girls made her skin crawl, and she shuddered.

Shelby scoffed. "I'm sorry the idea disgusts you so much."

"That's not it." But Luce *did* feel disgusted. Disgusted with herself. "I always . . . I thought I was the only—"

Shelby put her hands on her hips. "You thought every time you disappeared for seventeen years that Daniel just twiddled his thumbs? Earth to Luce, there is a Before You for Daniel. Or an In Between, or whatever." She paused to give Luce a sideways squint. "Are you really that self-involved?"

Luce was speechless.

Shelby grunted and turned to face the rest of the hall. "This estrogen force field needs to dissipate," she barked, waggling her fingers at them. "Move along. All of you. Now!"

As the girls scurried off, Luce pressed her head against the cold metal locker. She wanted to crawl inside it and hide.

Shelby leaned her back against the wall next to Luce's face. "You know," she said, her voice softening, "Daniel's a crap boyfriend. And a liar. He's lying to you."

Luce straightened up and went at Shelby, feeling her

cheeks flush. Luce might be pissed off at Daniel right now, but nobody talked smack about her boyfriend.

"Whoa." Shelby ducked away. "Calm down, there. Jeez." She slid down the wall to sit on the floor. "Look, I shouldn't have brought it up. It was one stupid night a long time ago and the guy was clearly miserable without *you*. I didn't know you then, so I thought all the lore about you two was . . . supremely boring. Which, if you must know, explains the huge grudge I've held with your name on it."

She patted the floor next to her, and Luce slid down the wall to sit too. Shelby gave a tentative smile. "I swear, Luce, I never thought I'd meet you. I definitely never expected you to be . . . cool."

"You think I'm cool?" Luce asked, laughing quietly to herself. "You were right about me being self-absorbed."

"Ugh, just what I thought. You're one of those impossible-to-stay-mad-at people, aren't you?" Shelby sighed. "Fine. I'm sorry for going after your boyfriend and, you know, hating you before I knew you. I won't do it again."

This was weird. The thing that could have driven two friends instantly apart was actually drawing them closer together. This wasn't Shelby's fault. Any flash of anger Luce felt about it was something she needed to take up with . . . Daniel. *One stupid night,* Shelby had said. But what had really happened?

Sunset found Luce walking down the rocky steps to the beach. It was cold outside, colder still as she got closer to the water. The day's last rays of light danced off thin sheets of cloud, staining the ocean orange, pink, and pastel blue. The calm sea stretched out in front of her, looking like a path to Heaven.

Until she got to the wide circle of sand, still blackened from Roland's bonfire, Luce didn't know what she was doing down there. Then she found herself crawling behind the tall lava rock where Daniel had tugged her away. Where the two of them had danced and then spent the precious few moments they'd had together fighting about something as stupid as the color of her hair.

Callie had once had a boyfriend at Dover whom she'd broken up with after a fight over a toaster. One of them had jammed the thing with an oversized New York bagel; the other one had flipped out. Luce couldn't remember all the details now, but she remembered thinking, *Who breaks up over a kitchen appliance?*

But it was never really about the toaster, Callie had told her. The toaster was just a symptom, something that represented everything else that was wrong between them.

Luce hated that she and Daniel kept getting into fights. The one on the beach, over her dye job, reminded her of Callie's story. It felt like a preview of some bigger, uglier argument on the way.

Bracing herself against the wind, Luce realized she'd come down here to try to trace where they'd gone wrong the other night. She was idiotically looking for signs in the water, some clue carved into the rough volcanic rock. She was looking everywhere except inside herself. Because what was inside Luce was just the vast enigma of her past. Maybe the answers were still somewhere in the Announcers, but for now, they remained frustratingly out of her grasp.

She didn't want to blame Daniel. She was the one who'd been naïve enough to assume that their relationship had been exclusive across time. But he'd never told her otherwise. So he'd practically set her up to walk right into this shock. It was embarrassing. And one more item to tick off on the long list of things that Luce thought she deserved to know and that Daniel didn't see fit to tell her.

She felt something she thought was rain, a drizzly sensation on her cheeks and her fingertips. But it was warm instead of cold. It was powdery and light, not wet. She turned her face toward the sky and was blinded by shimmering violet light. Not wanting to shield her eyes, she watched even when it grew so bright it hurt. The particles slowly drifted toward the water just offshore, falling into a pattern and limning the shape she'd know anywhere.

He seemed to have grown more gorgeous. His bare feet hovered inches off the water as he approached the shore. His broad white wings seemed to be edged with violet light and were pulsing nearly imperceptibly in the rough wind. It wasn't fair. The way he made her feel when she looked at him—awed and ecstatic and a little bit afraid. She could hardly think of anything else. Every annoyance or nagging frustration vanished. There was just that undeniable pull toward him.

"You keep turning up," she whispered.

Daniel's voice carried over the water. "I told you I wanted to talk to you."

Luce felt her mouth pucker up. "About Shelby?"

"About the danger you keep putting yourself in." Daniel spoke so plainly. She'd been expecting her mention of Shelby to elicit some reaction. But Daniel just cocked his head. He reached the wet edge of the beach, where the water foamed and rolled away, and floated just above the sand in front of her. "What about Shelby?"

"Are you really going to pretend like you don't know?"

"Hold on." Daniel lowered his feet to the ground, bending his knees in a deep plié when his bare soles touched the sand. When he straightened, his wings pulled backward, away from his face, and sent a wave of wind back with them. Luce got her first sense of how heavy they must be.

It took less than two seconds for Daniel to reach her, but when his arms slipped around her back and pulled her to him, he couldn't have come quickly enough.

"Let's not get off to another bad start," he said.

She closed her eyes and let him lift her off the ground. His mouth found hers and she tilted her face to the sky, letting the feel of him overwhelm her. There was no darkness, no more cold, just the lovely sensation of being bathed in his violet glow. Even the rush of the ocean was canceled out by a soft hum, the energy Daniel carried in his body.

Her hands were wrapped tight around his neck, then stroked the firm muscles on his shoulders, brushing the soft, thick perimeter of his wings. They were strong and white and shimmering, always so much bigger than she remembered. Two great sails extending from his sides, every inch of them perfect and smooth. She could feel a tension against her fingers, like touching a tightly stretched canvas. But silkier, and deliciously velvet soft. They seemed to respond to her touch, even extending forward to rub against her, pulling her closer, until she was buried in them, nestling deeper and deeper, and still never getting enough. Daniel shuddered.

"Is this okay?" she whispered, because sometimes he grew nervous when things between them started to heat up. "Does it hurt you?"

Tonight his eyes looked greedy. "It feels wonderful. Nothing compares."

His fingers glided along her waist, slipping inside her sweater. Usually, the softest caress from Daniel's hands made her go weak. Tonight his touch was more forceful. Almost rough. She didn't know what had gotten into him, but she liked it.

His lips traced hers, then drifted higher, following the bridge of her nose, coming down tenderly on each of her eyelids. When he pulled back, she opened her eyes and gazed at him.

"You are so beautiful," he whispered.

It was exactly what most girls would have wanted to hear—only, as soon as he said it, Luce felt ripped out of her body, replaced by someone else's.

Shelby's.

But not just Shelby's, because what were the odds that she had been the only one? Had other eyes and noses and cheekbones taken Daniel's kisses? Had other bodies huddled with him on a beach? Other lips tangled, other hearts pounded? Had other whispered compliments been exchanged?

"What's wrong?" he asked.

Luce felt sick. They could steam up windows with their kisses, but as soon as they started using their mouths for other things—like talking—everything got so complicated.

She turned her face away. "You lied to me."

Daniel didn't scoff or get angry, as she was expecting

him to—almost wanting him to. He sat down on the sand. He propped his hands on his knees and stared out at the frothy waves. "About *what,* exactly?"

Even as the words came out, Luce regretted where she was going. "I could take *your* approach—not tell you anything, ever."

"I can't tell you whatever it is you want to know if you won't tell me what's bothering you."

She thought about Shelby, but when she imagined playing the jealousy card, only to have him treat her like a child, Luce felt pathetic. Instead, she said, "I feel like we're strangers. Like I don't know you any better than anyone else."

"Oh." His voice was quiet, but his face was so infuriatingly stoic, Luce wanted to shake him. Nothing riled him up.

"You're holding me hostage out here, Daniel. I know nothing. I know no one. I'm lonely. Every time I see you, you've put up some new wall, and you never let me in. You never let me in. You dragged me all the way out here—"

She was thinking *to California,* but it was more than that. Her past, what limited conception of it that she had, rolled out in her mind like the dropped reel of a movie, unwinding onto the floor.

Daniel had dragged her much, much further than California. He'd dragged her through centuries of fights like this one. Through agonizing deaths that caused pain to everyone around her—like those nice old people she'd visited last week. Daniel had ruined that couple's life. Killed their daughter. All because he'd been some hotshot angel who saw something he wanted and went after it.

No, he hadn't just dragged her to California. He'd dragged her into a cursed eternity. A burden that should have been his alone to bear. "I am suffering—me and everyone who loves me—for your curse. For all time. Because of you."

He winced as though she'd struck him. "You want to go home," he said.

She kicked the sand. "I want to go back. I want you to take back whatever it was you did to get me into this. I just want to live and die a normal life and break up with normal people over normal things like toasters, not the supernatural secrets of the universe that you don't even trust me with."

"Hold on." Daniel's face had gone completely white. His shoulders stiffened and his hands were shaking. Even his wings, which moments ago had seemed so powerful, looked frail. Luce wanted to reach out and touch them, as if somehow they would tell her whether the pain she saw in his eyes was real. But she held her ground.

"Are we breaking up?" he asked, his voice weak and low.

"Are we even together, Daniel?"

He got to his feet and cupped her face. Before she could jerk away, she felt the heat subside from her cheeks. She closed her eyes, trying to resist the magnetic force of his touch, but it was so strong, stronger than anything else.

It erased her anger, left her identity in tatters. Who was she without him? Why did the pull toward Daniel always defeat anything that pulled her away? Reason, sensibility, self-preservation: None of them could ever compete. It must have been part of Daniel's punishment. That she was bound to him forever, like a marionette to its puppeteer. She knew she shouldn't want him with every fiber of her being, but she couldn't help herself. Gazing at him, feeling his touch—the rest of the world faded into the background.

She just wished loving him didn't always have to be so hard.

"What's this business about wanting a toaster?" Daniel whispered in her ear.

"I guess I don't know what I want."

"I do." His eyes were intent, holding hers. "I want you."

"I know, but—"

"Nothing will ever change that. No matter what you hear. No matter what happens."

"But I need more than to be wanted. I need for us to be together—actually together."

"Soon. I promise. All of this is only temporary."

"So you've said." Luce saw that the moon had risen overhead. It was brilliant orange and waning, a quiet blaze. "What did you want to talk to me about?"

Daniel tucked her blond hair behind her ear, examining the lock for way too long. "School," he said with a hesitancy that made her think he was being less than truthful. "I asked Francesca to look after you, but I wanted to see for myself. Are you learning anything? Are you having an okay time?"

She felt the sudden urge to brag to him about her work with the Announcers, about her talk with Steven and the glimpses she'd had of her parents. But Daniel's face looked more eager and open than she had seen it all evening. He seemed to be trying to avoid a fight, so Luce decided to do the same.

She closed her eyes. She told him what he needed to hear. School was fine. She was fine. Daniel's lips came down on hers again, briefly, hotly, until her whole body was tingling.

"I have to go," he said at last, getting to his feet. "I shouldn't even be here, but I cannot keep myself away from you. I worry about you in every waking moment. I love you, Luce. So much it hurts."

She closed her eyes against the beat of his wings and the sting of the sand he raised in his wake.

TEN

NINE DAYS

An echoing series of whooshes and clangs cut through the song of ospreys. A long, singing note of metal scraping metal, then the clash of the thin silver blade glancing off its opponent's guard.

Francesca and Steven were fighting.

Well, no—they were fencing. A demonstration for the students who were about to stage matches of their own.

"Knowing how to wield a sword—whether it's the light foils we're using today, or something as dangerous as a cutlass—is an invaluable skill," Steven said, slicing the point of his sword through the air in short, whiplike movements. "The armies of Heaven and Hell rarely engage in battle, but when they do"—without looking, he snapped his blade sideways toward Francesca, and without looking, she brought her sword up and parried the blow—"they remain untouched by modern warfare. Daggers, bows and bolts, giant flaming swords, these are our eternal tools."

The duel that followed was for show, merely a lesson; Francesca and Steven weren't even wearing masks.

It was late in the morning on Wednesday, and Luce was seated on the deck's wide bench between Jasmine and Miles. The entire class, including their two teachers, had changed out of their regular clothes into the white outfits fencers always wore. Half the class held black mesh face masks in their hands. Luce had arrived at the supply closet just after the last face mask had been snagged, which hadn't bothered her at all. She was hoping to avoid the embarrassment of having the entire class witness her cluelessness: It was obvious from the way the others were making lunges at the sides of the deck that they had been through these practices before.

"The idea is to present as small a target for your opponent as possible," Francesca explained to the circle of students surrounding her. "So you set your weight on one foot and lead with your sword foot, and then rock back and forth—into striking range and then away."

She and Steven were suddenly engaged in a rush of jabs and parries, making a dense clatter as they expertly fought off each other's blows. When her blade glanced wide to the left, he lunged forward, but she rocked back, sweeping her sword up and around and onto his wrist. *"Touché,"* she said, laughing.

Steven turned to the class. *"Touché,* of course, is French for 'touched.' In fencing, we count points by touches."

"Were we fighting for real," Francesca said, "I'm afraid that Steven's hand would be lying bloody on the deck. Sorry, darling."

"Quite all right," he said. "Quite. All. Right." He threw himself sideways at her, almost seeming to rise off the ground. In the frenzy that followed, Luce lost track of Steven's sword as it crisscrossed through the air again and again, nearly slicing into Francesca, who ducked sideways just in time and resurfaced behind him.

But he was ready for her and knocked her blade away before dropping the point of his and striking out at her instep.

"I'm afraid you, my dear, have gotten off on the wrong foot."

"We'll see." Francesca raised a hand and smoothed

her hair, the two of them staring at each other with murderous intensity.

Each new round of violent play caused Luce to tense up in alarm. She was used to being jittery, but the rest of the class was also surprisingly jittery today. Jittery with excitement. Watching Francesca and Steven, not one of them could keep still.

Until today, she'd wondered why none of the other Nephilim played on any of Shoreline's varsity sports teams. Jasmine had scrunched up her nose when Luce asked whether she and Dawn were interested in swim team tryouts in the gym. In fact, until she'd overheard Lilith in the locker room this morning yawning that every sport except fencing was "exquisitely boring," Luce had figured the Nephilim just weren't athletic. But that wasn't it at all. They just chose carefully what to play.

Luce winced as she imagined Lilith, who knew the French translation for all the fencing terms Luce didn't even know in English, throwing her svelte, spiteful self into an attack. If the rest of the class were one-tenth as skilled as Francesca and Steven, Luce was going to end up a pile of body parts by the end of the session.

Her teachers were obvious experts, stepping lithely in and out of lunges. Sunlight glinted off their swords, off their white padded vests. Francesca's thick blond waves cascaded out in a gorgeous halo around her shoulders as she spun around Steven. Their feet wove patterns on the deck with such grace, the match looked almost like a dance.

The expressions on their faces were dogged and full of a brutal determination to win. After those first few touches, they were evenly matched. They must have been getting tired. They'd been fencing for more than ten minutes without a hit. They began to fence so quickly that the arcs of their blades all but disappeared; there were only a fine fury and a faint buzz in the air and the constant crack of their foils against one another.

Sparks began to fly each time their swords connected. Sparks of love or hatred? There were moments when it almost looked like both.

And that unnerved Luce. Because love and hate were supposed to stand cleanly on opposite sides of the spectrum. The division seemed as clear as . . . well, angels and demons would once have seemed to her. Not anymore. As she watched her teachers in awe and fear, memories of last night's argument with Daniel fenced through her mind. And her own feelings of love and hate—or if not quite hate, a building fury—knotted up within her.

A cheer rang out from her classmates. It felt like Luce had only blinked, but she had missed it. The point of Francesca's sword jabbed into Steven's chest. Close to the heart. She pressed against him to the point where her thin blade bent into an arc. Both of them stood still for a moment, looking each other in the eye. Luce couldn't tell whether this, too, was part of the show.

"Right through my heart," Steven said.

"As if you had one," Francesca whispered.

The two teachers seemed momentarily unaware that the deck was full of students.

"Another win for Francesca," Jasmine said. She tipped her head toward Luce and dropped her voice. "She comes from a long line of winners. Steven? Not so much." The comment seemed loaded, but Jasmine just bounded lightly off the bench, slid her mask over her face, and tightened her ponytail. Ready to go.

As the other students started bustling around her, Luce tried to picture a similar scene between her and Daniel: Luce taking the upper hand, holding him at the mercy of her sword as Francesca had Steven. It was, frankly, impossible to imagine. And that bothered Luce. Not because she wanted to lord it over Daniel, but because she didn't want to be the one ruled over either. The night before, she'd been too much at his mercy. Remembering that kiss made her anxious, flushed, and overwhelmed—and not in a good way.

She loved him. But.

She should have been able to think the phrase without tacking on that ugly little conjunction. But she couldn't. What they had right now was not what she wanted. And if the rules of the game were always going to stay this way, she just didn't know if she even wanted to play. What kind of match was she for Daniel? What kind of match was he for her? If he'd been drawn to other girls . . . at some point he must have wondered, too. Could someone else give them each a more level playing field?

When Daniel kissed her, Luce knew in her bones that he was her past. Folded into his embrace, she was desperate for him to remain her present. But the second their lips parted, she couldn't *really* be sure he was her future. She needed the freedom to make that decision one way or the other. She didn't even know what else was out there.

"Miles," Steven called. He was fully back in teacher mode, sheathing his sword in a narrow black leather case and nodding to the northwest corner of the deck. "You'll match with Roland over here."

On her left, Miles leaned in to whisper, "You and Roland go back a ways—what's his Achilles heel? I am *not* going to lose to the new kid."

"Um . . . I don't really . . ." Luce's mind went blank. Looking over at Roland, whose mask already covered his face, she realized how very little she really knew about him. Other than his catalog of black-market goods. And his harmonica playing. And the way he'd made Daniel laugh so hard that first day at Sword &

Cross. She'd still never found out what they'd been talking about . . . or what Roland was *really* doing at Shoreline anyway. When it came to Mr. Sparks, Luce was definitely in the dark.

Miles patted her knee. "Luce, I was kidding. There's no way that guy's *not* going to kick my ass." He stood up, laughing. "Wish me luck."

Francesca had moved to the other side of the deck, near the entrance to the lodge, and was sipping a bottle of water. "Kristy and Millicent, take this corner," she told two Nephilim girls with pigtails and matching black sneakers. "Shelby and Dawn, come match right here." She gestured to the corner of the deck directly in front of Luce. "The rest of you will watch."

Luce was relieved her own name hadn't been called. The more she saw of Francesca and Steven's teaching method, the less she understood it. One intimidating demonstration took the place of any real instruction. Not watch and learn, but straight to watch and excel. As the first six students took their places on the deck, Luce felt huge pressure to pick up the entire art of fencing right away.

"*En garde!*" Shelby bellowed, lunging backward into a squat with the tip of her sword just inches from Dawn, whose sword was still sheathed.

Dawn's fingers were zigzagging through her short black hair, pinning sections of it back with a brimming handful of butterfly clips. "You can't *en-garde* me while I'm prepping for battle, Shelby!" Her high voice got even higher when she was frustrated. "What were you, raised by wolves?" she huffed through the last plastic barrette between her teeth. "Okay," she said, drawing her sword. "Now I'm ready."

Shelby, who had been holding her deep lunge throughout Dawn's primp session, now straightened up and looked down at her rough nail beds. "Wait, do I have time for a manicure?" she said, psyching Dawn out just long enough to allow her to drop into an offensive stance and swing her sword around.

"How uncouth!" Dawn barked, but to Luce's surprise, she instantly ratcheted up her swordsmanship, swishing her blade skillfully through the air and knocking Shelby's aside. Dawn was a fencing badass.

Next to Luce, Jasmine was doubled over laughing. "A match made in Hell."

A smile had crept onto Luce's face, too, because she'd never met anyone as unshakably upbeat as Dawn. At first, Luce had suspected phoniness, a façade—where Luce came from, the South, that always-happy bit wouldn't have been real. But Luce had been impressed by how quickly Dawn rebounded after that day on the yacht. Dawn's optimism seemed to know no limits. By now, it was hard for Luce to be around the girl without chuckling. And it was especially hard when Dawn was focusing her girly cheer on beating the crap out of someone as bleakly opposite as Shelby.

Things between Luce and Shelby were still a little weird. She knew it, Shelby knew it, even the Buddha night-light in their room seemed to know it. The truth was, Luce kind of enjoyed seeing Shelby fighting for her life while Dawn happily attacked her.

Shelby was a steady, patient fighter. Where Dawn's technique was showy and eye-catching, her limbs whirling in a virtual tango across the deck, Shelby was careful with her lunges, almost as if she had only so many to ration out. She kept her knees bent and never gave up anything.

Yet she'd said she had given up on Daniel after one night. Had been quick to say it was because of Daniel's feelings for Luce—that they interfered with everything else. But Luce didn't believe her. Something was weird about Shelby's confession; something didn't match up with Daniel's reaction when Luce had almost-sort-of brought it up the night before. He'd acted like there wasn't anything to tell.

A loud thump snapped Luce back to attention.

Across the deck, Miles had somehow landed on his back. Roland hovered over him. Literally. He was flying.

The enormous wings that had unfurled from Roland's shoulders were as large as a great cape and feathered like an eagle's, but with a beautiful golden marbling woven through their dark pinions. He must have had the same slits cut into his fencing garb that Daniel had in his T-shirt. Luce had never seen Roland's wings before, and like the other Nephilim, she couldn't stop staring. Shelby had told her that only a very few Nephilim had wings, and none of them went to Shoreline. Seeing Roland's come out in a battle, even a practice swordfight, sent a ripple of nervous excitement through the crowd.

The wings commanded so much attention, it took Luce a moment to realize that the tip of Roland's sword was hovering just over Miles's breastbone, pinning him to the ground. Roland's bright white fencing suit and golden wings cut a stark silhouette against the dark, lush trees bordering the deck. With his black mesh mask pulled down, Roland looked even more intimidating, more menacing than if she'd been able to see his face. She hoped his expression would look playful, because he really had Miles in a vulnerable situation. Luce jumped to her feet to go to him, surprised to find her knees shaking.

"Ohmigod*Miles*!" Dawn called out from across the deck, forgetting her own battle just long enough for Shelby to go in with a whip-over, touch Dawn's unshielded chest, and score the winning point.

"Not the most sportsmanlike way to win," Shelby said, sheathing her sword. "But sometimes that's the way it goes."

Luce hurried past them and the rest of the Nephilim

who weren't engaged in duels to Roland and Miles. Both were panting. By then Roland had settled to the ground, his wings retracted inside his skin. Miles looked fine; it was Luce who couldn't stop trembling.

"You got me." Miles laughed nervously, pushing away the point of the sword. "Didn't see your secret weapon coming."

"Sorry, man," Roland said sincerely. "Didn't mean to unleash the wings on you. Sometimes that just happens when I get going."

"Well, good game. Up until then, anyway." Miles raised his right hand to be helped off the ground. "Do they say 'good game' in fencing?"

"No, no one says that." Roland flipped up his mask with one hand and, grinning, dropped the sword from his other. He grasped Miles's hand and pulled him up in one swift move. "Good game yourself."

Luce let out her breath. Of course Roland wasn't really going to harm Miles. Roland was offbeat and unpredictable, but he wasn't *dangerous,* even if he had sided with Cam that last night in the Sword & Cross cemetery. But there was no reason to fear him. Why had she been so nervous? Why couldn't she get her heart to stop racing?

Then she understood why. It was because of Miles. Because he was the closest friend she had at Shoreline. All she knew was that recently, every time she was around Miles, it made her think of Daniel, and how a lot of things between them were sort of dragging. And how sometimes, secretly, she wished Daniel could be little bit more like Miles. Cheerful and easygoing, attentive and naturally sweet. Less caught up in things like being damned since the dawn of time.

A flash of white rushed past Luce and straight into Miles's arms.

Dawn. She leaped onto Miles, her eyes closed and her mouth in an enormous grin. "You're alive!"

"Alive?" Miles set her back down on her feet. "I barely got the wind knocked out of me. Good thing you've never come to watch one of the football games."

Standing behind Dawn, watching as she petted Miles where the sword had skimmed his white vest, Luce felt oddly embarrassed. It wasn't like *she* wanted to be petting Miles, right? She just wanted . . . she didn't know what she wanted.

"Want this?" Roland appeared at her side, handing her the mask he'd been using. "You're up next, aren't you?"

"Me? No." She shook her head. "Isn't the bell about to ring?"

Roland shook his head. "Nice try. Just own it, and no one's going to know you've never fenced before."

"I doubt that." Luce fingered the thin mesh screen. "Roland, I have to ask you—"

"No, I wasn't going to run Miles through. Why did everyone get so freaked out?"

"I know that. . . ." she tried to smile. "It's about Daniel."

"Luce, you know the rules."

"What rules?"

"I can get a lot of things, but I can't get Daniel for you. You're just going to have to wait it out."

"Wait, Roland. I know he can't be here right now. But what rules? What are you talking about?"

He pointed behind her. Francesca was beckoning toward Luce with a finger. The other Nephilim had all taken seats on the benches, except for a few students who looked like they were preparing to fence. Jasmine and a Korean girl named Sylvia, two tall, skinny boys whose names Luce could never keep straight, and Lilith, standing alone, examining the blunt rubber tip of her sword with careful scrutiny.

"Luce?" Francesca said in a low voice. She motioned to the space on the deck in front of Lilith. "Take your place."

"Trial by fire." Roland whistled, patting Luce on the back. "Show no fear."

There were only five other students standing in the middle of the deck, but to Luce, it felt as though there were a hundred.

Francesca stood with her arms folded casually over her chest. Her face was serene, but to Luce it looked like a forced serenity. Maybe she intended for Luce to lose in the most brutal, embarrassing match possible. Why else would she pit Luce against Lilith, who towered over Luce by at least a foot, and whose fiery red hair protruded from behind her mask like a lion's mane?

"I've never done this," Luce said lamely.

"It's okay, Luce, you don't need to be skilled yet," Francesca said. "We're trying to gauge your relative capacity. Just remember what Steven and I showed you at the start of the session and you'll do fine."

Lilith laughed and whipped the point of her foil in a broad Z. "The mark of zero, loser," she said.

"Showing off the number of friends you have?" Luce asked. She remembered what Roland had said about showing no fear. She slid the mask down over her face, took her foil from Francesca. Luce didn't even know how to hold it. She fumbled with the handle, wondering whether to put it in her right or left hand. She wrote right-handed, bowled and batted with her left.

Lilith was already looking at her like she wished Luce were dead, and Luce knew she couldn't afford the time to test out her swing in both hands. Did they even call it a swing in fencing?

Wordlessly, Francesca moved behind her. She stood with her shoulders brushing Luce's back, practically folding her narrow body around Luce and taking Luce's left hand, and the sword, in hers.

"I'm left-handed too," she said.

Luce opened her mouth, unsure whether or not to protest.

"Just like you." Francesca leaned around her and gave Luce a knowing look. As she repositioned her grip, something warm and tremendously soothing flowed through Francesca's fingers into Luce. Strength, or maybe courage—Luce didn't understand how it worked, but she was grateful.

"You'll want a light grip," Francesca said, directing Luce's fingers around the hilt under the guard. "Grip too tightly and your direction of the blade becomes less nimble, your defensive moves more limited. Grip too lightly and the blade can be spun out of your hands."

Her smooth, thin fingers guided Luce's to hold the curved grip of the sword's hilt just under the guard. With one hand on the sword and the other on Luce's shoulder, Francesca galloped lightly sideways one step, blocking out the move.

"Advance." She moved forward, thrusting the sword in Lilith's direction.

The redheaded girl ran her tongue across her teeth and glared at Luce with something like middle child syndrome.

"Disengage." Francesca moved Luce back as if she were a chess piece. She stepped away and circled to face Luce, whispering, "The rest is just gilding the lily."

Luce swallowed. Gilding the what?

"En garde!" Lilith practically shouted. Her long legs were bent, and her right arm was holding the foil straight at Luce.

Luce retreated, two quick galloping steps; then, when she felt at a safe enough distance, lunged forward with her sword extended.

Lilith dipped deftly to the left of Luce's sword, spun around, then came back from below with her own, clashing against Luce's. The two blades slid against each other until they reached a midpoint, then held. Luce had to put all her strength into stopping Lilith's foil with the pressure of her own. Her arms were shaking, but she was surprised to find she could hold Lilith back in this position. At last Lilith broke away and backed off. Luce watched her dip and spin a few times, and began to figure her out.

Lilith was a grunter, making tons of effort-filled noise. It was a bit of misdirection. She would make a huge noise and feint in one direction, then whip the point of her foil around in a high, tight arc to try to get past Luce's defenses.

So Luce tried the same move. When she swung the tip of her sword back around to get her first point, just south of Lilith's heart, the girl let out a deafening roar.

Luce winced and backed away. She didn't think she'd even touched Lilith very hard. "Are you okay?" she called out, about to lift her mask.

"She's not hurt," Francesca answered for Lilith. A smile parted her lips. "She's angry that you're beating her."

Luce didn't have time to wonder what it meant that Francesca seemed suddenly to be enjoying herself, because Lilith was barreling toward her once again, sword poised. Luce raised her sword to meet Lilith's, turning her wrist to clash three times before they disengaged.

Luce's pulse was racing and she felt good. She sensed an energy coursing through her that she hadn't felt in a long time. She was actually *good* at this, almost as good as Lilith, who looked like she'd been bred to skewer people with sharp things. Luce, who had never even picked up a sword, realized she actually had a chance to win. Just one more point.

She could hear the other students cheering, some even calling out her name. She could hear Miles, and she thought she could hear Shelby, which really egged her on. But the sound of their voices was woven through with something else. Something staticky and too loud. Lilith fought as fiercely as ever, but suddenly Luce was having a hard time concentrating. She backed up and blinked, looking into the sky. The sun was obscured by the overhanging trees—but that wasn't all. A growing fleet of shadows was stretching forth from the branches, like ink stains extending right above Luce's head.

No—not now, not in public with everyone watching,

and not when it might cost her this match. Yet no one else even noticed them, which seemed impossible. They were making so much noise it was impossible for Luce to do anything but cover her ears and try to block them out. She raised her hands to her ears, which made her sword tip skyward, confusing Lilith.

"Don't let her freak you out, Luce. She's toxic!" Dawn chirped from the bench.

"Use the *prise de fer*!" Shelby called. "Lilith sucks at the *prise de fer*. Correction: Lilith sucks at *everything*, but especially the *prise de fer*."

So many voices—more, it seemed, than there were people on the deck. Luce winced, trying to block it all out. But one voice separated from the crowd, as though it were whispering into her ear from just behind her head. Steven:

"Screen out the noise, Luce. Find the message."

She whipped her head around, but he was on the other side of the deck, looking toward the trees. Was he talking about the other Nephilim? All the noise and chatter they were making? She glanced at their faces, but they weren't even talking. So who was? For the briefest moment, she caught Steven's eyes, and he lifted his chin toward the sky. As if he were gesturing at the shadows.

In the trees above her head. The announcers were *speaking*.

And she could *hear* them. Had they been speaking all along?

Latin, Russian, Japanese. English with a southern accent. Broken French. Whispers, singing, bad directions, lines of rhyming verse. And one long bloodcurdling scream for help. She shook her head, still holding Lilith's sword at bay, and the voices overhead stayed with her. She looked at Steven, then Francesca. They showed no signs, but she knew they heard it. And she knew they knew she was listening too.

For the message behind the noise.

All her life she'd heard the same noise when the shadows came—whooshing, ugly, wet noise. But now it was different. . . .

Clash.

Lilith's sword collided with Luce's. The girl was snorting like an angry bull. Luce could hear her own breath inside the mask, panting as she tried to hold Lilith's sword. Then she could hear so much more among all the voices. Suddenly she could focus on them. Finding the balance just meant separating the static from the significant stuff. But how?

Il faut faire le coup double. Après ca, c'est facile a gagner, one of the Announcers whispered in French.

Luce had just two years of high school French to go on, but the words touched her somewhere deeper than her brain. It wasn't just her head understanding the message. Somehow her body knew it too. It seeped into her, right down to the bone, and she remembered: She'd been in a place like this before, in a sword fight like this, a standoff like this.

The Announcer was recommending the double cross, a complicated fencing move in which two separate attacks came one right after the other.

Her sword slid down her opponent's and the two of them broke away. A moment sooner than Lilith, Luce lunged forward in one clean intuitive motion, thrusting her sword point right, then left, then flush against the side of Lilith's rib cage. The Nephilim cheered, but Luce didn't stop. She disengaged, then came straight back a second time, plunging the tip of her foil into the padding near Lilith's gut.

That was three.

Lilith dashed her sword to the deck, tore off her mask, and gave Luce a terrifying scowl before making quickly for the locker room. The rest of the class was on their feet, and Luce could feel her classmates surrounding her. Dawn and Jasmine hugged her from both sides, giving dainty little squeezes. Shelby came forward next for a high five, and Luce could see Miles waiting patiently behind her. When it was his turn, he surprised her, swooping her off the deck and into a long, tight hug.

She hugged him back, remembering how awkward

she'd felt earlier when she'd gone to him after his match, only to find that Dawn had gotten to him first. Now she was just glad to have him, glad of his easy and honest support.

"I want fencing lessons from you," he said, laughing.

In his arms, Luce looked up at the sky, at the shadows lengthening from the long branches. Their voices were softer now, less distinct, but still clearer than they'd ever been before, like a static-filled radio she'd been listening to for years that had finally been tuned in. She couldn't tell whether she was supposed to be grateful or afraid.

ELEVEN

EIGHT DAYS

"Hold on." Callie's voice boomed across the line. "Let me pinch myself to make sure I'm not—"

"You're not dreaming," Luce said into her borrowed cell phone. Reception was spotty from her position at the edge of the woods, but Callie's sarcasm came through loud and clear. "It's really me. I'm sorry I've been such a crap friend."

It was Thursday after dinner, and Luce was leaning up against the stout trunk of a redwood tree behind her dorm. To her left was a rolling hill and then the cliff, and beyond that, the ocean. There was still a little amber light in the sky over the water. Her new friends would all be in the lodge making s'mores, telling demon stories around the hearth. It was a Dawn-and-Jasmine social event, part of the Nephilim Nights Luce was supposed to have helped organize, but all she'd really done was request a few bags of marshmallows and some dark chocolate from the mess hall.

And then she'd escaped out to the shadowy fringe of the woods to avoid everyone at Shoreline and reconnect with a few other important things:

Her parents. Callie. And the Announcers.

She'd waited until tonight to call home. Thursdays chez Price meant her mom would be out playing mahjongg at the neighbors' and her dad would have gone to the local movie theater to watch the Atlanta opera on simulcast. She could handle their voices on the ten-plus-year-old answering machine message, could manage to leave a thirty-second voice mail saying she was petitioning hard for Mr. Cole to let her off campus for Thanksgiving—and that she loved them very much.

Callie wasn't going to let her off so easy.

"I thought you could only call on Wednesdays," Callie was saying now. Luce had forgotten the strict telephone policy at Sword & Cross. "At first I stopped making plans on Wednesdays, waiting for your call,"

Callie went on. "But after a while, I kinda gave up. How did you get a cell phone, anyway?"

"That's it?" Luce asked. "How did I get a cell phone? You're not mad at me?"

Callie let out a long sigh. "You know, I thought about being mad. I even practiced this whole fight in my mind. But then we both lose." She paused. "And the thing is, I just miss you, Luce. So I figured, why waste time?"

"Thank you," Luce whispered, close to tears—happy ones. "So, what's been going on with you?"

"Unh-unh. I'm in charge of this conversation. That's your punishment for dropping off my radar. And what I want to know is: What's going on with that guy? I think his name started with a C?"

"Cam." Luce groaned. *Cam* was the last guy she'd told Callie about? "He didn't turn out to be . . . the kind of guy I thought he was." She paused for a moment. "I'm seeing someone else now, and things are really . . ." She thought of Daniel's glowing face, the way it had darkened so quickly during their last meeting outside her window.

Then she thought of Miles. Warm, dependable, charmingly no-drama Miles, who'd invited her home to his family's house for Thanksgiving. Who ordered pickles on his hamburgers at the mess hall now even though he didn't like them—just so he could pick them off and give them to Luce. Who tilted his head up when he laughed so that she could see the sparkle in his Dodgers-cap-shaded eyes.

"Things are good," she finally said. "We've been hanging out a lot."

"Ooh, bouncing around from one reform school boy to the next. Living the dream, aren't you? But this one sounds serious, I can hear it in your voice. Are you going to do Thanksgiving together? Bring him home to face the wrath of Harry? Hah!"

"Um . . . yeah, probably," Luce mumbled. She wasn't totally sure whether she'd been talking about Daniel or Miles.

"My parents are insisting on some big family reunion in Detroit that weekend," Callie said, "which I am boycotting. I wanted to come visit, but I figured you'd be locked up in reformville." She paused, and Luce could picture her curled up on her bed in her dorm room at Dover. It seemed like a lifetime ago since Luce had been at school there herself. So very much had changed. "If you'll be home, though, *and* bringing reform school boy, try and stop me."

"Okay, but Callie—"

Luce was interrupted by a squeal. "So it's settled? Imagine: In one week we'll be curled up on your couch, catching up! I'll make my famous kettle corn to help us through the boring slide shows your dad will show. And your crazy poodle will be going berserk. . . ."

Luce had never actually been to Callie's brownstone

in Philadelphia, and Callie had never actually been to Luce's house in Georgia. They'd both only seen pictures. A visit from Callie sounded so perfect, so exactly what Luce needed right now. It also sounded utterly impossible.

"I'll look up flights right now."

"Callie—"

"I'll email you, okay?" Callie hung up before Luce could even respond.

This was not good. Luce flipped the phone shut. She shouldn't have felt like Callie was intruding by inviting herself to Thanksgiving. She should have felt great that her friend still wanted to see her. But all she felt was helpless, homesick, and guilty for perpetuating this stupid cycle of lies.

Was it even possible to just be normal and happy anymore? What on earth—or beyond it—would it take for Luce to be as content with her life as someone like Miles seemed to be? Her mind kept circling around Daniel. And she had her answer: The only way she could be carefree again would be to have never met Daniel. To have never known true love.

Something rustled in the treetops. A frigid wind assailed her skin. She hadn't been concentrating on an Announcer specifically, but she realized—just as Steven had told her—that her wish for answers must have summoned one.

No, not one.

She shivered, looking up into the tangle of branches. Hundreds of stealthy, murky, foul-smelling shadows.

They flowed together in the high redwood branches over her head. Like someone in the clouds had tipped over a giant pot of black ink that had spread across the sky and dripped down into the canopy of the trees, bleeding one branch into another until the forest was a solid wash of blackness. At first it was almost impossible to tell where one shadow stopped and the next one began, which shadow was real and which an Announcer.

But soon they began to morph and make themselves obvious—slyly at first, as if they were moving innocently in the fading light of the day—but then more boldly. They pinched themselves free from the branches they'd been occupying, wrenching their tendrils of blackness down, down, close to Luce's head. Beckoning or threatening her? She steeled herself but couldn't catch her breath. There were too many. It was too much. She gasped for air, trying not to panic, knowing it was already too late.

She ran.

She started south, back toward the dorm. But the swirling black abyss in the treetops just moved with her, hissing along the lower branches of the redwoods, drawing closer. She felt the icy pinpricks of their touch on her shoulders. She yelped as they groped for her, swatting them away with her bare hands.

She changed course, swung herself around in the

opposite direction, toward the Nephilim lodge to the north. She would find Miles or Shelby or even Francesca. But the Announcers wouldn't let her go. Immediately, they slithered ahead, swelling out in front of her, swallowing the light and blocking the path to the lodge. Their hissing drowned out the distant murmurs of the Nephilim campfire, making Luce's friends seem impossibly far away.

Luce forced herself to stop and take a deep breath. She knew more about the Announcers than she ever had before. She should be *less* afraid of them. What was her problem? Maybe she knew she was getting closer to something, some memory or information that could alter the course of her life. And her relationship with Daniel. The truth was, she wasn't just terrified of the Announcers. She was terrified of what she might see within them.

Or hear.

Yesterday, Steven's mention of tuning out the Announcers' noise had finally clicked—she could listen in on her past lives. She could cut through the static and focus on what she wanted to know. What she needed to know. Steven must have meant to give her this clue, must have known she would listen and take her new knowledge straight to the Announcers.

She turned and stepped back into the dark solitude of the trees. The whooshing sounds from the Announcers quieted and settled.

The darkness under the branches engulfed her in cold and the peaty smell of decomposing leaves. In the twilight, the Announcers crept forward, settling into the dimness all around her, camouflaging themselves again among the natural shadows. Some of them moved swiftly and stiffly, like soldiers; others had a nimble grace. Luce wondered whether their appearances reflected anything about the messages they contained.

So much about the Announcers still felt impenetrable. Tuning them in wasn't intuitive, like fiddling with an old radio dial. What she'd heard yesterday—that one voice among the riot of voices—had come to her by accident.

The past might have been unfathomable to her before, but she could feel it pressing up against the dark surfaces, waiting to break into the light. She closed her eyes and cupped her hands together. There, in the darkness, her heart pounding, she willed them to come out. She called on those coldest, darkest things, asking them to deliver her past, to illuminate her and Daniel's story. She called on them to solve the mystery of who he was and why he had chosen her.

Even if the truth broke her heart.

A rich, feminine laugh rang out in the forest. A laugh so clear and full, it felt as if it were surrounding Luce, bouncing off the branches in the trees. She tried to trace its origin, but there were so many shadows gathered—Luce didn't know how to pinpoint the source. And then she felt her blood go cold.

The laughter was hers.

Or had once been hers, back when she was a child. Before Daniel, before Sword & Cross, before Trevor . . . before a life full of secrets and lies and so many unanswerable questions. Before she'd ever seen an angel. It was too innocent a laugh, too carefree to belong to her anymore.

A breath of wind swirled in the branches overhead, and a scattering of brown redwood needles broke off and showered to the ground. They pattered like raindrops as they joined a thousand predecessors on the mulchy forest floor. Among them was one large frond.

Thick and feathery, fully intact, it drifted slowly down somehow outside the power of gravity. It was black instead of brown. And instead of falling to the ground, it drifted lightly onto Luce's outstretched palm.

Not a frond, but an Announcer. As she leaned down to examine it more closely, she heard the laughter again. Somewhere inside, another Luce was laughing.

Gently, Luce gave the Announcer's prickly edges a pull. It was more pliant than she expected, but cold as ice and tacky against her fingers. It grew larger at the lightest touch. When it had grown to about a square foot, Luce released it from her grip and was pleased to watch it hover at eye level in front of her. She made a special effort to focus—on hearing, on tuning out the world around her.

Nothing at first, and then—

One more rising laugh sang out from within the shadow. Then the veil of blackness shredded and an image inside became clear.

This time, Daniel was the first one to come into view.

Even through the Announcer's screen, it was heaven to see him. His hair was a couple of inches longer than he wore it now. And he was tan—his shoulders and the bridge of his nose were both a deep, golden brown. He wore trim navy swim trunks, snug around his hips, the kind she'd seen in family pictures from the seventies. He made them look so good.

Behind Daniel was the verdant edge of a thick, dense rain forest, lush green but bright with berries and white flowers that Luce had never seen before. He stood at the lip of a short but dramatic cliff, which looked down at a sparkling pool of water. But Daniel kept glancing up, toward the sky.

That laugh again. And then Luce's own voice, broken apart by giggles. "Hurry up and get down here!"

Luce leaned forward, closer to the window of the Announcer, and saw her former self treading water in a yellow halter-top bikini. Her long hair danced around her, floating on the water's surface like a deep black halo. Daniel kept an eye on her but was also still glancing overhead. The muscles on his chest were tensing up. Luce had a bad feeling she already knew why.

The sky was filling with Announcers, like a flock of enormous black crows, a cloud so thick they blocked the sun. The long-ago Luce in the water noticed nothing, saw nothing. But watching all those Announcers flit and gather in the humid air of that rain forest, in an image *made* by an Announcer, had the Luce in the forest feeling suddenly dizzy.

"You make me wait forever," long-ago Luce called up to Daniel. "Pretty soon I'm going to freeze."

Daniel tore his eyes away from the sky, looking down at her with a broken expression. His lip was trembling and his face was ghostly white. "You won't freeze," he told her. Were those *tears* Daniel was wiping away? He closed his eyes and shivered. Then, arcing his hands over his head, he pushed off the rock and dove.

Daniel surfaced a moment later, and long-ago Luce swam toward him. She wrapped her arms around his neck, her face bright and happy. Luce watched it all play out with a mixture of sickness and satisfaction. She wanted her former self to have as much of Daniel as she could get, to feel that innocent, ecstatic closeness of being with the person she loved.

But she knew, just as Daniel knew, as the swarm of Announcers knew, exactly what was going to happen as soon as this Luce pressed her lips to his. Daniel was right: She wasn't going to freeze. She was going to combust in a horrifying burst of flames.

And Daniel would be left to mourn her.

But he wasn't the only one. This girl had had a life, friends, and a family who loved her, who would be devastated when they lost her.

Suddenly, Luce was enraged. Furious with the curse that had been hanging over her and Daniel. She had been innocent, powerless; she didn't understand a thing about what was going to happen. She still didn't understand *why* it happened, why she always had to die so quickly after finding Daniel.

Why it hadn't happened to her yet in this life.

The Luce in the water was still alive. Luce wouldn't—couldn't let her die.

She grabbed at the Announcer, curling its edges in her fists. It twisted and bent, contorting the swimmers' images like a fun-house mirror might. Inside its screen, the other shadows were descending. The swimmers were running out of time.

In frustration, Luce screamed and swung her fists at the Announcer—first one, then the other, raining blows upon the scene before her. She struck out at it again and again, heaving and crying as she tried her best to stop what was going to transpire.

Then it happened: Her right fist broke through and her arm sank in up to her elbow. Instantly, she felt the shock of a temperature change. The heat of a summer sunset spreading across her palm. Gravity shifted. Luce couldn't tell which way was up or down. She felt her stomach recoiling and feared she was going to throw up.

She could go through. She could save her old self. Tentatively, she stretched her left arm forward. It, too, disappeared into the Announcer, like passing through a bright, clammy sheet of Jell-O that rippled and widened as if it could just let her through.

"It wants me to," she said aloud. "I can do this. I can save her. I can save my life." She leaned back slightly and then thrust her body into the Announcer.

There was sunlight, so bright she had to close her eyes, and a warmth so tropical a sheen of sweat immediately broke out on her skin. And a nauseating scene of gravity tilting and upending, like at the height of a dive. In a moment she'd be falling—

Except something had hold of her left ankle. And her right. That something was pulling Luce very forcefully backward.

"No!" Luce cried out, because she could see now, could see, far below, a burst of yellow in the water. Too bright to be the halter top of her bathing suit. Was long-ago Luce already burning up?

Then it all vanished.

Luce was yanked roughly back into the cool, dim patch of redwood trees behind the Shoreline dorm. Her skin felt cold and clammy and her balance was all screwed up and she fell flat on her face in the dirt and redwood needles on the forest floor. She rolled over and saw two figures in front of her, but her vision was spinning so much she couldn't even tell who they were.

"I thought I'd find you here."

Shelby. Luce shook her head and blinked a few times. Not just Shelby, but Miles, too. Both of them looked exhausted. Luce *was* exhausted. She glanced at her watch, not surprised by now to see how long she'd spent glimpsing the Announcer. It was after one in the morning. What were Miles and Shelby still doing up?

"Wh-What . . . what were you trying to . . . ," Miles stammered, pointing at the place where the Announcer had been. She looked over her shoulder. It had splintered into hundreds of shadowy pine needles that rained down, brittle enough to turn to ash where they landed.

"I think I'm going to be sick," Luce muttered, rolling to the side and aiming behind a nearby tree. She heaved a few times, but nothing came up. She closed her eyes, racked with guilt. She'd been too weak and too late to save herself.

A cool hand reached around and pulled her short blond waves back from her face. Luce saw Shelby's frayed black yoga pants and flip-flopped feet and felt a wave of gratitude.

"Thanks," she said. After a long moment, she wiped her mouth and unsteadily got to her feet. "Are you mad at me?"

"What mad? I'm *proud* of you. You figured it out.

Why do you even need someone like me anymore?" Shelby gave Luce a one-shoulder shrug.

"Shelby—"

"No, I'll tell you why you need me," Shelby blurted. "To keep you out of catastrophes like the one you almost just threw yourself into! Willy-nilly, might I add. What were you trying to do? Do you know what happens to people who go *inside* Announcers?"

Luce shook her head.

"Me neither, but I doubt it's pretty!"

"You just have to know what you're doing," Miles said suddenly from behind them. His face looked paler than normal. Luce must really have shaken him up.

"Oh, and I presume *you* know what you're doing?" Shelby challenged.

"No," he mumbled. "But one summer my parents made me take a workshop with this old angel who knew how, okay?" He turned to Luce. "And the way you were doing it? Wasn't even close. You really scared me, Luce."

"I'm sorry." Luce winced. Shelby and Miles were acting like she'd betrayed them by coming out here alone. "I thought you guys were going to the campfire behind the lodge."

"We thought *you* were going," Shelby shot back. "We were there for a while, but then Jasmine started crying about how Dawn had disappeared, and the teachers got all weird, especially when they realized you were missing too, so the party kinda broke up. So then I mention casually to Miles that I kind of sort of have an idea what you might be up to and that I'm off to find you and suddenly he's Mr. Superglue—"

"Wait a minute," Luce broke in. "Dawn *disappeared*?"

"Probably not," Miles offered. "I mean, you know how she and Jasmine are. They're just flighty."

"But it was her party," Luce said. "She wouldn't miss her own party."

"That was what Jasmine kept saying," Miles offered. "She didn't come to the room last night, and wasn't at mess this morning, so finally Frankie and Steven instructed us all to go back to the dorms, but—"

"Twenty bucks says Dawn's mugging down with some non-Neph greaseball in the woods around here." Shelby rolled her eyes.

"No." Luce had a bad feeling about this. Dawn had been so excited about the campfire. She'd ordered T-shirts online even though there was no way in the world she'd be able to convince any of the Nephilim kids to wear them. She wouldn't just disappear—not of her own volition. "How long has she been gone?"

⁂

When the three of them came out of the woods, Luce was even more shaken up. And not just about Dawn. She was shaken by what she'd seen in the Announcer.

Watching death close in on her former self was agony, and this was the first time she had seen it. Daniel, on the other hand, had had to watch it hundreds of times. Only now could she understand why he'd been so cold to her when they first met: to save them both the trauma of going through another gruesome death. The reality of Daniel's plight began to overwhelm her, and she was desperate to see him.

Crossing the lawn to the dorm, Luce had to shade her eyes. Powerful flashlights were sweeping over the campus. A helicopter droned in the distance, its searchlight tracing the shoreline, sweeping back and forth along the beach. A wide line of men in dark uniforms walked along the path from the Nephilim lodge to the mess hall, slowly scanning the ground.

Miles said, "That's standard formation for search parties. Form a line and leave no inch of ground uncovered."

"Oh God," Luce said under her breath.

"She really is missing." Shelby winced. "Not good karma."

Luce broke into a jog toward the Nephilim lodge. Miles and Shelby followed. The path, decked with flowers and so pretty in the daylight, now looked overgrown with shadow. Ahead of them, the campfire in the pit had faded to glowing embers, but all the lights were on at the lodge, inside each of the two stories, and all around the deck. The great A-frame building was ablaze and looked formidable in the dark night.

Luce could see the scared faces of a lot of the Nephilim kids who were sitting on the benches around the deck. Jasmine was crying, her red knit cap tugged low on her head. She was holding Lilith's stiff hand for support as two cops with notebooks ran through a bunch of questions. Luce's heart went out to the girl. She knew how horrific that process could be.

The cops swarmed around the deck, passing out blown-up black-and-white photocopies of a recent photograph of Dawn that someone had printed off the Internet. Glancing down at the low-resolution image, Luce was surprised to see how much Dawn *did* resemble her— at least, before she'd dyed her hair. She remembered talking the morning after she'd done it, how Dawn kept joking about their not being Twinkies anymore.

Luce covered her gasp with her hand. Her head hurt as she began to add up so many things that hadn't made sense. Until now.

The awful moment on the life raft. Steven's harsh warning about keeping it a secret. Daniel's paranoia about "dangers" he'd never explained to Luce. The Outcast who'd lured her off campus, the threat that Cam had destroyed in the forest. The way Dawn looked so much like her in the fuzzy black-and-white photograph.

Whoever took Dawn had been mistaken. It was Luce they wanted.

TWELVE

⁓ ‡ ⁓

SEVEN DAYS

Friday morning, Luce's eyes blinked open and fell on the clock. Seven-thirty a.m. She'd barely gotten any sleep—she was a mess, worried sick about Dawn and still angry about the past life she'd witnessed the day before via the Announcer. It was so eerie to have seen the moments leading up to her death. Would they all have been like that? Her mind kept running up against the same roadblock over and over again:

If it hadn't been for Daniel . . .

Would she have had a shot at a normal life, a

relationship with someone else, getting married, having kids, and growing old like the rest of the world? If it hadn't been for Daniel falling in love with her ages ago, would Dawn be missing right now?

These questions were all detours, which eventually flowed back to the most important one: Would love be different with someone else? Was love even possible with someone else? Love was supposed to be easy, wasn't it? Then why did she feel so tormented?

Shelby's head swung down from the top bunk, her thick blond ponytail dropping behind her like a heavy rope. "Are you as freaked out by all this as I am?"

Luce patted the bed for Shelby to scoot down and sit next to her. Still in her thick red flannel pajamas, Shelby slid onto Luce's bed, bringing two giant bars of dark chocolate with her.

Luce was going to say she couldn't possibly eat, but as the scent of the chocolate wafted to her nose, she peeled back the bronze foil and gave Shelby a tiny smile.

"Hits the spot," Shelby said. "You know that thing I said last night about Dawn making out with some greaseball? I feel really bad about it."

Luce shook her head. "Oh, Shel, you didn't know. You can't feel bad about that." She, on the other hand, had plenty of reason to feel sick over what had happened to Dawn. Luce had spent so much time already feeling responsible for the deaths of people near her—Trevor, then Todd, then poor, poor Penn. Her throat closed up at the thought of adding Dawn to the list. She wiped a silent tear away before Shelby could see. It was getting to a point where she was going to have to quarantine herself, to stay away from everyone she loved so that they could be safe.

A knock on their door made Luce and Shelby both jump. The door opened slowly. Miles.

"They found Dawn."

"What?" Luce and Shelby asked, sitting up in unison.

Miles dragged Luce's desk chair over to the bed and sat facing the girls. He took his cap off and wiped his forehead. It was beaded with sweat, like he'd come running across campus to tell them.

"I couldn't sleep last night," he said, turning the cap in his hands. "I was up early, walking around. I ran into Steven and he told me the good news. The people who took her brought her back around sunrise. She's shaken up, but she's not hurt."

"That's a miracle," Shelby murmured.

Luce was more dubious. "I don't get it. They just brought her back? Unharmed? When does that ever happen?"

And how long had it taken whoever they were to realize they had the wrong girl?

"It wasn't that simple," Miles admitted. "Steven was involved. He rescued her."

"From who?" Luce practically shouted.

Miles shrugged, rocking back on two legs of the chair. "Beats me. I'm sure Steven knows, but, uh, I'm not exactly his first choice for pillow talk."

The idea made Shelby hoot. That Dawn had been found, unharmed, seemed to relax everyone except Luce. Her body was growing numb. She couldn't stop thinking: *It should have been me.*

She got out of bed and grabbed a T-shirt and jeans from her closet. She had to find Dawn. Dawn was the only person who could answer her questions. And even though Dawn would never understand, Luce knew she owed her an apology.

"Steven did say that the people who took her won't be back anymore," Miles added, watching Luce worriedly.

"And you believe him?" Luce scoffed.

"Why shouldn't he?" a voice asked from the open doorway.

Francesca was leaning up against the threshold in a khaki trench coat. She was radiating calm, but she didn't seem exactly happy to see them. "Dawn is home now and she's safe."

"I want to see her," Luce said, feeling ridiculous standing there in the tattered T-shirt and running shorts she'd slept in.

Francesca pursed her lips. "Dawn's family picked her

up an hour ago. She'll be back at Shoreline when the time is right."

"Why are you acting like nothing happened?" Luce threw up her arms. "Like Dawn wasn't kidnapped—"

"She wasn't kidnapped," Francesca corrected. "She was borrowed, and it turned out to be a mistake. Steven handled it."

"Um, is that supposed to make us feel better? She was *borrowed*? For what?"

Luce searched Francesca's features—and saw nothing but levelheaded calm. But then something in Francesca's blue eyes changed: They narrowed, then widened, and a silent plea passed from Francesca to Luce. Francesca wanted Luce not to show what she suspected in front of Miles or Shelby. Luce didn't know why, but she trusted Francesca.

"Steven and I expect that the rest of you will be quite shaken up," Francesca continued, widening her gaze to include Miles and Shelby. "Classes are canceled today, and we'll be in our offices if you'd like to come by and talk." She smiled in that dazzling angelic way of hers, then turned on her high heels and clicked down the hallway.

Shelby got up and shut the door behind Francesca. "Can you believe she used the term 'borrowed' to refer to a human being? Is Dawn a library book?" She balled her hands up. "We have to do something to take our minds off this. I mean I'm glad Dawn's safe, and I trust Steven—I think—but I'm still thoroughly creeped out."

"You're right," said Luce, looking over at Miles. "We'll distract ourselves. We could go for a walk—"

"Too dangerous." Shelby's eyes darted from side to side.

"Or watch a movie—"

"Too inactive. My mind will drift."

"Eddie said something about a soccer game during lunch," Miles threw out.

Shelby clamped a hand over her forehead. "Need I remind you I am *done* with Shoreline boys?"

"How about a board game—"

Finally Shelby's eyes lit up. "How about the game of life? As in . . . your past lives? We could do that thing where we track down your relatives again. I could help you."

Luce chewed on her lower lip. Punching through that Announcer yesterday had seriously rocked her foundation. She was still physically disoriented, emotionally exhausted, and that didn't even begin to address how it had made her feel about Daniel.

"I don't know," she said.

"You mean, more of what you were doing yesterday?" Miles asked.

Shelby cranked her head around and glared at Miles. "Are you still here?"

Miles picked up a pillow that had fallen on the floor

and chucked it at her. She swatted it back at him, seeming impressed with her own reflexes.

"Okay, fine. Miles can stay. Mascots are always handy. And we may need someone to throw under a bus. Right, Luce?"

Luce closed her eyes. Yes, she was dying to know more about her past, but what if it was as hard to swallow as it had been the day before? Even with Miles and Shelby at her side, she was scared to try again.

But then she remembered the day Francesca and Steven had glimpsed the Sodom and Gomorrah Announcer in front of the class. Afterward, the other students had reeled, but Luce kept thinking that whether or not they had glimpsed that gruesome scene didn't matter in the least: It would still have happened. Just like her past.

For the sakes of all her former selves, Luce couldn't turn away now. "Let's do it," she said to her friends.

※

Miles gave the girls a few minutes to get dressed, and they reconvened in the hallway. But then Shelby refused to go out to the forest where Luce had summoned the Announcers.

"Don't look at me like that. Dawn just got nabbed, and the woods are dark and creepy. I don't really want to be next, you know?"

That was when Miles insisted it would be good for

Luce to try to practice summoning the Announcers somewhere new, like the dorm room.

"Just whistle and bring 'em running," he said. "Make those Announcers your bitches. You know you want to."

"I don't want them to start lurking around here, though," Shelby said, turning to Luce. "No offense, but a girl likes her privacy."

Luce wasn't offended. But it wasn't like the Announcers ever really stopped following her, regardless of when she summoned them. She didn't want the shadows dropping by the dorm room unannounced any more than Shelby did.

"The thing with the Announcers is demonstrating control. It's like training a new puppy. You just have to let it know who's boss."

Luce cocked her head at Miles. "Since when do you know so much useful stuff about the Announcers?"

Miles blushed. "I may not always 'apply myself' in class, but I am capable of a few things."

"So what? She just stands there and summons?" Shelby asked.

Luce stood on Shelby's rainbow-colored yoga mat in the center of the room and thought about how Steven had coached her. "Let's open a window," she said.

Shelby hopped up to raise the sash of the broad window, letting in a fresh blast of chilling sea air. "Good idea. Makes it more hospitable."

"And cold," Miles said, pulling up the hood of his sweatshirt.

Then the two of them sat on the bed facing Luce, as if she were a performer on a stage.

She closed her eyes, trying not to feel on the spot. But instead of thinking of the shadows, instead of summoning them in her mind, all she could think of was Dawn and how terrified she must have been the night before, how she must be feeling even now, back with her family. She'd bounced back after the freakish incident on the yacht, but this was so much more serious. And it was Luce's fault. Well, Luce's *and* Daniel's, for bringing her here.

He kept saying he was taking her to a safer place. Now Luce wondered whether all he was really doing was making Shoreline dangerous for everyone else.

A gasp from Miles made Luce open her eyes. She looked just above the window, where a large charcoal-gray Announcer was pressed against the ceiling. At first it looked like it could have been a normal shadow, cast by the floor lamp Shelby moved into the corner when she did her Vinyasa. But then the Announcer began to spread across the ceiling until the room looked as if it had been given a deathly coat of paint, leaving a cold, foul-smelling wake over Luce's head. Out of her reach.

The Announcer she hadn't even summoned—the

Announcer that could contain, well, *anything*—was taunting her.

She inhaled nervously, remembering what Miles had said about control. She concentrated so fiercely that her brain began to hurt. Her face was red and her eyes were strained to the point where she was going to have to just give up. But then:

The Announcer buckled, sliding down to Luce's feet like a thick bolt of dropped fabric. Squinting, she discerned a smaller, plumper brownish shadow hovering over the larger, darker one, tracing its movements, almost the way a sparrow might fly closely in line with a hawk. What was this one after?

"Incredible," Miles whispered. Luce tried to let Miles's words sink in as a compliment. These things that had terrorized her all her life, that made her miserable? That she had always feared? Now they served her. Which really was kind of incredible. It hadn't occurred to her until she'd seen the intrigue on Miles's face. For the first time, she felt pretty badass.

She controlled her breathing and took her time guiding it off the floor and into her hands. Once the large gray Announcer was within reach, the smaller one poured to the floor like a golden bend of the light from the window, blending in with the hardwood planks.

Luce took the edges of the Announcer and held her breath, praying that the message inside was more innocent than yesterday's. She tugged, surprised to feel this shadow give her more resistance than any of the others had. It looked so sheer and insubstantial, but felt stiff in her hands. By the time she'd coaxed it into a window about a foot square, her arms were aching.

"This is the best I can do," she told Miles and Shelby. They stood up, drawing close.

The gray veil within the Announcer lifted, or Luce thought it did, but then another gray veil lay underneath. She squinted until she saw the gray texture roiling and moving, realizing it wasn't the shadow she was seeing anymore: The gray veil they were looking at was a thick cloud of cigarette smoke. Shelby coughed.

The smoke never really cleared, but Luce's eyes got used to it; soon she could see a broad half-moon table with a red felt top. Playing cards were arrayed in neat rows across its surface. A row of strangers sat crowded at one side. Some looked jumpy and nervous, like the bald man who kept loosening his polka-dot tie and whistling under his breath. Others looked exhausted, like the hairsprayed woman ashing a cigarette into a half-full glass of something. Her gloopy mascara was wearing off her upper lashes, leaving a seam of black grit under her eyes.

And across the table, a pair of hands were flying through a deck of cards, expertly flipping over a card at a time to each person at the table. Luce inched closer to

Miles so she could get a better look. She was distracted by the flashing neon lights from a thousand slot machines just beyond the tables. That was before she saw the dealer.

She thought she'd get used to seeing versions of herself in the Announcers. Young, hopeful, ever naïve. But this was different. The woman dealing cards in the seedy casino wore a white oxford shirt, snug black pants, and a black vest that bulged at the chest. Her fingernails were long and red, with sequins sparkling on both pinkies, and she kept using them to flick her black hair out of her face. Her focus hovered just above the hairlines of the players, so she never really looked anyone in the eye. She was three times as old as Luce, but there was still *something* between them.

"Is that you?" Miles whispered, trying hard not to sound horrified.

"No!" Shelby said flatly. "That broad is *old*. And Luce only lives to be seventeen." She shot Luce a nervous look. "I mean, in the past, that's been the deal. This time, though, I'm sure she'll live to a ripe old age. Maybe as old as this lady. I mean—"

"Enough, Shelby," Luce said.

Miles shook his head. "I have *so* much catching up to do."

"Okay, if it's not me, we must be . . . I don't know, somehow related." Luce watched as the woman cashed out chips for the bald man with the tie. Her hands looked sort of like Luce's. The way her mouth set was similarly serious. "Do you think it's my mom? Or my sister?"

Shelby was scribbling notes furiously on the inside back cover of a yoga manual. "Only one way to find out." She flashed her notes at Luce: *Vegas: Mirage Hotel and Casino, night shift, table stationed near the Bengal tiger show, Vera with the Lee press-on nails.*

She looked back at the dealer. Shelby was a stickler for the details that Luce never noticed. The dealer's name tag read VERA in lopsided white letters. But the image was starting to wobble and fade. Soon the whole image broke apart into tiny shadow shreds that fell to the floor and curled up like the ash from burning paper.

"But wait, isn't this the past?" Luce asked.

"Don't think so," Shelby said. "Or, at least, it's not far in the past. There was an ad for the new Cirque du Soleil in the background. So what do you say?"

Go all the way to Las Vegas to find this woman? A middle-aged sister would probably be easier to approach than parents well into their eighties, but still. What if they made it all the way to Vegas and Luce choked again?

Shelby nudged her. "Hey, I must really like you if I'm agreeing to go to Vegas. My mom was a waitress there for a couple of years when I was a kid. I'm telling you, it's Hell on earth."

"How would we get there?" Luce asked, not wanting

to ask Shelby if they could borrow SAEB's car again. "How far is Vegas, anyway?"

"Too far to drive." Miles spoke up. "Which is fine with me because I've been wanting to practice stepping through."

"Stepping through?" Luce asked.

"Stepping through." Miles knelt down on the ground and brushed the fragments of the shadow together in his palms. They looked almost tired, but Miles kept kneading them with his fingers until they formed a loose, messy ball. "I told you I couldn't sleep last night. I sort of broke into Steven's office through the transom."

"Yeah, right." Shelby balked. "You flunked levitation. You're definitely not good enough to float in through the transom."

"And *you're* not strong enough to drag the bookcase over," Miles said. "But I am, and I have this to show for myself." He grinned, holding up a thick black tome titled *An Announcer How-To: Summon, Glimpse, and Travel in Ten Thousand Easy Steps.* "I also have an enormous bruise on my shin from a poorly planned exit through the transom, but anyway . . ." He turned to Luce, who was having a hard time not ripping the book from his hands. "I was thinking, with your obvious talent for glimpsing, and my superior knowledge—"

Shelby snorted. "What'd you read, point three percent of the book?"

"A very useful point three percent," Miles said. "I think we might be able to do this. And not end up lost forever."

Shelby cocked her head suspiciously but didn't say anything else. Miles kept kneading the Announcer in his palm, then began stretching it out. After a minute or two, it had grown into a sheet of gray almost the size of a door. Its edges were wobbly and it was almost translucent, but when he pressed it away from his body a little, it seemed to take a firmer shape, like a plaster cast after being set to dry. Miles reached for the left side of the dark rectangle, feeling around its surface, searching for something.

"That's weird," he muttered, trolling the Announcer with his fingers. "The book says if you make the Announcer area large enough, the surface tension reduces by a ratio that allows for penetration." He sighed. "There's supposed to be a—"

"Great book, Miles." Shelby rolled her eyes. "You're a real expert now."

"What are you looking for?" Luce asked, stepping close behind Miles. Suddenly, watching his hands rove, she saw it.

A latch.

She blinked and the image vanished, but she knew where it had been. She reached around Miles and pressed her own hand against the left side of the

Announcer. *There.* The touch of it against her fingers made her gasp.

It felt like the kind of heavy metal latch with a bolt and hasp used to lock a garden gate. It was freezing, and rough with invisible rust.

"Now what?" Shelby said.

She looked back at her two very baffled friends, shrugged, fiddled with the lock, then slowly slid the invisible bolt to the side.

With its lock released, a shadow door swung up, almost knocking the three of them backward.

"We did it," Shelby whispered.

They were gazing into a long, deep, red-black tunnel. It was clammy inside and smelled like mildew and watered-down cocktails made with cheap liquor. Luce and Shelby looked at each other uncertainly. Where was the blackjack table? Where was the woman they'd been looking at before? A red glow pulsed from deep within, and then Luce could hear slot machines ringing, coins clinking into pay baskets with a clatter.

"Cool!" Miles said, grabbing for her hand. "I read about this part, it's a transitional phase. We just have to keep going."

Luce reached for Shelby's hand, gripping it tightly as Miles stepped inside the clammy darkness—and pulled the three of them through.

They walked only a couple of feet forward, about far

enough to reach the real door of Luce and Shelby's dorm room. But as soon as the cloudy gray Announcer door sealed shut behind them with a deeply unnerving *pffffft*, their Shoreline room was gone. What had been a deep, glowing velvety red in the distance suddenly became bright white. The white light shot forward, enveloping them, filling their ears with sound. All three of them had to shield their eyes. Miles pressed ahead, drawing Luce and Shelby behind him. Otherwise, Luce might have been paralyzed. Both her palms were sweating inside her friends' hands. She was listening to a single chord of music, loud and perfectly sonorous.

Luce rubbed her eyes, but it was the foggy curtain of Announcer that was obscuring the view. Miles reached forward and gently rubbed at it with a circular motion, until it started to peel away, like old paint chips flaking off a ceiling. And from each falling flake, blasts of arid desert air shot through the murky coolness, warming Luce's skin. As the Announcer fell to pieces at their feet, the view before them suddenly made sense: They were looking down at the Las Vegas Strip. Luce had only seen it in pictures, but now she had the tip of the Paris Las Vegas Hotel's Eiffel Tower at eye level in the distance.

Which meant they were very, very high. She dared a glance down: They were standing outside, on a roof somewhere, with the edge only a foot or two beyond their toes. And beyond that—the rush of Vegas traffic, the heads of a line of palm trees, an elaborately lit swimming pool. All at least thirty stories down.

Shelby let go of Luce's hand and began pacing the boundaries of the brown cement roof. Three identical long, rectangular wings extended from a center point. Luce spun around, taking in three hundred and sixty degrees of bright neon lights, and beyond the Strip, a range of far-off barren mountains, lit up eerily by the city's light pollution.

"Damn, Miles," Shelby said, hopping over skylights to explore more of the roof. "That step-through was amazing. I am almost attracted to you right now. Almost."

Miles dug his hands in his pockets. "Um . . . thanks?"

"Where exactly are we?" Luce asked. The difference between her solo tumble through the Announcer and this experience was like night and day. This was so much more civilized. It hadn't made anyone want to throw up. Plus, it had actually worked. At least, she thought it had. "What happened to the view we had before?"

"I had to zoom out," Miles said. "I figured it would look weird if the three of us stepped out of a cloud in the middle of the casino floor."

"Just a tad," Shelby said, tugging on a locked door. "Any brilliant ideas about how to get down from here?"

Luce grimaced. The Announcer was trembling in

tatters at their feet. She couldn't imagine it had the strength to help them now. No way off this roof and no way back to Shoreline.

"Never mind! I'm a genius," Shelby called from across the roof. She was hunched over one of the skylights, wrestling with a lock. With a grunt, she pried it open, then lifted a hinged pane of glass. She stuck her head through, motioning for Luce and Miles to join her.

Cautiously, Luce peered down through the open skylight into a large, opulent bathroom. There were four generous-sized stalls on one side, a line of raised marble sinks facing a gilded mirror on the other. A mauve plush settee was set up in front of a vanity, and a single woman sat there, looking into the mirror. Luce could only see the top of her black bouffant hair, but her reflection showed a heavily made-up face, thick bangs, and a French-manicured hand reapplying an unnecessary coat of red lipstick.

"As soon as Cleopatra's gone through that tube of lipstick, we'll just shimmy on down," Shelby whispered.

Below them, Cleopatra stood up from the vanity. She smacked her lips together and wiped a stray red stain off her teeth. Then she marched toward the door.

"Let me get this straight," Miles said. "You want me to 'shimmy' into a women's bathroom?"

Luce took one more look around the desolate roof.

There was really only one way in. "If anyone sees you, just pretend you went in the wrong door."

"Or that you two were making out in one of the stalls," Shelby added. "What? It's Vegas."

"Let's just go." Miles was blushing as he lowered himself feet-first through the window. He extended his arms slowly, until his feet hovered just over the high marble top of the vanity.

"Help Luce down," Shelby called.

Miles moved to lock the bathroom door, then raised his arms to catch Luce. She tried to mimic his smooth technique, but her arms were wobbly as she lowered herself through the skylight. She couldn't see much below her, but felt Miles's strong grip around her waist sooner than she'd expected.

"You can let go," he said, and when she did, he lowered her gracefully to the floor. His fingers spread out around her rib cage, just a thin black T-shirt away from her skin. His arms were still around her when her feet touched the tile. She was about to thank him, but when she looked up into his eyes, she got tongue-tied.

She backed out of his grasp too quickly, mumbling apologetically for tripping over his feet. Both of them leaned up against the vanity, nervously avoiding eye contact by staring at the wall.

That should not have happened. Miles was just her friend.

"*Hello!* Anyone going to help me?" Shelby's ribbed-stockinged feet were dangling from the skylight, kicking impatiently. Miles moved under the window and roughly grabbed her belt, easing her down by the waist. He released Shelby a lot more quickly, Luce noticed, than he had released her.

Shelby bounded across the gold-tiled floor and un-locked the door. "Come on, you two, what are you waiting for?"

On the other side of the door, glamorously made-up black-clad waitresses bustled by in sequined high heels, trays of cocktail shakers balanced in the crooks of their arms. Men in expensive dark suits crowded around blackjack tables, where they whooped like teenage boys each time a hand was dealt. There were no slot machines clanking and banging on an endless loop here. It was hushed, and exclusive, and endlessly exciting—but it wasn't anything like the scene they had watched in the Announcer.

A cocktail waitress approached them. "May I help you?" She lowered her stainless steel tray to scrutinize them.

"Ooh, caviar," Shelby said, scooping up three blini and handing one to the others. "You guys thinking what I'm thinking?"

Luce nodded. "We were just going downstairs."

When the elevator doors opened onto the bright and glaring lobby of the casino, Luce had to be pushed out by Miles. She could tell they'd finally come to the right place. The cocktail waitresses were older, tired, showing a lot less flesh. They didn't glide across the stained orange carpet; they thumped. And the patrons looked much more like the ones they had seen crowding the table in the glimpsing: overweight, middle-class, middle-aged, sad, wallet-emptying automatons. All they had to do now was find Vera.

Shelby maneuvered them through a cramped maze of slot machines, past clots of people at roulette tables shouting at the tiny ball as it spun in the wheel, past big, boxy games at which people blew on dice and threw them and then cheered at the outcome, down a row of tables offering poker and strange games with names like Pai Gow, until they came to a cluster of blackjack tables.

Most of the dealers were men. Tall, hunched-over, oily-haired men, bespectacled gray-mustached men, one man wearing a surgical mask over his face. Shelby didn't slow to gape at any of them, and she was right not to: There, at the far back corner of the casino, was Vera.

Her black hair was swept up in a lopsided bun. Her pale face looked thin and saggy. Luce didn't feel the same emotional outpouring she'd felt when she looked at her previous life's parents in Shasta. But then again, she still didn't know who Vera was to her besides a tired, middle-aged woman holding a deck of cards out for a half-asleep redheaded woman to cut. Sloppily, the redhead picked up the deck in the middle; then Vera's hands started flying.

Other tables in the casino were overcrowded, but the redhead and her diminutive husband were the only two people at Vera's. Still, she put on a good show for them, snapping the cards out with an easy dexterity that made the work look effortless. Luce could see an elegant side of Vera that she hadn't noticed before. A flair for the dramatic.

"So," Miles said, shifting his weight next to Luce. "Are we gonna . . . or . . ."

Shelby's hands were suddenly on Luce's shoulders, practically wedging her into one of the empty leather seats at the table.

Though she was dying to stare, Luce avoided eye contact at first. She was nervous that Vera might recognize her before she even had a chance. But Vera's eyes passed over each of them with only the mildest of interest, and Luce remembered how different she looked now that she'd bleached her hair. She tugged at it nervously, not sure what to do next.

Then Miles plunked down a twenty-dollar bill in front of Luce, and she remembered the game she was supposed to be playing. She slid the money across the table.

Vera raised a penciled-in eyebrow. "Got ID?"

Luce shook her head. "Maybe we could just watch?"

Across the table, the redhead was nodding off, her head falling onto Shelby's stiff shoulder. Vera rolled her eyes at the whole scene and pushed Luce's money back, pointing at the neon billboard advertising Cirque du Soleil. "Circus is that way, kids."

Luce sighed. They were going to have to wait until Vera got off work. And by then she'd probably be even less interested in talking to them. Feeling defeated, Luce reached out to take Miles's money back. Vera's fingers were drawing away just as Luce's swept over the money, and their fingertips kissed. Both of them snapped up their heads. The weird shock briefly blinded Luce. She sucked in her breath. She looked deep into Vera's wide hazel eyes.

And she saw everything:

A two-story cabin in a snowy Canadian town. Webs of ice on the windows, wind soughing at the panes. A ten-year-old girl watching TV in the living room, rocking a baby on her lap. It was Vera, pale and pretty in acid-washed jeans and Doc Martens, a thick navy turtleneck rising to her chin, a cheap wool blanket bunched up between her and the back of the couch. A bowl of popcorn on the coffee table, reduced to a handful of cold, unpopped kernels. A fat orange cat prowling the mantel, hissing at the radiator. And Luce—Luce was her sister, the baby sister in her arms.

Luce felt herself rocking in her seat at the casino, aching to remember all of this. Just as quickly, the impression faded, replaced by another.

Luce as a toddler chasing Vera, up the stairs, down the stairs, the worn wide steps beneath her thumping feet, her chest tight from breathless laughter, when the doorbell sounded and a fair, slick-haired boy arrived to pick Vera up for a date, and she stopped and straightened her clothes and turned her back, turned away. . . .

A heartbeat later and Luce was a teenager herself, with a mess of curly shoulder-length black hair. *Sprawled on Vera's denim bedspread, the coarse fabric somehow a comfort, flipping through Vera's secret diary. He loves me, Vera had scrawled again and again and again, her handwriting getting loopier and loopier. And then the pages pulled away, her sister's angry face looming, the tracks of her tears clear. . . .*

And then again, a different scene, Luce older still, maybe seventeen. She braced herself for what was coming.

Snow pouring from the sky like soft white static. Vera and a few friends ice-skating on the frozen pond behind their house, gliding in swift circles, happy and laughing, and at the frayed icy edge of the pond, Luce crouched down, the cold seeping through her thin clothes while she laced up her skates, in a hurry, as usual, to catch up with her sister. And beside her, a warmth she didn't have to look at to identify, Daniel, who was silent, moody, his skates already tightly laced. She could feel the urge to kiss him—and yet no shadows were visible. The evening and everything about it were star-dotted and glittering, endlessly clear and full of possibility.

Luce searched for the shadows, then realized that their absence made sense. These were Vera's memories. And the snow made everything harder to see. Still, Daniel must know, as he had known when he dove into that lake. He must have sensed it every single time. Did he ever care what became of people like Vera after Luce was killed?

There came a bursting sound from Luce's side of the lake, like the letting out of a parachute. And then: A blooming shot of red-hot fire in the middle of a blizzard. A huge column of bright orange flames shooting into the sky at the edge of the pond. Where Luce had been. The other skaters rushed senselessly toward it, barreling across the pond. But the ice was melting, rapidly, catastrophically, sending their skates plunging through to the frigid water underneath. Vera's scream echoed through the blue night, her frozen look of agony all that Luce could see.

In the casino, Vera yanked her hand back, shaking it as if she'd been burned. Her lips quivered a few times before they formed the words: "It's you." She shook her head. "But it can't be."

"Vera," Luce whispered, reaching her hand out again to her sister. She wanted to hold her, to take all the pain Vera had ever been caused and transfer it to herself.

"No." Vera shook her head, backing away and wagging a finger at Luce. "No, no, no." She backed into the dealer at the table behind her, tripping over him and sending a giant stack of poker chips cascading off the table. The colored disks slid across the floor, causing a ripple of oohs and aahs from gamblers who leaped from their seats to scoop them up.

"Dammit, Vera!" a squat man bellowed over the din. As he waddled to their table in a cheap gray polyester suit and scuffed black shoes, Luce shared a worried glance with Miles and Shelby. Three underage kids wanted nothing to do with the pit boss. But he was still chewing Vera out, his lip curled up in disgust. "How many times—"

Vera had found her feet again but kept staring, terrified, at Luce, as if Luce were the devil instead of her sister a lifetime removed. Vera's kohl-lined eyes were white with terror as she stammered, "She c-c-can't be here."

"Christ," the pit boss muttered, checking out Luce and her friends, then speaking into a walkie-talkie. "Get me security. Got a coupla hoodlum kids."

Luce shrank back between Miles and Shelby, who said through gritted teeth, "How about one of those step-throughs, Miles?"

Before Miles could reply, three men with enormous wrists and necks appeared and towered over them. The pit boss waved his hands. "Take them to the pen. See what other kind of trouble they've been in."

"I've got a better idea," a girl's voice growled from behind the wall of security guards.

All heads whipped around to find the voice, but only Luce's face lit up. "Arriane!"

The tiny girl flashed Luce a grin as she sidled through the crowd. With five-inch platform wedges, her hair done up all crazy, and her eyes nearly swallowed by dark eyeliner, Arriane fit in with the casino's weird clientele perfectly. Nobody seemed to know quite what to make of her, least of all Shelby and Miles.

The pit boss veered over to confront Arriane. He reeked of shoe polish and cough medicine.

"Do you need to be taken to the pen, too, missy?"

"Ooh, sounds fun." Arriane's eyes widened. "Alas, I'm overbooked tonight. I've got front-row tickets to Blue Man Group, and of course there's dinner with Cher after the show. One more thing I know I had to do . . ." She tapped her chin, then looked over at Luce. "Ah yes—get these three guys the hell out of here. 'Scuse us!" She blew a kiss at the fuming pit boss, shrugged an apology at Vera, and snapped her fingers.

Then all the lights went out.

THIRTEEN

SIX DAYS

Rushing them through the labyrinth of the dark casino, Arriane moved as if she had night vision.

"Stay cool, you three," she sang. "I'll have you out of here in a flash."

She held Luce's wrist in a tight grip, and Luce in turn held Miles's hand; Miles held Shelby's, as she cursed at the indignity of having to bring up the escape caboose.

Arriane led them unerringly, and though Luce

couldn't see what she was doing, she could hear people grunt and exclaim as Arriane shouldered them aside. "Sorry 'bout that!" she'd call. "Whoops!" and "Excuse me!"

She took them down dark hallways packed with anxious tourists using their cell phones as flashlights. Up darker staircases, stuffy with disuse and crammed with empty cardboard boxes. Finally she kicked open an emergency exit, ushering them through it and into a dark, narrow alley.

The alleyway was tucked between the Mirage and another towering hotel. A row of Dumpsters sent out the foul odor of expensive rotting food. A trickle of acid-green gutter water formed a vile little river, splitting the alley in half. Straight ahead, in the middle of the bright, bustling neon-lit Strip, an old-fashioned black street clock struck twelve.

"Ahhh." Arriane inhaled deeply. "The beginning of another glorious day in Sin City. I like to start it off right, with a big breakfast. Who's hungry?"

"Um . . . er . . . ," Shelby stammered, looking at Luce, then Arriane, then at the casino. "What just . . . How did . . ."

Miles's gaze was fixed on the shiny, marbled scar that spanned one side of Arriane's neck. Luce was used to Arriane by now, but it was clear that her friends didn't know what to make of her.

Arriane waved her finger at Miles. "This guy looks like he can eat his weight in waffles. Come on, I know a filthy diner."

As they clipped up the alley toward the street, Miles turned to Luce and mouthed, "That was *awesome*."

Luce nodded. It was all she could do to keep up with Arriane as she jogged across the Strip. *Vera.* She couldn't get over it. All those memories, glimpsed in a flash. They'd been painful and startling, and she could only imagine what it had been like for Vera. But for Luce, they had also been deeply satisfying. More than with any of her glimpses through the Announcers so far, this time she felt as if she'd *experienced* one of her past lives. Strangely, she'd also seen something she'd never even thought about: Her previous selves had lives. Lives that had been full and meaningful before Daniel had shown up.

Arriane led them to an IHOP, a squat brown stucco building that looked so ancient it could have predated everything else on the Strip. It seemed more claustrophobic and sadder than other IHOPs.

Shelby led the way inside, pushing through the glass doors, chiming the cheap jingle bells duct-taped to the top. She grabbed a fistful of mints from the bowl by the register before claiming a booth in the far back corner. Arriane slid in next to her, while Luce and Miles took the other side of the cracked orange leather booth.

With a whistle and a quick circular gesture, Arriane ordered a round of coffee from the plump, pretty waitress with the pencil stuck in her hair.

The rest of them focused on the thick, spiral-bound laminated menu. Turning the pages was a battle against the ancient maple syrup welding the whole thing together—and a good way to avoid talking about the trouble they'd just narrowly escaped.

Finally Luce had to ask. "What are you doing here, Arriane?"

"Ordering something with a funny name. Rooty Tooty, I guess, since they don't have Moons Over My Hammy here. I can never decide."

Luce rolled her eyes. Arriane didn't need to act so coy. It was obvious her rescue effort hadn't been coincidental. "You know what I mean."

"These are strange days, Luce. I figured I'd pass them in an equally strange city."

"Yeah, well, they're almost over. Aren't they, according to the truce timeline?"

Arriane put down her coffee cup and cradled her chin in her palm. "Well, hallelujah. They are teaching you something at that school after all."

"Yes and no," Luce said. "I just overheard Roland saying something about how Daniel would be counting down the minutes. He said it had something to do with a truce, but I didn't know exactly how many minutes we were talking about."

Beside her, Miles's body seemed to have stiffened at the mention of Daniel. When the waitress arrived to take their orders, he barked his out first, practically shoving the menu back at her. "Steak and eggs, rare."

"Oooh, *manly*," Arriane said, eyeing Miles approvingly in the midst of the eeny, meeny, miny, moe game she was playing on her menu. "Rooty Tooty Fresh 'N Fruity it is." She enunciated as properly as the Queen of England might, keeping a remarkably straight face.

"Pigs in a blanket for me," Shelby said. "Actually, make that an egg-white omelet, no cheese. Aw, what the hell. Pigs in a blanket."

The waitress turned to Luce. "How 'bout you, hon?"

"Breakfast Sampler." Luce smiled apologetically on behalf of her friends. "Scrambled, hold the meat."

The waitress nodded, padding off toward the kitchen.

"Okay, so what else did you hear?" Arriane asked.

"Um." Luce started playing with the carafe of syrup next to the salt and pepper. "There was some talk of, you know, End Times."

Snickering, Shelby splashed three little tubs of creamer into her coffee. "End Times! You actually buy into that crap? I mean, how many millennia have we been waiting around for that? And humans think they've been patient for a mere couple thousand years! Hah. Like anything is ever going to change."

Arriane looked about a second away from putting

Shelby in her place, but then she set down her coffee. "How rude of me to not even introduce myself to your friends, Luce."

"Um, we know who you are," Shelby said.

"Yeah, there was a whole chapter on you in my eighth-grade History of Angels textbook," Miles said.

Arriane clapped. "And they told me that book had been banned!"

"Seriously? You're in a textbook?" Luce laughed.

"Why so surprised? You don't find me historic?" Arriane turned back to Shelby and Miles. "Now, tell me all about yourselves. I need to know who my girl's been palling around with."

"Lapsed nonbelieving Nephilim." Shelby raised her hand.

Miles stared at his food. "And the ineffectual great-great-great-to-the-nth-degree-grandson of an angel."

"That's not true." Luce bumped Miles's shoulder. "Arriane, you should have seen how he helped us step through this shadow tonight. He was great. That's why we're here, because he read this book and the next thing you know, he could—"

"Yeah, I was wondering about that," Arriane said sarcastically. "But what concerns me more is this one." She gestured at Shelby. Arriane's face was much graver than Luce was accustomed to. Even her manic light blue eyes looked steady. "It's not a good time to be a lapsed anything right now. Everything's in flux, but there will be a reckoning. And you will have to choose one side or the other." Arriane stared deliberately at Shelby. "We all have to know where we stand."

Before anyone could respond, the waitress reappeared, wielding a huge brown plastic tray of food.

"Well, how's this for speedy service?" she asked. "Now, which one of you had the pigs—"

"Me!" Shelby startled the waitress with the quickness of her reach for the plate.

"Anybody need any ketchup?"

They shook their heads.

"Extra butter?"

Luce pointed down at the ice cream scoop of butter already on her pancakes. "We're all set. Thanks."

"If we need anything," Arriane said, beaming down at the whipped cream happy face on her plate, "we'll holler."

"Oh, I know *you* will." The waitress chuckled, tucking the tray under her arm. "Holler like the world's about to end, this one will."

After she left, Arriane was the only one who ate. She plucked a blueberry from the pancake's nose, popped it into her mouth, and licked her fingers with relish. Finally she glanced around the table.

"Dig in," Arriane said. "There's nothing good about cold steak and eggs." She sighed. "Come on, guys.

You've read the history books. Don't you know the drill—"

"I haven't," Luce said. "I don't know any drills."

Arriane sucked meditatively on her fork. "Good point. In that case, allow me to present my version to you. Which is more fun than the history books anyway because I won't censor the big fights and curses and all the sexy stuff. My version has everything but 3-D, which, I have to say, is totally overrated. Did you see that movie with"—she noticed the blank looks on their faces. "Oh, never mind. Okay, it starts millennia ago. Now, do I need to catch you up on Satan?"

"Waged an early power struggle against God." Miles's voice was a monotone, as if he were repeating a third-grade lesson plan while he speared a bit of steak with his fork.

"Before then they were super-tight," Shelby added, dousing her pigs in blankets with syrup. "I mean, God called Satan his morning star. So it's not like Satan wasn't worthy or beloved."

"But he would rather reign in Hell than serve in Heaven," Luce chimed in. She might not have read the Nephilim histories, but she'd read *Paradise Lost*. Or at least, the CliffsNotes.

"*Very* nice." Arriane beamed, leaning toward Luce. "You know, Gabbe was big friends with Milton's daughters back in the day. *She* likes to take credit for that phrase, and I'm all 'Aren't you enough people's darling already?' But whatever." Arriane moved in on a forkful of Luce's eggs. "Damn, these are *good*. Can we get some hot sauce over here?" she bellowed toward the kitchen. "Okay, where were we?"

"Satan," Shelby said through a mouthful of pancake.

"Right. So. Say what you will about El Diablo Grande, but he is"—Arriane tossed her head—"somewhat responsible for introducing the idea of free will among angels. I mean: He really gave the rest of us something to think about. On which side do you throw your weight? Given the choice, a whole lotta angels fell."

"How many?" Miles asked.

"The Fallen? Enough to cause something of a stalemate." Arriane looked thoughtful for a moment, then grimaced and called out to the waitress. "Hot sauce! Does it exist in this establishment?"

"What about the angels who fell, but didn't side with—" Luce broke off, thinking of Daniel. She was aware that she was whispering, but this felt like a really big thing to be discussing in the middle of a diner. Even a mostly empty diner in the middle of the night.

Arriane lowered her voice too. "Oh, there are plenty of angels who fell but still technically ally with God. But then there are those who threw in with Satan. We call them demons, even though they're just fallen angels who made really poor choices.

"Not like it's been easy for anyone. Since the Fall,

angels and demons have been neck and neck, split down the middle, yada yada yada." She slathered butter into the pancake's nose. "But all that may be about to change."

Luce looked down at her eggs, unable to eat.

"So, um, before, you seemed to be suggesting that my allegiance had something to do with that?" Shelby looked slightly less doubtful than she usually did.

"Not yours exactly." Arriane shook her head. "I know it feels like we've all been hanging in the balance forever. But in the end, it's going to come down to one powerful angel choosing a side. When that happens, the scale finally tips. *That's* when it matters which side you're on."

Arriane's words reminded Luce of being locked all the way up in that tiny chapel with Miss Sophia, how she kept saying the fate of the universe had something to do with Luce and Daniel. It had sounded crazy at the time, and Miss Sophia *was* evil bananas. And even though Luce wasn't certain exactly what everyone was talking about, she knew it had to do with Daniel coming back around.

"It's Daniel," she said softly. "The angel who can tip the scales is Daniel."

It explained the agony he carried all the time, like a two-ton suitcase. It explained why he'd been away from her so long. The only thing it didn't explain was why there seemed to be some question in Arriane's mind about which side the scales would tip onto. Which side would win the war.

Arriane opened her mouth, but instead of answering, she attacked Luce's plate again. *"Can I get some freaking hot sauce over here?"* she yelled.

A shadow fell over their table. "I'll give you something *fiery*."

Luce looked behind her and recoiled at the sight: A very tall boy in a long brown trench coat, unbuttoned so that Luce could see a flash of something silver tucked inside his belt. He had a shaved head, a slim, straight nose, a mouthful of perfect teeth.

And white eyes. Eyes utterly empty of color. No irises, no pupils, none at all.

His strange, vacant expression reminded Luce of the Outcast girl. Though Luce hadn't seen that girl closely enough to figure out what was wrong with her eyes, she now had a pretty good guess.

Shelby looked at the boy, swallowed hard, and tucked into her breakfast. "Nothing to do with me," she mumbled.

"Save it," Arriane said to the boy. "You can put it on the fist sandwich I'm about to serve you." Luce watched wide-eyed as tiny Arriane stood up and wiped her hands on her jeans. "BRB, guys. Oh, and Luce, remind me to berate you for this when I get back." Before Luce could ask what this guy had to do with her, Arriane had grabbed him by the earlobe, twisted hard, and slammed his head down on the glass display counter near the bar.

The noise shattered the lazy, late-night quiet of the restaurant. The guy yelped like a child as Arriane twisted his ear the other way and climbed on top of him. Bellowing in pain, he started bucking his lean body until he'd flung Arriane off and onto the glass case.

She rolled along its length and came to a stop at the end, knocking over a towering lemon meringue pie, then leaped to her feet on the bar. She somersaulted back toward him and caught him in a headlock with her legs, then set to work pounding his face with her small fists.

"Arriane!" the waitress shrieked. "Not my pies! I try to be tolerant! But I have my livelihood to look after!"

"Aw, fine!" Arriane shouted. "We'll take it to the kitchen." She released the guy, slid to the floor, and booted him with her platform heel. He blindly stumbled toward the door that led to the diner's kitchen. "Come on, you three," she called to their table. "Might as well learn something."

Miles and Shelby threw down their napkins, reminding Luce of the way kids at Dover used to drop everything and run screaming through the halls yelling "Fight! Fight!" anytime there was the slightest rumor of a scuffle.

Luce followed behind, a little more hesitantly. If Arriane was suggesting that this guy had showed up because of her, it raised a lot of other hairy questions. What about the people who'd taken Dawn? And that arrow-shooting Outcast girl Cam had killed at Noyo Point?

A loud slam sounded from inside the kitchen and three terrified men in dirty aprons rushed out. By the time Luce made it past them through the swinging door, Arriane was holding down the boy with her foot on his head while Miles and Shelby tied him up with the kind of twine used to secure a tenderloin. His empty eyes stared up at Luce, but also through her.

They'd gagged him with a kitchen rag, so when Arriane taunted, "You want to chill out for a little bit? In the meat cooler?" the boy could only groan. He'd stopped putting up any kind of fight.

Grabbing him by the collar, Arriane dragged him across the floor and into the walk-in refrigerator, gave him a few more kicks for good measure, then calmly shut the door. She dusted off her hands and turned to Luce with a ticked-off look on her face.

"Who's after me, Arriane?" Luce's voice was shaking.

"A lot of people, babe."

"Was that"—Luce thought back to her meeting with Cam—"an Outcast?"

Arriane cleared her throat. Shelby coughed.

"Daniel said he couldn't be with me because he attracted too much attention. He said I'd be safe at Shoreline, but they came there, too—"

"Only because they traced you leaving campus. *You* attract attention too, Luce. And when you're out in the world tearing up casinos and the like, we can sense it. That goes for the bad guys, too. That's why you're at that school in the first place."

"What?" It was Shelby. "You guys are just hiding her with us? What about our safety? What if these Outcasts people just showed up on campus?"

Miles said nothing, just looked with alarm from Luce to Arriane.

"You didn't understand that the Nephilim camouflage you?" Arriane asked. "Daniel didn't tell you about their—whatever, protective coloration?"

Luce's mind rolled back to the night Daniel dropped her off at Shoreline. "Maybe he did say something about a shield, but—" There had been so many other things racing through her mind that night. It had been enough to try to process Daniel's leaving her. Now she felt a queasy wave of guilt. "I didn't understand. He didn't elaborate, just kept saying I had to stay on campus. I thought he was being too protective."

"Daniel knows what he's doing." Arriane shrugged. "Most of the time." She poked her tongue at the corner of her mouth thoughtfully. "Okay, sometimes. Every now and then."

"So you mean whoever's after her can't see her when she's with a bunch of Nephilim?" This was Miles, who seemed to have found his tongue again.

"Actually, the Outcasts can't see at all," Arriane said. "They were blinded during the Revolt. I was getting to that part of the story—it's good! The putting out of eyes and all that Oedipal jazz." She sighed. "Oh, well. Yeah, the Outcasts. They can see the burning of your soul—which is a lot more difficult to discern when you're with a bunch of other Nephilim."

Miles's eyes grew wide. Shelby was chewing nervously on her nails.

"So that's how they mistook Dawn for me."

"It's how meat-cooler boy found you tonight, anyway," Arriane said. "Hell, it's how I found you too. You're like a candle in a dark cave out here." She grabbed a can of whipped cream from the counter and shot a squirt into her mouth. "I like a little nondairy pick-me-up after a brawl." She yawned, which made Luce look up at the green digital clock on the counter. It was two-thirty in the morning.

"Well, as much as I love kicking asses and taking names, it's way past curfew for you three." Arriane whistled through her teeth and a thick blob of an Announcer bled out from the shadows under the prep tables. "I never do this, okay? If anyone asks, I *never* do this. Traveling by Announcers is ver-ry dangerous. Hear that, hero?" She bopped Miles on his forehead, then flicked her fingers open. The shadow bounced instantly into a perfect door shape in the middle of the kitchen. "But I'm on the clock here and it's the fastest way to get you guys home and to safety."

"Nice," Miles said, like he was taking notes.

Arriane shook her head at him. "Don't get any ideas. I'm taking you back to school, where you will stay"— she made eye contact with each of them—"or you're going to have to answer to me."

"You're coming with us?" Shelby asked, finally showing just a little glimmer of awe toward Arriane.

"Looks that way." Arriane winked at Luce. "You've turned into some kind of firecracker. Someone's gotta keep an eye on you."

✵

Stepping through with Arriane was even smoother than it had been on the way to Vegas. It felt like coming inside after being out in the sun: The light was a little dimmer when you walked through the door, but you blinked a few times and got used to it.

Luce was almost disappointed to find herself back in her dorm room after the flash and excitement of Las Vegas. But then she thought of Dawn, and of Vera. *Almost* disappointed. Her eyes settled on all the familiar signs that they were back: two unmade bunk beds, the clutter of plants on the windowsill, Shelby's yoga mats stacked in the corner, Steven's copy of Plato's *Republic* sitting bookmarked on Luce's desk—and one thing she was not expecting to see.

Daniel, dressed all in black, tending a blazing fire in the hearth.

"Aaaugh!" Shelby screamed, tumbling back into Miles's arms. "You scared the hell out of me! And in my own place of sanctuary. Not cool, Daniel." She shot Luce a dirty look, like she'd had something to do with his appearance.

Daniel ignored Shelby, just said calmly to Luce, "Welcome back."

She didn't know whether to run to him or burst into tears. "Daniel—"

"*Daniel?*" Arriane gasped. Her eyes widened as if she'd seen a ghost.

Daniel froze, clearly not having expected to encounter Arriane, either. "I—I just need her for a moment. Then I'll go." He sounded guilty, even scared.

"Right," Arriane said, gripping Miles and Shelby by the scruffs of their neck. "We were just leaving. *None* of us saw you here." She herded the others before her. "We'll catch you later, Luce."

Shelby looked like she couldn't get out of their dorm

room quickly enough. Miles's eyes looked stormy, and they stayed fixed on Luce until Arriane practically threw him into the hall, slamming the door behind them with a great boom.

Then Daniel came to Luce. She closed her eyes and let the brush of his nearness warm her. She breathed him in, glad to be home. Not home to Shoreline, but the home that Daniel made her feel. Even when she was in the strangest of places. Even when their relationship was a mess.

As it seemed to be now.

He wasn't kissing her yet, wasn't even taking her in his arms. It surprised her that she wanted him to do those things, even after all she had seen. The absence of his touch caused a pain deep within her chest. When she opened her eyes he was standing there, only inches away, poring over every part of her with his violet eyes.

"You scared me."

She'd never heard him say that. *She* was used to being the one who was afraid.

"Are you all right?" he asked.

Luce shook her head. Daniel took her hand and guided her wordlessly to the window, out of the warm room near the fire and back into the cold night, onto the rough ledge under the window where he'd come to her before.

The moon was oblong and low in the sky. The owls

were asleep in the redwoods. From up here Luce could see the waves breaking smoothly on the shore; on the other side of campus, a single light on high in the Nephilim lodge, but she couldn't tell whether it was Francesca's or Steven's.

She and Daniel sat down on the ledge and dangled their legs. They leaned against the slight slope of the roof behind them and looked up at the stars, which were dim in the sky, as if cloaked by the thinnest sheen of cloud. It wasn't long before Luce began to cry.

Because he was mad at her or she was mad at him. Because her body had just been through so much, in and out of Announcers, across state lines, into the recent past and right back here. Because her heart and her head were tangled up and confused, and being close to Daniel mucked everything up even more. Because Miles and Shelby seemed to hate him. Because of the plain horror on Vera's face when she recognized Luce. Because of all the tears that her sister must have cried for her, and because Luce had hurt her all over again by showing up at her blackjack table. Because of all of her other bereaved families, sunk into sadness because their daughters had the bad luck to be the reincarnation of a stupid girl in love. Because thinking of those families made Luce desperately miss her parents back in Thunderbolt. Because she was responsible for Dawn's kidnapping. Because she was seventeen, and still alive, against thousands of years' worth of odds. Because she knew enough to fear what the future would bring. Because in the meantime it was three-thirty in the morning, and she hadn't slept in days, and she didn't know what else to do.

Now he held her, encasing her body in his warmth, drawing her into him and rocking her in his arms. She sobbed and hiccupped and wished for a tissue to blow her nose. She wondered how it was possible to feel so bad about so many things at once.

"Shhh," Daniel whispered. "Shhh."

A day ago, she'd been sick watching Daniel love her into oblivion in that Announcer. The inescapable violence sewn into their relationship had seemed insurmountable. But now, especially after talking with Arriane, Luce could feel something big coming on. Something shifting—maybe the whole world shifting—with Luce and Daniel hovering right on the edge. It was all around them, in the ether, and it affected the way she saw herself, and Daniel, too.

The helpless looks she'd seen in his eyes in those just-before-dying moments: Now they felt like—they *were*—the past. It reminded her of the way he'd looked at her after their first kiss in this life on the marshy beach near Sword & Cross. The taste of his lips on hers, the feel of his breath on her neck, his strong hands wrapped around her: It had all been so wonderful—except for the fear in his eyes.

But Daniel hadn't looked at her like that in a while.

The way he looked at her now surrendered nothing. He looked at her as if she were going to stick around, almost as if she had to. Things were different in this life. Everyone was saying it, and Luce could feel it, too: a revelation growing ever larger inside her. She'd watched herself die, and she'd survived it. Daniel didn't have to shoulder his punishment alone anymore. It was something they could do together.

"I want to say something," she said into his shirt, wiping her eyes on her sleeve. "I want to talk before you say anything."

She could feel his chin brushing the top of her head. He was nodding.

"I know you have to be careful about what you tell me. I know I've died before. But I'm not going anywhere this time, Daniel, I can feel it. At least, not without a fight." She tried to smile. "I think it will help us both to stop treating me like a fragile piece of glass. So I'm asking you, as your friend, as your girlfriend, as, you know, the love of your life, to let me in a little more. Otherwise I just feel isolated and anxious and—"

He caught her chin with his finger and tilted her head up. He was eyeing her curiously. She waited for him to interrupt, but he didn't.

"I didn't leave Shoreline to spite you," she continued. "I left because I didn't understand why it mattered. And I put my friends in danger because of it."

Daniel held her face in front of his. The violet in his

eyes practically glowed. "I have failed you too many times before," he whispered. "And in this life maybe I've erred on the side of caution. I should have known you'd test whatever boundary you were given. You wouldn't be . . . the girl I loved if you didn't." Luce waited for him to smile down at her. He didn't. "There's just so much at stake this time around. I've been so focused on—"

"The Outcasts?"

"They're the ones who took your friend," Daniel said. "They can barely identify right from left, let alone which side they're working for."

Luce thought back to the girl Cam had shot with the silver arrow, to the good-looking empty-eyed boy in the diner. "Because they're blind."

Daniel looked down at his hands, rubbing his fingers together. He looked as if he might be sick. "Blind but very brutal." He reached up and traced one of her blond curls with his finger. "You were smart to dye your hair. It kept you safe when I couldn't get there fast enough."

"Smart?" Luce was horrified. "Dawn could have *died* because I got my hands on a cheap bottle of bleach. How is that smart? If . . . if I dyed my hair black tomorrow, you mean the Outcasts would suddenly be able to find me?"

Daniel shook his head roughly. "They shouldn't have found their way onto this campus at all. They should never have been able to get their hands on any of you. I am working night and day to keep them from you—from this whole school. Someone's aiding them, and I don't know who—"

"Cam." What else would he have been doing here?

But Daniel shook his head. "Whoever it is will regret it."

Luce crossed her arms over her chest. Her face still felt hot from crying. "I guess this means I don't get to go home for Thanksgiving?" She closed her eyes, trying not to picture her parents' crestfallen faces. "Don't answer that."

"Please." Daniel's voice was so earnest. "It's only for a little while longer."

She nodded. "The truce timeline."

"What?" His hands gripped her shoulders tightly. "How did you—"

"I know." Luce hoped he couldn't feel that her body had begun to tremble. It got worse when she tried to act more assured than she felt. "And I know that at some point soon, you will tip the balance between Heaven and Hell."

"Who told you that?" Daniel was arching his shoulders back, which she knew meant he was trying to keep his wings from unfurling.

"I figured it out. A lot goes on here when you're not around."

A hint of envy flashed through Daniel's eyes. At first, it felt almost good to be able to provoke that in him, but Luce didn't want to make him jealous. Especially with so many bigger things at hand.

"I'm sorry," she said. "The last thing you need right now is me distracting you. What you're doing . . . it sounds like a pretty big deal."

She left it at that, hoping Daniel would feel comfortable enough to tell her more. This was the most open, honest, and mature conversation they'd had, maybe ever.

But then, too soon, the cloud she hadn't even known she'd been dreading passed over Daniel's face. "Put all of that out of your head. You don't know what you think you know."

Disappointment flooded through Luce's body. He was still treating her like a child. One step forward, ten steps back.

She gathered her feet under her and stood up on the ledge.

"I know one thing, Daniel," she said, staring down at him. "If it were me, there wouldn't be a question. If it were *me* the whole universe was waiting on to tip the scales, I would just pick the side of good."

Daniel's violet eyes stared straight ahead, into the shadowy forest.

"You would just pick good," he repeated. His voice

sounded both numb and desperately sad. Sadder than she'd ever heard him sound before.

Luce had to resist the urge to crouch down and apologize. Instead, she turned, leaving Daniel behind her. Wasn't it obvious that he was supposed to pick good? Wouldn't anyone?

FOURTEEN

FIVE DAYS

Someone had ratted them out.

On Sunday morning, while the rest of the campus was still eerily calm, Shelby, Miles, and Luce sat in a row on one side of Francesca's office, waiting to be interrogated. Her office was larger than Steven's—brighter, too, with a high, sloping ceiling and three large windows facing the forest to the north, each with thick lavender velvet curtains, parted to show a shocking blue sky. A large framed photograph of a galaxy, hanging over the tall marble-topped desk, was the only piece of art in the room. The baroque chairs they sat on were chic but uncomfortable. Luce couldn't stop fidgeting.

"'Anonymous tip,' my ass," Shelby muttered, quoting the harsh email they'd each received from Francesca this morning. "This immature tattling reeks of Lilith."

Luce didn't think it was possible that Lilith—or any of the students, really—would have known they'd left campus. Someone else had looped their teachers in.

"What's taking them so long?" Miles nodded toward Steven's office on the other side of the wall, where they could hear their teachers arguing in low voices. "It's like they're coming up with a punishment before they've even heard our side of the story!" He bit his lower lip. "What *is* our side of the story, by the way?"

But Luce wasn't listening. "I really don't see what's so difficult," she said under her breath, more to herself than the others. "You just pick a side and move on."

"Huh?" Miles and Shelby said in unison.

"Sorry," Luce said. "It's just . . . you know what Arriane was saying about tipping the scales the other night? I brought it up to Daniel, and he got all weird. Seriously, how is it not obvious that there's a right answer here and a wrong one?"

"It's obvious to me," Miles said. "There's a good choice and a bad choice."

"How can you say that?" Shelby asked. "That kind

of thinking is exactly what got us into this mess in the first place. Blind faith! Blanket acceptance of a practically obsolete dichotomy!" Her face was turning red and her voice had gotten loud enough that Francesca and Steven could probably hear. "I am so sick of all these angels and demons taking sides—blah blah blah, they're evil! No, *they're* evil! On and on—like they know what's best for everyone in the universe."

"So you're suggesting Daniel side with evil?" Miles scoffed. "Bring on the end of the world?"

"I don't give a damn what Daniel does," Shelby said. "And frankly, I find it hard to believe that it's all up to him, anyway."

But it had to be. Luce couldn't think of any other explanation.

"Look, maybe the lines aren't as clear-cut as we're taught they are," Shelby continued. "I mean, who says Lucifer is so bad—"

"Um, everyone?" Miles said, looking to Luce for support.

"Wrong," Shelby barked. "A group of very persuasive angels trying to preserve the status quo. Just because they won a big battle a long time ago, they think it gives them the right."

Luce watched Shelby's eyebrows bunch up as she slumped against the rigid back of her chair. Her words made Luce think of something she'd heard somewhere else. . . .

"The victors rewrite history," she murmured. That was what Cam had said to her that day at Noyo Point. Wasn't that what Shelby meant? That the losers ended up with a bad rap? Their viewpoints were both similar—only, Cam, of course, was legitimately evil. Right? And Shelby was just talking.

"Exactly." Shelby nodded at Luce. "Wait—what?"

Just then, Francesca and Steven walked through the door. Francesca lowered herself into the black swivel chair at her desk. Steven stood behind her, his hands resting lightly on the back of the chair. He looked as breezy in his jeans and crisp white shirt as Francesca looked severe in her tailored black dress with the rigid square-cut neckline.

It brought to Luce's mind Shelby's talk about blurred lines, and the connotations of words like *angel* and *demon*. Of course it was superficial to make judgments based solely on Steven's and Francesca's clothing, but then again, it wasn't just that. In a lot of ways, it was easy to forget which one of them was which.

"Who wants to go first?" Francesca asked, resting her interlaced manicured hands on the marble desktop. "We know everything that happened, so don't even bother contesting those details. This is your chance to tell us why."

Luce inhaled deeply. Though she hadn't been prepared for Francesca to turn over the floor so soon, she didn't want Miles or Shelby trying to cover for her. "It was my fault," she said. "I wanted to—" She looked at Steven's drawn expression, then down at her lap. "I saw something in the Announcers, something from my past, and I wanted to see more."

"And so you went for a dangerous joyride—an unauthorized passage through an Announcer, imperiling two of your classmates who really should have known better—the day after another one of your classmates was kidnapped?" Francesca asked.

"That's not fair," Luce said. "*You* were the one downplaying what happened to Dawn. We thought we were just going to look into something, but—"

"But . . . ?" Steven prodded. "But you realize now how utterly moronic that line of thinking was?"

Luce gripped her chair's armrests, trying to fight back tears. Francesca was cross with all three of them, but it seemed that all of Steven's fury was coming down solely on Luce. It wasn't fair.

"Yes, okay, we snuck out of school and went to Vegas," she said finally. "But the only reason we were in danger was because *you* kept me in the dark. You knew someone was after me and you probably even know why. I wouldn't have left campus if you'd just told me."

Steven stared Luce down with eyes like fire. "If you're saying we honestly have to be *that* explicit with you, Luce, then I am disappointed." He cupped a hand on Francesca's shoulder. "Perhaps you were right about her, dear."

"Wait—" Luce said.

But Francesca made a stop sign with her hand. "Need we also be explicit about the fact that the opportunity you've been given at Shoreline for educational and personal growth is—for you—a once-in-a-thousand-lifetimes experience?" A pink flush rose on her cheeks. "You've created a very awkward situation for us. The main school"—she gestured to the south portion of campus—"has its detentions and its community service programs for students who step out of line. But Steven and I don't have a system of punishment in place. We've been fortunate until now to have students who did not overstep our very lenient boundaries."

"Until now," Steven said, looking at Luce. "But Francesca and I both agree that a swift and severe sentence must be handed down."

Luce leaned forward in her chair. "But Shelby and Miles didn't—"

"Exactly." Francesca nodded. "Which is why, when you are dismissed, Shelby and Miles will report to Mr. Kramer in the main school for community service. Shoreline's annual Harvest Fest food drive begins tomorrow, so I'm sure you'll have your work cut out for you."

"What a crock of—" Shelby broke off, looking up at Francesca. "I mean, Harvest Fest sounds like my kind of *fun*."

"What about Luce?" Miles asked.

Steven's arms were crossed and his complicated hazel eyes peered down at Luce over the tortoiseshell rims of his glasses. "Effectively, Luce, you're grounded."

Grounded? That was it?

"Class. Meals. Dorm," Francesca recited. "Until you hear differently from us, and unless you are under our strict supervision—these are the only places you will be permitted. And *no* dipping into Announcers. Understand?"

Luce nodded.

Steven added: "Do not test us again. Even our patience comes to an end."

⁂

Class-Meals-Dorm didn't leave Luce with a lot of options on a Sunday morning. The lodge was dark, and the mess hall didn't open for brunch until eleven. After Miles and Shelby shuffled off reluctantly toward Mr. Kramer's community service boot camp, Luce had no choice but to go back to her room. She closed the window shade, which Shelby always liked to leave open, then sank into her desk chair.

It could have been worse. Compared to the stories of cramped cinder-block cells for solitary confinement at Sword & Cross, it almost seemed like she was getting off easy. No one was slapping a pair of wristband tracking devices on her. In fact, Steven and Francesca had basically given her the same restrictions Daniel had. The difference was, her teachers really *could* watch over her night and day. Daniel, on the other hand, wasn't supposed to be there at all.

Annoyed, she powered up her computer, half expecting her access to the Internet to be suddenly restricted. But she logged on just as usual and found three emails from her parents and one from Callie. Maybe the bright side of being grounded was that she'd be forced to finally stay in better contact with her friends and family.

To: lucindap44@gmail.com
From: thegaprices@aol.com
Sent: Friday, 11/20 at 8:22am
Subject: Turkey-dog

Check out this picture! We dressed Andrew up as a turkey for the neighborhood autumn block party. As you can tell from the bite marks on the feathers: He loved it. What do you think? Should we make him wear it again when you come for Thanksgiving?

To: lucindap44@gmail.com
From: thegaprices@aol.com
Sent: Friday, 11/20 at 9:06am
Subject: PS

Your dad read my email and thought it might have made you feel bad. No guilt trip intended, sweetie. If you're allowed to come home for Thanksgiving, we'd love it. If you can't, we'll reschedule for another time. We love you.

To: lucindap44@gmail.com
From: thegaprices@aol.com
Sent: Saturday, 11/21 at 12:12am
Subject: no subject

Just let us know either way? xoxo, Mom

Luce held her head in her hands. She'd been wrong. All the grounding in the world wouldn't make it easier for her to respond to her parents. They'd dressed their poodle up as a turkey, for crying out loud! It broke her heart to think of letting them down. So she procrastinated by opening Callie's email.

To: lucindap44@gmail.com
From: callieallieoxenfree@gmail.com
Sent: Friday, 11/20 at 4:14pm
Subject: HERE IT IS!

I believe the flight reservation below speaks for itself. Send me your address and I'll take a cab when I get in on Thursday morning. My first time in Georgia! With my long-lost

best friend! It's going to be soooo peachy! See you in
SIX DAYS!

In less than a week, Luce's best friend would be showing up for Thanksgiving at her parents' house, her parents
would be expecting her, and Luce would be right here,
grounded in her dorm room. An enormous sadness engulfed her. She would have given anything to go to them,
to spend a few days with people who loved her, who would
give her a break from the exhausting, confusing couple of
weeks she'd spent shackled within these wooden walls.

She opened a new email and composed a hasty message:

To: cole321@swordandcross.edu
From: lucindap44@gmail.com
Sent: Sunday, 11/22 at 9:33am

Hi, Mr. Cole.

Don't worry, I'm not going to beg you to let me go home for
Thanksgiving. I know a hopeless waste of effort when I see
one. But I don't have the heart to tell my parents. Will you let
them know? Tell them I'm sorry.

Things here are fine. Sort of. I am homesick.

Luce

A thumping knock at the door made Luce jump—and click Send on the email without proofreading it first for typos or embarrassing admissions of emotion.

"Luce!" Shelby's voice called from the other side. "Open up! My hands are full of Harvest Fest crap. I mean, *bounty*." The thuds continued on the other side of the door, louder now, with the occasional whimpering grunt thrown in.

Pulling open the door, Luce found a panting Shelby, sagging under the weight of an enormous cardboard box. She had several stretched-out plastic bags threaded through her fingers. Her knees trembled as she staggered into the room.

"Can I help with something?" Luce took the feather-light wicker cornucopia that was resting on Shelby's head like a conical hat.

"They put me on Decorations," Shelby grumbled, heaving the box onto the ground. "I'd give anything to be on Garbage, like Miles. Do you even know what happened the last time someone made me use a hot-glue gun?"

Luce felt responsible for both Shelby's and Miles's punishments. She pictured Miles combing the beach with one of those trash-poking sticks she'd seen convicts using on the side of the road in Thunderbolt. "I don't even know what Harvest Fest is."

"Obnoxious and pretentious, that's what," Shelby

said, digging through the box and tossing onto the floor plastic bags of feathers, tubs of glitter, and a ream of autumn-colored construction paper. "It's basically a big banquet where all of Shoreline's donors come out to raise money for the school. Everyone goes home feeling all charitable because they unloaded a few old cans of green beans on a food bank in Fort Bragg. You'll see tomorrow night."

"I doubt it," Luce said. "Remember, I'm grounded?"

"Don't worry, you'll be dragged to this. Some of the biggest donors are angel advocates, so Frankie and Steven have to put on a show. Which means the Nephilim all have to be there, smiling pretty."

Luce frowned, glancing up at her non-Nephilim reflection in the mirror. All the more reason she should stay right here.

Shelby cursed under her breath. "I left the stupid paint-by-number turkey centerpiece in Mr. Kramer's office," she said, standing up and giving the box of decorations a kick. "I have to go back."

When Shelby pushed past her toward the door, Luce lost her balance and started to tumble, tripping over the box and snagging her foot on something cold and wet on the way down.

She landed face-first on the wood floor. The only thing breaking her fall was the plastic bag of feathers, which popped, shooting colorful fluff out from under her. Luce looked back to see how much damage she had done, expecting Shelby's eyebrows to be joined in exasperation. But Shelby was standing still with one hand pointing toward the center of the room. A smog-brown Announcer was quietly floating there.

"Isn't that a little risky?" Shelby asked. "Summoning an Announcer an hour after getting busted for summoning an Announcer? You really don't listen at all, do you? I kind of admire that."

"I didn't summon it," Luce insisted, pulling herself up and picking the feathers out of her clothes. "I tripped and it was just there, waiting or something." She stepped closer to examine the hazy, dun-colored sheet. It was as flat as a piece of paper and not large for an Announcer, but the way it hung in the air in front of her face, almost daring her to reject it, made Luce nervous.

It didn't seem to need her to guide it into shape at all. It hovered, barely moving, looking like it could have floated there all day.

"Wait a minute," Luce murmured. "This came in with the other one the other day. Don't you remember?" This was the strange brown shadow that had flown in tandem with the darker shadow that took them to Vegas. They'd both come in through the window Friday afternoon; then this one had disappeared. Luce had forgotten about it until now.

"Well," Shelby said, leaning against the ladder of the bunk bed. "Are you going to glimpse it or what?"

The Announcer was the color of a smoky room, noxious brown and mistlike to the touch. Luce reached for it, running her fingers along its clammy limits. She felt its cloudy breath brush back her hair. The air around this Announcer was humid, even briny. A far-away croon of seagulls echoed from within.

She shouldn't glimpse it. Wouldn't glimpse it.

But there was the Announcer, shifting from a smoky brown mesh into something clear and discernible, independently of Luce. There was the message cast by its shadow coming to life.

It was an aerial view of an island. At first, they were high above, so that all Luce could see was a small swell of steep black rock with a fringe of tapered pine trees ringing its base. Then, slowly, the Announcer zoomed in, like a bird swooping down to roost in the treetops, its focus a small, deserted beach.

The water was murky from the claylike silver sand. A scattering of boulders reckoned with the smooth intentions of the tide. And standing inconspicuously between two of the tallest rocks—

Daniel was staring at the sea. The tree branch in his hand was covered in blood.

Luce gasped as she leaned closer and saw what Daniel was looking at. Not the sea, but a bloody mess of a man. A dead man, lying stiff on the sand. Each time the waves reached the body, they receded stained a deep, dark red. But Luce couldn't see the wound that had killed the man. Someone else, in a long black trench coat, was crouched over the body, tying it up with thick braided rope.

Her heart thudding, Luce looked again at Daniel. His expression was even, but his shoulders were twitching.

"Hurry up. You're wasting time. The tide's going out now, anyway."

His voice was so cold, it made Luce shiver.

A second later, the scene in the Announcer disappeared. Luce held her breath until it dropped to the ground in a heap. Then, across the room, the window shade Luce had pulled down earlier rattled open. Luce and Shelby shot each other an anxious look, then watched as a gust of wind caught the Announcer and lofted it up and out the window.

Luce clutched Shelby's wrist. "You notice everything. Who else was there with Daniel? Who was crouched over that"—she shivered again—"guy?"

"Gee, I don't know, Luce. I was kind of distracted by the *dead body*. Not to mention the bloody *tree* your boyfriend was holding." Shelby's attempt to be sarcastic was diminished by how terrified she sounded. "So he killed him?" she asked Luce. "Daniel killed whoever that was?"

"I don't know." Luce winced. "Don't say it like that. Maybe there's a logical explanation—"

"What do you think he was saying at the end?" Shelby asked. "I saw his lips move but I couldn't make it out. I hate that about Announcers."

Hurry up. You're wasting time. The tide's going out now, anyway.

Shelby hadn't heard that? How callous and unremorseful Daniel sounded?

Then Luce remembered: It wasn't that long ago that she couldn't hear the Announcers either. Before, their noises used to be just that—noises: rustlings and thick, wet whooshes through treetops. It was Steven who'd told her how to tune in the voices inside. In a way, Luce almost wished he hadn't.

There had to be more to this message. "I have to glimpse it again," Luce said, stepping toward the open window. Shelby tugged her back.

"Oh, no you don't. That Announcer could be anywhere by now, and you're under dorm arrest, remember?" Shelby pushed Luce down in her desk chair. "You're going to stay right here while I go down to Kramer's office to retrieve my turkey. We're both going to forget this ever happened. Okay?"

"Okay."

"Good. I'll be back in five minutes, so don't disappear on me."

But as soon as the door closed, Luce was out the window, climbing to the flat part of the ledge where she and

Daniel had sat the night before. Putting what she'd just seen out of her mind was impossible. She had to summon that shadow again. Even if it got her in more trouble. Even if she saw something she didn't like.

The late morning had turned gusty, and Luce had to crouch down and hold on to the slanting wooden shingles to keep her balance. Her hands were cold. Her heart felt numb. She closed her eyes. Every time she tried to summon an Announcer, she remembered how little training she'd had. She'd always just been lucky—if watching your boyfriend look down at someone he'd just murdered could be considered luck.

A damp brushing crept along her arms. Was it the brown shadow, the ugly thing that showed her an even uglier thing? Her eyes shot open.

It was. Creeping up her shoulder like a snake. She yanked it off and held it in front of her, trying to spin it into a ball with her hands. The Announcer rejected her touch, floating backward, out of her reach just past the roof's edge.

She looked down two stories to the ground below. A trail of students were leaving the dorm to head to the mess hall for brunch, a stream of color moving along a sheet of bright green grass. Luce teetered. Vertigo hit, and she felt herself falling forward.

But then the shadow rushed like a football player, knocking her back against the slope of the roof. There she stayed, stuck against the shingles, panting as the Announcer yawned open again.

The smoky veil diffused into light, and Luce was back with Daniel and his bloody branch. Back to the caw of seagulls circling overhead and the stench of rotting surf along the shore, the sight of icy waves crashing on the beach. And back to the two figures huddled on the ground. The dead one was all tied up. The living one stood to face Daniel.

Cam.

No. It had to be a mistake. They hated one another. Had just waged a huge battle against one another. She could accept that Daniel did dark things to protect her from the people who were after her. But what foul thing would ever make him seek out Cam? Work alongside Cam—who took pleasure in killing?

They were in a heated discussion of some sort, but Luce couldn't make out the words. She couldn't hear anything over the clock in the middle of the terrace, which had just struck eleven. She strained her ears, waiting for the gongs to cease.

"Let me take her to Shoreline," she finally heard Daniel plead.

This must have been right before she arrived in California. But why should Daniel have to ask Cam's permission? Unless—

"Fine," Cam said evenly. "Take her as far as the

school and then find me. Don't screw up; I'll be watching."

"And then?" Daniel sounded nervous.

Cam ran his eyes over Daniel's face. "You and I have work to do."

"No!" Luce screamed, slashing at the shadow with her fingers in anger.

But as soon as she felt her hands break through the cold, slippery surface, she regretted it. It broke into spent fragments, settling into an ashy pile at her side. Now she couldn't see anymore. She tried to gather the fragments up the way she'd seen Miles do, but they were quivering and unresponsive.

She grabbed a fistful of the worthless pieces, sobbing into them.

Steven had said that sometimes the Announcers distorted what was real. Like the shadows cast on the cave wall. But that there was always some truth to them too. Luce could feel the truth in the cold, soggy pieces, even as she wrung them out, trying to squeeze out all her agony.

Daniel and Cam weren't enemies. They were partners.

FIFTEEN

FOUR DAYS

"More Tofurky?" Connor Madson—a towheaded kid from Luce's biology class and one of Shoreline's student waiters—stood over her with a silver platter at the Harvest Fest on Monday night.

"No, thanks." Luce pointed down at the thick stack of lukewarm fake meat slices still on her plate.

"Maybe later." Connor and the rest of the scholarship wait staff at Shoreline were suited up for the Harvest Fest in tuxedos and ridiculous pilgrim hats. They glided past each other on the terrace, which was nearly unrecognizable as the swanky-casual place to grab some pancakes before class; it had been transformed into a full-fledged outdoor banquet hall.

Shelby was still grumbling as she moved from table to table, adjusting place cards and relighting candles. She and the rest of the Decorations Committee had done a beautiful job: Red-and-orange silk leaves had been strewn across the long white tablecloths, fresh-baked dinner rolls were arranged inside gold-painted cornucopias, heat lamps took the edge off the brisk ocean breeze. Even the paint-by-number turkey centerpieces looked stylish.

All the students, the faculty, and about fifty of the school's biggest donors had turned out in their finest for the dinner. Dawn and her parents had driven up for the night. Though Luce hadn't gotten a chance to talk to Dawn yet, she looked recovered, even happy, and had waved to Luce cheerfully from her seat next to Jasmine.

Most of the twenty or so Nephilim were seated together at two adjacent circular tables, with the exception of Roland, who was sitting in a faraway corner with a mysterious date. Then the mysterious date stood up, lifted her broad rosebud-shaped hat, and gave Luce a sneaky little wave.

Arriane.

Despite herself, Luce smiled—but a second later, she

felt close to tears. Watching those two snickering to-gether reminded Luce of the sickeningly sinister scene she had glimpsed in the Announcer the day before. Like Cam and Daniel, Arriane and Roland were supposed to be on opposite sides, but everybody knew they were a team.

Still, that felt different somehow.

Harvest Fest was supposed to be a last pre-Thanksgiving hurrah before classes were dismissed. Then everyone else would have another Thanksgiving, a real Thanksgiving, with their families. For Luce, it was the *only* Thanksgiving she was going to get. Mr. Cole hadn't written her back. After yesterday's grounding and then the rooftop revelation, she was having a hard time feeling thankful for much of anything.

"You're hardly eating," Francesca said, spooning a great dollop of shiny mashed potatoes onto Luce's plate. Luce was growing more attuned to the thrilling glow that fell over everything when Francesca was talking to her. Francesca possessed an otherworldly charisma, sim-ply by virtue of being an angel.

She beamed at Luce like there'd been no meeting in her office yesterday, like Luce wasn't under lock and key.

Luce had been given the seat of honor at the expan-sive faculty head table, next to Francesca. All the donors came by in a stream to shake hands with the faculty. The three other students at the head table—Lilith, Beaker

Brady, and a Korean girl with a dark bob Luce didn't know—had applied for their seats in an essay contest. All Luce had had to do was piss off her teachers enough that they were afraid to let her out of their sight.

The meal was finally wrapping up when Steven leaned forward in his chair. Like Francesca, he displayed none of yesterday's venom. "Make sure Luce introduces herself to Dr. Buchanan."

Francesca popped the last bite of a buttered corn bread muffin into her mouth. "Buchanan's one of the biggest supporters of the school," she told Luce. "You might have heard of his Devils Abroad program?"

Luce shrugged as the waiters reappeared to clear the plates.

"His ex-wife had angel lineage, but after the divorce he shifted some of his alliances. Still"—Francesca glanced at Steven—"a very good person to know. Oh, hello, Ms. Fisher! How nice of you to come."

"Yes, hello." An elderly woman with an affected British accent, a bulky mink coat, and more diamonds around her neck than Luce had ever seen before extended a white-gloved hand to Steven, who stood up to greet her. Francesca rose too, leaning forward to greet the woman with a kiss on either cheek. "Where's my Miles?" the woman asked.

Luce jumped up. "Oh, you must be Miles's . . . grandmother?"

"Good heavens, no." The woman recoiled. "Don't have children, never married, boo-hoo-hoo. I am Ms. Ginger Fisher, from the NorCal branch of the family tree. Miles is my great-nephew. And you are?"

"Lucinda Price."

"Lucinda Price, yes." Ms. Fisher looked down her nose at Luce, squinting. "Read about you in one or another of the histories. Though I can't recall what it was exactly that you did—"

Before Luce could respond, Steven's hands were on her shoulders. "Luce is one of our newest students," he boomed. "You'll be happy to know that Miles has really gone out of his way to make her feel comfortable here."

Ms. Fisher's squinty eyes were already looking past them, searching the crowded lawn. The guests had mostly finished eating, and now Shelby was lighting the tiki torches staked into the ground. When the torch closest to the head table grew bright, it illuminated Miles, leaning over the next table to clear away some plates.

"Is that my grand-nephew—*waiting tables?*" Ms. Fisher pressed a gloved hand to her forehead.

"Actually," Shelby said, butting into the conversation, the torch lighter in one hand, "he's the trash—"

"Shelby." Francesca cut her off. "I think that tiki torch near the Nephilim tables has just burned out. Could you fix it? *Now?*"

"You know what?" Luce said to Ms. Fisher. "I'll go

get Miles and bring him over. You must be eager to catch up."

Miles had traded in the Dodgers cap and sweatshirt for a pair of brown tweed slacks and a bright orange button-down shirt. Kind of a bold choice, but it looked good.

"Hey!" He waved her over with the hand that wasn't balancing a stack of dirty plates. Miles didn't seem to mind busing tables. He was grinning, in his element, chatting with everyone at the banquet as he cleared their plates.

When Luce approached, he put the plates down and gave her a big hug, squeezing her closer at the end.

"Are you okay?" he asked, tilting his head to one side so that his brown hair flopped over his eyes. He didn't seem used to the way his hair moved without his cap on, and he flicked it quickly back. "You don't look so good. I mean—you *look* great, that's not what I meant. *At all.* I really like that dress. And your hair looks pretty. But you also look kind of"—he frowned—"down."

"That's disturbing." Luce kicked the grass with the toe of her black high heel. "Because this is the best I've felt all night."

"Really?" Miles's face lit up just long enough for him to take it as a compliment. Then it fell. "I know it must suck being grounded. If you ask me, Frankie and Steven are blowing this way out of proportion. Keeping you under their thumbs all night—"

"I know."

"Don't look now, I'm sure they're watching us. Oh, great." He groaned. "Is that my aunt Ginger?"

"I just had the pleasure." Luce laughed. "She wants to see you."

"I'm sure she does. Please don't think all my relatives are like her. When you meet the rest of the clan at Thanksgiving—"

Thanksgiving with Miles. Luce had completely forgotten about that.

"Oh." Miles was watching her face. "You don't think Frankie and Steven are going to make you stay *here* on Thanksgiving?"

Luce shrugged. "I figured that was what 'until further notice' meant."

"So that's what's making you sad." He put a hand on Luce's bare shoulder. She'd been regretting the sleeveless dress until now, until his fingers lay across her skin. It was nothing like Daniel's touch—which was electrifying and magical every time—but it was comforting nonetheless.

Miles stepped closer, lowering his face to hers. "What is it?"

She looked up into his dark blue eyes. His hand was still on her shoulder. She felt her lips parting with the truth, or what she knew of the truth, ready to pour out from inside her.

That Daniel wasn't who she'd thought he was.

Which maybe meant *she* wasn't who she'd thought she was. That everything she'd felt about Daniel at Sword & Cross was still there—it made her dizzy to think about it—but now everything was also so different. And that everyone kept saying that this lifetime was different, that it was time to break the cycle—but no one could tell her what that meant. That maybe it didn't end with Luce and Daniel together. That maybe she was supposed to shake herself free and do something on her own.

"It's hard to put it all into words," she said finally.

"I know," Miles said. "I have a hard time with that myself. Actually, there's something I've sort of been wanting to tell you—"

"Luce." Francesca was suddenly standing there, practically wedging herself between them. "It's time to go. I'll be escorting you back to your room now."

So much for doing something on her own.

"And Miles, your aunt Ginger and Steven would like to see you."

Miles tossed Luce one last sympathetic smile before trudging across the terrace toward his aunt.

The tables were clearing out, but Luce could see Arriane and Roland cracking up near the bar. A cluster of Nephilim girls crowded around Dawn. Shelby was standing beside a tall boy with bleached-blond hair and pale, almost white skin.

SAEB. It had to be. He was leaning into Shelby, clearly still interested, but she was clearly still pissed off.

So pissed off, she didn't even notice Luce and Francesca walking nearby—but her ex-boyfriend did. His gaze hung on Luce. The pale not-quite-blue of his eyes was eerie.

Then someone shouted that the after-party was moving down to the beach, and Shelby snagged SAEB's attention by turning her back on him, saying he'd better not follow her to the party.

"Do you wish you could join them?" Francesca asked as they moved further from the commotion of the terrace. The noise and the wind both quieted as they walked along the gravel path back toward the dorm, passing rows of hot-pink bougainvillea. Luce began to wonder whether Francesca was responsible for the overriding tranquility.

"No." Luce liked all of them well enough, but if she were to attach the word *wish* to anything right now, it wouldn't be to go to some party on the beach. She would wish . . . well, she wasn't sure for what. For something having to do with Daniel, that much she knew—but what? That he would tell her what was going on, perhaps. That instead of protecting her by withholding knowledge, he would fill her in on the truth. She still loved Daniel. Of course she did. He knew her better than anyone. Her heart raced every time she saw him. She yearned for him. But how well, really, did she know him?

Francesca fixed her eyes on the grass lining the path

to the dorm. Very subtly, her arms extended out at either side, like a ballet dancer at the barre.

"Not lilies and not roses," she murmured under her breath as her narrow fingertips started to tremble. "What was it, then?"

There came a soft thrashing sound, like the roots of a plant being pulled from a garden bed, and suddenly, miraculously, a border of moonbeam-white flowers sprang up on either side of the path. Thick and lush and a foot tall, these weren't just any flowers.

They were rare and delicate wild peonies, with buds as big as baseballs. The flowers Daniel had brought Luce when she was in the hospital—and maybe other times before. Edging the path at Shoreline, they shimmered in the night like stars.

"What was that for?" Luce asked.

"For you," Francesca said.

"For what?"

Francesca touched her briefly on the cheek. "Sometimes beautiful things come into our lives out of nowhere. We can't always understand them, but we have to trust in them. I know you want to question everything, but sometimes it pays to just have a little faith."

She was talking about Daniel.

"You look at me and Steven," Francesca went on, "—and I know we can be confusing. Do I love him? Yes. But when the final battle comes, I'll have to kill him.

That's just our reality. We both know exactly where we stand."

"But you don't trust him?"

"I trust him to be true to his nature, which is a demon's. You need to trust that those around you will be true to their natures. Even when it may appear that they are betraying who they are."

"What if it's not that easy?"

"You're strong, Luce, independent of anything or anyone else. The way you responded yesterday in my office, I could see it in you. And it made me very . . . glad."

Luce didn't feel strong. She felt foolish. Daniel was an angel, so his true nature had to be good. She was supposed to blindly accept that? And what about her true nature? Not as black-and-white. Was Luce the reason things between them were so complicated? Long after she'd stepped into her room and closed the door behind her, she couldn't get Francesca's words out of her head.

❈

About an hour later, a knock on the window made Luce jump as she sat staring at the dwindling fire in the hearth. Before she could even get up, there was a second knock on the pane, but this time it sounded more hesitant. Luce rose from the floor and went to the window. What was Daniel doing here again? After making such a huge deal about how unsafe it was to see each other, why did he keep turning up?

She didn't even know what Daniel wanted from her—other than to torment her, the way she'd seen him torment those other versions of her in the Announcers. Or, as he put it, *loved* so many versions of her. Tonight all she wanted from him was to be left alone.

She flung open the wooden shutters, then pushed up the pane, knocking over yet another one of Shelby's thousand plants. She braced her hands on the sill, then plunged her head into the night, ready to rip into Daniel.

But it wasn't Daniel standing on the ledge in the moonlight.

It was Miles.

He'd changed out of his fancy clothes, but he'd left off the Dodgers cap. Most of his body was in shadow, but the outline of his broad shoulders was clear against the deep blue night. His shy smile brought an answering smile to her face. He was holding a gold cornucopia full of orange lilies plucked from one of the Harvest Fest centerpieces.

"Miles," Luce said. The word felt funny in her mouth. It was tinged with pleasant surprise, when a moment ago she'd been so prepared to be nasty. Her heartbeat picked up, and she couldn't stop grinning.

"How crazy is it that I can walk from the ledge outside my window to yours?"

Luce shook her head, stunned too. She'd never even been to Miles's room on the boys' side of the dorm. She didn't even know where it was.

"See?" His smile broadened. "If you hadn't been grounded, we never would have known. It's really pretty out here, Luce; you should come out. You're not scared of heights or anything?"

Luce wanted to go out on the ledge with Miles. She just didn't want to be reminded of the times she'd been out there with Daniel. The two of them were so different. Miles—dependable, sweet, concerned. Daniel—the love of her life. If only it were that simple. It seemed unfair, and impossible, to compare them.

"How come you're not at the beach with everyone?" she asked.

"Not *everyone's* down at the beach." Miles smiled. "You're here." He waved the cornucopia of flowers in the air. "I brought these for you from the dinner. Shelby's got all those plants on her side of the room. I thought you could put these on your desk."

Miles shoved the wicker horn through the window at her. It was brimming with the glossy orange flowers. Their black stamens shivered in the wind. They weren't perfect, a few were even wilting, but they were so much lovelier than the larger-than-life peonies Francesca had made bloom. *Sometimes beautiful things come into our lives out of nowhere.*

This was maybe the nicest thing anyone had done for

her at Shoreline—up there with the time Miles had broken into Steven's office to steal the book so he could
help Luce learn how to step through a shadow. Or the
time Miles had invited her to have breakfast, the very
first day he met her. Or how quick Miles had been to include her in his Thanksgiving plans. Or the utter absence
of resentment on Miles's face when he'd been assigned
garbage duty after she'd gotten him in trouble for sneaking out. Or the way Miles . . .

She could go on, she realized, all night. She carried
the flowers across the room and set them on her desk.

When she came back, Miles was holding out a hand
for her to step through the window. She could make up
an excuse, something lame about not breaking
Francesca's rules. Or she could just take his hand, warm
and strong and safe, and let herself glide through. She
could forget Daniel for just a moment.

Outside, the sky was an explosion of stars. They glittered in the black night like Ms. Fisher's diamonds—but
clearer, brighter, even more beautiful. From here, the
redwood canopy east of the school looked dense and
dark and foreboding; to the west were the ceaselessly
churning water and the distant glow of the bonfire blazing down on the blustery beach. Luce had noticed these
things before from the ledge. Ocean. Forest. Sky. But all
the other times she'd been out here, Daniel had consumed her focus. Almost blinded her, to the point where
she'd never really taken in the scene.

It truly was breathtaking.

"You're probably wondering why I came over," Miles said, which made Luce realize they'd both been silent for a while. "I started to tell you this earlier, but— I didn't—I'm not sure—"

"I'm glad you came by. It was getting a little boring in there, staring at the fire." She gave him half a smile.

Miles stuffed his hands in his pockets. "Look, I know you and Daniel—"

Luce involuntarily groaned.

"You're right, I shouldn't even bring this up—"

"No, that wasn't why I groaned."

"It's just . . . You know I like you, right?"

"Um."

Of course Miles liked her. They were friends. Good friends.

Luce chewed her lip. Now she was playing dumb with herself, which was never a good sign. The truth: Miles *liked* her. And she *liked* him, too. Look at the guy. With his ocean-blue eyes and the little chuckle he gave every time he broke into a smile. Plus, he was hands down the nicest person she had ever met.

But there was Daniel, and before him there'd been Daniel too, and Daniel again and again and—it was endlessly complicated.

"I'm botching this." Miles winced. "When all I really wanted to do was say goodnight."

She looked up at him and found that he was looking

down at her. His hands came out of his pockets, found her hands, and clasped them in the space between their chests. He leaned down slowly, deliberately, giving Luce another chance to feel the spectacular night all around them.

She knew that Miles was going to kiss her. She knew she shouldn't let him. Because of Daniel, of course—but also because of what had happened when she'd kissed Trevor. Her first kiss. The only kiss she'd ever had with anyone besides Daniel. Could being tied to Daniel be the reason Trevor died? What if the second she kissed Miles, he . . . she couldn't even bear to think about it.

"Miles." She pressed him back. "You shouldn't do this. Kissing me is"—she swallowed—"dangerous."

He chuckled. Of course he would, because he didn't know anything about Trevor. "I think I'll take my chances."

She tried to pull back, but Miles had a way of making her feel good about almost everything. Even this. When his mouth came down on hers, she held her breath, waiting for the worst.

But nothing happened.

Miles lips were feather-soft, kissing her gently enough that he still felt like her good friend—but with just enough passion to prove there was more where this one came from. If she wanted it.

But even if there were no flames, no scorched skin,

no death or destruction—and why weren't there?—the kiss was still supposed to *feel* wrong. For so long, all her lips had wanted were Daniel's lips, all the time. She used to dream about his kiss, his smile, his gorgeous violet eyes, his body holding hers. There was never supposed to be anyone else.

What if she'd been wrong about Daniel? What if she could be happier—or happy, period—with another guy?

Miles pulled away, looking happy and sad at the same time. "So, goodnight." He turned away, almost like he was going to bolt back toward his room. But then he turned back. And took her hand. "If you ever feel like things aren't working out, you know, with . . ." He looked up at the sky. "I'm here. Just wanted you to know."

Luce nodded, already battling a rolling wave of confusion. Miles squeezed her hand, then took off in the other direction, bounding over the sloping shingled roof, back toward his side of the dorm.

Alone, she traced her lips where Miles's had just been. The next time she saw Daniel, would he be able to tell? Her head hurt from all the ups and downs of the day, and she wanted to crawl into bed. As she slipped back through the window into her room, she turned one last time to take in the view, to remember how everything had looked on the night when so many things had changed.

But instead of the stars and trees and crashing waves, Luce's eyes fixed on something else behind one of the roof's many chimneys. Something white and billowing. An iridescent pair of wings.

Daniel. Crouched, only half hidden from view, just feet away from where she and Miles had kissed. His back was to her. His head was hanging.

"Daniel," she called out, feeling her voice catch on his name.

When he turned to face her, the drawn look on his face was one of absolute agony. As if Luce had just ripped his heart out. He bent his knees, unfurled his wings, and took off into the night.

A moment later, he looked like just another star in the sparkling black sky.

SIXTEEN

❧ ‡ ❧

THREE DAYS

At breakfast the next morning, Luce could hardly eat anything.

It was the last day of classes before Shoreline dismissed the students for Thanksgiving break, and Luce was already feeling lonely. Loneliness in a crowd of people was the worst kind of loneliness, but she couldn't help it. All the students around her were chattering happily about going home to their families. About the girl or guy they hadn't seen since summer break. About the parties their best friends were throwing over the weekend.

The only party Luce was going to this weekend was the pity party in her empty dorm room.

Of course, a few other students from the main school were staying put over the break: Connor Madson, who had come to Shoreline from an orphanage in Minnesota. Brenna Lee, whose parents lived in China. Francesca and Steven were staying, too—surprise, surprise—and were hosting a Thanksgiving dinner-for-the-displaced in the mess hall Thursday night.

Luce was holding out one hope: That Arriane's threat to keep an eye on her included Thanksgiving break. Then again, she'd barely seen the girl since Arriane had taken the three of them back to Shoreline. Only for that brief moment at Harvest Fest.

Everyone else was checking out in the next day or two. Miles to his family's one-hundred-plus-person catered event. Dawn and Jasmine to their families' joint gathering at Jasmine's Sausalito mansion. Even Shelby— though she hadn't said a word to Luce about going back to Bakersfield—had been on the phone with her mom the day before, groaning, "*Yes. I know. I'll be there.*"

It was the worst possible time for Luce to be left alone. The stew of her inner turmoil grew thicker every day, until she didn't know how to feel about Daniel or anyone else. And she couldn't stop cursing herself for how stupid she'd been the night before, letting Miles go so far.

All night long, she kept arriving at the same conclusion: Even though she was upset with Daniel, what had happened with Miles wasn't anyone's fault but hers. She was the one who'd cheated.

It made her physically ill to think of Daniel sitting out there, watching, saying nothing as she and Miles kissed; to imagine how he must have felt when he took off from her roof. The way she'd felt when she first heard about whatever had happened between Daniel and Shelby—only worse, because this was bona fide cheating. One more thing to add to the list of proofs that she and Daniel could not seem to communicate.

A soft laugh brought her back to her uneaten breakfast.

Francesca was gliding around the tables in a long black-and-white polka-dotted cape. Every time Luce glanced over at her, she had that saccharine smile stuck on her face and was deep in conversation with one student or another, but Luce still felt under heavy scrutiny. As if Francesca could bore into Luce's mind and know exactly what had made Luce lose her appetite. Like the wild white peonies that had disappeared without a trace from their border overnight, so too could Francesca's belief disappear that Luce was strong.

"Why so glum, chum?" Shelby swallowed a large wedge of bagel. "Believe me, you didn't miss that much last night."

Luce didn't answer. The bonfire on the beach was the furthest thing from her mind. She'd just noticed Miles trudging to breakfast, much later than he usually did. His Dodgers cap was tugged low over his eyes, and his shoulders looked a little stooped. Involuntarily, her fingers went to her lips.

Shelby was waving flamboyantly, both arms over her head. "What is he, blind? Earth to Miles!"

When she finally caught his attention, Miles gave their table a clumsy wave, practically tripping over the to-go buffet. He waved again, then disappeared behind the mess hall.

"Is it me or has Miles been acting like a total spaz recently?" Shelby rolled her eyes and imitated Miles's goofy stumble.

But Luce was dying to stumble after him and—

And what? Tell him not to feel embarrassed? That the kiss had been her fault, too? That having a crush on a train wreck like her was only going to end badly? That she liked him, but so many things about it—them—were impossible? That even though she and Daniel were fighting right now, nothing could ever really threaten their love?

"Anyway, like I was saying," Shelby continued, refilling

Luce's coffee from the bronze carafe on the table. "Bonfire, hedonism, blah blah blah. These things can be so tedious." One side of Shelby's mouth flinched to an almost-smile. "Especially, you know, when you're not around."

Luce's heart unclenched just a little. Every once in a while, Shelby let in the tiniest ray of light. But then her roommate quickly shrugged, as if to say *Don't let it go to your head.*

"No one else appreciates my Lilith impersonation. That's all." Shelby straightened her spine, heaved her chest forward, and made the right side of her top lip quiver disapprovingly.

Shelby's Lilith impersonation had never failed to crack Luce up. But today all she could manage was a thin closed-mouth smile.

"Hmmm," Shelby said. "Not that you'd care what you missed at the party. I noticed Daniel flying away over the beach last night. You two must have had a lot to catch up on."

Shelby had seen Daniel? Why hadn't she mentioned it sooner? Could anyone else have seen him?

"We didn't even talk."

"That's hard to believe. He's usually so full of orders to give you—"

"Shelby, Miles kissed me," Luce interrupted. Her eyes were closed. For some reason, that made it easier to confess. "Last night. And Daniel saw everything. He took off before I could—"

"Yeah, that would do it." Shelby let out a low whistle. "This is kind of huge."

Luce's face burned with shame. Her mind couldn't shake the image of Daniel taking flight. It felt so final.

"So is it, you know, *over* between you and Daniel?"

"No. Never." Luce couldn't even hear that phrase without shuddering. "I just don't know."

She hadn't told Shelby the rest of what she'd glimpsed in the Announcer, that Daniel and Cam were working together. Were secret pals, as far as she could tell. Shelby wouldn't know who Cam was, anyway, and the history was way too complicated to explain. Besides, Luce wouldn't be able to stand it if Shelby, with her oh-so-deliberately-controversial views about angels and demons, tried to make a case that a partnership between Daniel and Cam wasn't that big a deal.

"You know Daniel's gonna be all screwed up over it right now. Isn't that Daniel's big thing—the *undying* devotion you two share?"

Luce stiffened in her white iron chair.

"I wasn't being sarcastic, Luce. So maybe, I don't know, Daniel's been involved with other people. It's all pretty nebulous. The take-home message, like I said before, is that there was never a question in his mind that you were the only one that mattered."

"That's supposed to make me feel better?"

"I don't claim to be in the business of making you feel better, I'm just trying to illustrate a point. For all Daniel's annoying aloofness—and there's plenty of it—the guy's clearly devoted. The real question here is: Are you? As far as Daniel knows, you could drop him as soon as someone else comes along. Miles has come along. And he's obviously a great guy. A little sappy for my taste, but—"

"I would never drop Daniel," Luce said aloud, desperately wanting to believe it.

She thought about the horror on his face the night they'd argued on the beach. She was stunned when he'd been so quick to ask: *Are we breaking up?* Like he suspected that was a possibility. Like she hadn't swallowed whole his entire insane story about their endless love when he'd told her under the peach trees at Sword & Cross. She had swallowed it, in one single believing gulp, ingesting all its fissures, too—the jagged pieces that made no sense but begged her to believe them at the time. Now, every day, another of them gnawed at her insides. She could feel the biggest one rising up in her throat:

"Most of the time, I don't even know why he likes me."

"Come on," Shelby groaned. "Do not be one of those girls. *He's too good for me, wah wah wah.* I'll have to punt you over to Dawn and Jasmine's table. That's their expertise, not mine."

"I don't mean it like that." Luce leaned in and dropped her voice. "I mean, ages ago, when Daniel was, you know, *up there,* he chose me. Me, out of everyone else on earth—"

"Well, there were probably a lot fewer options back then— Ouch!" Luce had swatted her. "Just trying to lighten the mood!"

"He chose me, Shelby, over some big role in Heaven, over some elevated position. That's pretty major, don't you think?" Shelby nodded. "There had to be more to it than just him thinking I was cute."

"But . . . you don't know what it was?"

"I've asked, but he's never told me what happened. When I brought it up, it was almost like Daniel couldn't remember. And that's crazy, because it means we're both just going through the motions. Based on thousands of years of some fairy tale neither one of us can even back up."

Shelby rubbed her jaw. "What else is Daniel keeping from you?"

"That's what I plan on finding out."

Around the terrace, time had marched on; most of the students were heading to class. The scholarship waiters were hurrying to bus the plates. At a table closest to the ocean, Steven was drinking coffee alone. His glasses were folded up and resting on the table. His eyes found Luce's, and he held her gaze for a long time, so long that—even after she stood up to go to class—his intense, watchful expression stuck with her. Which was probably his point.

※

After the longest, most mind-numbing PBS special on cell division ever seen, Luce walked out of her biology class, down the stairs of the main school building, and outside, where she was surprised to see the parking lot completely packed. Parents, older siblings, and more than a few chauffeurs formed one long line of vehicles the likes of which Luce hadn't seen since the car-pool lane at her middle school in Georgia.

Around her, students hurried out of class and zig-zagged toward the cars, wheeling suitcases in their wake. Dawn and Jasmine hugged goodbye before Jasmine got into a town car and Dawn's brothers made room for her in the back of an SUV. The two of them were only splitting up for a few hours.

Luce ducked back into the building and slipped out the rarely used rear door to trek across the grounds to her dorm. She definitely could not deal with goodbyes right now.

Walking under the gray sky, Luce was still a guilty wreck, but her conversation with Shelby had left her feeling a bit more in control. It was screwed up, she knew it, but having kissed someone else made her feel like she finally had a say in her relationship with Daniel. Maybe she'd get a reaction out of him, for a change. She could apologize. He could apologize. They could make lemonade or whatever. Break through all this crap and really start talking.

Just then, her phone buzzed. A text from Mr. Cole:

Everything's taken care of.

So Mr. Cole had passed on the news that Luce wasn't coming home. But he'd conveniently left out of his text whether or not her parents were still speaking to her. She hadn't heard from them in days.

It was a no-win situation: If they wrote to her, she felt guilty about not writing them back. If they didn't write to her, she felt responsible for being the reason they couldn't reach out. She still hadn't figured out what to do about Callie.

She thumped up the stairs of the empty dorm. Each step echoed hollowly in the cavernous building. No one was around.

When she made it to her room, she expected to find Shelby already gone—or at least, to see her suitcase packed and waiting by the door.

Shelby wasn't there, but her clothes were still strewn all over her side of the room. Her puffy red vest was still on its peg, and her yoga gear was still stacked in the corner. Maybe she wasn't leaving until tomorrow morning.

Before Luce had even fully closed the door behind her, someone knocked on the other side. She stuck her head into the hallway.

Miles.

Her palms grew damp and she could feel her heartbeat pick up. She wondered what her hair looked like, whether she'd remembered to make her bed this morning, and how long he'd been walking behind her. Whether he'd seen her dodge the caravan of Thanksgiving farewells, or seen the pained look on her face when she'd checked her text messages.

"Hi," she said softly.

"Hi."

Miles had on a thick brown sweater over a collared white shirt. He was wearing those jeans with the hole in the knee, the ones that always made Dawn jump up to follow him so she and Jasmine could swoon from behind him.

Miles's mouth twitched into a nervous smile. "Wanna do something?"

His thumbs were tucked under the straps of his navy blue backpack and his voice echoed off the wood walls. It crossed Luce's mind that she and Miles might be the only two people in the entire building. The thought was both thrilling and nerve-wracking.

"I'm grounded for eternity, remember?"

"That's why I brought the fun to you."

At first Luce thought Miles was referring to himself, but then he slid his backpack off one shoulder and unzipped the main compartment. Inside was a treasure trove of board games: Boggle. Connect Four. Parcheesi. The *High School Musical* game. Even travel Scrabble. It was so nice, and so not awkward, Luce thought she might cry.

"I figured you were going home today," she said. "Everyone else is leaving."

Miles shrugged. "My parents said it was cool if I stayed. I'll be home again in a couple of weeks, and besides, we have different opinions on the perfect vacation. Theirs is anything worthy of a write-up in the *New York Times* Styles section."

Luce laughed. "And yours?"

Miles dug a little deeper into his bag, pulling out two packets of instant apple cider, a box of microwave popcorn, and a DVD of the Woody Allen movie *Hannah and Her Sisters*. "Pretty humble, but you're looking at it." He smiled. "I asked you to spend Thanksgiving with me, Luce. Just because we're changing venues doesn't mean we have to change our plans."

She felt a grin spread across her face, and held open the door for Miles to come in. His shoulder brushed hers when he passed, and they locked eyes for a moment. She felt Miles almost sway on his heels, as if he was going to double back and kiss her. She tensed up, waiting.

But he just smiled, dropped his backpack in the middle of the floor, and started to unload Thanksgiving.

"Are you hungry?" he asked, waving a packet of popcorn.

Luce winced. "I am really bad at making popcorn."

She was thinking of the time she and Callie nearly burned down their dorm at Dover. She couldn't help it. It made her miss her best friend all over again.

Miles opened the door of the microwave. He held up a finger. "I can press *any* button with this finger, and microwave most anything. You're lucky I'm so good at it."

It was weird that earlier she'd been torn up over kissing Miles. Now she realized he was the only thing making her feel better. If he hadn't come over, she'd be spiraling into another guilty black abyss. Even though she couldn't imagine kissing him again—not because she didn't want to, necessarily, but because she knew it wasn't right, that she couldn't do that to Daniel . . . that she didn't *want* to do that to Daniel—Miles's presence was extremely comforting.

They played Boggle until Luce finally understood the rules, Scrabble until they realized the set was missing half its letters, and Parcheesi until the sun went down outside the window and it was too dim to see the board without turning on a light. Then Miles stood up and lit the fire, and slid *Hannah and Her Sisters* into the DVD player on Luce's computer. The only place to sit and watch the movie was on the bed.

Suddenly, Luce felt nervous. Before, they'd just been two friends playing board games on a weekday afternoon. Now the stars were out, the dorm was empty, the fire was crackling, and—what did that make them?

They sat next to each other on Luce's bed, and she couldn't stop thinking about where her hands were, whether they looked unnatural if she kept them pinned across her lap, whether they'd brush against Miles's fingertips if she rested them at her sides. Out of the corner of her eye, she could see his chest moving when he breathed. She could hear him scratch the back of his neck. He'd taken his baseball cap off, and she could smell the citrusy shampoo in his fine brown hair.

Hannah and Her Sisters was one of the few Woody Allen movies she'd never seen, but she could not make herself pay attention. She'd crossed and uncrossed her legs three times before the opening titles rolled.

The door swung open. Shelby barreled into the room, took one look at Luce's computer monitor, and blurted, "Best Thanksgiving movie ever! Can I watch with—" Then she looked at Luce and Miles, sitting in the dark on the bed. "Oh."

Luce bolted up off the bed. "Of course you can! I didn't know when you were leaving to go home—"

"Never." Shelby flung herself on the top bunk, sending a small earthquake down to Luce and Miles on the bottom bunk. "My mom and I got in a fight. Don't ask, it was utterly boring. Besides, I'd much rather hang out with you guys, anyway."

"But Shelby—" Luce couldn't imagine getting in a fight so big it kept her from going home on Thanksgiving.

"Let's just enjoy the genius of Woody in silence," Shelby commanded.

Miles and Luce shot each other a conspiratorial look. "You got it," Miles called up to Shelby, giving Luce a grin.

Truthfully, Luce was relieved. When she settled back into her seat, her fingers did brush against Miles's, and he gave them a squeeze. It was only for a moment, but it was long enough to let Luce know that, at least as far as Thanksgiving weekend was concerned, things were going to be okay.

SEVENTEEN

TWO DAYS

Luce woke to the scrape of a hanger dragging across the bar in her closet.

Before she could see who was responsible for the noise, a mound of clothes bombarded her. She sat up in bed, pushing her way out from under the pile of jeans, T-shirts, and sweaters. She plucked an argyle sock off her forehead.

"Arriane?"

"Do you like the red one? Or the black?" Arriane

was holding two of Luce's dresses up against her tiny frame, swaying as she modeled each one.

Arriane's arms were bare of the awful tracking wristband she'd had to wear at Sword & Cross. Luce hadn't noticed until now, and she shuddered to remember the cruel voltage sent coursing through Arriane whenever she stepped out of line. Every day in California, Luce's memories of Sword & Cross grew hazier, until a moment like this one jolted her back into the turmoil of her stay there.

"Elizabeth Taylor says only certain women can wear red," Arriane continued. "It's all about cleavage and coloring. Luckily, you've got both." She freed the red dress from its hanger and tossed it on the pile.

"What are you doing here?" Luce asked.

Arriane put her tiny hands on her hips. "Helping you pack, silly. You're going home."

"Wh-What home? What do you mean?" Luce stammered.

Arriane laughed, stepping forward to take one of Luce's hands and tug her out of bed. "Georgia, my peach." She patted Luce's cheek. "With good old Harry and Doreen. And apparently some friend of yours is also flying in."

Callie. She was actually going to get to see Callie? And her parents? Luce wobbled where she stood, suddenly speechless.

"Don't you want to spend Thanksgiving with your fam?"

Luce was waiting for the catch. "What about—"

"Don't worry." Arriane tweaked Luce's nose. "It was Mr. Cole's idea. We've got to keep up the ruse that you're still just down the road from your parents. This seemed the simplest and most fun way to go about it."

"But when he texted me yesterday, all he said was—"

"He didn't want to get your hopes up until he had every little thing taken care of, including"—Arriane curtseyed—"the perfect escort. One of them, anyway. Roland should be here any second."

A knock on the door.

"He's so good." Arriane pointed to the red dress still in Luce's hand. "Throw that baby on."

Luce quickly shimmied into the dress, then ducked into the bathroom to brush her teeth and hair. Arriane had presented her with one of those rare *Jump!—How high?* situations. You didn't bother with questions. You just leaped.

She emerged from the bathroom, expecting to see Roland and Arriane doing something Roland-and-Arriane-esque, like one of them standing on top of her suitcase while the other tried to zip it up.

But it wasn't Roland who had knocked.

It was Steven and Francesca.

Shit.

The words *I can explain* formed on the tip of Luce's

tongue. Only, she had no idea how to talk herself out of this situation. She looked to Arriane for help. Arriane was still tossing Luce's sneakers into the suitcase. Didn't she know the kind of major trouble they were about to be in?

When Francesca stepped forward, Luce braced herself. But then the wide bell sleeves of Francesca's crimson turtleneck engulfed Luce in an unexpected hug. "We came to wish you well."

"Of course, we'll miss you tomorrow at what we with tongue in cheek refer to as the Dinner for the Displaced," Steven said, taking Francesca's hand and prying her away from Luce. "But it's always best for a student to be with family."

"I don't understand," Luce said. "You knew about this? I thought I was grounded until further notice."

"We spoke with Mr. Cole this morning," Francesca said.

"And you weren't grounded as punishment, Luce," Steven explained. "It was the only way we could ensure you'd be safe under our charge. But you're in good hands with Arriane."

Never one to overstay her welcome, Francesca was already steering Steven toward the door. "We hear your parents are anxious to see you. Something about your mother filling up a freezer with pies." She winked at Luce, and both she and Steven waved, and then they were gone.

Luce's heart swelled at the prospect of getting home to her family.

But not before it went out to Miles and Shelby. They'd be crestfallen if she went home to Thunderbolt and abandoned them here. She didn't even know where Shelby was. She couldn't leave without—

Roland stuck his head through Luce's open door. He looked professional in his pinstriped blazer and crisp white collared shirt. His black-and-gold dreads were shorter, spikier, making his dark, deep-set eyes even more striking.

"Is the coast clear?" he asked, shooting Luce his familiar devilish grin. "We've got a hanger-on." He nodded at someone behind him—who appeared a moment later with duffel bag in hand.

Miles.

He flashed Luce a wonderfully unembarrassed grin and took a seat on the edge of her bed. An image of introducing him to her parents ran though Luce's mind. He'd take off his baseball cap, shake both of their hands, compliment her mom's half-finished needlepoint . . .

"Roland, what part of 'top-secret mission' don't you understand?" Arriane asked.

"It's my fault," Miles admitted. "I saw Roland heading over here . . . and I forced it out of him. That's why he's late."

"As soon as this guy heard the words *Luce* and *Georgia*"—Roland jerked his thumb at Miles—"it took him about a nanosecond to pack."

"We kind of had a Thanksgiving deal," Miles said, looking only at Luce. "I couldn't let her break it."

"No." Luce bit back a smile. "He couldn't."

"Mmm-hmm." Arriane raised an eyebrow. "I just wonder what Francesca would have to say about this. Whether someone should run it by your parents first, Miles—"

"Aw, come on, Arriane." Roland waved his hand dismissively. "Since when do you check in with authority? I'll look out for the kid. He won't get into any trouble."

"Get into any trouble where?" Shelby barged into the room, her yoga mat swinging from a string across her back. "Where are we going?"

"Luce's house in Georgia for Thanksgiving," Miles said.

In the hallway behind Shelby, a bleached-blond head hovered. Shelby's ex-boyfriend. His skin was ghost-white, and Shelby was right: There was something odd about his eyes. How pale they were.

"For the last time, I said *goodbye,* Phil." Shelby quickly shut the door in his face.

"Who was that?" Roland asked.

"My skeeze-and-a-half ex-boyfriend."

"Seems like an interesting guy," Roland said, staring at the door, distracted.

"Interesting?" Shelby snorted. "A restraining order would be interesting." She took one look at Luce's suitcase, then at Miles's duffel, then haphazardly started throwing her belongings into a squat black trunk.

Arriane threw up her hands. "Can't you do anything without an entourage?" she asked Luce. Then, turning to Roland, "I assume you want to take responsibility for this one, too?"

"That's the holiday spirit!" Roland laughed. "We're going to the Prices' for Thanksgiving," he told Shelby, whose face lit up. "The more the merrier."

Luce couldn't believe how perfectly everything was working out. Thanksgiving with her family *and* Callie *and* Arriane and Roland *and* Shelby *and* Miles. She couldn't have scripted this any better.

Only one thing nagged at her. And it seriously nagged.

"What about Daniel?"

She meant: *Does he know about this trip already?* and *What's the real story between him and Cam?* and *Is he still mad at me about that kiss?* and *Is it wrong that Miles is coming too?* and also *What are the odds of Daniel showing up at my parents' house tomorrow even though he says he can't see me?*

Arriane cleared her throat. "Yes, what about Daniel?" she repeated quietly. "Time will tell."

"So do we have plane tickets or something?" Shelby asked. "Because if we're flying, I need to pack my serenity kit, essential oils, and heating pad. You don't want to see me at thirty-five thousand feet without them."

Roland snapped his fingers.

Near his feet, the shadow cast by the open door peeled itself off the hardwood planks, rising the way a trapdoor might to lead down to a basement. A gust of cold swept up from the floor, followed by a bleak blast of darkness. It smelled like wet hay as it shrank into a small, compact sphere. But then, at a nod from Roland, it ballooned into a tall black portal. It looked like the sort of door that would lead to a restaurant kitchen, the swinging kind with a round glass window in the top. Only, this one was made out of dark Announcer fog, and all that was visible through the window was a darker, swirling blackness.

"That looks just like the one I read about in the book," Miles said, clearly impressed. "All I could manage was a weird sort of trapezoidal window." He smiled at Luce. "But we still made it work."

"Stick with me, kid," Roland said, "and you'll see what it's like to travel in style."

Arriane rolled her eyes. "He's such a show-off."

Luce cocked her head at Arriane. "But I thought you said—"

"I know." Arriane put up a hand. "I know I repeated that whole spiel about how dangerous Announcer travel is. And I don't want to be one of those sucky do-as-I-say-not-as-I-do angels. But we all agreed—Francesca and Steven, Mr. Cole, everyone—"

Everyone? Luce couldn't group them together

without seeing a glaring missing piece. Where was Daniel in all of this?

"Besides." Arriane smiled proudly. "We're in the presence of a master. Ro's one of the very best Announcer travelers." And then, in a whispered aside to Roland, "Don't let it go to your head."

Roland swung open the Announcer's door. It groaned and creaked on shadow hinges and swung open onto a dank, yawning pit of emptiness.

"Um . . . what is it again that makes traveling by Announcer so dangerous?" Miles asked.

Arriane pointed around the room, at the shadow under the desk lamp, behind Shelby's yoga mat. All of the shadows were quivering. "An untrained eye might not know which Announcer to step through. And believe us, there are always uninvited lurkers, waiting for someone to accidentally open them."

Luce remembered the sickly brown shadow she'd tripped over. The uninvited lurker that had given her the nightmarish glimpse of Cam and Daniel on the beach.

"If you pick the wrong Announcer, it's very easy to get lost," Roland explained. "To not have any idea where—or when—you're stepping through to. But as long as you stick with us, you don't have anything to worry about."

Nervously, Luce pointed into the belly of the Announcer. She didn't remember the other shadows they'd stepped through looking quite so murky and dark. Or maybe she just hadn't known the consequences until now. "We're not just going to pop up in the middle of my parents' kitchen, are we? Because I think my mom might pass out from the shock—"

"Please." Arriane clucked her tongue, guiding Luce, then Miles, and then Shelby to stand before the Announcer. "Have a little faith."

⚜

It was like pushing through a murky wet fog, clammy and unpleasant. It slid and coiled over Luce's skin and stuck in her lungs when she breathed. An echo of ceaseless white noise filled up the tunnel like a waterfall. The two other times Luce had traveled by Announcer, she'd felt lumbering and hurried, catapulting though darkness to come out somewhere light. This was different. She'd lost track of where and when she was, even of who she was and where she was going.

Then there was a strong hand yanking her out.

When Roland let her go, the echoing waterfall trickled to a drip, and a whiff of chlorine filled her nose. A diving board. A familiar one, under a lofty arched ceiling lined with broken stained-glass panels. The sun had passed over the high windows, but its light still cast faint colored prisms onto the surface of an Olympic-size pool. Along the walls, candles flickered in stone recesses, throwing off a dim, useless light. She'd recognize this church-gymnasium anywhere.

"Oh my God," Luce whispered. "We're back at Sword and Cross."

Arriane scanned the room quickly and without affection. "As far as your parents are concerned when they pick us up tomorrow morning, you've been here all along. Got it?"

Arriane acted as if returning to Sword & Cross for the night was no different than checking into a nondescript motel. The jolt back to this part of her life, however, hit Luce like a slap across the face. She hadn't liked it here. Sword & Cross was a miserable place, but it was a place where things had *happened* to her. She'd fallen in love here, had watched a close friend die. More than anywhere else, this was a place where she had changed.

She closed her eyes and laughed bitterly. She'd known *nothing* then compared to what she knew now. And yet she'd felt surer of herself and her emotions than she could imagine ever feeling again.

"What the hell is this place?" Shelby asked.

"My last school," Luce said, glancing at Miles. He seemed uneasy, huddling next to Shelby against the wall. Luce remembered: They were good kids—and though she'd never talked much about her time here, the Nephilim rumor mill could easily have filled their minds with enough vivid details to paint one scary night at Sword & Cross.

"Ahem," Arriane said, looking at Shelby and Miles. "And when Luce's parents ask, you guys go here too."

"Explain to me how this is a school," Shelby said. "What, do you swim and pray at the same time? That's a level of freakish efficiency you'd never see on the West Coast. I think I just got homesick."

"You think this is bad," Luce said, "you should see the rest of campus."

Shelby scrunched up her face, and Luce couldn't blame her. Compared to Shoreline, this place was a gruesome sort of Purgatory. At least, unlike the rest of the kids here, they'd be gone after tonight.

"You guys look drained," Arriane said. "Which is good, because I promised Cole we'd lie low."

Roland had been leaning against the diving board, rubbing his temples, the Announcer shards quivering at his feet. Now he stood up and began to take charge. "Miles, you're going to bunk up with me in my old room. And Luce, your room's still empty. We'll roll in a cot for Shelby. Let's all drop our bags and meet back at my room. I'll use the old black-market network to order a pizza."

The mention of pizza was enough to shake Miles and Shelby out of their comas, but Luce was taking longer to adjust. It wasn't that weird for her room to still be empty. Counting on her fingers, she realized she'd been gone from this place less than three weeks. It felt like so much longer, like every day had been a month, and it was impossible for Luce to imagine Sword & Cross without any of the people—or angels, or demons—who had made up her life here.

"Don't worry." Arriane stood next to Luce. "This place is like a reject revolving door. People come and go all the time because of some parole issue, crazy parents, whatever. Randy's off tonight. No one else gives a damn. If anyone gives you a second look—just give 'em a third one. Or send them over to me." She made a fist. "You ready to get out of here?" She pointed at the others already following Roland out the door.

"I'll catch up with you guys," Luce said. "There's something I need to do first."

⭔

In the far east corner of the cemetery, next to her father's plot, Penn's grave was modest but neat.

The last time Luce had seen this cemetery, it had been coated in a thick felt of dust. The aftermath of every angel battle, Daniel had told her. Luce didn't know whether the wind had carried the dust away by now, or whether angel dust just disappeared over time, but the cemetery seemed to be back to its neglected old self. Still ringed by an ever-advancing forest of kudzu-strangled live oaks. Still barren and depleted under the no-color sky. Only, there was something missing, something vital Luce couldn't put her finger on, but that still made her feel lonely.

A sparse layer of dull green grass had grown up and around Penn's grave, so it didn't look so jarringly new, compared to the centuries-old graves surrounding it. A bouquet of fresh lilies lay in front of the simple gray tombstone, which Luce stooped down to read:

PENNYWEATHER VAN SYCKLE-LOCKWOOD
A DEAR FRIEND
1991–2009

Luce inhaled a jagged breath, and tears sprang to her eyes. She'd left Sword & Cross before there'd been time to bury Penn, but Daniel had taken care of everything. It was the first time in several days that her heart ached for him. Because he had known, better than she would have known herself, exactly how Penn's tombstone should read. Luce knelt down on the grass, her tears flowing freely now, her hands combing the grass uselessly.

"I'm here, Penn," she whispered. "I'm sorry I had to leave you. I'm sorry you got mixed up with me in the first place. You deserved better than this. A better friend than me."

She wished her friend were still here. She wished she could talk to her. She knew Penn's death was her fault, and it almost broke her heart.

"I don't know what I'm doing anymore, and I'm scared."

She wanted to say she missed Penn all the time, but what she really missed was the idea of a friend she could have known better if death hadn't taken her away too soon. None of it was right.

"Hello, Luce."

She had to wipe away the tears before she could see Mr. Cole standing on the other side of Penn's grave. She'd gotten so used to her crisply elegant teachers at Shoreline that Mr. Cole looked almost frumpy in his bunched-up tawny suit, with his mustache, and his brown hair parted straight as a ruler just above his left ear.

Luce scrambled to her feet, sniffling against her wrist. "Hi, Mr. Cole."

He smiled kindly. "You're doing well over there, I hear. Everyone says you're doing very well."

"Oh . . . n-no . . . ," she stammered. "I don't know about that."

"Well, I do. I also know your parents are very happy to get to see you. It's good when these things can work out."

"Thank you," she said, hoping he understood how grateful she was.

"I won't keep you but for just one question."

Luce waited for him to ask her about something deep and dark and over her head about Daniel and Cam, good and evil, right and wrong, trust and deceit. . . .

But all he said was "What did you do to your hair?"

Luce's head was upside down in the sink in the girls' bathroom down the hall from the Sword & Cross cafeteria. Shelby carried in the last two slices of cheese pizza stacked on a paper plate for Luce. Arriane held out a bottle of cheap black hair dye—the best Roland could do on such short notice, but not a bad match for Luce's natural color.

Neither Arriane nor Shelby had questioned Luce about her sudden need for a change. She'd been grateful for that. Now she saw they'd only been waiting for her to be in a vulnerable half-dyed position to begin their inquisition.

"I guess Daniel will be pleased," Arriane said in her coyest leading-question tone of voice. "Not that you're doing this for Daniel. Are you?"

"Arriane," Luce warned. She wasn't going there. Not tonight.

But Shelby seemed to want to. "You know what I've always liked about Miles? That he likes you for who you are, not for what you do with your hair."

"If you two were going to be that obvious about it, why didn't you guys come down in your Team Daniel and Team Miles T-shirts?"

"We should order those," Shelby said.

"Mine's in the laundry," Arriane said.

Luce tuned them out, focusing instead on the warm

water and the strange confluence of things flowing over her head, into her scalp, and down the drain: Shelby's stubby fingers had helped with Luce's first dye job, back when Luce thought that was the only way to start afresh. Arriane's first act of friendship toward Luce had been the command to chop off her black hair, to make her look like Luce. Now their hands worked through Luce's scalp in the same bathroom where Penn had rinsed her clean of the meat loaf Molly had dumped on her head her first day at Sword & Cross.

It was bittersweet, and beautiful, and Luce couldn't figure out what any of it meant. Only that she didn't want to hide anymore—not from herself, or from her parents; not from Daniel, or even from those who sought to harm her.

She'd been seeking a cheap transformation when she first got out to California. Now she realized that the only worthwhile way to make a change was to earn a real one. Dying her hair black wasn't the answer either—she knew she wasn't there yet—but at least it was a step in the right direction.

Arriane and Shelby stopped arguing over which guy was Luce's soul mate. They looked at her silently and nodded. She felt it before she even saw her reflection in the mirror: The heavy weight of melancholy, one she hadn't even known she was shouldering, had lifted from her body.

She was back to her roots. She was ready to go home.

EIGHTEEN

THANKSGIVING

When Luce stepped through the front door of her parents' house in Thunderbolt, everything was just the same: The coatrack in the foyer still looked like it was about to topple under the weight of too many jackets. The smell of dryer sheets and Pledge still made the house feel cleaner than it was. The floral couch in the living room was faded from the morning sun that fell through the blinds. A stack of tea-stained southern decorating magazines covered the coffee table, favorite pages bookmarked with grocery receipts, for the distant time when her parents' dream came true of the mortgage's being paid off and their finally having a little extra money for remodeling. Andrew, her mom's hysterical toy poodle, trotted over to sniff the guests and give the back of Luce's ankle a familiar chomp.

Luce's dad set down her duffel in the foyer, draping an easy arm around her shoulder. Luce watched their reflection in the narrow entryway mirror: father and daughter.

His rimless glasses slipped down on his nose as he kissed the crown of her back-to-black hair. "Welcome home, Lucie," he said. "We missed you around here."

Luce closed her eyes. "I missed you, too." It was the first time in weeks she hadn't lied to her parents.

The house was warm and full of intoxicating Thanksgiving scents. She inhaled and could instantly picture every foil-wrapped dish staying hot in the oven. Deep-fried turkey with mushroom stuffing—her dad's specialty. Apple-cranberry sauce, light-as-air yeast rolls, and enough pumpkin-pecan pies—her mom's—to feed the whole state. She must have been cooking all week.

Luce's mom took hold of her wrists. Her hazel eyes were a little damp around the edges. "How are you, Luce?" she asked. "Are you all right?"

It was such a relief to be home. Luce could feel her eyes grow damp too. She nodded, folding into her mom for a hug.

Her mother's chin-length dark hair was sculpted and sprayed, like she'd just been to the beauty parlor the day before. Which, knowing her, she probably had. She looked younger and prettier than Luce remembered. Compared to the elderly parents she'd tried to visit in Mount Shasta—even compared to Vera—Luce's mom seemed happy and alive, untainted by sorrow.

It was because she'd never had to feel what the others had felt, losing a daughter. Losing Luce. Her parents had made their whole life around her. It would destroy them if she died.

She could not die the way she had in the past. She could not wreck her parents' life this time around, now that she knew more about her past. She would do whatever it took to keep them happy.

Her mom gathered the coats and hats of the four other teenagers who were standing in her foyer. "I hope your friends brought their appetites."

Shelby jerked her thumb at Miles. "Be careful what you wish for."

It was just like Luce's parents not to mind a carful of last-minute guests at their Thanksgiving table.

When her dad's Chrysler New Yorker had rolled through Sword & Cross's tall wrought iron gates just before noon, Luce had been waiting for him. She hadn't been able to sleep at all the night before. Between the strangeness of being back at Sword & Cross and her nerves about mingling such an odd Thanksgiving crew the next day—her mind would not settle down.

Luckily, the morning had passed without incident; after giving her dad the longest, tightest hug she'd ever given someone, she'd mentioned that she had a few friends without places to go for the holiday.

Five minutes later, they were all in the car.

Now they were milling around Luce's childhood home, picking up framed pictures of her at different awkward ages, gazing out the same French windows she'd been gazing out over bowls of cereal for more than a decade. It was kind of surreal. As Arriane bounded into the kitchen to help her mom whip some cream, Miles peppered her dad with questions about the enormous piece-of-junk telescope in his office. Luce felt a swell of pride in her parents for making everyone feel welcome.

The sound of a car horn outside made her jump.

She perched on the sagging couch and lifted a slat of the window blind. Outside, a red-and-white taxi was idling in front of the house, coughing exhaust into the cold fall air. The windows were tinted, but the passenger could be only one person.

Callie.

One of Callie's knee-high red leather boots extended from the back door, planting itself on the concrete sidewalk. A second later, Luce's best friend's heart-shaped face came into view. Callie's porcelain skin was flushed, her auburn hair shorter, cut at a sleek angle close to her chin. Her pale blue eyes glittered. For some reason, she kept glancing back inside the cab.

"Whatcha looking at?" Shelby asked, pulling up another slat so she could see. Roland slid in on Luce's other side and looked out too.

Just in time to see Daniel slide out of the taxi—

Followed by Cam, from the front seat.

Luce sucked in her breath at the sight of them.

Both guys were wearing long, dark coats, like the coats they'd worn on the shore in the scene she'd glimpsed. Their hair gleamed in the sunlight. And for a moment, just a moment, Luce remembered why she'd originally been intrigued by them both at Sword & Cross. They were *beautiful*. There was no getting around it. Surreally, unnaturally stunning.

But what the hell were they doing here?

"Right on time," Roland murmured.

On her other side, Shelby asked, "Who invited them?"

"My thoughts exactly," Luce said, but she couldn't help swooning a little at the sight of Daniel. Even though things between them were a mess.

"Luce." Roland was chuckling at her expression as she watched Daniel. "Don't you think you should answer the door?"

The doorbell rang.

"Is that Callie?" Luce's mom called from the kitchen over the whir of the stand mixer.

"Got it!" Luce shouted back, feeling a cold pain spread through her chest. Of course she wanted to see Callie. But more overwhelming than her joy at seeing her best friend, she realized, was her hunger to see Daniel. To touch him, to hold him and breathe him in. To introduce him to her parents.

They would be able to see, wouldn't they? They'd be able to tell that Luce had found the person who had changed her life forever.

She opened the door.

"Happy Thanksgiving!" a high southern voice drawled. Luce had to blink a few times before her brain could connect with the sight before her eyes.

Gabbe, the most beautiful and the most perfectly mannered angel at Sword & Cross, was standing on Luce's porch in a pink mohair sweater dress. Her blond hair was a gorgeous frenzy of braids, pinned up into little swirls on top of her head. Her skin had a soft, lovely shimmer—not unlike Francesca's. She held a bouquet of white gladiolas in one hand and a frosty white plastic ice cream tub in the other.

Next to her, her bleached-blond hair grown brown at the roots, stood the demon Molly Zane. Her torn black jeans matched her frayed black sweater, like she was still following Sword & Cross's dress code. Her facial piercings had multiplied since the last time Luce had seen her. She had a small black cast iron kettle balanced in the crook of her arm. She was glaring at Luce.

Luce could see the others walking up the long, curving walk. Daniel had Callie's suitcase hoisted up over his shoulder, but it was Cam who was leaning in, smiling, his hand on Callie's right forearm as he chatted with her. She didn't seem to know whether to be slightly nervous or absolutely charmed.

"We were just in the neighborhood." Gabbe beamed, holding out the flowers to Luce. "I made my homemade vanilla ice cream, and Molly brought an appetizer."

"Shrimp Diablo." Molly lifted up the lid of her kettle, and Luce breathed in a spicy garlic broth. "Family recipe." Molly slapped the lid back down, then pushed past Luce into the foyer, stumbling over Shelby in her path.

"Excuse *you*," they said gruffly at the same time, eyeing each other suspiciously.

"Oh, good." Gabbe leaned in to give Luce a hug. "Molly's made a friend."

Roland took Gabbe into the kitchen, and Luce had her first clear view of Callie. When they locked eyes, they couldn't help themselves: Both girls broke into involuntary grins and ran toward one another.

The impact of Callie's body knocked the wind out of Luce, but it didn't matter. Their arms were flung around each other, each girl's face buried in the other's hair; they were laughing the way you laugh only after too long a separation from a very good friend.

Reluctantly, Luce pulled away and turned to the two guys standing a few feet back. Cam looked as he always did: controlled and at ease, slick and handsome.

But Daniel looked uncomfortable—and he had good reason to be. They hadn't spoken since he'd seen her kiss Miles, and now they were standing with Luce's best friend and Daniel's enemy-turned- . . . whatever Cam was to Daniel now.

But—

Daniel was *in her home.* Within shouting distance of her parents. Would they lose it if they knew who he really was? How did she introduce the guy who was responsible for a thousand of her deaths, whom she was magnetically drawn to almost all the time, who was impossible and elusive and secretive and sometimes even mean, whose love she didn't understand, who was *working with the devil,* for crying out loud, and who—if he thought showing up here uninvited with that demon was a good idea—maybe didn't know her very well at all.

"What are you doing here?" Her voice was bone-dry because she couldn't talk to Daniel without talking to Cam, too, and she couldn't talk to Cam without wanting to throw something heavy at him.

Cam spoke first. "Happy Thanksgiving to you, too. We heard your house was the place to be today."

"We ran into your friend here at the airport," Daniel added, using the flat tone he spoke in when he and Luce were in public. It was more formal, making her yearn to be alone with him so they could just be real. And so she could grab him by the lapels of his stupid coat and shake him until he explained everything. This had gone on long enough.

"Got to talking, shared a cab," Cam picked up, winking at Callie.

Callie smiled at Luce. "Here I was picturing some intimate gathering at the Price household, but this is so much better. Now I can get the real scoop."

Luce could feel her friend searching her face for clues about what the deal was with these two guys. Thanksgiving was about to get really awkward, really fast. This was not the way things were supposed to go.

"Turkey time!" her mother called from the doorway. Her smile changed into a confused grimace when she saw the crowd outside. "Luce? What's going on?" Her old green-and-white-striped apron was tied around her waist.

"Mom," Luce said, gesturing with her hand, "this is Callie, and Cam, and . . ." She wanted to reach out to put her hand on Daniel, something, anything to let her mom know that he was special, that this was the one. To let him know, too, that she still loved him, that everything between them was going to be okay. But she couldn't. She just stood there. ". . . Daniel."

"Okay." Her mom squinted at each of the newcomers. "Well, um, welcome. Luce, honey, can I have a word?"

Luce went to her mother at the front door, holding up a finger to let Callie know she'd be right back. She followed her mother through the foyer, through the dim hallway hung with framed pictures from Luce's childhood, and into her parents' cozy, lamplit bedroom. Her mom sat down on the white bedspread and crossed her arms. "Feel like telling me anything?"

"I'm so sorry, Mom," Luce said, sinking down on the bed.

"I don't want to shut anyone out of a Thanksgiving meal, but don't you think we need to draw the line somewhere? Wasn't one unexpected carful of people enough?"

"Yes, of course you're right," Luce said. "I didn't invite all these people. I'm as stunned as you are that they all showed up."

"It's just that we have so little time with you. We love to meet your friends," Luce's mom said, stroking her hair. "But we cherish our time with you more."

"I know this is such a huge imposition, but Mom"— Luce turned her cheek into her mother's open palm— "he is special. Daniel. I didn't know he was going to come, but now that he's here, I need this time with him as much as I need it with you and Dad. Does that make any sense?"

"Daniel?" her mom repeated. "That beautiful blond boy? You two are—"

"We're in love." For some reason, Luce was trembling. Even though she had her doubts about their relationship, saying out loud, to her mother, that she loved Daniel made it seem true—made her remember that she did, despite everything, truly love him.

"I see." When her mom nodded, her sprayed brown curls stayed in place. She smiled. "Well, we can't very well kick out everyone else but him, can we?"

"Thank you, Mom."

"Thank your father, too. And honey? Next time, a little more advance notice, please. If I'd known you were bringing home 'the one,' I would have grabbed your baby album from the attic." She winked, planting a kiss on Luce's cheek.

❊

Back in the living room, Luce ran into Daniel first.

"I'm glad you got to be with your family after all," he said.

"I hope you're not mad at Daniel for bringing me," Cam put in, and Luce searched for haughtiness in his voice but found none. "I'm sure you'd both rather I weren't here, but"—he looked at Daniel—"a deal's a deal."

"I'm sure," Luce said coolly.

Daniel's face gave nothing away. Until it darkened. Miles had come in from the dining room.

"Um, hey, your dad's about to make a toast." Miles's eyes were fixed on Luce in a way that made her think he was trying hard not to meet Daniel's stare. "Your mom told me to ask where you wanted to sit."

"Oh, wherever. Maybe next to Callie?" A mild panic struck Luce as she thought about all the other guests and the need to keep them as far away from each other as possible. And Molly away from just about everyone. "I should have done a seating chart."

Roland and Arriane had made quick work of setting up the card table at the edge of the dining room table, so the banquet now stretched into the living room. Someone had thrown down a gold-and-white tablecloth, and her parents had even busted out their wedding china. Candles were lit and goblets of water filled. And soon Shelby and Miles were carrying in steaming bowls of green beans and mashed potatoes while Luce took her seat between Callie and Arriane.

Their intimate Thanksgiving dinner was now serving twelve: four humans, two Nephilim, six fallen angels (three each on the side of Good and Evil), and one dog dressed as a turkey, with his bowl of scraps under the table.

Miles went for the seat directly across from Luce—until Daniel flashed him a menacing look. Miles backed off, and Daniel was just about to sit down when Shelby slid right in. Smiling with a little look of victory, Miles sat on Shelby's left, across from Callie, while Daniel, looking vaguely annoyed, sat to her right, across from Arriane.

Someone was kicking Luce under the table, trying to get her attention, but she kept her eyes on her plate.

Once everyone was seated, Luce's father stood up at the head of the table, facing her mother at the foot. He clanked his fork against his glass of red wine. "I've been known to make a long-winded speech or two this time of year." He chuckled. "But we've never served so many hungry-looking kids before, so I'll just cut to the chase. I'm thankful for my sweet wife, Doreen, my best kid, Lucie, and all of you for joining us." He fixed on Luce, drawing his cheeks in the way he did when he was especially proud. "It's wonderful to see you prospering, growing into a beautiful young lady with so many great friends. We hope they'll all come again. Cheers, everyone. To friends."

Luce forced a smile, avoiding the shifty glances all her "friends" were sharing.

"Hear, hear!" Daniel broke the exquisitely awkward silence, raising his glass. "What good is life without trusty, reliable friends?"

Miles barely looked at him, plunging a serving spoon

deep into the mashed potatoes. "Coming from Mr. Reliable himself."

The Prices were too busy passing dishes at opposite ends of the table to notice the dirty look Daniel directed at Miles.

Molly was spooning the Shrimp Diablo appetizer no one had yet touched in a growing heap on Miles's plate. "Just say uncle when you've had enough."

"Whoa, Mo. Save some heat for me." Cam reached to take the kettle of shrimp. "Say, Miles. Roland told me you showed off some mad skills fencing the other day. I bet the girls went crazy." He leaned forward. "You were there, right, Luce?"

Miles had his fork poised in midair. His large blue eyes looked confused about Cam's intentions, and as if he was hoping to hear Luce say that yes, the girls—herself included—had indeed gone crazy.

"Roland also said Miles lost," Daniel said placidly, and speared a piece of stuffing.

At the other end of the table, Gabbe cut the tension with a loud and satisfied purr. "Oh my God, Mrs. Price. These Brussels sprouts are a little taste of Heaven. Aren't they, Roland?"

"Mmm," Roland agreed. "They really bring me back to a simpler time."

Luce's mother began reciting the recipe while Luce's dad went on about local produce. Luce was trying to enjoy this rare time with her family, and Callie leaning in to whisper that everyone seemed pretty cool, especially Arriane and Miles—but there were too many other situations to monitor. Luce felt like she might have to defuse a bomb at any moment.

A few minutes later, passing the stuffing around the table a second time, Luce's mother said, "You know, your father and I met when we were right around your age."

Luce had heard the story thirty-five hundred times before.

"He was the quarterback at Athens High." Her mother winked at Miles. "The athletic ones drove the girls wild in those days, too."

"Yep, the Trojans were twelve and two my varsity year." Luce's dad laughed, and she waited for his token line. "I just had to show Doreen I wasn't as much of a tough guy off the field."

"I think it's great what a strong marriage you two have," Miles said, grabbing yet another of Luce's mother's famous yeast rolls. "Luce is lucky to have parents who are so *honest* and *open* with her and each other."

Luce's mom beamed.

But before she could respond, Daniel butted in. "There's much more to love than *that*, Miles. Wouldn't you say, Mr. Price, that a *real* relationship is more than just easy fun and games? That it takes some effort?"

"Of course, of course." Luce's father patted his lips

with his napkin. "Why else would they call marriage a commitment? Sure, love has its ups and downs. That's life."

"Well said, Mr. P.," Roland said, with a soulfulness beyond his smooth seventeen-year-old-looking face. "God knows, I've seen some ups and downs."

"Oh, come on," Callie chimed in, to Luce's surprise. Poor Callie, taking everyone here at face value. "You guys make it sound so heavy."

"Callie's right," Luce's mom said. "You kids are young and hopeful, and you really should just be having fun."

Fun. So that was the goal right now? Was fun even possible for Luce? She glanced at Miles. He was smiling. "I'm having fun," he mouthed.

That made all the difference to Luce, who looked around the table again and realized that despite everything, she was having fun too. Roland was making a show of tonguing a shrimp at Molly, who laughed for possibly the first time in history. Cam tried doting on Callie, even offering to butter her roll, which she declined with raised eyebrows and a shy shake of her head. Shelby ate like she was training for a competition. And someone was still playing footsie with Luce underneath the table. She met Daniel's violet eyes. He winked, giving her butterflies.

There was something remarkable about this gathering.

It was the liveliest Thanksgiving they'd had since Luce's grandmother died and the Prices stopped going to the Louisiana bayou for the holiday. So this was her family now: all these people, angels, demons, and whatever else they were. For better or worse, complicated, treacherous, full of ups and downs, and even at times fun. Just like her dad had said: That was life.

And for a girl who had had some experience with dying, life—period—was the thing for which Luce was suddenly overwhelmingly thankful.

"Well, I've had just about enough," Shelby announced after a few more minutes. "You know. Food. Everyone else done? Let's wrap this up." She whistled and made a lasso gesture with her finger. "I'm eager to get back to that reform school we all go to—um—"

"I'll help clear the table." Gabbe jumped up and started stacking plates, dragging a reluctant Molly into the kitchen with her.

Luce's mom was still shooting her furtive glances, trying to see the gathering through her daughter's eyes. Which was impossible. She'd latched on to the Daniel idea pretty quickly and kept looking back and forth between the two of them. Luce wanted a chance to show her mom that what she and Daniel had was solid and wonderful and unlike anything else in the world, but there were too many other people around. Everything that should have been easy felt hard.

Then Andrew stopped chewing on the felt feathers around his neck and started yipping at the door. Luce's dad stood up and reached for the dog's leash. What a relief. "Somebody wants his after-dinner walk," he announced.

Her mother stood up, too, and Luce followed her to the door and helped her into her pea coat. Luce handed her dad his scarf. "Thank you guys for being so cool tonight. We'll do the dishes while you're gone."

Her mom smiled. "You make us proud, Luce. No matter what. Remember that."

"I like that Miles," Luce's dad said, clipping Andrew's leash to his collar.

"And Daniel is . . . just remarkable," her mom said to her dad in a leading tone of voice.

Luce's cheeks flushed and she glanced back at the table. She gave her parents a please-don't-embarrass-me look. "Okay! Have a nice long walk!"

Luce held open the door and watched them walk out into the night with the eager dog practically choking on his leash. The cold air through the open door was refreshing. The house was hot, with so many people filling it up. Just before her parents disappeared down the street, Luce thought she saw a flash of something outside.

Something that looked like a wing.

"Did you see that?" she said, not sure who she was addressing.

"What?" her father called, turning back. He looked so full and happy that it almost broke Luce's heart.

"Nothing." Luce forced a smile as she closed the door. She could feel someone right behind her.

Daniel. The warmth that made her sway where she stood.

"What did you see?"

His voice was icy, not with anger but with fear. She looked up at him, reaching for his hands, but he had turned the other way.

"Cam," he called. "Get your bow."

Across the room, Cam's head shot up. "Already?"

A whizzing sound outside the house silenced him. He moved away from the window and reached inside his blazer. Luce saw the flash of silver, and she remembered: the arrows he'd collected from the Outcast girl.

"Tell the others," Daniel said before turning to face Luce. His lips parted and the desperate look on his face made her think that he might kiss her, but all he did was say, "Do you have a storm cellar?"

"Tell me what's happening," Luce said. She could hear water running in the kitchen, Arriane and Gabbe singing harmony on "Heart and Soul" with Callie while they did the dishes. She could see Molly's and Roland's skittish expressions as they cleared the table. And suddenly, Luce knew that this Thanksgiving dinner was all an act. A cover-up. Only, she didn't know for what.

Miles appeared at Luce's side. "What's going on?"

"Nothing you need to be concerned with," Cam said. Not rudely, just stating the facts. "Molly. Roland."

Molly put down her stack of dishes. "What do you need us to do?"

It was Daniel who answered, speaking to Molly as if they were suddenly on the same side. "Tell the others. And find shields. They'll be armed."

"Who?" Luce asked. "The Outcasts?"

Daniel's eyes landed on her and his face fell. "They shouldn't have found us tonight. We knew there was a chance, but I really didn't want to bring this here. I'm sorry—"

"Daniel." Cam interrupted him. "All that matters now is fighting back."

A heavy knocking thudded through the house. Cam and Daniel moved instinctively toward the front door, but Luce shook her head. "Back door," she whispered. "Through the kitchen."

They all stood for a moment and listened to the creak of the back door opening. Then came a long and piercing scream.

"Callie!" Luce took off running through the living room, shuddering to imagine what scene her best friend was facing. If Luce had known the Outcasts would show up, she would not have let Callie come. She would never have come home at all. If anything bad happened, Luce would never forgive herself.

Swinging through her parents' kitchen door, Luce saw Callie, shielded behind Gabbe's narrow frame. She was safe, at least for now. Luce exhaled, almost collapsing backward into the wall of muscle that Daniel, Cam, Miles, and Roland had formed behind her.

Arriane stood in the whitewashed doorway, a giant butcher block raised high in her hands. She looked ready to bash someone Luce couldn't quite see yet.

"Good evening." A guy's voice, stiff with formality.

When Arriane lowered the butcher's block, there in the doorway stood a tall, lean boy in a brown trench coat. He was very pale, with a narrow face and a strong nose. He looked familiar. Cropped bleached-blond hair. Blank white eyes.

An Outcast.

But Luce had seen him somewhere else before.

"*Phil?*" Shelby cried. "What the hell are you doing here? And what happened to your eyes? They're all—"

Daniel turned on Shelby. "You know this Outcast?"

"*Outcast?*" Shelby's voice quaked. "He's not a— He's my sorry-ass ex— He's—"

"He's been using you," Roland said, as if he knew something the rest of them didn't. "I should have known. Should have recognized him for what he was."

"But you didn't," the Outcast said, his voice eerily calm. He reached inside his trench coat and, from an inner pocket, pulled out a silver bow. From his other pocket came a silver arrow, which he swiftly nocked. He pointed it at Roland, then swept across the crowd, aiming at each of them in turn. "Please forgive my barging in. I've come to fetch Lucinda."

Daniel stepped toward the Outcast. "You'll *fetch* no one and nothing," he said, "except a swift death unless you leave right now."

"Sorry, no, can't do that," the boy responded, his muscled arms still holding the silver arrow taut. "We've had time to prepare for this night of blessed restitution. We will not leave empty-handed."

"How could you, Phil?" Shelby whimpered, turning to Luce. "I didn't know . . . Honestly, Luce, I didn't. I just thought he was a creep."

The boy's lips curled up in a smile. His horrible, depthless white eyes were straight out of a nightmare. "Give her to me without a fight, or none of you will be spared."

Then Cam burst out in a long, deep belly laugh. It shook the kitchen and made the boy in the doorway twitch uncomfortably.

"You and what army?" Cam said. "You know, I think you're the first Outcast I've ever met with a sense of humor." He glanced around the cramped kitchen. "Why don't you and I take this outside? Get it over with, shall we?"

"Gladly," the boy replied, a flat smile on his pale lips.

Cam rolled his shoulders back as if he were working out a knot—and there, right where his shoulder blades came together, an enormous pair of golden wings split through his gray cashmere sweater. They unfurled behind him, taking up most of the kitchen. Cam's wings were so bright they were almost blinding as they pulsed.

"Holy Hell," Callie whispered, blinking.

"More or less," Arriane said as Cam arched his wings backward and plowed past the Outcast boy, through the door and into the backyard. "Luce will explain, I'm sure!"

Roland's wings unfurled with a sound like a great flock of birds taking flight. The lamplight in the kitchen highlighted their dark gold and black marbling as he squeezed out the door after Cam. Molly and Arriane were right behind him, butting into each other, Arriane pressing her glowing iridescent wings ahead of Molly's cloudy bronze ones, sending off what looked like little electric sparks as they hustled out the door. Next was Gabbe, whose fluffy white wings spread open as gracefully as a butterfly's, but with such speed they sent a rush of floral-scented wind through the kitchen.

Daniel took Luce's hands in his. He closed his eyes, inhaled, and let his massive white wings unfurl. Fully extended, they would have filled the entire kitchen, but Daniel reined them in, close to his body. They shimmered and glowed and looked altogether too beautiful.

Luce reached out and touched them with both hands. Warm and satin smooth on the outside, but inside, full of power. She could feel it coursing through Daniel, into her. She felt so close to him, understood him completely. As if they'd become one.

Don't worry. Everything's going to be fine. I'll always take care of you.

But what he said aloud was "Stay safe. Stay here."

"No," she pleaded. *"Daniel."*

"I'll be right back." Then he arched his wings backward and flew out the door.

Left alone inside, the unangelic gathered together. Miles was pressed against the back door, gaping out the window. Shelby had her head in her hands. Callie's face looked as white as the refrigerator.

Luce slipped a hand into Callie's. "I guess I have a few things to explain."

"Who is that boy with the bow and arrow?" Callie whispered, flinching but still holding tight to Luce's hand. "Who *are* you?"

"Me? I'm just . . . me." Luce shrugged, feeling a chill spread through her. "I don't know."

"Luce," Shelby said, clearly trying not to cry. "I feel like such a chump. I swear I had no idea. The stuff I told him, I was just venting. He was always asking about you, and he was a good listener, so I . . . I mean, I had no idea what he really was . . . I would never, never—"

"I believe you," Luce said. She moved to the window, next to Miles, looking out onto the small wooden deck her dad had built a few years ago. "What do you think he wants?"

In the yard, fallen oak leaves had been raked into neat piles. The air smelled like a bonfire. Somewhere in the distance, a siren was going off. At the foot of the deck's three steps, Daniel, Cam, Arriane, Roland, and Gabbe stood side by side, facing the fence.

No, not the fence, Luce realized. They faced a dark crowd of Outcasts, standing at attention with their silver arrows aimed at the row of angels. The Outcast boy was not alone. He'd amassed an army.

Luce had to steady herself against the counter. Aside from Cam, the angels were unarmed. And she'd already seen what those arrows could do.

"Luce, stop!" Miles called after her, but she was already rushing out the door.

Even in the darkness, Luce could see that all the Outcasts had similar expressionless good looks. There were just as many girls as boys, all of them pale and dressed in the same brown trench coats, with closely cropped bleached-blond hair for the boys and tight, almost white ponytails for the girls. The Outcasts' wings arched out from their backs. They were in very, very bad shape—tattered and frayed and revoltingly filthy, practically caked with dirt. Nothing at all like the glorious wings of

Daniel or Cam, or any of the angels and demons Luce knew. Standing in solidarity, with their strange empty eyes staring out, their heads tilted in different directions, the Outcasts made a horrible nightmare of an army. Only, Luce could not wake up.

When Daniel noticed her standing with the others on the deck, he doubled back and seized her hands. His perfect face looked wild with fear. *"I told you to stay inside."*

"No," she whispered. "I won't stay locked up while the rest of you fight. I can't just keep watching people around me die for no reason."

"No reason? Let's have this fight another time, Luce." His eyes kept darting toward the dark line of Outcasts near the fence.

She balled up her fists at her sides. *"Daniel—"*

"Your life is too precious to squander in a temper tantrum. Get inside. *Now.*"

A loud shriek rang out in the middle of the yard. The front line of ten Outcasts raised their weapons toward the angels and loosed their arrows. Luce's head shot up just in time to catch the sight of something—some*one*—catapulting off the roof.

Molly.

She flew down from it, a dark clot wielding two garden rakes, twirling them like batons in each of her hands.

The Outcasts heard but couldn't see her coming. But Molly's rakes twirled, tilling the arrows from the air as if they were crops in a field. She landed on her black combat boots, the dull-ended silver arrows thudding and rolling along the ground, looking about as harmless as twigs. But Luce knew better.

"There will be no mercy now!" an Outcast—Phil—bellowed from the other side of the yard.

"Get her inside, and get the starshots!" Cam shouted at Daniel, mounting the railing of the deck and pulling out his own silver bow. In quick succession, he nocked and loosed three streaks of light. The Outcasts writhed as three of their ranks vanished in puffs of dust.

With lightning speed, Arriane and Roland darted around the yard, sweeping up arrows with their wings.

A second line of Outcasts was advancing, readying a new volley of arrows. When they were on the brink of shooting, Gabbe leaped onto the railing of the deck.

"Hmmm, let's see." With a fierce look in her eyes, she pointed the tip of her right wing at the ground below the Outcasts.

The lawn shuddered, and then a clean seam of earth—the length of the backyard and a few feet wide—split wide open.

Taking at least twenty Outcasts deep into the black chasm.

They bellowed hollow, lonely cries on the way down.

Down to God-knew-where. The Outcasts behind them skidded, halting just in front of the awful gorge Gabbe had pulled from nowhere. Their heads moved from left to right as if to help their blind eyes make sense of what just happened. A few more Outcasts teetered on the edge and tumbled in. Their wails grew fainter—until no sound could be heard. An instant later, the earth creaked like a rusty hinge and closed back up.

Gabbe drew her downy wing back to her side with the utmost elegance. She wiped her brow. "Well, that should help."

But then another bright shower of silver splinters rained from the sky. One of them thunked into the top step of the deck at Luce's feet. Daniel yanked the arrow out of the wooden step, wound up his arm, and flung it sharply, like a lethal dart, straight into the forehead of an advancing Outcast.

There was a flash of light, like a camera flash, and then: The white-eyed boy didn't even have time to cry out at the impact—he just vanished into thin air.

Daniel's eyes raced over Luce's body, and he patted her down, as if in disbelief that she was still alive.

At her side, Callie gulped. "Did he just— Did that guy really—"

"Yes," Luce said.

"Don't do this, Luce," Daniel said. "Don't make me drag you inside. I have to fight. You have to get away from here. *Now.*"

Luce had seen enough to agree. She turned back toward the house, reaching for Callie—but then, through the open doorway of the kitchen, she caught a brutal glimpse of Outcasts.

Three of them. *Standing inside her house.* Silver bows aimed to shoot.

"No!" Daniel bellowed, rushing to shield Luce.

Shelby lurched out of the kitchen and onto the deck, slamming the door behind her.

Three distinct thumps of arrows struck the other side of the door.

"Hey, she's exonerated!" Cam called from the lawn, nodding at Shelby briefly before bashing an arrow into an Outcast girl's skull.

"Okay, new plan," Daniel muttered. "Find someplace to take cover somewhere nearby. All of you." He addressed Callie and Shelby and, for the first time all night, Miles. He grabbed Luce by the arms. "Stay away from the starshots," he pleaded. "Promise me." He kissed her quickly, then shooed them all against the back wall of the deck.

The glow of so many angels' wings was brilliant enough that Luce, Callie, Shelby, and Miles had to shade their eyes. They crouched down and crawled along the deck, shadows of the railing dancing before them, while Luce directed everyone to the side yard. To shelter. There had to be some, somewhere.

More Outcasts stepped out from the shadows. They

appeared in the high branches of faraway trees, came ambling out from around the raised garden beds and the termite-eaten old swing set Luce had used as a kid. Their silver bows gleamed in the moonlight.

Cam was the only one on the other side with a bow. He never paused to count how many Outcasts he was picking off. He just loosed arrow after arrow with deadly precision into their hearts. But for each one that vanished, another seemed to appear.

When he ran out of arrows, he wrenched the wooden picnic table out of its decade-old rut in the ground and held it in front of him with one arm like a shield. Volley after volley of arrows bounced off the tabletop and fell to the ground at his feet. He just stooped, plucked, and fired; stooped, plucked, and fired.

The others had to get more creative.

Roland beat his golden wings with such force that the air around him sent the arrows back in the direction they had come from, taking out the unseeing Outcasts several at a time. Molly charged the line again and again, her rakes spiraling like a samurai's swords.

Arriane yanked Luce's old tire swing from its tree and twirled it like a lasso, deflecting arrows into the fence, while Gabbe raced around, picking them up. She spun and slashed like a dervish, taking out any Outcast who got too close, smiling sweetly as the arrows bit their skin.

Daniel had commandeered the Prices' rusted iron horseshoes from under the porch. He pitched them at the Outcasts, sometimes knocking three of them senseless with one horseshoe as it ricocheted off their skulls. Then he would pounce on them, slip the starshots from their bows, and drive the arrows into their hearts with his bare hands.

At the edge of the deck, Luce caught sight of her father's storage shed and motioned for the other three to follow. They rolled over the railing to the grass below and, ducking, hurried to the shed.

They were almost at the entrance when Luce heard a quick whiz in the air. Callie cried out in pain.

"Callie!" Luce whirled around.

But her friend was still there. She was rubbing her shoulder where the arrow had grazed her, but otherwise, she was unharmed. "That totally stings!"

Luce reached out to touch her. "How did you . . . ?"

Callie shook her head.

"Get down!" Shelby shouted.

Luce dropped to her knees, tugging the others down with her and pulling them inside the shed. Among the dirty shadows of Luce's dad's tools, lawn mower, and old sporting equipment, Shelby crawled over to Luce. Her eyes glistened and her lip was quivering.

"I can't believe this is happening," she whispered, grabbing hold of Luce's arm. "You don't know how sorry I am. It's all my fault."

"It's not your fault," Luce said quickly. Of course Shelby hadn't known who Phil really was. What he really wanted from her. What this night would bring. Luce knew what it was like to carry around guilt for doing something you didn't understand. She wouldn't have wished it on anyone. Least of all Shelby.

"Where is he?" Shelby asked. "I could kill that sorry-ass freak."

"No." Luce held Shelby back. "You're not going out there. *You* could get killed."

"I don't get it," Callie said. "Why would anyone want to hurt you?"

That was when Miles stepped toward the entrance to the shed, into a beam of moonlight. He was carrying one of Luce's father's kayaks over his head.

"Nobody's going to hurt Luce," he said as he stepped outside with it.

Right into the battle.

"Miles!" Luce screamed. "Come back—"

She rose to her feet to take off after him—then froze, stunned by the sight of him chucking the kayak right into one of the Outcasts.

It was Phil.

His blank eyes gaped and he cried out, falling to the grass as the kayak struck him. Pinned and helpless, his dirty wings writhed on the ground.

For an instant Miles looked proud of himself—and

Luce felt a little bit proud too. But then a short Outcast girl stepped forward, cocked her head like a dog listening to a silent whistle, raised her silver bow, and aimed point-blank at Miles's chest.

"No mercy," she said tonelessly.

Miles was defenseless against this strange girl, who looked like she had no understanding of mercy, not even for the nicest, most innocent kid in the world.

"Stop!" Luce cried out, her heart pounding in her ears as she ran out of the shed. She could sense the battle going on around her, but all she could see was that arrow, poised to enter Miles's chest. Poised to kill yet another of her friends.

The Outcast girl's head canted on her neck. Her vacant eyes turned on Luce, then widened slightly, like, just as Arriane had said, she really could see the burning of Luce's soul.

"Don't shoot him." Luce held out her hands in surrender. "I'm the one you want."

NINETEEN

THE TRUCE IS BROKEN

The Outcast girl lowered her bow. When the arrow re-laxed along its bowstring, the string made a creaking sound, like an attic door opening. Her face was as calm as a still pond on a windless day. She was Luce's height, with clear, dewy skin, pale lips, and dimples even in the absence of a smile.

"If you wish the boy to live," she said, her voice flat, "I will yield to you."

Around them, the others had stopped fighting. The

tire swing rolled to a stop, thudding against the corner of the fence. Roland's wings slowed to a soft beating and carried him down to earth. Everyone was still, but the air was charged with an electric silence.

Luce could feel the weight of so many gazes falling on her: Callie, Miles, and Shelby. Daniel, Arriane, and Gabbe. Cam, Roland, and Molly. The blind gazes of the Outcasts themselves. But she couldn't wrench herself away from the girl with the depthless white eyes.

"You won't kill him . . . just because I say not to?" Luce was so baffled, she laughed. "I thought you wanted to kill me."

"Kill *you*?" The girl's mechanical voice lilted upward, registering surprise. "Not at all. We would die for you. We want you to come with us. You are the last hope. Our entrance."

"Entrance?" Miles voiced what Luce was too surprised to say. "To what?"

"To Heaven, of course." The girl peered at Luce with her dead eyes. "You are the price."

"No." Luce shook her head, but the girl's words knocked around inside her mind, echoing in a way that made her feel so hollow she could barely stand.

Entrance into Heaven. The price.

Luce didn't understand. The Outcasts would take her, and do what? Use her as some sort of bargaining chip? This girl couldn't even see Luce to know who she was. If Luce had learned one thing at Shoreline, it was that no one could keep the myths straight. They were too old, too convoluted. Everyone knew there was a history, one Luce had been involved in for a long time, but nobody seemed to know *why*.

"Don't listen to her, Luce. She's a monster." Daniel's wings were trembling. As if he thought she might be tempted to go. Luce's shoulders began to itch, a hot prickling that left the rest of her body cold.

"Lucinda?" the Outcast girl called.

"Okay, hold on a minute," Luce said to the girl. She turned to Daniel. "I want to know: What is this truce? And don't tell me 'nothing,' and don't tell me you can't explain. Tell me the truth. You owe it to me."

"You're right," Daniel said, surprising Luce. He kept sneaking glances at the Outcast, as if she might spirit Luce away at any moment. "Cam and I drew it up. We agreed to put aside our differences for eighteen days. All angels and demons. We came together to hunt down other enemies. Like them." He pointed to the Outcast.

"But why?"

"Because of you. Because you needed time. Our end goals may be different, but for now, Cam and I—and all of our kin—we work as allies. We have one priority in common."

The glimpse Luce had seen in the Announcer, that sickening scene with Daniel and Cam working together . . . that was supposed to be okay because they'd agreed upon a truce? To give *her* time?

"Not that you even stuck by the truce." Cam spat in Daniel's direction. "What good is a truce if you don't honor it?"

"You didn't stand by it either," Luce said to Cam. "You were in the forest outside Shoreline."

"Protecting you!" said Cam. "Not taking you out on moonlight parades!"

Luce turned to Arriane. "Whatever the truce is—or isn't—once it's over, does that mean that . . . Cam's suddenly the enemy again? And Roland, too? This doesn't make any sense."

"Say the word, Lucinda," the Outcast said. "I will take you far from all of this."

"To what? To where?" Luce asked. There was something appealing about just getting away. From all the heartache and struggle and confusion.

"Don't do something you'll regret, Luce," Cam warned. It was strange the way he sounded like the voice of reason, compared to Daniel, who looked practically paralyzed.

Luce glanced around her for the first time since leaving the shed. The fighting had ceased. The same felt of dust that had coated the cemetery at Sword & Cross now caked the grass of the backyard. While their group of angels seemed fully intact and accounted for, the

Outcasts had lost most of their army. About ten stood at a distance, watching. Their silver bows were lowered.

The Outcast girl was still waiting for Luce to answer. Her eyes shone in the night and her feet inched backward as the angels pressed closer to her. When Cam approached, the girl raised her silver bow again, slowly, and pointed it at his heart.

Luce watched him stiffen.

"You don't want to go with the Outcasts," he told Luce, "especially not tonight."

"Don't tell her what she does or doesn't want." Shelby butted in. "I'm not saying she should go with the albino freaks or anything. Just everybody quit babying her and let her do her own thing for once. It's, like, *enough* already."

Her voice boomed across the yard, making the Outcast girl jump. She turned to aim her arrow at Shelby.

Luce sucked in her breath. The silver arrow quivered in the Outcast's hands. She pulled back on the bowstring. Luce held her breath. But before the girl could shoot, her glossy eyes widened. The bow tumbled from her hands. And her body disappeared in a dim gray flash of light.

Two feet behind where the Outcast girl had stood, Molly lowered a silver bow. She had shot the girl cleanly in the back.

"What?" Molly barked as the whole group turned to gape at her. "I like that Nephilim. She reminds me of someone I know."

She jerked an arm to gesture at Shelby, who said, "Thanks. Seriously. That was cool."

Molly shrugged, oblivious to the towering dark presence rising up behind her. The Outcast boy Miles had beaten to the ground with the kayak. Phil.

He swung the kayak behind his body, as if it were a baseball bat, and batted Molly clear across the lawn. She landed with a grunt on the grass. Tossing the kayak aside, the Outcast reached into his trench coat for one last shining arrow.

His dead eyes were the only expressionless part of his face. The rest of him—his snarl, his brow, even his cheekbones—looked utterly ferocious. His white skin seemed stretched across his bony skull. His hands looked more like claws. Anger and desperation had changed him from a pale and strange but good-looking guy into an actual monster. He raised his silver bow and took aim at Luce.

"I've been patiently waiting for my chance with you for weeks. Now, I don't mind being a little more forceful than my sister," he growled. "You *will* come with us."

On either side of Luce, silver bows were raised. Cam brought his out from inside his coat once again, and Daniel scrambled to the ground to pick up the bow that the Outcast girl had just dropped. Phil seemed to expect this. His face twisted into a dark smile.

"Do I need to kill your lover to get you to join me?"

he asked, pointing his arrow now at Daniel. "Or do I need to kill them all?"

Luce stared at the strange, flat tip of the silver arrow, less than ten feet from Daniel's chest. No chance Phil would miss from this range. She'd seen the arrows extinguish a dozen angels tonight with that paltry flash of light. But she'd also seen an arrow glance off Callie's skin, like it was nothing more than the dull stick it appeared to be.

The silver arrows killed angels, she suddenly realized, not humans.

She leaped in front of Daniel. "I won't let you hurt him. And your arrows can't hurt me."

A sound escaped from Daniel, a weird half-laugh, half-sob. She turned to him, wide-eyed. He looked afraid, but more than that, he looked guilty.

She thought of the conversation they'd had under the gnarled peach tree at Sword & Cross, the first time he'd told her about her reincarnations. She remembered sitting with him on the beach in Mendocino when he talked of his place in Heaven before her. What a struggle it had been to get him to open up about those early days. She still felt like there was more. There had to be more.

The creak of the bowstring snapped her attention back to the Outcast, who was pulling back the silver arrow. Now it was aimed at Miles. "Enough talk," he said.

"I'll take your friends out one at a time until you surrender to me."

In her mind, Luce saw a bright blink of light, a swirl of color, and a whirling montage of her lives flashing before her eyes—her mom and dad and Andrew. The parents she'd seen in Mount Shasta. Vera ice-skating on the frozen pond. The girl she'd been, swimming under the waterfall in a yellow halter-top bathing suit. Other cities, homes, and times she couldn't recognize yet. Daniel's face from a thousand different angles, under a thousand different lights. And blaze after blaze after blaze.

Then she blinked and was back in the yard. The Outcasts were drawing closer, huddling together and whispering to Phil. He kept waving them back, agitated, trying to focus on Luce. Everyone was tense.

She saw Miles staring at her. He must have been terrified. But no, not terrified. He was *fixating* on her with so much intensity that his gaze seemed to vibrate her very core. Luce grew woozy and her vision clouded. What followed was an unfamiliar sensation of something being lifted off her. Like a casing being removed from her skin.

And she heard her voice say, "Don't shoot. I surrender."

Only, it was echoing and disembodied, and Luce hadn't actually said the words. She followed the sound with her eyes, and her body grew rigid at what she saw.

Another Luce standing behind the Outcast, tapping him on the shoulder.

But this was no glimpse of a former life. This was *her*, in her skinny black jeans and plaid shirt with the missing button. With her black hair cropped and newly dyed. With her hazel eyes taunting the Outcast. With the burning of her same soul clearly visible to him. Clearly visible to all the other angels, too. This was a mirror image of her. This was—

Miles's doing.

His gift. He had splintered Luce off into a second self, just as he'd told her he could on her very first day at Shoreline. *They say it's easy to do with the people you, like, love,* he'd said.

He loved her.

She couldn't think about that right now. While everyone's eyes were drawn to the reflection, the real Luce retreated two steps and hid inside the shed.

"What's happening?" Cam barked at Daniel.

"I don't know!" Daniel whispered hoarsely.

Only Shelby seemed to understand. "He did it," she said under her breath.

The Outcast swung his bow around to aim at this new Luce. Like he didn't quite trust the victory.

"Let's do this," Luce heard her own voice saying in

the middle of the yard. "I can't stay here with them. Too many secrets. Too many lies."

A part of her did feel that way. That she couldn't keep going on like this. That something had to change.

"You will come with me, and join my brothers and my sisters?" the Outcast said, sounding hopeful. His eyes made her nauseated. He held out his ghostly white hand.

"I will," Luce's voice projected.

"Luce, no." Daniel sucked in his breath. "You can't."

Now the remaining Outcasts raised their bows at Daniel and Cam and the rest of them, lest they interfere.

Luce's mirror stepped forward. Slipped her hand inside Phil's. "Yes, I can."

The monster Outcast cradled her in his stiff white arms. There was a great flap of dirty wings. A stale cloud of dust stormed up from the ground. Inside the shed, Luce held her breath.

She heard Daniel gasp as Luce's mirror and the Outcast soared up and out of the backyard. The rest of them looked incredulous. Except for Shelby and Miles.

"What the hell just happened?" Arriane said. "Did she really—"

"No!" Daniel cried. "No, no, no!"

Luce's heart ached as he tore at his hair, spun in a circle, and let his wings bloom out to their full size.

Immediately, the fleet of remaining Outcasts spread

their own dingy brown wings and took flight. Their wings were so thin, they had to beat frantically just to stay in the air. They were closing in on Phil. Trying to form a shield around him so he could take Luce wherever he thought he was taking her.

But Cam was faster. The Outcasts were probably twenty feet in the air when Luce heard one final arrow loose from its bow.

Cam's arrow wasn't meant for Phil. It was meant for Luce.

And his aim was perfect.

Luce froze as her mirror image disappeared in a great bloom of white light. In the sky, Phil's tattered wings shuddered open. Empty. A horrible roar escaped his mouth. He started to swoop back toward Cam, followed by his army of Outcasts. But then he stopped midway. As if he'd realized there was no more reason to go back.

"So it begins again," he called down to Cam. To all of them. "It could have ended peacefully. But tonight you've made a new sect of immortal enemies. Next time we will not negotiate."

Then the Outcasts disappeared into the night.

Back in the yard, Daniel barreled into Cam, throwing him to the ground. "What's *wrong* with you?" he yelled, his fists wailing down on Cam's face. "How could you?"

Cam strained to stop him. They rolled over each other on the grass. "It was a better end for her, Daniel."

Daniel was seething, tackling Cam, slamming his head into the dirt. Daniel's eyes blazed. "I'll kill you!"

"You *know* I'm right!" Cam shouted, not fighting back at all.

Daniel froze. He closed his eyes. "I don't know anything now." His voice was ragged. He'd been gripping Cam by the lapel, but now he just slumped to the ground, burying his face in the grass.

Luce wanted to go to him. To fall on him and tell him everything was going to be okay.

Except it wasn't.

What she'd seen tonight was too much. She felt sick from watching herself—Miles's mirror image of her—die from the starshot.

Miles had saved her life. She couldn't get over it.

And the rest of them thought Cam had ended it.

Her head swam as she stepped forward from the shadows of the shed, planning to tell the others not to worry, that she was still alive. But then she sensed the presence of something else.

An Announcer was quivering in the doorway. Luce stepped out of the shed and approached it.

Slowly, it broke free of a shadow cast by the moon. It slithered along the grass toward her for a few feet, picking up a dirty coat of dust left by the battle. When it reached Luce, it shuddered up and rose along her body, until it hovered blackly over her head.

She closed her eyes and felt herself raising her hand to meet it. The darkness fell to rest in her palm. It made a cold sizzling sound.

"What is that?" Daniel's head snapped around at the noise. He raised himself from the ground. *"Luce!"*

She stayed put as the others gasped at the sight of her standing in front of the shed. She didn't want to glimpse an Announcer. She'd seen enough for one night. She didn't even know why she was doing this—

Until she did. She wasn't looking for a vision, she was looking for a way out. Something far away enough to step through to. It had been too long since she'd had a moment to think on her own. What she needed was a break. From everything.

"Time to go," she said to herself.

The shadow door that presented itself in front of her wasn't perfect—it was jagged around the edges and it stank of sewage. But Luce parted its surface anyway.

"You don't know what you're doing, Luce!" Roland's voice reached her at the edge of the doorway. "It could take you anywhere!"

Daniel was on his feet, jogging toward her. "What are you doing?" She could hear the profound relief in his voice that she was still alive, and the sheer panic that she could manipulate the Announcer. His anxiety only spurred her on.

She wanted to look back to apologize to Callie, to thank Miles for what he'd done, to tell Arriane and Gabbe not to worry the way she knew they were going to anyway, to leave word for her parents. To tell Daniel not to follow her, that she needed to do this for herself. But her chance to break free was closing. So she stepped forward and called over her shoulder to Roland, "Guess I'll just have to figure it out."

Out of the corner of her eye, she saw Daniel rushing toward her. Like he hadn't believed until now that she would do it.

She felt the words rising up in her throat. *I love you.* She did. She did forever. But if she and Daniel *had* forever, their love could wait until she figured out a few important things about herself. About her lives and the life she had ahead of her. Tonight there was only time to wave goodbye, take a deep breath, and leap into the dismal shadow.

Into darkness.

Into her past.

EPILOGUE

PANDEMONIUM

"What just happened?"

"Where'd she go?"

"Who taught her how to do that?"

The frantic voices in the backyard sounded wobbly and distant to Daniel. He knew the other fallen angels were arguing, looking for Announcers in the shadows of the yard. Daniel was an island, closed off to everything but his own agony.

He had failed her. He had failed.

How could it be? For weeks he'd run himself ragged, his only goal to keep her safe until the moment when he could no longer offer her protection. Now that moment had come and gone—and so had Luce.

Anything could happen to her. And she could be anywhere. He had never felt so hollow and ashamed.

"Why can't we just find the Announcer she stepped through, put it back together, and go after her?"

The Nephilim boy. Miles. He was on his knees, combing the grass with his fingers. Like a moron.

"They don't work that way," Daniel snarled at him. "When you step into time, you take the Announcer with you. That's why you never do it unless . . ."

Cam looked at Miles, almost pityingly. "Please tell me Luce knows more about Announcer travel than you do."

"Shut up," Shelby said, standing over Miles protectively. "If he hadn't thrown Luce's reflection, Phil would have taken her."

Shelby looked guarded and afraid, out of place among the fallen angels. Years ago, she'd had a crush on Daniel—one he'd never requited, of course. But until tonight, he'd always thought well of the girl. Now she was just in the way.

"You said yourself Luce would be better off dead than with the Outcasts," she said, still defending Miles.

"The Outcasts *you* all but invited here." Arriane

stepped into the conversation, turning on Shelby, whose face reddened.

"Why would you assume some Nephilim child could detect the Outcast?" Molly challenged Arriane. "You were at that school. *You* should have noticed something."

"All of you: *Quiet.*" Daniel couldn't think straight. The yard was crammed with angels, but Luce's absence made it feel utterly empty.

He could hardly stand to look at anyone else. Shelby, for walking straight into the Outcast's easy trap. Miles, for thinking he had some stake in Luce's future. Cam, for what he'd tried to do—

Oh, that moment when Daniel thought he'd lost her to Cam's starshot! His wings had felt too heavy to lift. Colder than death. In that instant, he'd given up all hope.

But it was only a trick of the eye. A thrown reflection, nothing special under ordinary circumstances, but tonight the last thing Daniel had been expecting. It had given him a horrible shock. One that had nearly killed him. Until the joy of her resurrection.

There was still hope.

As long as he could find her.

He'd been stunned, watching Luce open up the shadow. Awed and impressed and painfully attracted to her—but more than all of that, stunned. How many times had she done it before without his even knowing?

"What do you think?" Cam asked, coming up beside

him. Their wings drew toward each other, that old magnetic force, and Daniel was too drained to pull away.

"I'm going after her," he said.

"Good plan." Cam sneered. "Just 'go after her.' Anywhere in time and space across the several thousand years. Why should you need a strategy?"

His sarcasm made Daniel want to tackle him a second time.

"I'm not asking for your help or your advice, Cam."

Only two starshots remained in the yard: the one he'd picked up from the Outcast Molly had killed, and the one Cam had found on the beach at the beginning of the truce. There would have been a nice symmetry if Cam and Daniel had been working as enemies right now—two bows, two starshots, two immortal foes.

But no. Not yet. They had to eliminate too many others before they could turn on each other again.

"What Cam means"—Roland stood between them, speaking to Daniel in a low voice—"is that this might take some team effort. I've seen the way these kids flop through the Announcers. She doesn't know what she's doing, Daniel. She's going to get into trouble pretty quick."

"*I know.*"

"It's not a sign of weakness to let us help," Roland said.

"I can help," Shelby called. She'd been whispering with Miles. "I think I might know where she is."

"You?" Daniel asked. "You've helped enough. Both of you."

"Daniel—"

"I know Luce better than anyone in the world." Daniel turned away from all of them, toward the dark, empty space in the yard where she'd stepped through. "Far better than any of you ever will. I don't need your help."

"You know her past," Shelby said, walking in front of him so that he had to look at her. "You don't know what she's been through these past few weeks. I'm the one who's been around while she glimpsed her past lives. I'm the one who saw her face when she found the sister she lost when you kissed her and she . . ." Shelby trailed off. "I know you all hate me right now. But I swear to— Oh, whatever it is you guys believe in. You can trust me from here on out. Miles, too. We want to help. We're *going* to help. Please." She reached for Daniel. "Trust us."

Daniel wrested himself away from her. Trust as an activity had always made him uneasy. What he had with Luce was unshakable. There was never any need even to work on trust. Their love just *was*.

But for all eternity, Daniel had never been able to find faith in anyone or anything else. And he didn't want to start now.

Down the street, a dog yipped. Then again, louder. Closer.

Luce's parents, coming back from their walk.

In the dark yard, Daniel's eyes found Gabbe's. She was standing close to Callie, probably consoling her. She'd already retracted her wings.

"Just go," Gabbe mouthed to him in the desolate, dust-filled backyard. What she meant was *Go get her.* She would handle Luce's parents. She would see that Callie got home. She would cover all the bases so that Daniel could go after what mattered. *We'll find you and help you as soon as we can.*

The moon drifted out from behind a mist of cloud. Daniel's shadow lengthened on the grass at his feet. He watched it swell a little, then began to draw up the Announcer inside it. When the cool, damp darkness brushed against him, Daniel realized that he hadn't stepped through time in ages. Looking back was not normally his style.

But the motions were still in him, buried in his wings or his soul or his heart. He moved quickly, peeling the Announcer off his own shadow, giving it a quick pinch to separate it from the ground. Then he threw it, like a piece of potter's clay, onto the air directly in front of him.

It formed a clean, finite portal.

He had been a part of every one of Luce's past lives. There was no reason he wouldn't be able to find her.

He opened the door. No time to waste. His heart would take him to her.

He had an innate sense that something bad was just

around the bend, but a hope that something incredible was waiting in the distance.

It had to be.

His burning love for her coursed through him until he felt so full he didn't know whether he would fit through the portal. He wrapped his wings close against his body and bounded into the Announcer.

Behind him, in the yard, a distant commotion. Whispers and rustling and shouts.

He didn't care. He didn't care about any of them, really.

Only her.

He whooped as he broke through.

"Daniel."

Voices. Behind him, following, getting closer. Calling his name as he tunneled deeper and deeper into the past.

Would he find her?

Without question.

Would he save her?

Always.

PASSION

THE NEXT BOOK IN THE FALLEN SERIES

SUMMER 2011

WWW.FALLENBOOKS.COM

DELACORTE PRESS

LAUREN KATE grew up in Dallas, went to school in Atlanta, and started writing in New York. She is the author of the international bestseller *Fallen* and *The Betrayal of Natalie Hargrove*. She lives in Los Angeles with her husband and is learning how to surf.

OFFICIALLY NOTED